Death by Alligator

A Sadie Snow Historical Cozy Mystery: Book 1

Marsha Whitney

Jaeval

JAEVAL PRESS

DEATH BY ALLIGATOR

Contents

Dedication

T o Gene, my most ardent cheerleader, and to our girls, Allegra, Eve, and Janeen. And thanks to Keller for the tech support. I am grateful to all of my family and friends for their love, support, patience, and confidence in me. We're all in this world together and I'm happy to say that I'm surrounded by kind, generous, thoughtful, and powerfully creative people. Let's create a world full of love, joy, and peace.

Chapter One

April 14, 1865 Evening

Behind the Curtain at Ford's Theater in Washington D.C.

"**B**ang!" Evangeline Bright stood in the wings at Ford's Theater mentally rehearsing her lines. The tall redhead heard it over the shouts and uproarious laughter from the audience.

What in the Sam Hill? Was that revelers out in the street still celebrating the end of the war? Or a new bit of business to spice up the show?

With her, by the prompter's desk, call boy Will Ferguson ran his fingers through his mop of curly brown hair and hissed, "Oh, Laws! I'm in for it now. That stack of books I preset for our next scene... they musta fell over!"

She grasped the plush red-velvet curtain between two fingers, then peeked out at the powdered and jeweled crowd. Fellow actor John Booth, lean, athletic, and mustachioed, vaulted the rail of the president's box.

The flags below the box tangled around his legs and Evangeline heard them tear... "rrriiip," as he dragged them down. A puff of blue smoke drifted down, bringing the smell of spent gun powder to mingle with the overwhelming perfume of 1500 theatergoers.

Only feet away from Evangeline and Will, Booth landed, "thump," in the white spotlights of center stage. He wobbled amid a twisted mass of shredded patriotic flags, previously arranged in honor of Lincoln's and Grant's presence. Evangeline tried to move her feet backwards. She couldn't budge.

The lone actor onstage, 28-year-old comedian Harry Hawk, who had just delivered the funniest line of the play with a wide, thin-lipped grin, had no such problem. With raw fear showing in his big, deep-set, dark eyes, he began a slow retreat from the crazed-looking Booth, who now rose from his off-balance crouch and stomped one shiny riding boot to rid himself of red, white, and blue tangles.

Booth limped forward, shouting into the shocked silence beyond, "The South shall be free! I have done it. Virginia is avenged!" With his black eyes sparkling in the spotlights, he brandished aloft an enormous, long, glinting, double-edged Bowie knife.

Evangeline was used to seeing Booth in his black frock coat with blue flannel shirt and tall riding boots. But she'd never seen him with his hair disarrayed and face blanched of all color. He drew his white lips back over his gleaming teeth and, with a wild look, started toward Hawk.

Is John Booth crazy?

Evangeline's feet finally woke up in response to a deep bass voice shouting, "Stop that man." A shriek rose from the president's box,, "My husband's been shot," and the audience took up the cry with shouts of, "The president's been shot." Evangeline backed through the darkness toward her dressing room. *What on earth has John done?*

She stopped a few moments for thought. *I was probably seen at the National Hotel with Booth and his wild-eyed secessionist friends. I can't stay in Washington. Police will think I had something to do with it.* Changing course, she headed for the costumes and props rooms.

This will be epic. I never should have gone with John to hear Lincoln's speech. He nearly foamed at the mouth when the president called for suffrage for colored men.

She entered the props room. The resourceful actress rummaged around until she found what she was looking for. A handful of people clattered by, outside in the hallway. She stood stock still.

Policemen looking for me already?

There'll be a terrible uproar.

A round-up of all his friends.

Ford's theater will probably be closed tighter than a bank vault after this.

But I'm an actress.

I can be somebody else for a while. But who? Hurry. No time to decide now. I'll just give myself options and figure that out later.

From the theater's costume room, she searched until she found a medium-sized brown-tweed men's suit. *Hurry. They're probably searching for me right now.*

She folded it quickly, placed it in the 'Little all,' and added a pair of brown high-heeled men's boots, only one size too large for her, with matching men's socks that some fellow actor had thoughtfully stashed inside. *Maybe the toes of the socks will fill up the ends of the shoes.* A top hat went upside down into the roomy small bag.

Faster. She grabbed a pair of gloves bigger than her hands and slapped them in the hat.

The costumes hanging on the ladies' rack caught her eye. *I wore this green silk dress on stage. It's much fancier than my normal clothing. I better take it, too.*

Into the bag she tossed the dress, the matching jacket, and a lovely coordinating hat with feathers. *Hoops? Impossible.*

The fashion of the day called for steel hoops to spread a lady's skirt in a giant bubble, all around her. *I can't take hoops in a carpet bag.* She added needles and sewing thread to alter it for wear without hoops.

Enough. Now get out of here.

Wait. Not yet. I need make up, if I am to change into somebody else.

Be quick. In the extensive make-up room, Evangeline gathered brown false whiskers, mustache, eyebrows, and a brown men's-hairstyle wig of yak hair. Into the hat they went.

On top of that went a bottle of spirit gum with a brush applicator, alcohol and cotton wads, a brunette lady's wig, flesh-colored wig netting, crochet hook, and embroidery needles used in wig making.

That should do it.

Now, go.

No. One more thing. On her way out, she dodged back into the props room.

Cigars. She gathered a handful of chubby long cigars and a cigar holder. *The blasted smell of that spirit gum will give me away if I don't cover it with something else.*

She snapped the bag closed and made her way through the murky halls to her dressing room. After gathering her few personal items and not bothering to change out of costume, she eased her way down the back corridors of the theater. She looked over her shoulder, then hurried out into the driving rain.

Evangeline scampered across 10th St. through the downpour, dodging around milling theater-goers and groups of overwrought neighbors who'd heard about the shooting. As she climbed the front steps of Petersen's boarding house, a tall young man with heavy brows and long thin nose greeted her.

"You were on stage in the play at Ford's theater this evening?"

As she was still in her costume and full stage make up, Evangeline could hardly deny it. "Yes. Why do you ask?"

"We'll need to take a statement from you. It'll only take a few minutes. Come this way, please," and he headed down the front passageway.

"What's this about? Can't it wait? I've a splitting headache."

"No, miss. It can't wait...Here. Dry your face," and he produced a folded white handkerchief.

Evangeline heard the Secretary of War Edwin Stanton wheezing before she ever saw him. The aide ushered her into the back parlor that now smelled of stale cigar smoke. "Evangeline Bright, well-known actress, sir," said the aide.

The big, balding, bespectacled Pittsburgh lawyer with foot-long, salt-and-pepper, chin whiskers coughed into his handkerchief and after some moments pointed to a chair and said, "Sit here. Now, tell us what happened at the theater tonight."

Evangeline sat, slid the little bag beneath her chair, and promptly answered, "I was standing behind the curtain waiting to go on, when I heard a loud noise that must have been a shot. I looked out and saw someone jump onto the stage. When he started waving around a big knife I went backstage."

To the white-collared clerical man with pad and pencil at the small desk in the corner, Stanton said, "Did you get all that?"

The man nodded and, still writing, with the other hand made a gesture like lowering a window. Stanton said to Evangeline, "Slow down. The recorder can only write so fast. Did you recognize the person who jumped?"

"I think, umm, I did."

Stanton's knee jiggled up and down nervously and he raised his voice. "Well, speak up, girl. Who was it?"

"It was John Booth, sir."

"And what's your relationship with John Wilkes Booth, Miss Bright?" said Secretary Stanton.

Evangeline looked him straight in the eye and said, "I've known the whole family since Edwin, that's his older brother, hired me in New York. John is just an actor whom I admire. I've felt privileged to work with him occasionally."

"Are you friends?"

"Not really."

"Are you in a romance with him?"

Evangeline's eyes flashed. "Absolutely not," she said.

"Who else is involved with Booth in this matter?"

"I have no idea."

"What more do you know about the President's shooting?"

"Nothing at all."

Stanton paused and looked away for half a minute.

The air is all gone from this room. Let's open a window. She didn't. Evangeline listened to the multitude of voices in the hall and a buzzing roar from the chaotic crowd outside in the street.

I wonder? What is he thinking?

Her eyes roamed the room. In the lamplight she noticed a ceramic pitcher with glasses on a tray. *A drink of water would be welcome.* Then he motioned her out. Her first thought was, *Is that all? I could've done better than that!*

From the noisy corridor, the aide stepped in. "Sir, the doctor says the president probably won't last the night."

The president's dying. Good Lord. This can't be happening.

Stanton sighed and wiped his face with his handkerchief. Then he said, "We've seen Hawk, Keene, and this one. How many of the others have you rounded up for me?"

"I have six waiting out here, sir. "

"Out of what? Forty-five cast and crew? All right, but we are going to need to see Hawk again."

As she was leaving, he said, "Make sure he doesn't slip away somewhere. Arrest him. $1000 bond should do it."

Evangeline gulped. She couldn't get away fast enough.

Laura Keene, famous, exquisitely beautiful, 39-year-old British actress and theater manager who starred in tonight's production, approached her in the hall. The front of her light dress was soaked in huge red blotches. Laura's dark ringlets bounced on her shoulders as she looked down at herself. In a dazed voice, she said, "I tried to make him more comfortable. I held his head on my lap. That's his blood."

Lincoln's blood. Fear backed up in Evangeline's throat and she was a child, with bitter medicine in her mouth. *Have to get to my room. It's freezing in here.*

With her every step the bell that clanged endlessly inside her head moved her closer to feral.

The president is dying!

My crazy friend John shot him.

And I was there.

They'll think I helped.

She passed the front parlor. Mrs. Lincoln stood entirely alone, in her bonnet and gloves, next to a solitary marble-top table in the center of the room. "Why didn't he shoot me? Why didn't he shoot me? Why didn't..."

Ahhh.

My chest hurts.

She's crazy, too.

Am I? Crazy...

Dreaming?

Can't stop. Shaking.

Evangeline was a wild stallion with pounding heart, rolling eyes, and quivering flesh.

I. Can't. Do. This...

Oh, yes, I can!

Control yourself. Evangeline stopped wandering the halls and found her room. She sank onto the armchair. Some deep breaths later, head between her knees, she calmed herself enough to think.

What next? Loosen this tight French twist.

She pulled off her hat, removed hairpins, and shook her damp red curls loose. With a sigh of relief, she moved over and sat on the edge of the bed.

I feel like I'm stranded on a floating iceberg with a polar bear hunting right behind me. Argh! Stop it.

She threw up her hands in disgust. Then she peeled off her sopping wet theater costume and rubbed her arms warm with a towel.

How could I have gotten involved with someone who could shoot our president? She wiped the make-up from her face and became even more chilled by washing with soap, cloth, and the cold water in her basin.

I guess I was never really part of John Booth's group of anarchists. Or Dr. Mary Walker's hospital group either, for that matter.

She pulled on a warm hand-knitted wool nightgown and socks. Evangeline sighed deeply and shed some of her tension from the evening. As she relaxed, she let herself lapse into that time of sunshine, rubber boots, and baskets when she enjoyed foraging trips with nurse and poet, Walt Whitman...

"Oh, look... a clump of willow saplings that're just the right size," said Evangeline, known to everyone in Washington as an up-and-coming young actress. She pointed, then squished toward the stand of tall branches with long, green, pointed leaves. From the nearby oak, a mockingbird's song trilled and soared.

The country air smelled fresh, especially in contrast to the sweet antiseptic odors of chloroform and ether in the hospital tents. The grapevine handles of her old baskets felt rough in her hands as their cargo weighed her down.

"I can't carry much more, Evangeline. This is a good mix of herbs and bark, but let's strip some of this willow, too. Dr. Walker's almost out of pain medication," Walt said. "And I see some fever bark over there," he said, indicating a large shrub.

"All right, but I have to get back to the theater soon. Let's just bundle some of the larger branches and balance them atop our baskets so we can start back to town. I'll help you strip them tomorrow."

"The earlier we can turn this bounty into tinctures, the sooner those poor wounded can find relief."

Evangeline gave up her reverie, but now she felt utterly alone. *What am I going to do?*

No job. No boyfriend... Who needs George, anyway, that two-timer.

No family - she counted them off on her fingers. *Mama died alone in the sanitarium. God rest her tender soul. Father, plus my brother and sister, are all chasing their fortunes out west. Aunt Cora, my true soulmate...*

Tears plopped onto her blanket. She just gave in and had a good blubbering cry.

She cried for lost loved ones. She cried for family, so far away. She cried for a lost love. She cried for President and Mrs. Lincoln. She cried for the country.

She cried for clever kind Aunt Cora. And she cried for Ford's theater, her stunted acting career, and her jobless self. Then, she gave a final sniff, rubbed her eyes, and sat, staring at the wall.

Wait.

She sat up straight, eyes wide.

I forgot the letter from Aunt Cora's solicitor about the bequest...and the key he sent me!

She found them in the drawer of her bedside table. The envelope was addressed to 'Miss Sarah (a.k.a. Sadie) Snow.'

My real name!

Everybody here knows me as Evangeline Bright.

If I can get away from here, I can turn back into Sadie and not get sucked into this investigation.

Last week I couldn't take time to decide about a sale for Aunt Cora's house, because I was too busy learning new lines for our upcoming show... but now... a tiny cabin in Florida might be just what I need.

But travel... as a single woman? Difficult.

I would be very noticeable.

I don't want 'noticeable.'

A companion? No. I'm safer on my own.

I would blend in much better as a man.

How long could I act that part?

She set her jaw.

Evangeline pulled out her double-sided carpet bag and very deliberately turned the plain tweed side out. *I can act like a man as long as necessary.*

I can do it until Florida.

Aunt Cora, you are a lifesaver. Thank you.

Into the bag she put lacy underwear-chemises, drawers, no corset! - and two changes of casual wear - Long skirts, a silk one in 'mauvine,' an astonishing new shade of purple, and the other in fine grey cotton, and matching blouses, with long sleeves and high necklines.

I did nothing wrong. But try to convince them of that.

On top of these she placed detachable collars, belts, a hat, and comfortable shoes. *The newspaper articles make Florida and the St. John's River sound beautiful. Perhaps I'll see exotic birds.*

She added a Garibaldi shirt in white cotton, a navy blue paletot, and a purple paisley shawl, plus her favorite gold brooch and a chatelain with pad and pencil.

Secretary Stanton didn't tell me to stay. If I'm pulled into this investigation, who knows what could happen.

Have to get out of here.

NOW.

Well...not now. Be sensible.

I can't get any kind of transportation tonight.

And I'm so tired I can't wiggle.

Tomorrow, then.

The sturdy trousers, shirt, boots, and knife that she used for foraging she threw on top of the other items. She added her knee-length blue skirt and matching trousers that she wore when working with Dr. Walker. *Put in these two tie-on pockets to wear under the slits in my casual skirts. I won't need these when I'm dressed as a man. Men's clothing already has plenty of pockets.*

She looked around her small room for items that she might need. After pitching in a few more things, she checked her cash.

Steamer fare from the Potomac to Charleston before the war was $1.50. I'll take out at least $10 to keep in the money clip. The rest she folded and put into another tie-on pocket. *I'll wear this under my trousers to keep my funds extra safe, when I travel as Charles Snow.*

Evangeline laid out her clothes and tie-on money stash, with the money clip in her right pants pocket, for the next morning. She set her two travel bags and her black umbrella by the door.

Closing her eyes momentarily, the spent young woman willed her tiredness away.

With a sigh, she sat in front of her little mirror and braided her curly red hair. *I look tired.*

She took the sharp scissors from her sewing kit and cut her waist-length braids to shoulder length. Then she evened the bob, bound the cut ends of the braids, and stowed the hair in her carpet bag.

Keep going.

Evangeline hastily dry fit and trimmed the eyebrows, mustache, goatee, and side-whiskers that she would wear tomorrow. *These pieces feel like bristle brushes under my fingers.*

When she was satisfied, she returned the scissors to the sewing kit and placed it in her carpet bag. *One more thing.*

Her last preparation was to stuff strips of plain writing paper under the inside band of the top hat until, with repeated tries, the traditional topper fit over what was left of her hair and the men's wig.

I'm exhausted. But I am ready. Now, I need a mental alarm for 4 am. She pinched her wrist four times and finally allowed her head to sink into the pillow on her small bed. "Ahhh."

She closed her eyes. *Soon I'll put many miles between Ford's theater and Evangeline Bright. Tomorrow I get to play my biggest, most important role yet.*

Chapter Two

April 15, 1865 Very Early Morning

Leaving Petersen Boardinghouse

I t was a dark and gloomy night — and, as she peered out her window at four a.m. into the pitch black, Evangeline supposed the morning wouldn't be much better. She could still hear voices from the crowds in the street outside.

She yawned and stretched like a tabby cat. Then she got to work. First, she lifted her flickering candle, held a cigar to the flame, and drew on the chubby wad of tobacco until it spewed forth acrid smoke. Choking slightly, she laid it on a dish to allow it to perfume her new persona. She returned the candle to its holder on the wall.

Next, she sat at her dressing table and opened the bottle of spirit gum. She brushed a thin layer of the liquid on the back sides of the false eyebrows, mustache, and whiskers.

Whew. These fumes are enough to make a lesser woman faint. And cigar smoke, too. Ugh. How can people smoke these things?

She puffed on the cigar again to keep it from going out. *Blech.* The actress laid the hairpieces aside and gazed at herself in the mirror. With great care she brushed the pungent liquid onto her own eyebrows and other areas of her face where she needed the false hair.

After a minute and another puff on the cigar, she touched her finger to the back of the false mustache. *Still wet.* While she waited for the gum to become tacky, she dressed in the brown tweed suit, socks and high-heel men's boots. *This extra three inches will make me five foot ten. That will do.*

Evangeline took another puff, then pinned her now-chin-length curls back from her face and flat against her scalp. *Lovely.* Again, she touched her face. *Good, it's ready to stick.* She carefully attached her new facial hair and pinned in place the brown men's wig. *Hello, Charles Snow.*

It was five a.m. when 'Charles Snow,' feeling queasy from the cigar, donned slightly large gloves and top hat, and hooked the handle of the black umbrella over 'his' wrist. *UGG. I know it would add to my manly image to be seen smoking the cigar this morning, but I won't get very far if I'm vomiting. I'll just carry it as a prop.*

All right. Here I go. Goodbye, Evangeline Bright.

'He' lifted the two travel bags and strode out of the boarding house and into the pale morning light. *No guard at the door.*

Charles looked over his shoulder several times as he maneuvered his heavy bags around the large groups of anxious people. Strong odors of stale perspiration and fear assailed his nostrils as he brushed shoulders with many unwashed people.

Hurry. Get a move on, he thought, as he waited for a heavily loaded quartermaster's mule train to lumber up the street. *Crikey. These mules couldn't possibly move any slower.* In front of him, an animal deposited a pile of fresh manure, leaving a cloud of pungent steam rising from the slick cobbles.

Many people greeted him as he hurried on his way.

A tall brown man said, "Good morning. Is there any news?"

An old stooped fellow, with intense grief on his face, asked, "How is the president?"

Still another, a burly very black man said, "Is there no hope?"

In answer to these inquiries, Charles just shook his head. He saw many more negroes than whites. He heard all around him soft prayers and tearfully expressed outpourings of grief. They blended into a sort of hymn of supplication.

Get going. Faster.

Charles sped on toward the Potomac river. He could just hear the bawling of cows penned up on grounds of the unfinished Washington monument. *Cheerful thought for the morning...Butchers will slaughter some of them on site today to feed the Union soldiers.*

Emaciated government horses wandered the street, heads down, searching for grass. Hogs rooted in dark corners and chickens, that somebody was fattening for a future Sunday dinner, scurried away from the sound of his steps.

The gray clouds overhead promised rain. *Please, please, please don't let it rain until I'm inside, where it's dry. This gum will come unstuck if it gets wet. Then my goatee will slip down to my gullet.*

An ambulance approached, one of a seemingly endless stream, bringing more tattered skeletal wounded to the 21 military hospitals. From down a side street came the noises from yet more companies of Union soldiers drilling. "Hup, two, three, four, Hup, two, three..."

Oops. His heel slid on a slippery smelly patch of cobbles.

Is that footsteps? Someone running after me? He turned to look. The sounds receded into the distance.

Charles rushed on, past dim shapes of pine trees. He drew in a big deep breath. *That fresh pine scent is welcome.*

The boughs glistened with last night's rain, which had cleansed the air. It now smelled fresher, damp, faintly fishy, and a bit like the hardwood fires burning in the boilers of nearby paddleboats, steaming by on the Potomac. *All I need is one ocean-going sidewheeler. Please, God. Help me find a steamer that will give me passage.*

Just short of the docks, he stopped and set down the bags. He touched his new coarse whiskers. *Good. Still there.* He looked behind him. *No pursuers.* He heaved a big sigh, then peered out across the quarter mile span of dark water.

When I was here before the war, Washington was a sleepy southern town with genteel aristocracy, a population of 60,000 souls, and plenty of space.

Now the town is bursting with 250,000 people, including soldiers and the 5000 prostitutes who live in 450 brothels just 11 blocks south of the theater.

No, Washington. I won't miss you or your artillery caissons rolling up and down the city streets at all hours.

Ahoy. Here comes a fellow from one of those packets.

Better find my handkerchief to hold onto these whiskers.

A pale thin young man in a grey wool lounge jacket with matching waistcoat, trousers and greying blonde hair tied back, approached Charles. He fanned six tickets of different sizes in front of him.

"Good day, sir. I have here tickets that'll allow you to travel on the packet of yer choice this very morning," said the huckster. "Where are you headed today?"

Charles pulled out his linen square and covered his mouth, while he coughed slightly. He cleared his throat.

Speaking in a deep throaty voice through the handkerchief, he said, "I need to go to Savannah. Could you arrange that, good man?"

"With pleasure, sir. These here steamers are chartered to the Union army. They been carrying Union troops and supplies. But they're privately owned. Now that the war is over, a couple of 'em are headed down to Savannah to pick up prisoners of war, what just got released. They are real happy to have payin' passengers. Which of these two on the end do you fancy?"

Charles asked, "How much is the fare, sir?"

"Well, that would be $4.25 fer a cabin."

Plump drops of rain splattered the displayed tickets. *Oh, noo, no, no. Not now, when I'm so close.* Charles pulled out his money clip and pointed to the newer of the two steamers. "Here is a fiver. If you'll carry my bags to my cabin on board and arrange some breakfast to be taken there, you can keep the change."

"Done," he said, and pocketed the five dollars. "I'm Abraham. Come this way, sir."

Charles handed over the bags and followed him up a gangplank.

Abraham hailed a tight-muscled crew member, who had a pleasant face, and said, "Your new passenger fer cabin six, Pete."

"Thanks, Abe," the deckhand replied. "Show him on around. I'll just grab the key from the peg and be there in a minute."

They walked along the outside railing until Abraham stopped at the door of a cabin. "Here's your ticket. Yer made a good choice, sir. This here is the *Helen Getty,* as used to be a Confederate blockade runner, called the *Saint John's,* afore she was captured in '63. They wouldn't of got her, but she run aground in South Carolina waters comin' back from Nassau. She's real fast, too, now as they put in a new boiler, and engine, and all that."

Pete jogged up and unlocked the door. He pulled it open. "Welcome aboard the *Helen Getty,* with Nick King at the helm. Here's your key," he said, as he laid the key on the table by the narrow bunk. "Breakfast is at eight bells, dinner two bells."

"That's eight a.m. and five p.m., right?"

"Yes, sir. We take four-hour shifts, with a bell every half hour. And cabin 18 is set aside as our drinks room, where you can purchase any extras. Now, if that's all, I'll be gettin' on." He saluted and jogged off.

Abraham set Charles's bags inside, then said, "I'll be back in a bit with yer breakfast." He turned and followed the deckhand.

Just in time, too. There goes my eyebrow.

April 15, 1865 Early Morning Aboard the *Helen Getty* Bound for Savannah

I wonder which would draw more attention – arranging to have a waiter bring all my meals to the cabin, which will deplete available funds quickly, or speaking very little during meals and worrying that these eyebrows will fall into the soup?

Charles finished the ham and biscuit. He drank his tea. *I am so tired. I wonder if those creaks and groans are going to continue all the way to Savannah? Sounds like a threshing machine.*

Lulled by the motion of the ship, he relaxed and felt the anxiety of the last hours leave him. Eventually, he napped.

At 4:45 p.m. he walked into the pleasant dining room, which smelled of roast beef and potatoes. *I'll try one dinner in the dining room and then take it from there.*

He sat at a table with eight place-settings and other travelers soon joined him. "Cough. Cough." Through his handkerchief he said to his dinner companions, "This biting sea air... sorry for the cough."

"Yes, it's very bracing this time of year. Perhaps a little brandy will help," said an elderly, very upright gentleman to his left. Small bottles of brandy were at all the place settings and two pitchers of water graced each table. He helpfully poured some into a tumbler for Charles and passed it over.

If this doesn't dissolve the spirit gum, nothing will. He sipped and coughed.

Seated on his right, a lady in a blue bonnet tossed her head, setting the bonnet's ribbons bouncing. She said, "This table has a raised rim running all around the outside. Do they think we are all babies?"

Her officious companion said, "No, my dear. This edging is called a fiddle. It's there to keep plates and utensils from falling off when the steamer lurches."

And lurch it did, as they were being served their first course of roast meat, potatoes, and vegetables of various kinds. The meal finished with dessert of pies, puddings, and cheese.

This must be the fastest I've ever eaten a meal. But I don't think anybody noticed. They all seem in a big hurry to get back out onto the deck.

He rose and mingled with a large group of travelers, who exited the dining room and moved purposefully along the deck. *Why are they all going into that one cabin?*

Many people went into and out of the cabin. Curious, Charles allowed himself to be carried along with the crowd into a room, where a bar was railed off and a bar keeper, noticeable in suspenders and a red apron, was giving out liquor. *Ahh. The 'drinks room.' Hmm. Wine and spirits of all sorts. and malt liquors. and lemonade. and ice!*

That reminds me of the perfectly square ice cube in a lemonade I had at the fashionable National Hotel in Washington, where John Booth and his rebel friends used to meet. "Gulp."

The barman said, "I'm Sam, your mixologist, ladies and gentlemen. Everybody's asking. This here is a cash bar. The brandy put down on the dinner table may be used at pleasure and is included in your fare. But everything procured here is charged extra. Please pay for your drinks when you order them."

And deplete my funds before I even reach my destination? Charles edged out of the crowd and enjoyed the view of a grand sunset as he returned to his cabin, where he stayed, except for meals.

CHAPTER THREE

April 16–21, 1865

ABOARD THE "HELEN GETTY" TO SAVANNAH, MAKING WIGS

O n his second day aboard, Charles ate a breakfast of omelettes and more sausage and ham than he was used to consuming. Then he returned to his cabin and indulged in a little light sewing.

It's pretty calm this morning. I might as well work on my wig. Charles removed from his carpetbag the thick braids of his red hair, which he had cut at Petersen's.

My little room at Petersen's seems far away this morning. But it can't be far enough away to suit me. Though it was bigger than this berth.

On his bunk he assembled the flesh-colored, silk-net, foundation material, plus scissors, crochet hook and other items for wig-making. *So much hair - it's going to take forever.*

A chignon, I think. He unbound one braid and laid it on the bunk with the loose ends facing him. Then he cut off and rounded the edges of a piece of the net fabric.

If this steamboat doesn't stay steady, my hands will look like pincushions. Don't want blood stains on those fine big gloves. He hemmed this thin light base with tiny stitches.

Many of his future hours at sea were spent in the repetitive motions of pulling, with the fine crochet hook, and then knotting the cut ends of red hair through the cloth.

I wish I could attach more than a very few hairs at a time. But then, what else do I have to do?

On the night of the 19th the engine noise increased. "Chun, Chung, CHUNG." *That clanking and rattling of metal must mean we're going into Charleston for supplies.* Charles stayed in his cabin and altered the dress taken from Ford's theater.

Later that evening, bells sounded and soon the regular noises resumed.

A night and another two days of continuous motion and noise at sea saw Charles complete a long hair 'switch' and an intricate chignon, both fully ready to be pinned to his shorn locks.

And it brought them to the port of Savannah, Georgia. *At last. I am so ready to be off this steamer.*

Charles disembarked in Savannah with everyone else. *Now, to find some big impersonal hotel, where I can remove this fake beard.*

He walked along River Street, where many buildings smelled of mildew and cooked cabbage.

Is that fried chicken I smell? It can't be.

Wandering away from the river, he found streets lined with shops. On Broughton Street in Savannah's premier shopping district, he found his hotel. *Oh! Four stories of red brick...Marshall House.*

This looks like a pretty highfalutin place. A long iron veranda ran across the front of the property for 120 feet. It was a full 12 feet wide and 12 feet high. He went inside. The stylish young brunette lady behind the counter introduced herself as Madge. Charles inquired about availability and price of the rooms, then he said, "I expect to entertain my sister. Is this place respectable?"

Madge said, "I came here from San Francisco last year and I wouldn't set foot in some of these hotels around here. They are going to hell in a handbasket. But I can promise you, sir, there will be no Tomfoolery in our hotel."

"I'm glad to hear it. I'll take a single for tonight." He paid his fees and signed the guest registry.

She rang a bell and a bald man in a neat navy uniform appeared. "John, please show Mr., uh..." She consulted the book. "... Mr. Snow to his room." Charles accepted the proffered key, then relinquished it and his bags to John, and followed him through gaslit corridors.

Ooo, a courtyard atrium. With trees. And best of all, a back door.

"She gave you one of our newly renovated rooms, sir. It's a real pretty blue, like a bird's egg, with a mahogany fourposter featherbed. Until last month we were operated as a Union hospital. But now we have several illustrious guests living here."

"Really?"

"A newspaper man, Mr. Joel Chandler Harris, is writing funny stories. I like the ones about tricky animals. 'Heh, heh.' Yessir. In one book, a negro fellow called Uncle Remus tells about those talking critters. Here we are." With a flourish, he opened the door of Charles's room.

This is a mansion, compared to the steamer berth I've inhabited for the last week.

"Thank you," said Charles, "for the service and the interesting update." He tipped the helpful man generously.

It will be such a relief to be done with these whiskers. I know I can't just rip them off, but I really want to.

A knock sounded at the door. "I have your hot water and soap to wash, sir."

Whew. Luckily, I am still a 'sir.'

As soon as he was alone, he shed the itchy men's wig. He slowly removed the false hair and spirit gum from his face.

Sadie inspected herself in the mirror. *Welcome back, Sadie.*

Then she ever-so-gently washed her sore reddened skin with soap and warm water.

CHAPTER FOUR

April 22–24, 1865

FINDING THE "E.W. HALL"

The next morning Sadie stretched to her full height of five feet seven inches. *Ahhh. Nothing like a full night's rest on a thick soft mattress, which isn't moving, to make me feel human again. Time to get to work.* She took everything out of her carpet bag and laid it on the bed. *Now, presto-chango.*

She turned her carpet bag inside out to the flowered side. *This side is so much prettier anyway.*

She repacked most of her things. *If they are looking for me, they are looking for a redhead. I need this brunette ladies' wig, my plainest dress, and proper shoes.* After dressing, she added a straw boater hat over the wig.

I hope it's too early to see anyone out and about. Sadie Snow exited the back door of the Marshall House Hotel.

She walked through the sleepy early-morning streets of Savannah. No one challenged the upright conservative lady, who carried a bag in each hand.

If the police are looking for me, maybe I'm far enough away that they won't be looking here... and not for a brunette. I'll be quick.

As she neared the docks, the smell of fried chicken became stronger. *That has to be fried chicken.*

She turned a corner and saw a young negress entrepreneur in a purple and gold head scarf, putting the final adjustments to a portable food stand that was piled high with hot, crispy, golden-brown, fried chicken.

Sadie smiled and said, "That smells heavenly. Are you open for business now?"

The girl smiled back. "Yes, I sure am. I jest killed these hens this mornin'. They been battered and deep-fried crisp in hot oil, fresh as you can get. An' I have some fresh-baked, hot-buttered cornbread, an' some very frisky bottled cider, too. Would you like some?"

A bargain was struck and Sadie sank her teeth into a crunchy tender drumstick. "I need to get to Jacksonville. What do you know about the steamers going south?"

"Well, you has to make a choice. Smaller 'coastal steamers' go on th' inside sea route and are slower. The outside ones goes farther out ta sea, maybe 10 or 15 mile."

"Which is better, do you think?"

"Oh, I love the inside route and it's more pop'lar, 'cause of the famous wild scenery of the Sea Islands..."

"What do you mean?"

"When I go there, I'm always got up a' mornin' by noisy chirruping barn swallows. And ospreys holler tuh each other from these giant basket nests inna toppa trees. I like best the pretty feathery white egrets, what strut aroun' like royalty." She stirred the batter for some more cornbread.

"Big ol' pelicans and blue herons an' horny owls fill the air, an' ducks, too. People can allus get 'em a tasty turkey or a deer. The sakes, now... mean ol' hogs root there, under thuh oaks. Black bears go there, mos' times. You ever eat a bear?"

"No."

"A big un, sure 'nuff, can feed a gang." She poured batter. "An' the snake birds, an' sea cows, and otters, an', o' course, gators are everywhere in the water."

Sadie gulped. She shivered head to toe. Her voice came out squeaky as she said, "Snake birds? You mean you have snakes with wings?"

"No. O' course not." The girl laughed. "They's big black birds, what look like turkeys with long black necks like snakes."

Sadie relaxed. "That does sound wild. I can tell that you really love it," said Sadie, through a mouth full of cornbread. "Thanks for the delicious food and the information. Good luck with your business."

"Lord bless you!"

Sadie carried her carpetbag in her left hand and tucked the small bag under her left arm. Then she munched the rest of the way to the docks.

Hmm, coastal steamer or an outside ocean one?

Travelers are more likely to spend a lot of time on deck of a coastal steamer, which might not be a good thing for me.

Staying in my cabin could cause questions and suspicion.

I guess I don't need scenic. I need fast. How do I find a fast steamer for the next leg of my journey?

Lady luck smiled and Sadie found a berth on a 147-foot side-wheel steamer, the *E.W. Hall,* leaving at noon for Jacksonville, by way of the outside sea route. She boarded and settled in.

They left the dock right at noon and passed down the river toward the sea.

The land is low on either side. Look at that. People with hoes, wading ankle deep in water. Those must be rice paddies.

By two p.m. they were at sea, miles from the coast. *Nothing much to see here, except seagulls, which follow in our wake.*

A squall brought gray clouds, whipping wind, and slanted rain. *No chance of a pretty sunset this evening.*

Then lady luck frowned and the fugitive spent that evening and the next day until midnight battling something that had not plagued her before, seasickness.

A teaspoon of the digestive tincture I made when working with Dr. Mary Walker should help.

More than one teaspoon was needed, but it helped alleviate her discomfort. At midnight the *E.W. Hall* stopped.

She opened her cabin door and looked out on the mostly dark deck. "Are we there?" she said to a rugged deckhand in a striped navy and white shirt.

"No, Miss. We are at Fernandina. We have to wait a few hours for high tide. Cap'n says it's dead easy to get stuck on that there sandbar at the mouth of the St. John's. But don't worry none. We can float right on over at high tide."

"Thank you." She looked out over a calm sea, with moonlight reflected off thousands of tiny riplets on the immense sheet of water.

A huge full moon shone golden on the horizon, with its light shimmering across the dimpled surface.

Welcome to Florida, Sadie.

She went back to her bunk. Her last thought before sleep claimed her was, *I like this gentle rocking and rhythmic splashing of the water on the hull.*

Sunrise was a yellow, red, orange, cobalt blue, purple, and pearly white affair. It spread forever in all directions and was reflected in a glassy sea.

A pod of 60 or 80 dolphins exploded in the water. They splashed and cavorted, transforming the placid scene. *Ooo, how they jump.*

Sadie heard a deckhand call out to another, "Toss the Jacob's ladder overboard."

From the railing she watched them. One had a thatch of blond hair under his dark blue wool flat hat and the other had coal black hair. They wrestled a sort of flexible ladder, made of wooden rungs and ropes, overboard.

'Thud.' It hit the side. Seagulls scolded.

A small boat puttered along beside the *E.W. Hall.*

Hmm, that man just reached out to the side of our steamer and grabbed at the bottom rung. Uncomfortable way to come aboard.

Pilot? Guess they need more than high tide to help get them over an ever-changing sandbar.

Sadie went back to her cabin and repacked her carpet bag. On the top went the red chignon and some hair pins. She tied an orange band around her straw boater and repacked it.

And she pleated and neatly folded a large, orange-and-white polka-dot silk scarf on top of it all. *Ready. Time to join the other travelers on deck.*

The river, broad and beautiful, was marred by a battery of ominous 32-pounders, cannons looking over the sand bank. The banks were covered with a dense thicket of palmetto. *My goodness. Smell those magnolias. And those are the biggest oaks I ever saw. Beautiful...* They stopped at Mayville and Yellow Bluff to deliver mail and some goods.

Fishing villages? Fishermen and small creeks seem to go together here.

At 10 a.m. on the morning of the 24th, they arrived in Jacksonville, a disappointment.

CHAPTER FIVE

April 24, 1865 Morning

AT JACKSONVILLE, FLORIDA DOCKS, FINDING THE "KATIE ASBELL"

*W*hat a dilapidated place. *She stood silent, perfectly paralyzed with amazement. Dirt streets? Stores and houses not numbered?*

Compared to Washington and New York and other northern cities, where I've been working lately, Jacksonville is pathetic.

Sadie disembarked with everyone else. She overheard another traveler, who said in a deep bass voice, "No. I promise you, my dear, it used to be full of shops. More than 2,000 souls lived here. People gave dinner parties and played cards. They danced. But it has changed occupiers four times during the war. It has become a mere skeleton of its former self."

I need a private place to take off this wig. She walked past abandoned shops. *Hmm, that one, with the rickety door slightly ajar, nobody around that I can see, no bad smells, no sounds coming from there...*

She stepped into the entryway and stood still a moment, listening. *Nothing.*

Off came the brunette wig. She ran her fingers through her short red hair, removing pins and massaging her scalp.

The hair pins went back into her smoothed bob and then fastened the chignon at the back of her head. *Bright, orange-and-white, polka-dot scarf at my neck to change the look of this white dress.*

And, on top, my straw boater hat with its orange band to finish the look. I'm ready to be me.

She readjusted the items in her carpet bag, snapped it closed, turned to leave, — and looked straight into the glittering black eyes of a man with glossy, slicked-back hair, a trim black van dyke beard, and small mustache.

The devil?

Can't get out to run.

Fight.

She edged backwards and changed her stance. *Who is he?*

Silk top hat? In this weather?

Black wool fitted jacket with embroidered shiny red silk waistcoat. Definitely not police.

He continued to stare, with a calculating look.

Then he turned on his heel and strode away. His ultra-fashionable, wide, billowing, pinstriped trousers flapped around his legs.

Dear God.

Whew.

How much did he see?

She told herself, *Self, hurry up. Go find another paddleboat and get out of here.*

With every nerve on high alert, Sadie rushed back to the dock. *Need a smaller boat.*

She saw a small split-paddle stern-wheeler by the name of *Katie Asbell.*

"Does this ship go to Enterprise?" she said to the tall hard-muscled young man working with ropes on deck.

"Yes, in about five minutes. And we have a berth available. Do you want to book passage?"

"How much do you charge?"

"It is $1.75 one-way, $3.25 round-trip."

"Yes, all right. I'll take the one way, please."

"You planning to stay a while?" He moved more ropes.

"Maybe." *His muscles really ripple under that tight knit shirt.*

"You know, it's cheaper to buy your return ticket now."

"Yes, I noticed that. My education did run to math, algebra, logical reasoning..." she said, with some heat.

"Sorry, if I offended you. Just trying to help. Come on aboard. I'm Noah Asbell, by the way." Over his shoulder, he said to a group of men headed down the gangplank, "Abel, when you finish offloading the gator, help this lady get situated. We are burning daylight here."

Great Caesar's ghost. Four muscular deckhands, who balanced on their shoulders a 12-foot-long alligator lashed to a 12-foot-long board, marched heavily down the plank straight toward her. As they passed, she could read the tag on its leg: 'Oskey's General Store, Souvenir Handbags, Shoes, Belts, and Suitcases.'

What is that? A do-it-yourself kit? A shiver ran up her spine.

His eyeballs just turned toward me. Yick.

Both leathery eyelids closed halfway. *He looks as if he's summing me up as a candidate for his next meal. Ugh.*

I expected beautiful exotic birds. But alligators? What am I getting myself into?

She gathered her bags and started up the gang plank.

After a few minutes, with fare and keys sorted, Sadie stopped at her door a moment to talk with Abel, the young fit deckhand. *He could be a relative, but his chin-length hair is more orange. He's exactly my height*

A fashionable five-foot tall, blue-eyed brunette in a big black bonnet emerged from the cabin next door.

The lady said, "Can you tell me why we must change steamers yet again? I just get settled and then I have to move."

Oh, dear. How will she get around on the steamer in that skirt? My fussy neighbor is festooned with so many yards of fine white gauze that she looks like a five-tiered wedding cake.

Abel said, "Sorry for your inconvenience, Mrs. Maas. On Florida's rivers, big side-wheelers would not do. Sometimes the curves on the Saint John's are so tight that long steamers can get stuck. And only stern-wheelers can hope to push their way through the masses of floating water weeds that clog the creeks in the southern reaches of the Saint John's."

"Well, thank you. It's done now," she said, dismissively.

And to Sadie, she said, "Hello. I'm Ava. Would you care to promenade with me on the deck?"

Why not? No government agents will be all the way out here. "I'm Sadie, and yes. Let's enjoy the fresh air and see the sites."

They pushed their way toward the bow. *Ava's skirt is waaaaay too wide for this passageway.*

The steamer chugged past a huge grove of magnolias and for a few moments the air smelled of lemons.

"Good morning," Ava said to a winsome, blue-eyed, blonde woman, who stood looking out. "I'm Ava, and this is Sadie. Won't you join us?"

She's very lithe. Except for a bit of a tummy bulge. Very pretty, with that heart shaped face.

"Kat Ashley. I'm sorry, but I wouldn't be very good company. I'm somewhat seasick."

The boat pitched the ladies sideways and Sadie grabbed the rough wooden handrail to steady herself.

A tall man, with shaved shiny-bald head and brown eyes that crinkled at the corners rushed up to them. "There you are, Kat." His ginger handlebar mustache and long ginger goatee looked more suitable to a billy goat.

His wide welcoming smile with sparkling white teeth seemed to be intended for Kat, but extended to Sadie and Ava, as well.

That man's a smile on feet.

Kat reacted like a parched flower offered water. She bloomed momentarily, then settled and said, "Ladies, this is Buck Stotts. Buck, meet my new friends, Sadie and Ava. I think I might go back to my cabin and lie down a few minutes."

"Nonsense, Kat. The fresh air will do you a world of good," said Buck. He took her arm in a supportive manner.

The little group headed once more toward the bow, with Ava, compressing her giant hooped skirt as much as possible, in the lead.

Coming toward them at speed was a hefty man of medium height, with a big belly, receding blond hair and blue eyes in an affable round face. Ava introduced him as her husband, Mr. Bram Maas.

"Mrs. Maas. Ava, my dear," he said.

He looks like the wealthy Dutchmen I saw in New York — white shirt with 10-inch-wide collar, dark green vest, knee pants, high white knee socks, square-toed shoes, and a tall wide-brimmed black hat.

He twitched his enormous reddish-brown up-curled mustache. *It's a set of ox horns attached to his face.*

He burst out, "O folly, fudge, and flummediddle, Ava. You know I hold you in highest esteem, but your adoption of every latest fashion is, at times, totally impractical."

The couple hurried on toward the bow, with Ava, once again in the lead.

"Well, I just wanted a stroll to take some air."

She is 'strolling' the narrowest of decks, 18 inches wide, in her huge bubble skirt.

"The problem, dear husband, is this deck is not of sufficient area to allow comfortable passage."

"I'm having no trouble, but you will insist upon your high fashion, though it pinches or cuts off your breathing or obscures the very ground upon which you tread."

Ignoring his criticism, she forged valiantly ahead. "I think I might quite like to stop in Piccolata, Mr. Maas.

"We could take that stage coach ride over to Saint Augustine. It's only three hours, and Aaaa... AAaa... AAAA."

"Oh, my goodness," said Kat Ashley, from behind them.

"Aaagh. Aaaa."

"I don't believe my eyes, "Kat said. "She has toppled over headfirst into the companionway."

"Ohhh. EEeeee. Help," Ava said, wiggling her legs in the air.

"What happened?" said Kat.

"I was compressing my skirt as much as I could... but it still stuck out some... in the front. I leaned forward to look... my foot slipped... and... and my hoops... Ohhhhhhh. Get me out of here," Ava said, her voice muffled by yards of fabric.

Mary Merritt, one of a pair of little white-haired vacationing ladies, approached the dramatic scene from the other direction. "Gracious. Mercy me."

Martha, her sister, stepped from behind her and said, "I saw it all very clearly. That lovely voluminous skirt covered up the opening. She stepped over the edge and fell right in. I think she was pushed by her...catapulted by her...her, yes, by her hoops."

"I demand that you release me," said Ava, her voice floating up from the stairs below. She kicked and bicycled her legs frantically.

Sadie said, "Be calm, Ava. That skirt has inverted over your head."

"I don't want commentary. I want down," came her faint shout.

The fashionable lady twisted and bucked. She churned her legs.

"Better stay still, Ava. Those hoops are holding you up," said Sadie.

She continued to twist and kick.

"If you keep on kicking, I fear you'll dislodge the hoops and fall down the stairwell. You are in danger of being seriously hurt."

"Oh. I can't bear it. Everybody is standing around looking at my drawers," was her muffled reply.

Sadie turned and rushed to find the captain.

Ava unleashed a new wave of thrashing.

"Keep those boat men away," Ava said.

The hoops settled on one side.

"Clatter. Thunk."

"Eek."

On one side they caught firm 18 inches lower.

Onlookers gasped.

That side of Ava dropped farther down into the stairwell.

Ava shrieked.

She suddenly stopped moving.

A moan floated up from the depths of the stairwell.

"I am so embarrassed. I could die."

Oblivious to her danger, the little woman gave one more giant angry kick, accompanied by an anguished cry. "HEEEeeahh."

They heard her faint sobs.

Mary leaned over the nest of fabric, steel bands, and legs. "Take two deep breaths, Misses Maas. Now, are you hurt? Anything broken?"

"N-no. "Hiccup." "N-nothing broken."

"Glad to hear you are all right," said Mary.

"All right? No. I don't think I am. I'm angry."

An onlooker said, "Heavens to Betsy. Her skirt's inverted. Most improper. We can't let her just dangle upside down there in the midst of all those steel hoops. Poor dear."

Kat said, "Where is Mr. Maas? There you are, sir. Do something, Mr. Maas."

Bram seemed unaware of her peril. He stifled a smile and said, "By thunder, my fair pet. You are disarrayed of many roses, and five yards of flounce or flummediddle, which skirted the lower part of your dress."

Then he relented. "All right. This has gone on long enough. Don't cry, Ava. I'll have you out in a minute."

He didn't bat an eyelash at seeing his wife suspended upside down, kicking her bloomered legs.

He grabbed said diminutive wife by the ankles and unceremoniously hoisted her, legs first, up and out of the gaping hole.

When he managed to get her upright, he clasped her to his chest in a great bearhug that lasted a full five minutes.

Noah Asbell arrived with Sadie in his wake. "Has anyone been hurt?"

When Bram finally let her go, Ava said to all those assembled, "I have only a small scratch and some bumps."

The skirt hoops, however, were not so lucky.

Could this lady possibly get into any more trouble on this trip?

Sadie distanced herself from the group to explore. Climbing the almost-straight-up stairs of the companionway was fairly easy, though the skirt kept getting in the way. She went to the top and emerged into bright sunshine.

What is the sense in wearing a long skirt that tangles around your ankles? In view of Ava's accident, I'm going to wear my knee-length skirt and trousers tomorrow.

From the top-most level, the hurricane deck, Sadie admired the view. *If I were to paint a picture of this forest, I would need a great variety of different greens.*

Magnificent oaks stood with stately elderberry trees and pines behind the cypress, whose 'knees' made a fence to keep intruders away from the bank. Curly grey-green moss dangled from every branch. And the saw-toothed palmettos grew more and more abundant as they traveled farther south.

Noah stepped out of the pilot house and walked to where Sadie stood. *Ha. I see silver-green branches of mistletoe. Too bad there's no one to kiss*, he thought.

A sweet smell arose from a large stand of shiny-leafed trees. The scent perfumed the air as they cruised by. "Mmm," she said.

"Yes. Late-blooming oranges. It's a perfect spring day, all right." Great numbers of blue herons and white-plumed egrets lifted from the tops of trees and wheeled away into the distance, to escape the disturbance of the noisy steamboat engines.

"You know that I'm Noah Asbell, the captain of this steamer. May I know your name, please?"

"Sadie Snow, math prodigy and logical thinker," she said, with a wry smile.

"Again, sorry about that. Are you visiting the St. John's River for a vacation?" he said.

Before she could answer, a fat three-foot-long, orangeish-brown snake fell from an overhanging cypress tree and landed with a wet 'plop' right in front of them. Sadie jumped back and gave a strangled scream. "Ack!"

Noah said, "Oh, what a beauty. Look at those bright red blotches between the black borders." He reached over and picked it up behind its head. "It won't hurt you. This is a harmless corn snake. They're non-venomous. Want a closer look?"

He held it out toward her and she danced backwards a few more steps. "No, thanks."

"Some people keep these as pets, because they're so pretty."

"Not me. Get rid of that thing."

"All right." He laughed and dangled it over the rail. Then he leaned out and dropped it overboard, far out of the path of the paddle.

Sadie looked away. *How embarrassing. He was actually laughing at me. He thinks I'm weak — that I need to be rescued. I hate that.* Without another word, Sadie headed for the companionway ladder and rushed down as far as she could go.

I'll avoid him, brush him off.

She found herself on the cargo deck. *Cackling and clucking? Ahh. Crates of live chickens, labeled* '50c each, eggs 10c per dozen.' *These red hens are not pleased with all the noise and confusion down here.* She hurried around the corner.

Ooo, bolts of colorful fabric from across the world. Going to Enterprise? A peek under the muslin covers showed glorious shades of deep blue, majestic purple, jade green, and soft dove gray.

She stroked the slippery silk with her fingertips. *Mmm, I can just imagine the feel of a blouse in the cobalt blue as it slides smooth against my skin.*

An earthy smell reached her nose and she heard a low nicker. She walked around a pile of boxes. *I thought so. A hobbled mule.* She sat on a hogshead of sugar and fed him bits of grass from the floor.

Wonder what's in those barrels? The sacks of flour will probably end up as next week's bread and biscuits.

She wandered around among more boxes and barrels. *Ohhh. A big wicker basket labeled* 'Rosenbush Bakery, Green Cove Springs.' She lifted the lid. *Empty. Maybe they trade them out, every time they stop there.*

Mmm. The smell of cured tobacco. And those covered bushel baskets are labeled 'SALT.' Seems like a lot. Maybe for preserving things? I read something about Florida saltworks, active during the war.

The dinner bell rang and Sadie made her way to the dining room.

CHAPTER SIX

April 24, 1865

ABOARD THE "KATIE ASBELL" FROM JACKSONVILLE TO PALATKA

H er friends from that morning sat at a table for eight. "Hi, Sadie. Over here. We have six and you make a seventh," said Ava, waving to Sadie, as if her trouble and embarrassment from her morning was forgotten.

"Thank you," said Sadie and she walked toward their party.

Kat and Buck are sitting together at the far end laughing with Ava and Bram. Then the two nice older ladies are sitting across from each other. Two end places left. Which one?

"Hello. I'm Mary. Come sit next to me." She patted the seat beside her. "And this is my sister, Martha, " she said, gesturing. "I'm sorry, I don't know your name."

"I'm Sadie," she said with a smile to the little lady. "Have you come a long way to see the beauties of Florida, Mary?"

"Not really. We have a place south of Saint Augustine and we just love the Saint John's. We used to come here often, but the blockades stopped all that, you know."

All right, Sadie. You opened that door, and now, if asked, where are you going to say you came from? Oh bother.

Sadie opened her mouth to continue the conversation, when her eyes met the black ones of her devil from the morning.

She gasped.

He took the seat across from her.

"Good evening, ladies. I'm Neville. Neville Beaumont. Hasn't it been a beautiful day?" he said, in a most charming manner.

No. This can't be happening. On the other hand, what better time to use my acting skills to find out more about this man.

Hold your body like his. Mimic his movements to put yourself into a similar state. What are his real emotions?

Introductions were made around the table, with Sadie watching, mimicking, and learning.

Then Sadie, wishing to divert attention from herself, focused on the delicious-smelling meat and vegetable stew with biscuits and separate bowls of vegetables, just brought to table.

She said to the server, a tall skinny young boy with a shock of chin-length dark curls, "This smells wonderful. What kind of meat is it?"

The young man's brown eyes, framed by dark heavy brows, looked down at his feet and he said, "This is venison, Miss. Very fresh, it is."

"And I don't recognize this pod vegetable. What is it?"

"Oh, fried okra, Miss. It's just come in. It grows in hot weather. Very tender, Miss."

"Thank you. You are most helpful. What's your name?"

"Christian, Miss."

My table mates keep looking at this 'Neville Beaumont.'

"Where are you from, Mr. Beaumont?" said Mary.

Watching.

"I have a plantation near Savannah Georgia, and I thought I would come down here and see how Florida has fared during the war. I might invest."

"Does your place have a name?" said Bram.

"Why, yes. It's called *Windsweep* and we grow mostly cotton and tobacco. What do you do, Mr. Maas?"

"Please, call me Bram. We hail from New Amsterdam and I trade all up and down the Hudson River. Ava here runs our emporium, Maas Brothers, in New York."

"And you, Mr. Stotts?"

"Insurance, Neville, insurance. I travel a lot for my company, Guaranteed Mutual."

Christian set on the table a yellow cake topped with lightly-browned, glazed, yellow fruit.

"Ohhh, lovely. What is this?" Sadie said, in an attempt to change the subject.

"Pineapple upside-down cake, Miss. It's a specialty in these parts, as we have a very fine pinery nearby."

"Thank you. I'm sure we'll all enjoy it." *Now everyone be quiet and eat your cake.*

After many satisfied "Ooo's" and "Ahh's," Kat wiped her lips and said, "I believe I will go out on deck. We should be arriving in Palatka soon. I am curious about the place."

"Me, too," came a chorus of voices from around the table.

"Well, gents, can I interest either of you in a friendly game of poker?" said Neville.

"Lots of fuss changing steamers, don't you know," said Bram, as a half-hearted excuse.

"Would love to, but let's make it tomorrow," came the excuse from Buck.

He still has glossy, slicked-back hair and a black van dyke beard. Something secret about him. I'm undecided. Am I wrong about Neville?

Those at her table stood and ambled out on the deck to watch the *Katie Asbell* dock at Palatka.

"He's nice, that Neville," said Ava, on the arm of Bram. "And quite a swell. I heartily approve of his attire."

The boy Christian came and stood for a few minutes next to Sadie at the railing.

He finally said, "I think there are 30 or 40 families living here now. Some left during the war, but many just came back. I stayed here some during the war."

"How very beautiful." *Palatka's up on a high bluff.*

"I'm off duty. Would you like me to show you around?" he said.

"That would be splendid. Thank you."

As soon as the gang plank went down, Sadie and the young server sauntered off the steamer to explore Palatka.

They walked along the flat banks of the river, where tall oak trees sent roots down into the dark waters.

"Five or six stores used to sell lots of things along here. But now all that's left is the dry goods store," he said.

They wandered into an old weathered wooden structure. "Almost all of the buildings in town were built by Union troops during the Seminole war. They made small one-story houses for enlisted men and two-story ones for the officers. This was a supply depot."

"Hey there, Christian, Miss" said a wrinkled old man in a floppy hat. "I have sugar cane, fresh today, which sells at two cents per cane."

"Hey there, Curly," said the boy. "This is Miss Snow. We was just..."

"I'll have two of those, please," said Sadie. She handed over the money.

With a large sharp knife, he cut the canes into six-inch pieces, peeled them, and put them into a sack. He laid the knife on his table and handed the cane to Sadie.

"Thank you," she said and immediately offered some to the man and Christian.

They all chewed on the crunchy pithy cane. She watched her companions. *They chew, swallow, and spit.*

Sadie followed their lead and, after swallowing the sweet juice, she spat out the remaining stringy fibers.

"That's very good. I see why everybody likes it," she said.

Two men came in with venison to sell. "Hey, Curly. I have six saddles," said a short wiry fellow in blue plaid.

The second, who wore a faded red shirt, said, "And I have three. We're askin' a dollar and a half per saddle."

Christian said, "A saddle of venison is the hindquarters of a deer, separated from the fore. Hunters around here keep the forequarters for themselves and sell the hinds."

"I'm paying a dollar a saddle, " said Curly.

"You can have 'em all for a dollar and a quarter uh piece."

"Deal," said Curly, and the three headed outside to a wagon with a bay grazing nearby.

"He'll do good on that trade," said Christian, as they moved farther into the depths of the store. "He can sell it fast to the steamboats. They salt it and take it off to sell in Savannah and Boston."

In the dark interior Sadie spied bales of black wiry goods. She moved to inspect the substance.

Why do I have the eerie feeling that I'm being watched?

Christian said, "We call that stiff wiry stuff 'black moss.' Gathering moss is a very profitable business. It sells for \$.10 or \$.12 a pound."

Something moved in that dusty murky corner. She tensed.

"Folks take the green moss down from the trees and lay it in water or in heaps. Weeks later they spread it out to dry and pound it with sticks. Then they bale it up and sell it. Folks use it to stuff mattresses."

She moved back toward Christian in the dark.

The shape is following me.

In her loudest voice, she said, "Christian, I need to trim this cane. Would you get Curly's knife for me, please."

"He must 'a took it with him, Miss. It's not here."

"Let's go back, Christian. I'm feeling tired," she said and rushed from the building.

"All right. I'm on duty again soon, anyway. But first, I want to show you the 'Lookout.' We're almost there."

Sadie looked back and saw no one following them.

"See that big armory over there? The tower on top is where the soldiers kept 'lookout' for Seminole attackers."

She looked where he pointed.

Am I imagining things?

Watching us from atop the tower?

A man in a top hat. And he has a distinctive pointy Van Dyke beard.

Don't be daft. A lot of men have top hats.

Chapter Seven

April 25, 1865

Aboard the "Katie Asbell" from Palatka to Enterprise

Midmorning Sadie meandered along the passenger deck, her knee-length blue skirt and matching trousers flapping in the breeze.

Practical clothes today. Dr. Mary Walker would approve.

At the approach of the steamer, many white egrets, blue herons, and red ibis flew from their perches in trees beside the river. Ahead of her on the bow, she saw Buck and Kat standing at the railing.

They don't look like strangers to me. He looks at her like a cat ready to lap up cream.
"Hello, you two. Beautiful day isn't it?"

"Is it? I feel green," said Kat.

I don't remember seeing her at breakfast a while ago.

Sadie said, "We do seem to be twisting and turning more today. I have some digestive tincture that might help you feel better. Would you like me to bring you some?"

Kat replied in a faint voice, "Oh, yes. Please do."

"It'll just take a few moments to retrieve it from my cabin."

Now, what did I do with that blue bottle? Got it. She made her way back to the small dining room with the well-stoppered bottle.

In the adjoining galley, Cookie, a swarthy, aproned fellow, smiled at her request. He quickly brewed her a cup of strong hot tea.

She thanked him and added a teaspoon of the digestive tincture. She stoppered the bottle and pocketed it, then carried the cup to Kat.

"You're an angel."

Sadie said something she had heard Aunt Cora say many times. "We are all in this world together." And then, " I hope you feel better soon."

The *Katie Asbell* stopped mid-river and began to float back down the stream. "Why are we stopping?" she asked a nearby deckhand.

"This here is the best spring for filling our water tanks. We'll be here a few minutes."

Sadie continued along and opened the door to the small salon. *Oh. Smoky.*

"Hello, Shugah, lookin' for a frolic? Let me take off them trousers for ya. That there short skirt'll make it real easy," said a burly scruffy man, built like a New York city fire hydrant.

"Behave yourself and don't call me sugar," Sadie said and walked back out.

Huh. His waistcoat is embroidered shiny red silk, similar to that of Neville Beaumont's. Must be an 'embroidered-shiny-red-silk-vest' club around here somewhere.

She moved a chair to the bow and sat enjoying the scenery, the beautiful weather, and a lot of attention from the crew. *I guess it's still not that common for unaccompanied women to travel.*

A clean-shaven man, over six feet tall, approached her. "Hi. I'm first mate. My name is Shorty. Can I get anything for you? A more comfortable chair?"

"No, thanks. I have everything I need."

Two young fellows with carrot-colored hair approached. "Hello, Abel. Who's your friend?"

"Good day, Miss. My brother and I are the new hands Noah just hired. He answers to Adam. I thought as you might be getting thirsty out here. We brought lemonade and gingerbread."

"How kind." *And I was worried about being a woman traveling alone.*

Thus, her second day in Florida passed pleasantly.

Noah happened by. She ignored him. But she couldn't help noticing the tall commanding appearance of his retreating figure. *Hmm.*

After dinner a light sprinkle of rain sent most of the travelers into the salon to play cards and tell stories.

Kat playfully grabbed Sadie's hand and said, "Come on, Sadie. It'll be fun."

"Do join us," said Mary Merritt.

"All right. For a little while," said Sadie.

"Bram and Buck are with Neville, who is shuffling cards already. Doesn't that sweet man have lovely manners?" said Ava.

"Yes. Neville Beaumont's a real gentleman," said Kat. "Who is that loud, offensive, back-slapping person with them?"

"That's Luther Greim. He has no sense of social boundaries or proprieties," said Ava.

Unlikely companions. Neville, Bram, and Buck with that obnoxious man who accosted me this morning. Laughing and drinking. A roar of laughter came up as they slapped down the cards.

Luther's animated coarse voice could be heard all over the room. He said, "Bram Maas. Dutch name, isn't it? I heard of a real famous fella, New York poet, Washington Irving, what said that the Dutch smoke so much they become a lantern-jawed, smoke-dried, leather-hided race. Hahahah."

Bram removed his briar and silver pipe from his mouth and blew smoke on Luther. Everyone laughed.

Luther said, "Didja hear about them 12 Union ships sunk in the Saint John's by the Confederacy during the War? A confederate spy, Lola Sanchez by name, told the local militia leader when and right where the *Columbine* would be. HaHA. An' I bet I know what they were doin' when she told 'im. Ha, ha, ha, ha, ha." He waggled his bushy brown eyebrows.

"The militia set up artillery pieces an' sharp shooters along the river. They fired on the *Columbine* when it came into view. She sunk and 68 sailors was killed -- a lot of 'em were slaves, what done been freed. Ha, HA. Kin you imagine a US naval ship sunk by... BY A Horsey CAVALRY UNIT? Ha, ha, hah."

That's all we need - somebody stirring up more trouble between the north and the south. Luther is drunk.

Cookie walked through the room and said, "I see he's already well corned."

Luther asked, in a loud belligerent voice, "Buck, where's that pretty little red-headed wife a yours? She at home with your two little children?"

Buck paled. He stood and shook his fist in Luther's face. "Shut up, you cheater."

Luther stumbled up and grabbed Buck by the lapels. "Who are you calling a cheater?"

Uh oh.

Kat and Sadie jumped up.

Kat said, "Do something."

Sadie rushed to stand between the two men. "Luther, you're drunk. You need to stop bothering people and go sleep it off."

"You britches-wearing busybody. Quit sticking your nose in my business."

He slapped her hard, knocking her against the bulkhead. A great gush of warm blood spewed forth from her nose.

Ow, ow, ow, ow. That hurts like blazes. Then, *No complaining. No moaning.* As he started for her again, she regained her balance.

An onlooker shouted, "That'll teach 'er to stay out uh men's affairs, Luther."

Great Caesar's ghost.

He must weigh as much as two men put together.

"Hit 'im back, Girl. He ain't got no respec'," shouted an angry-sounding woman from the gathering crowd.

He charged.

She sidestepped and pivoted.

It's like fighting a bull.

He slammed into the bulkhead, then shook his head. "Yer can't get away from me. GRR." He pulled back his lips from yellow teeth, in a rictus grin.

A robust gal punched the air and shouted, "Smack 'im. Give 'im a good one."

"Stay out of it, Missus," hollered a slight man beside her.

"Rrraaar."

Luther roared and charged.

This time, Sadie moved toward him.

She leaned in, like a hug, with her head on his left shoulder.

In a flash, her left hand grabbed his right elbow and pinned the drunken man's wrist under her left arm pit.

She adjusted her feet, reached her right arm around his waist and pushed him forward, yanking down hard on his right elbow.

Her feet moved in front of his.

She looked over her left shoulder and pulled him in front of her.

Pull.

Push.

He toppled over her.

"Crash. Kerwham. Thud."

His huge head, body, then legs smacked hard on the deck.

He spat out blood.

He didn't get up.

"Did she just knock him down?" said Mary.

Ava said, "No, of course not. He tripped."

Sadie backed away.

Luther swarmed up. "You are mine, girlie," he raged. "I'm gonna teach you who wears the pants."

He lunged toward her. "Let me at her. She needs a good beating."

Buck and Bram pulled him back.

"I am gonna beat her within an inch of her life."

Luther broke away and lurched toward her.

"Watch out. He's wild."

Noah burst in. "What's going on?"

Luther punched him.

Noah stumbled backward a step.

He recovered.

His eyes were windows on his anger. It showed like two orange-flaming bonfires.

The fit, muscular boat-captain set his jaw.

He took a deep breath.

With every ounce of his muscle and considerable torque, he let fly a right hook to Luther's nose.

The bully kissed the deck again.

He stayed down.

After flexing his fingers, Noah checked the man for a breath. "He's all right. Cookie and Adam, take him to his cabin to sleep it off."

Oh great. He's saved me again.

Noah pulled a neatly folded clean white handkerchief from his pocket and handed it to Sadie. "You want to tell me why your nose is bleeding? Or why Luther was going for you?"

"He was drunk and looking for somebody to fight. I got in his way. End of story."

Noah raised his voice and said, "The show's over folks. We'll be in Enterprise within the hour. Please go to your cabins and get ready. The hotel is waiting for you with soft beds and good cooks."

CHAPTER EIGHT

April 25, 1865 Evening

AT BROCK HOUSE HOTEL IN ENTERPRISE, FLORIDA

"Woot, woot, woooot." The distinctive whistle blew its cheery 'We're-back-again-everyone' greeting. Fifty-year-old retired Pinkerton man, Michael MacNally, Mac to his friends, sat in a cushy deck chair on the Brock House front veranda, watching the *Katie Asbell* steam up to the dock. His old leg wound, from his days as an active agent, was barely hurting today.

Jacob Brock built his two and a half story white hotel on the shore of Lake Monroe in 1854 to sleep 50 people. He extended the Brock House verandas the full width of the south-facing building.

Guests, drawn by the warm climate, hunting, and fishing, traveled from the northern United States, Canada, and Europe to vacation on the sparkling lakeshore.

Sadie stood on the deck and watched the soaring flight of a red-tailed hawk, as Enterprise came into view. Its call of "cree, creee'" was swallowed in the sound of *Katie Asbell's* whistle.

Water lapped the shore below the hotel, the centerpiece in the Enterprise crown on Lake Monroe. A shell street ran behind it, past just four small weathered shops. A series of sandy lanes ran off in three directions to higgledy-piggledy placements of log houses that looked like small ships sailing in the scrub.

Beyond the road the town was surrounded by miles and miles of woods, thick palmetto brush, and swamps.

Brock House nestled below towering oaks and palms. Sadie thought, *I love those massive trees shading the hotel veranda. One, two, three...seven, eight, nine, ten tall pillars. We'll all be able to enjoy sitting on a veranda for views of Lake Monroe, while we're here.*

The handsome former detective, with slightly receding short silver hair, silver mustache, goatee and side whiskers, pushed his round rimless spectacles down.

He searched in the pockets of his loose khaki jacket for a cat treat. *Hmm, that seems to be my folding knife.* He dove into another. *Uh, pencil and pad.*

Beside him sat Jacob Brock's two grown daughters, Hattie and Jennie, in identical blue gingham dresses and bonnets, reflecting the scarcity of goods from mills in the north during the war. They knitted and waited for the procession of travelers to emerge from the paddlewheeler.

Hattie said, "The citrus bloom smells wonderful. It's awfully late this year, though, isn't it? "

He said, "Mmm." *All I want to smell is our dinner. And I hope that happens soon.*

Fluffy, the hotel's orange tabby mouser cat, nosed into one of Mac's many pockets. He dug out the treat and produced it for her. She circled and settled in his lap.

Mac's piercing blue eyes followed the redhead as she came off the steamboat. *Her way of walking, shoulders back and head held high.*

Unconventional clothes. Short skirt with trousers underneath? Tight bodice. Quite a womanly figure.

And as she neared, *those eyes. the vivid green of palm fronds. an intense light in them.*

Pipe smoke wafted Mac's way. *Our officious manager, come out of his lair, to judge our new inmates.*

Mr. Lavigne, his meerschaum clenched in his teeth and notebook at ready, strode onto the veranda and bid welcome to all of the guests as they arrived in ones and twos.

Mac heard the woman with the red hair say to her greeter, "Thank you. My, what a charming hotel."

A voice as sweet as orange-blossom honey. She's special — and not precisely what she professes to be.

The evening light grew rosy. Spring fragrances of late-blooming orange blossoms, from the surrounding groves, and gardenias, in the hedges, engulfed the veranda.

Sadie left her room. *Might as well wait for dinner on the veranda. I'll deal with the cottage in the morning.*

Sadie stepped out from the lobby just as Christian trotted up the steps to Mac with the latest issues of *Daily News and Herald* from Savannah and the *Charleston Daily News.*

"Thank you, son. Would you please put these old newspapers on the table over there, for others to read after dinner."

As he complied, she walked over beside Mac and looked over his shoulder. *Holy mackerel.* Her heart raced.

A headline read: $100,000 Reward! for Apprehension of John Wilkes Booth and Two of his Known Accomplices, John H. Surrat and David C. Harold in Connection with the Assassination of President Lincoln at Ford's theater on April 14, 1865.

Bram Maas, the trader, crossed the veranda with Ava and nodded at Mac. "Good evening. Folks call me Bram Maas."

Mac gave them a penetrating look as he said, "Welcome to Enterprise. I'm Mac. Glad to see new faces. We've been a bit cut off, what with war games going on in the back waters of the St. John's. Few guests have made it this far recently."

Neville Beaumont appeared and joined the conversation, saying, "Neville Beaumont. I can imagine. Before Fort Sumter, many of my friends, well-to-do plantation owners, industrialists, and important politicians, talked of coming here for the hunting."

Sadie caught sight of Mac looking at Neville speculatively. *Beware. Mac notices things.*

Noah chewed on a spearmint leaf as he came up the steps. "Evening, Mac. Just checking to make sure you got your newspapers. I know you paid $10 a year subscription fee for each of them. I've had to guard them, lest they magically disappear en route to you."

He is kind to everyone he meets. Too bad he thinks I'm a snowflake.

Noah pinched the bridge of his nose and rubbed his temples.

And awfully handsome, too. "Sniff." Smells like mint. Looks like he's hurting from that punch. I could be nicer.

"Headache?" she said.

"Yes. It's pounding."

"I have some medicine that really helps. And I could use some, too. Let me just run up to my room and get it. Perhaps you could get us some hot tea?"

"Will do. Thanks." In a very low voice, Noah said to himself, "Pretty and perceptive, too. Maybe one just has to get to know her."

CHAPTER NINE

April 26, 1865 6:30 a.m.

AT ENTERPRISE, FLORIDA DOCK

I hope that drunk, Greim, went ashore under his own steam, thought Noah.

"Christian, take a light and go check to see if Mr. Greim made it to the hotel or is still in his cabin."

"Aye, sir."

Christian returned moments later. "There is no sign of him, sir."

Good. "Then let's get this steamer on the river."

At 7 a.m. Noah eased *his Katie Asbell* away from the dock at Enterprise and headed for Jacksonville. He said to his first mate, "This sure beats the Ohio, doesn't it, Shorty?"

"Aye, Captain, that it does. Our Pittsburgh to New Orleans route was rough the last couple of years. Never could get warm in Pittsburgh."

"What do you think about spending some more time around here?"

"That'd suit me real good, Captain."

Jim, the stoker, came into the pilothouse. The muscular, sweaty, begrimed fellow said, "The door to the firebox's stuck again, Cap'n."

Again? "Well, do what you usually do, Jim. Tap that blasted latch with the claw hammer," said Noah.

"That's just it, Cap'n. I've searched everywhere for that hammer and can't find it nowhere."

"All right." He said, "You take the helm, Shorty. I need to stretch my legs anyway."

He and Jim climbed down the companionway ladder to the freight deck and searched again for the hammer. Noah said, as they looked, "Have you noticed any other tools missing, Jim?"

"Not that I can think of, sir."

After coming up empty-handed once again Noah said, "Go get mine out of my locker in my cabin. Here's the locker key."

"Aye, sir."

Noah climbed to the passenger deck and said to the cabin boy, "Come and give me a hand, Christian. I'm looking for a claw hammer that belongs in the engine room."

"Yes, sir. Captain, sir."

They searched all along the deck and rails. "It's not particularly valuable, but we can't have our tools walking off," said Noah.

Shorty called out from above, "Disturbance in the water starboard. Slow the engine by half." And he repeated the information through the speaking tube to the engine room.

Noah said, "Forget the search. That tremendous thrashing means trouble."

Christian said, "Something big has tore that water plumb up. Can't tell what it is."

As the steamer neared the foaming swirls Noah thought, *Gators. Congregated around a twirling log. With something red and shiny trailing along in the water.* "Oh, Lord God Almighty!"

Christian said, "It's a person. Somebody's in the water and about 20 gators have got 'im. They're going to chew him up."

"Gators don't chew. They just grab and roll. We better shoot those gators quick or he won't stand a chance."

Pete's already stationed on the freight deck to shoot any self-sacrificing gator that threatens to throw himself at our paddle wheel. But he's going to need help.

Noah started to his cabin for his gun. Over his shoulder he hurled the command, "Deckhands who can leave your posts, get your guns and shoot those gators. That's an order."

He was first to the rail with his rifle. "No need to point him out, Christian. It looks like a small tornado is churning up the water. And I'd wager that the furious sounds of those gator tails pounding the water can be heard a quarter of a mile away."

"Bang."

"Got one." He reloaded and shot again. Gun owners picked off gators, one by one, until the man's body floated alone languidly down the river.

"Good shooting, sir," said Christian.

"Thanks. This is a Whitworth rifle. People complain that muzzle loader rifles have only one shot, but with the telescopic sight, it's very accurate. At this range I could hardly miss."

Noah said, "Joe, join Pete on alligator watch from the bow. Plenty more could come while we have crew in the water. The rest of you deck hands stop what you're doing and stow your guns."

Christian said, "How are we going to get him out of the river?"

Like we always do. "Simple. Just like lifting a bale of cotton, only sideways and out of the water. Keep him in sight, Christian, while I go talk to Shorty."

He climbed up to the passenger deck, stowed his gun, then continued up to the pilothouse.

The first mate stood at the helm watching it all. "Is he alive, Captain?"

"I don't know. I haven't seen him move. But we have to get him out of the water. It should be easy and will be good training for the new hands."

"Yes, sir."

"Shorty, I trust you to not steer us into any logs, low overhanging trees, or the bank." He grinned. "But if you don't want to do this, I'll take the helm. Listen to my plan before you decide."

"Aye, sir."

"All right. You can consider this part of your training. We're going to a wide spot below him, then swing around and come up river until he's on the bow. After that, you'll need to maneuver to keep us with him.

"We'll lower the gangplank into the water next to him, take boat hooks and walk out and wrestle him onto the gangplank.

"Then we lift the boom and swing it around, giving those deckhands a little ride, lower the gangplank, and bring it onto the deck. Questions?"

"No, captain. We've done it a hundred times, when docking or loading freight."

"Yes, but you haven't done it in this narrow, twisty, winding river, in these shallows - so can you do this?"

Shorty said, "Captain, I don't see a problem. Just keep the snakes off the deck. I hate snakes."

"Right. Shorty, you'll need to navigate with very little wake, to a wide spot well below him - I think there's one a couple hundred yards ahead."

"Aye, sir."

"While you're doing that, I'll explain the plan to everyone and assign tasks, so they are all ready when our target is in range. I wouldn't want to have to try a second time."

"Aye, Captain."

"Then let's do it now. Shorty, the helm is yours."

Noah made his way down to the freight deck.

After he made sure that all the deckhands knew exactly what to do, Noah said, "Christian, let's pull out the gang plank. All right. Now push it. Heave it up to the edge until the wheels meet the combing. See those lines with block and tackle attached to either side of the gangplank? We might need those to haul the gang plank side to side or inboard later."

"Clank, clank, clank, clank."

"Adam and Abel are cranking winches that raise the free end of the boom and swing it, with the gang plank hanging below, out over the water."

The steamer turned in the water and headed back up river. Noah called out, "Here he comes. Easy now. Lower the boom," which moved it out farther away from the steamer.

"Too much. Bring her in some." The men cranked and adjusted until they lowered the gang plank into the water beside the body.

Two of the crew, 'Cookie,' a former circus man, and Jan, their agile server, jumped barefooted onto the inboard portion of the gang plank.

They saluted Noah with their 10-foot-long boat hooks. "Jest keep them Minié balls handy for the gators, Captain, and everything'll be hunkey dorey," said Jan.

Cheeky boy.

They walked out onto the gang plank. "He looks dead, Captain. He still has his red vest. I think it's that swell from Savannah, Mr. Beaumont."

They pulled the body toward them with the crooks on the tapered end of the boat hooks.

"Ye gods! There's another gator." They punched the snout of the gator away from the body with the iron balls on the ends of the boathooks and then danced back away.

"Crack. Crack." The gunmen on the bow killed the hungry reptile, which slid away underwater.

"Let's get done and get off this plank." Between them they wrestled the heavy water-logged, and mangled body onto the gangplank.

Noah shouted, "All right. Hold steady, now. Raise the boom."

"Clank, clank, clank." The gangplank lifted level with the deck of the steamer. "All right. Get busy heaving on those lines to pull them aboard."

It seemed like the whole crew joined to bring in the gangplank bearing their crew mates and the body.

Yay! Hooray! Cheers rose, when the rescuers finally jumped down on the deck among them.

What in the tarnation are we supposed to do with a dead body? Can't have it on board two days in this heat--all the way to Jacksonville.

And Jacksonville is still under martial law, with two regiments of negro Union troops up there.

"Well done, everyone, " said Noah. "Now let's get a look at this drowned man. Why, it's not Mr. Beaumont. That's Luther Greim."

We have to go back. "Adam, go find a sheet to wrap him. And get that old plank to lay him on. You two, carry him to his cabin. Lock the cabin door when you leave. The rest of you, back to your posts. We are going to Enterprise." He turned and headed for the pilothouse.

When he reached Shorty, Noah said, "We're only 15 minutes away from Enterprise. We'll take him back to the hotel. Mac will know what to do."

Chapter Ten

April 26, 1865 7:00 a.m.

At Brock House Hotel

S adie moved her chair and writing desk to the window of her second story room.

That's better. Now I can watch people going to and from the dock.

She bathed and dressed, then sat and enjoyed the ever-changing view. *Noah's leaving with the Katie Asbell. She's pretty, as steamers go. Two days up to Jacksonville and two days to get back. Four days till he's back.*

"Knock, Knock," sounded at the door. "It's Daisy, the housekeeper, Miss. I can come back later if..."

"No. No, come right in."

A sturdy five-foot-tall lass, with pink cheeks and light brown braids coiled around her ears, pushed a trolley with a huge wicker basket into the room.

She looks barely 20 years old.

"Thank you, Miss. I know it's early. I'll just get your linens for washing and, er, the chamber pot."

"I'm Sarah, but please, call me Sadie. Have you worked here long, Daisy?"

"Five years, Miss....uh, Sadie."

"Is it a good place to work?"

"Yes, but we are getting really busy. And you? Are you having a nice vacation?"

"Not exactly. I think I'm leaving today. Did you know a lady here by the name of Cora Bird?

"Yes. Oh, yes, Miss….uh, Sadie. Ever so nice she was. And Dr. Bird, too." She piled the damp towels in her basket.

"Cora Bird was my aunt, my father's sister. When her husband died, he left the cottage, Snow Bird Cottage, to her. Now she has left it to me."

"That's wonderful, Sadie."

"Except, that I don't know where it is and I have spent all my savings to get here. If I can't find it today, I'll have no place to stay."

"Oh, that's easy, Sadie. Go out the back of the hotel to the shell road. Turn right and walk fast about 10 minutes. And you're there. Lor, Miss, why are you crying?"

"Oh, Daisy. I could hug you." And she did. Tears flowed down her face. *Maybe they'll wash away the tension of the last few days.*

"It must be all the strain from the travel on top of grief. And worry… that I would get here and find nothing, leaving me penniless."

Not to mention the fear of getting tangled in an assassination plot.

Daisy's rough hand patted at Sadie's tears with a soft clean napkin that smelled of lemons. "Oh, Miss, if you need a job, maybe you could work here. I know we need more help. Mr. Brock is bringing in 20 new guests this evening. I don't know how I'll get everything done."

"That's a good idea, Daisy." She laughed through the last of her tears and Daisy laughed with her. "With the war over, and more tourists arriving, you'll be doing more laundry. I might get a job as a cleaner or laundress." *…at least temporarily, to put bread on the table until I can figure out something else.*

"We need more cooks, too. We are serving more meals in the dining room."

"Cook is out of the question, because I lack the skills." *Server would be too public — raise my chances of being identified as Evangeline Bright.*

"Let's go talk to Mr. Lavigne right now," said the enthusiastic girl.

"All right. Lead the way." *Daisy's limping. Is that usual, I wonder?*

Sadie knocked on the pine-plank door, which had a shiny name plate that said, "Guillaume Lavigne, Manager."

"Come," he said. He puffed on his meerschaum pipe as they entered the room. "What is it, Daisy?"

"Oh, Mr. Lavigne, I brought Miss Sadie..." Here she hesitated.

"Snow. Sadie Snow," Sadie supplied.

"Snow, to see about a job here in the hotel. Mr. Brock is bringing all those new guests and we really need more help."

Mr. Lavigne looked down his nose at Sadie, as if he were judging her and finding her 'not enough' in all categories. "And what do you think you can do here?"

"Daisy says she needs help. I could clean rooms," said Sadie.

"No. Afraid not. We don't have any budget for more cleaning staff."

"Well, perhaps I could do laundry for you."

"Out of the question. You are not strong enough."

"I'm a lot stronger than I look."

Daisy said, "But, Mr. Lavigne we really do need..."

"And you don't have the proper look to be one of our staff members," he said.

Ahh, so that's it. Trousers. Individualistic clothing equals what? Dishonest? Unreliable? Lazy? Incapable?

"Sorry, Daisy. You'll just have to work faster. My answer is no."

Breakfast is a hearty meal at Brock house. Sadie put her fork into a plate of eggs over- easy, ham, hot buttered biscuit, sausage, and sausage gravy.

The combined aromas of this food cause a cozy feeling inside of me. Hope my taste buds agree.

"Whoo, Hoot. Ring, ding, ding." *What is that? Sounds like the steamer whistle and bell. I thought it left for Jacksonville.*

All the diners looked out the large windows overlooking the dock.

She listened. That's either a threshing machine or the Katie Asbell is coming back. Mmm, good biscuit. I better hurry.

"Shorty, you take the helm. As soon as we get to the dock, I'll jump off and go tell Mac what we've got," Noah said. "And see that Greim's cabin door is locked before and after we move him."

Noah hit the dock running and made it to the veranda in record time. He said to Mac, who was in his usual chair with Fluffy stretching and yawning on his lap, "Put on your Pinkerton hat, Mac. We have a problem."

"I thought you might. What happened?"

"We found a body in the river. We think it's Luther Greim's. It's in pretty bad shape, what with the gators and all. It'll be really ripe if we take it to Jacksonville. And you know the political situation there. Suggestions?"

"The first thing we have to do is find out what caused his death. Why don't you bring it on inside and we'll have a look. While you do that, I'll just step inside and have a word with Mr. Lavigne." Fluffy leaped to the veranda and stretched paws, front, then back.

Lavigne said, "You want to bring in a what?"

"You heard me."

"No. Absolutely not. Under no circumstances..."

"Now look here, Guillaume. I don't see that we really have a choice. I think we must deal with it here," Mac said. It would waste valuable time to take it to Jacksonville. If you have a better plan, I'd be glad to hear it."

"No. He must take it to Jacksonville. We can do nothing here."

"We could send for a marshal. Then, by the time he gets here, we'll probably have it all sorted."

"No. We can't have a dead body in my beautiful hotel. You must take it to Jacksonville."

"He would be a bag of slime by the time Noah could get him to Jacksonville. Authorities would have no hopes of finding out what happened to him. And if there are political implications, both you and I could be in a lot of trouble for not dealing with it before all the evidence disappears. Who knows? It might be a simple case. Maybe he was drunk and walked off the steamer. Then we notify the next of kin and have a quiet burial. The end."

"Well, all right, we don't need any political trouble. Maybe we could put him in a back room until you find out what happened. Then we bury him."

"Good. But give me a back room with lots of light so I can examine him."

"Take him around to the back door. I will direct you."

The news passed through the dining room faster than whispers of an impending wedding at a quilting bee. Soon the whole hotel was abuzz.

"He was very drunk. Did he fall overboard?" said Mary Merritt, around a mouthful of biscuit.

"Or was he pushed? That's the question isn't it, my dear," said her sister Martha, with a shiver. "I suppose they'll want to talk to all of us, now."

Neville stood up from the breakfast table and patted his pockets. "Has anyone seen my snuff box?"

He received blank looks all around. Without waiting for an answer, he said, " I must have left it on the steamer. Better go check."

"Luther probably realized what a blighter he was and jumped overboard," said Bram. He forked another slice of ham onto his plate.

"To save us the trouble of pushing him," said Kat, who seemed to be eating only dry toast.

"Kat, really. You are scandalous," said Buck in mock horror.

Abel, Adam, Joe, and Christian carried Luther's bulky body on its makeshift stretcher around the outside of the hotel. "Quickly. Come this way. We don't want anyone to see," said Mr. Lavigne.

Noah and Mac followed them into a tiny storeroom, hastily cleared. The two windows let in a flood of natural sunlight.

Mac said, "This will do fine, Guillaume. Thank you."

Noah's crewmen deposited their heavy burden on a small clean cot. "Thank you, fellows. Get on back to the *Katie Asbell* now and start on the cabins. We need them clean for the customers we're picking up in Palatka this evening."

They chorused, "Cap'ain," and "Aye, sir." The men ambled off in the general direction of the dock.

"Was this death by alligator, Mac?" said Noah, as they unwrapped the body.

Mac pointed and said, "Look at these two round indentations on the back of his skull. Those weren't made by any gator. This was murder."

"Yes, it looks like someone hit him with a big heavy pair of spectacles that left identical depressions. Field glasses? The heavy base of a lamp? A tool made from two pipes?" Noah said.

"Or he fell with force against something like that," said Mac, with a sigh. "It's a start. Can you definitely identify him as this Luther Greim?"

"Yes. No doubt about it. His clothes are mostly intact, but he's lost his belt. Not unusual."

"Some gator is probably wearing it. How did he act with the other guests?"

"He seemed to be almost universally disliked."

"By whom, in particular?"

"He insulted almost everybody. He was involved in a poker game with Bram Maas, Neville Beaumont, and Buck Stotts right before we got to Enterprise. I was told that Buck accused him of cheating. When I arrived, Luther was throwing punches at Buck and me, and at a young woman, Sadie Snow, who got in his way."

"The redheaded woman?"

"That's right. He gave her a bloody nose and threatened to give her a beating, from what I heard."

"What happened, finally?"

"He hit me, so I knocked him out and the boys carried him to his cabin to sleep it off."

"What time was that?"

"We put him in his bunk at about five-thirty. Then docking required all my attention at about six and I checked on him at six-thirty, after all the passengers had gone ashore. It was dark by seven."

"When was the last time you saw him alive?"

"Last night, when I checked on him. This morning he wasn't in his cabin and I assumed that he'd come here to the hotel."

"Who stayed on board last night?"

"I did, of course, and all the crew, except Jan. His parents live in a little cabin across the lake."

"Noah, that fight gives you a motive for murder. It might have been self-defense."

"Me? I didn't kill him. All I did was restore order on my boat."

"I hear you, but don't go any farther than Jacksonville until we get this mess cleared up. I'm going to need statements from your crew members. Send them to the front veranda now, before you go, please."

"Thunderation, Mac. I have to get on the river. No way I can navigate those crooks and turns in the dark."

"I'll make it quick. But you know if I wait four days I won't get anything out of them. And I expect you back here in four days."

"I can't imagine that they know any more than what I just told you."

"You never know. And, Noah, you did the right thing, bringing him here. Thanks for your help. Oh. I'll need to see his luggage. Please send one of your boys up here with it."

Chapter Eleven

April 26, 1865 9:00 a.m.

At Brock House Hotel

No more drama for me. Sadie headed to her room.

Time to gather my things and find Aunt Cora's cottage. No time for goodbyes.

"Oh, Sadie. I've been looking for you," said Kat Ashley, who stopped her in the hall.

Not now, please, Kat.

"Do you have any more of that digestive medicine that you gave me yesterday? It helped so much last time."

"Yes, of course. Why don't you go to the kitchen and ask for a cup of very hot tea. Take it up to your room. Meanwhile I'll look through my bag for that bottle of tincture, then meet you there shortly."

"Is the tea really necessary? I don't like it very much."

"Yes, it is. This medicine is made with whiskey. That is, it has alcohol, which is not good for a baby. It could be important to evaporate some of the alcohol in boiling liquid, if you are, as I suspect, pregnant."

Neville whistled as he passed unnoticed by Abel and Adam with others of the steamer crew, near the dock.

"How much do you want for this rattlesnake skin, Gator?" said Abel to a weathered, somewhat hunched, barefooted man, who stood next to a hollowed-out pine-log, dugout canoe. It splashed as it floated in the surf.

They all clustered around a 12-foot alligator bound to an oak plank, which was displayed on the beach.

Noah hurried up to them and said, "You lot, get on up to the veranda and tell Mac what you know about Luther Greim. And get a move on. The *Katie Asbell* needs to leave here within the hour."

"Well, you done run off all my customers," said the old man to Noah, who'd been buying from the man for months and paid no attention to his frayed pants with rope belt, leathery wrinkled skin, hooded eyes under craggy brows, drooping salt and pepper mustache, and battered, four-inch-brimmed, palmetto hat.

"Hi, Gator. What you got there? Maybe I'm interested in buying."

"I'm glad you come back. I just missed you early this morning. I'll give you a deal on these."

Noah bought tanned hides, gators strapped on planks, and snake skins from the 'gator wrangler.'

As Noah was finishing with this transaction, Shorty came rushing up. "Christian just keeled over on deck. He's burning up with fever, and he said that he aches all over, especially his back. He didn't eat any breakfast either. It sounds like the yellow plague."

"Dash It! How in tarnation am I supposed to keep this steamer on schedule with people falling overboard and fainting with fever?"

Shorty said, "I can reassign his duties, but somebody's going to have to take care of him--and he might be contagious."

Noah heaved a great sigh. "All right. I'll go talk to Lavigne. They must have a back room where somebody can treat him until he's better. It usually runs its course in what? three or four days?" He turned and went back into the hotel.

"Mr. Asbell, you are completely unreasonable. First a dead body. And now you want to bring a sick man into my hotel?"

"I didn't plan this predicament, Mr. Lavigne. I understand this fever usually goes away in three or four days. I'll pay for a room for him for four nights and I will be back in four days."

"But who would take care of him?"

"Well, I don't know the answer to that. But there must be somebody who could bring him meals and that."

""We have a room where he can rest until you return, but... maybe yellow plague? I don't know."

"The boy might be fit as a fiddle in three days. Just until I come back? I'll pay you."

Kat and Sadie passed by the open office door. "Stop just a minute, Kat. Did he say yellow plague?" Sadie said.

She stopped and listened. Staff and other guests had also stopped and all crowded around to listen.

Lavigne repeated, louder this time, "But we have no medicine. We have no one to take care of him."

Total silence ensued, during which all those nearby suddenly seemed to be needed urgently elsewhere.

Sadie thought, *Do what you know is right.*

She spoke up. "If you'll let me, I think I can help. I saw many soldiers with those symptoms when I volunteered in field hospitals."

"You have experience in field hospitals?" said Lavigne, looking down his nose at her again.

Sadie could almost hear his judging voice say, "Not enough."

"I brought a small supply of fever bark with me. Nine out of 10 people who are treated with it recover fully. And since I don't have a job yet," she looked pointedly at Mr. Lavigne, "I can nurse him for three or four days."

"I can't say that I approve. This is most irregular."

"That seems to be our answer then," said Noah.

"Hmpf. Our only answer, Captain Asbell," said Mr. Lavigne. "We'll put him in the storeroom, next door to your Mr. Greim, and far away from everyone else."

"Agreed," said Noah.

Mr. Lavigne pouted his lips and said, "Can you start now, Miss Snow?"

"Yes. Let me just get Kat sorted. I need several things from my bag, plus a lemon, a lime, and some sugar. I will need to use your kitchen to make tea."

Mr. Lavigne raised his voice and said, "You are going to stop and have a cup of tea? Now? We're in the middle of a crisis, and you want TEA?"

"No. It's for the patient. Will you show me where I can work in the kitchen, please?"

His outburst attracted the attention of several guests. Mary Merritt, looking small and meek, approached them. "Can I do anything to help?"

Sadie said, "Yes, thank you. After I get Christian settled, could you stay with him for a few hours while I attend to something else?"

"Why, yes. I'll be glad to."

"Thank you. And now the kitchen, Mr. Lavigne?"

"Mrs. Flowers won't like you invading her territory. She'll have a fit."

CHAPTER TWELVE

April 26, 1865

ABOARD "KATIE ASBELL" AT BROCK HOUSE DOCK

N oah looked down at Christian, who writhed in pain on the deck of *Katie Asbell*. "Christian, we're going to take you to the hotel, where Miss Snow will give you some medicine to make you feel better."

"Unghh," was the only response.

"Why didn't you at least help him to his bunk?" he said to the crew members, who crowded around.

"We didn't rightly know what to do with him, Captain," said Abel.

"Well, go get that big plank. We're taking him to the room right next door to Greim. Lavigne said he'd meet us at the back door."

"Ahh, Mr. Lavigne, Miss Snow," said Noah. Would you hold those doors wide open, please? Thanks."

"It's right over here," said Mr. Lavigne. "The door is unlocked, and I aired it out. A cot and those two chairs were all Daisy could fit in here."

Sadie thought, *With all she has to do, he's having her move furniture?*

Mary came down the hall and Noah said, "Ahh. Miss Merritt. Careful. Perhaps you could go ahead of us?"

Noah's having a really bad morning. First Luther Greim and now this. "I brought the pain medication to ease Christian. Do you need some more this morning?" she said.

"No, thanks. I'm fine. I just need to get back on the river."

"Ahh. Here we are," said Lavigne.

"Careful, now," Noah said. Do you need anything else, Sadie?"

"Yes. Pull that chair up next to his cot, please. The other one can go next to the window at the foot of the bed, where Mary will get good light for reading. Thank you. And this big box will do for a table."

Sadie said, "Christian, I want you to take a spoonful of this now. It'll make you feel better."

Christian fluttered his eyelashes and opened his mouth half an inch. Sadie spooned in the willow bark and feverfew tincture.

"Swallow. Good. Now I'm going to go mix some medicine for the fever. But Mary is staying here with you."

"I'm going too, Chris. I'll be back Sunday," said Noah. "And I expect you to be up and r'aring' to go." He patted the boy's arm.

CHAPTER THIRTEEN

April 26, 1865 Afternoon

AT BROCK HOUSE HOTEL VERANDA, KITCHEN, SICKROOM

M ac stood up from his deck chair, dislodging Fluffy. He said to the cat, "Noah was right. His deckhands say they didn't hear any scuffles or a big splash last night."

They did tell me that Sadie Snow threw Luther to the deck. Improbable. Maybe they were fully corned, too.

He tossed Luther's 'luggage' over his shoulder and headed to his room for privacy. He glanced back and saw the curious cat trotting behind him.

"What kind of man has a set of saddlebags as his only luggage, Fluffy? A horseman, that's who. Come on in, cat. Let's see what Luther stored in here."

He spread out the contents on his bed.

The only unusual item that he found was an old notebook with dates and lists of items: Saddle. Spurs. Wagon. Horse. Mule. Head of cattleXXV.

Maybe it's an old list of provisions he needed. He bought 25 head of cattle?

Pages dated as far back as February 3,1862. The last one dated April 1865 - *This month.* And dollar amounts.

A business journal reflecting the sale of those things?

Then the last entry is for the sale? of 100 barrels of rum to a New Orleans purveyor of fine spirits? At a high price. Where would a horseman get barrels of rum?

He reached for the cat. "All I have are questions, Fluffy. Perhaps Sadie Snow and those other three poker players have some answers."

Outside in the well-ventilated, but warm kitchen, Sadie looked up and saw Mac, who said, "I was told I might find you here. I've been asked to look into the recent death. May I have a word, please, about Luther Greim?"

"Obnoxious."

"What's that?"

"If I get only one word to describe him, then that word is 'obnoxious.'"

"Yes. But I need to speak with you."

Uh.oh, she thought. *Blast it. I haven't thought of good answers for all his questions.*

"All right, but can we do it while I work? I'm in a bit of a hurry."

He took out a small notebook and pencil. "Yes. Let's start with your full name, the one in your family Bible, or recorded by your parish priest."

Tell the truth. "Sarah Snow."

"What other name have you used in the past?"

Zing. She walked into the kitchen cupboard and removed a saucepan and a quart, screw-top, canning jar from a shelf, along with a lemon and a lime from a basket. "Um. What other name? Why, uh, none." *Lie.*

"Where were you born?"

"Louisville, Kentucky." *True.*

"Where is your home?"

"Well, I've traveled quite a bit and cared for sick relatives. But now I hope to make this my home." *True, or rather, lie of omission.*

"How so?"

"My Aunt Cora Bird left Snow Bird Cottage to me. I will make that my home."

He raised his eyebrows. "I see. Are you now or have you ever been married?"

"No." *At least, that's true.*

"Are you employed outside your home? Have you been employed in the last five years?"

Don't answer that. Not with the president dead and the theater shut tight. She pumped the quart jar full of spring water, then poured it into the saucepan.

"Um, have I ever been employed? I told you. I have taken care of a sick relative."

"I'll need you to provide me with a detailed list of names and dates. Do you have any previous acquaintance with any of the other guests who traveled with you from Jacksonville?"

"No." *True.*

"Describe how you met Luther Greim."

"I stepped into the *Katie Asbell's* onboard lounge and he offered to remove my trousers."

"Is that when you slapped him?"

"I never slapped him. I told him to grow up."

"But I was told he gave you that black eye. That gives you a pretty good motive for murder."

"He knocked me against a bulkhead when I told him that he was drunk and needed to go sleep it off. "

"Some witnesses say you knocked him to the deck. Is that possible?"

Tell the truth. She picked up a lemon and, with a sharp knife, quickly removed the colored part of the rind, releasing a burst of fragrance. She repeated this with a lime.

She looked him in the eye and said, "I did not kill Luther Greim." She placed the zest in the saucepan. "Do I look like I could knock down a 250-pound man?"

"Point taken. Who would want to do him harm?"

"I suspect folks might have been lining up to kill him. He insulted just about everybody." She juiced the lemon and lime, removed the seeds, and added the juice to the saucepan.

"What else do you know about the man?"

"Nothing."

"Did you ever see him writing in a small notebook?"

"No." From a pouch labeled "Fever Bark," she measured eight teaspoons of bark chunks into the mixture.

"Did he ever say why he was on this trip?"

"Not to me." She measured a cup and a half of sugar, from a box on the counter, into the concoction. "Look at these beautiful pure crystals. Cook grudgingly unlocked it this morning." She placed the pan on the hot stove.

"What do you know about 100 barrels of rum?"

"You could give a really big party with it, I guess."

Mac suppressed a smile. "When was the last time you saw Luther Greim alive?"

"Noah's deckhands were carrying his fully-liquored form out of the lounge."

"What were your movements after that?"

"I packed my things and went ashore. Dinner in the dining room was pleasant. I conversed with some of the other guests in the front parlor until about seven, then went up to bed."

"Did you see or hear anything out of the ordinary last night? Someone where they shouldn't be? An oil lamp where you did not expect it? A strange noise?"

"I can't think of anything, but if I do, I'll let you know."

"All right. That's all, for now. Don't leave this area without talking to me first."

"Then I'm a suspect?"

"As someone who had a public argument with the man shortly before he died – yes, you are our number one suspect."

Crikey. If they don't hang me for conspiring to kill Lincoln, then they're going to pin this murder on me. I have to find out who did this. And fast.

Her quinine simmered for 45 minutes and then steeped for another 20 minutes. During that time, she thought about ways to investigate.

I need to start by getting friendly with those other three card players. Maybe they'll tell me something of use. And Mac, too. I need to be very friendly, even though he scares me.

She strained the cooled brew into the clean canning jar and screwed the lid tight. *Hmm. Those jars on the shelf are labeled.*

A quick search ensued. *Ahh. Pen and labels.*

She wrote on a label, "Quinine. Dosage: 1 teaspoon orally every eight hours, for three to seven days." She moistened the label and affixed it to the jar.

I am almost ready to go explore Aunt Cora's cottage - my cottage. It better be where Daisy said, or I have no bed for tonight.

She went back into the hotel and directed her steps toward Christian's small room. Christian was in a fitful doze when Sadie entered.

"He relaxed some after you gave him the willow and feverfew," said Mary.

"We should give him a little more. And he needs some of this quinine. Christian, can you wake up?"

She touched him lightly on the shoulder. "Please swallow a spoonful of this. It's sweet. Excellent. And another of this. Good."

He closed his eyes and sank back down into sleep.

"I'll leave these medicine bottles here, Mary. He can have more willow bark after four hours, if he needs it. And he must have another dose of quinine eight hours from now."

"All right. He seems settled. I'll just sit here at the foot of his bed and read my book," said Mary.

"I should be back around dinner time. Can I bring you anything, Mary, before I leave?"

"No, thanks. I'll listen to that mockingbird. I hope folks will leave us to enjoy the peace."

Chapter Fourteen

April 26, 1865 Late Afternoon

At Brock House Hotel

M ac stood in the hallway and tapped on Buck's door, with his gold-tipped ebony cane. "Are you looking for Buck?" said Ava, who came down the hall from the other direction.

"Good afternoon, Mrs. Maas. I need to speak with the three gentlemen who played cards with Luther Greim last night. Have you seen them?"

"Buck left with Kat a few minutes ago saying something about a stroll in the back garden," Ava said. "Bram and Neville are out shooting things, but they should be back pretty soon."

"Thank you. Would you please tell them I need to speak with them?"

"Yes, of course. Are they in any trouble?"

"No, I don't think so. I just need their help. I'm trying to understand what happened last night in the salon. Were you there during the poker game that ended in fisticuffs?"

"I saw the whole thing. It was quite a show. I'll be glad to tell you about it."

I want to talk to the men involved first. It took a lot of strength to overcome a 250 pound man. But I might as well see what she has to say.

"That would be helpful. The back parlor was empty when I passed a moment ago," he said, and gestured to a room down the hall. "Let's go in there."

When they were comfortably settled, Mac pulled out his notebook and pencil. "Let's start with your name. What is your full legal name?"

"My name? I thought this was about Luther Greim."

"It is. I just want to get all the details straight."

"Oh. All right. Ava Jansen Maas."

"Where were you born."

"I was born 25 years ago in New Amsterdam, but the English call it Manhattan."

"Where is your home, Mrs. Maas?"

"New Amsterdam. I like to visit other places but I want to live only there."

"And you are married? With children?"

"Yes, I'm married to Bram - you've met him, and no. No children."

She sounds wistful. "Are you employed?"

"Yes. I run our large family mercantile store, Maas Brothers, in New York."

"Do you have any previous acquaintance with any of the other guests who traveled with you from Jacksonville?"

"Um, did I know any of the other uh, guests, who traveled with us from Jacksonville? Er, no."

Oh, really. Why the stalling? Are you lying to me, Ava Maas?

"How long have you known Luther Greim?"

"To be perfectly honest, I just met him two days ago on the steamer from Jacksonville." She patted her chest. "Whew. It's warm today."

"Describe how you met."

"Oh, you know. He was one of the other passengers." She looked at the door.

"Did he have any enemies?"

"A great many, I would suspect." She paused. "He was odious."

"Where is he from?"

Ava angled her body toward the door and looked that direction. "Um. Where was he from? Oh, my. I honestly don't know."

"Did he say how he spent the war? Soldier? Sailor? Trader?"

"I hardly knew the man. How could I possibly say?"

"Did he ever mention why he was on this trip? Business? Vacation?"

"I never heard him say anything about it."

"What happened in the salon during the poker game?"

"Mr. Greim was being very coarse. He insulted everybody. He asked Buck about his wife and children. That's when Buck told him to shut up and accused him of cheating.

"Kat asked us to do something, and Sadie went over. She just told him he was drunk, to go sleep it off. He knocked her against the bulkhead. Blood spurted everywhere. He tripped in her slippery blood and fell. Then he yelled that he would beat her. The captain came. Greim hauled off and hit him. The captain knocked Mr. Greim out, but that didn't kill him. I saw that he was breathing. And deckhands carried him away."

"Did you see Mr. Greim after that?"

"No. We all went to our cabins and packed, preparatory to docking at Enterprise."

"Did you see or hear anything that you thought unusual last night? Someone where they weren't supposed to be? An oil lamp in a place that wasn't supposed to have light?"

"Not that I remember."

"Thank you, Mrs. Maas. Are you staying in Enterprise long?"

"Yes, we have three weeks here. Bram is very excited about the hunting and fishing."

"If you remember any details, don't hesitate to come to me. I'll likely be in a deck chair on the veranda."

"I will." She hurried out of the parlor like she was speeding to a fire.

CHAPTER FIFTEEN

April 26, 1865 Late afternoon

AT BROCK HOUSE HOTEL AND SNOW BIRD COTTAGE

S adie stepped out of the storage room, turned sickroom. She hurried past the door of the room where Luther's body lay, out the back door of the hotel, and into the warm afternoon.

At last. Free to go see the cottage that Aunt Cora bequeathed to me. A walk will do me good. Please, please, please let there be a cottage.

She approached the shell road, turned right, and strode forward, with her head held high, breathing the full fragrance of flowering trees.

Just look at the red and purple wild flowers on either side of the road. And the birds... how do they trill like that?

She began to sing to herself as she caught glimpses of red cardinals, blue jays, and bright yellow goldfinches in the hedges. She stopped. *That can't be it, can it?*

A freshly painted Italianate style pier and beam house, with white wooden latticework at the base, sat gleaming in the afternoon light.

This is where Daisy said it would be and she said it is nice. This must be it.

Sadie stood and gazed at the cottage. *I don't know what I expected, but it wasn't this. Paradise, indeed.*

But if it's been empty for months, how can it look so fresh?

A hipped metal roof with deep eaves rose high, to cool the house. At the center of the ridge was placed a big square cupola with three large four-paned windows.

Perfect for nature watching. The cupola's roof, a smaller version of the one below, provided pleasing symmetry.

Oh, I love it, already. The white clapboard cottage sat surrounded by a citrus grove, fragrant with bloom. Bees buzzed among the flowers and afternoon sun glinted off shiny jade leaves.

She picked a leaf and, crushing it between her fingers, breathed in the heady sweet scent. *A lemon tree? Marvelous. Thank you, Aunt Cora.*

A lump rose in her throat at the thought of Aunt Cora. Sadie was back in that lonely little room at Petersen's boardinghouse.

I remember reading the letter about Aunt Cora's death. That day, tears failed to wash away my sadness.

Tears threatened again, now. *When I was little, my visits with her were always filled with fun and laughter and love.*

Sometimes we talked of integrity. 'Do what you know is right, Sadie. Do what you've said you will do,' she'd say.

Sadie sniffed.

She was kind. She created this hideaway with hard work and love. And gave it to me.

Sadie sighed and continued up the red-brick herringbone-patterned path to the front steps.

She stopped at the five wide steps. *Oh, they narrow as they go up to the porch, like they're leading me in. And it looks like the porch wraps around the whole house.*

Up the steps she went. She set her bags on the front porch and stood in front of the paired entryway doors, with 12-paned glass windows in them, and a fan light above.

She fumbled around for the key given to her by her aunt's lawyer. One smooth turn and "Click." It opened. She put her bags in, then stepped inside and marveled to see that the hallway led to another door.

Cross ventilation? She investigated. *Imagine that. This house has four doors, one on either end of an east-west corridor and the other two doors on either end of a north-south corridor.*

At the sight of a staircase, she climbed up to explore the cupola. *Wonderful light. And Aunt Cora already arranged a chair and writing table by the window.*

A shiny brass object glinted at her from an upper shelf. *I will just stand on tiptoes and maybe I can reach it. Oh, my. A spyglass?*

She pulled it out to its full 18 inches and fitted it to her eye. *Aunt Cora, what did you do during the war?*

Back downstairs, she tried the back door and found it to be unlocked. *That's puzzling.* She locked the door. *I guess this key fits all the doors. Convenient.*

It's getting late. I really have to get back to relieve Mary. I'll just have to explore the rest tomorrow.

She locked the front door behind her and hurried back to the hotel. With a song in her heart, she pondered. *Spying? Probably not. Probably Birdwatching.*

Chapter Sixteen

April 26, 1865 Late Afternoon

At Brock House Hotel

Mac found Buck deep in conversation at a table in the back garden, with his shiny bald head inclined toward Kat. "Buck, may I talk with you a few minutes about Luther Greim?"

"Why, sure. Have a seat." His wide smile, framed by the upturned, ginger, handlebar mustache, returned.

"If you will excuse me, I have some things to do inside," said Kat, who rose and left.

"Certainly, Miss." He nodded, then turn to the man across from him. "Now, your full legal name, Buck?"

"Buck Stotts."

"Where were you born?"

"Southeastern Loosiana. New Orleans, to be exact."

"Where do you call 'home'?"

"I thought you were asking about Luther Greim?" Buck said, and he looked toward where Kat had disappeared into the hotel.

"I will. I just wanted to get accurate details. Where is your home?"

"That's hard to say. I travel for my business and you might find me in Florida today, and Georgia tomorrow." He laughed heartily.

"Are you married with children, Buck?"

"Well, now. Do you want to know about Luther Greim, or are you building a dossier on me?" He laughed again.

"We do need the facts, Mr. Stotts. Are you married? I understand Luther asked you about your wife and children. Is that correct?"

"Er, yes, he did. I mean, yes, I do have a wife and children north of Tampa. But I didn't want to discuss them with that Neanderthal."

"I understand you were upset about his mentioning your family and you abruptly accused him of cheating."

"He was cheating. I was brought up to be honest. That man didn't have an honest bone in his body."

"What did Luther do for a living?"

"I don't know. He was probably a robber. Hahaha."

Hmm. Nervous laugh. "What exactly is your business, Buck?"

"Insurance, Mac, insurance."

"Describe how you met Luther."

"Uhh, how I met him? Oh, he asked me to play a friendly game of poker."

"So, you didn't know him before this trip?"

Buck angled his shoes toward the building. "Did I know him from before. Um. No. No, I didn't know the man."

"Did you ever see him write in a small notebook?"

"No. I'd be surprised if he could read, let alone write."

"When was the last time you saw him alive?"

"Well, sir, the captain decked him, then the crew carried him off. That was it."

"Where were you last night from six-thirty?"

"I ate dinner, then went to bed."

"Can anyone verify that?"

"You mean, do I have an alibi? No. I didn't know I needed one."

"It's getting late, Buck. That's all, for now. Don't leave the area without talking to me first."

"You don't seriously think I killed that varmint?"

"You had a public fist fight with him. That gives you a good motive. Yes, you are a prime suspect."

CHAPTER SEVENTEEN

April 26, 1865 Late Afternoon

JACOB BROCK DOCKS THE "DARLINGTON" AT BROCK HOUSE HOTEL

The 'threshing machine sound' of the side-wheel steamer *Darlington* and its distinctive whistle signaled its arrival, before it came into view. As soon as it docked, owner and captain Jacob Brock, an imposing ruddy-faced gentleman with a goatee and drooping mustache, strode onto the dock and up to the hotel veranda.

"Mac. It's been too long," said Jacob.

"I see you survived those harsh Union prisons, Jacob. Stay around here a while and we'll fatten you up."

"Can't do it, Mac. I have to get my business back on its feet again. I brought 20 guests, this trip. And I have to go back for more in the morning. Do you know, I had to buy back the *Darlington* from those Union sons-of-guns. Think of it. Buy back my own boat."

Sadie stepped onto the veranda in time to hear Jacob's diatribe.

"It's good to have you and *the Darlington* back where you belong, Jacob."

Sadie sank onto a chair next to Martha and greeted her and Mac with a warm smile.

"Thanks, Mac. Well, hello. If it isn't Martha Merritt. How is your plantation doing? Did you ever catch the sneak thieves who were stealing your rum?" Jacob said.

Hmmm, plantation owner? Rum? thought Mac.

"Hello, Jacob, dear. Yes. We've taken steps to ensure that it won't happen again." She continued knitting a cylinder of very fine pink wool.

"Good evening. I'm Sadie Snow. I don't believe we've met," Sadie said to Jacob.

"Jacob Brock. Pleased to meet you, Sadie. You must be one of the guests that young Noah brought. A bright future, has that lad," he said.

Mac said, "Martha, tell me about your plantation."

"After Papa died Mary and I inherited 160 acres in Eau Gallie, next door to John Carroll Houston. He and Papa, with some neighbors founded Eau Gallie, you know.

Sadie said, "That's interesting. I'm new around here. Where is Eau Gallie?"

"It's on the coast about 150 miles south of Saint Augustine, dear. Come visit us."

"I might. Couldn't we go on horseback over to the coast from here?"

"Only if you like rattlesnakes, gators, and outlaws. No. We love the Saint John's River, so we take a coastal steamer up to Jacksonville specially so we can enjoy the river trip down to Enterprise."

"And we love having you and your sister here, Martha. I understand it's been three or four years since you've been here. Are you going to stay a while?" said Jacob.

"We've reserved through July. And our manager will be bringing us regular reports. We may have to go back home once in a while. But we want to cruise on the river. What do you say about a long-term pass, Jacob, to ride whenever we want?"

"Absolutely. Talk to Charles. He's acting as our bursar right now. And tell him I said he better give you a good deal."

"I'll do that, Jacob."

"He's a good son, Martha. When I get the *Hattie* and the *Florence* back, Charles will captain one of them. Well, I better get on folks. More later."

After he hurried off, Sadie said, "Martha, Jacob mentioned rum. Do you make rum on your plantation?"

"Yes. Ours is really a small operation compared to others, like Robert Gamble's 3,500 acres of sugarcane on his plantation south of Tampa. It's on the Little Manatee River. Since '62, Captain Archibald MacNeil has lived there. He was a Commissary agent for the Confederacy. Last I heard he had an enormous rum production there. And ran the blockades during the war. They made over 1,500 hogsheads of processed sugar last year, before the Union blew up their extraction mill. That was late '64."

Mac thought, *She's better than a newspaper.*

"It's all very hush-hush, but I understand that Judah Benjamin has been hiding out there since he fled Richmond at the beginning of April. He was the confederate Secretary of State, dear. They say he came into Florida on horseback under a false name, M. M. Bonfals."

"But do you use sugar to make rum? asked Sadie, rerouting Martha's flow.

"Some do, but we discovered we could make good rum from our molasses, a byproduct of our sugar production, by adding water and yeast. And it's very profitable."

"Jacob said somebody was stealing it?"

"We saw them the last time. It was that Luther Greim's gang. We recognized him on the *Katie Asbell*. While Mary and I were trying to figure out what to do, somebody did away with the man. Oh, my. I need more wool. Would you excuse me, please?"

"Just a minute, Martha. When was the last time you saw Luther Greim alive?"

"That would've been last night, when the deckhands carried him off, after the fight in the salon."

"Did you see any unusual occurrence after that? Anything at all that made you wonder?"

"Mmm, no, I don't think so. But if I think of anything, I will let you know."

After she left, Sadie blinked. "Whew. I never knew she was so talkative, or social, or ..."

"Knowledgeable?"

"Yes. She always seemed like just a sweet little lady."

"You have to watch out for those knitters. They sit in a corner and listen," said Mac, with a laugh. "You did a right good job of aiming her talk."

"Mac, you realize that's two more people who had reason to get rid of Luther Greim? What if they went to his cabin, while he was still blind drunk, got him up under some pretext, and pushed him overboard."

"Miss Snow. "

"Sadie. Please, call me Sadie."

"Sadie, neither of those ladies weighs over 98 pounds, sopping wet. Luther was 250 pounds, at least..."

"Yes, but it would only take a push."

What is she hiding? She's trying hard to implicate somebody else. Did she kill him?

"Sadie, thank you for getting that much information from her. But I'm not buying it. And now it's time to get ready for dinner. Good day."

Sadie made her way out to the kitchen in the yard behind the hotel. "May I have a sandwich and a cup of clear meat broth, please," she said to Mrs. Flowers, the short, stout chief cook, who was making preparations for the next day's meals.

"Yes, Miss Sadie. Everybody knows what you're doing for that boy. Here you are. A cup of broth for you, too. And put these cookies in your pocket. You need anything else?"

She handed Sadie the food on a pretty, round, copper food service tray covered by a fresh napkin. Her hand reached up to adjust the white cap over her sleeked-back gray hair.

"Could you spare a candle and matches? I may have to dose him during the night."

"Of course. We make these ourselves. They are beeswax and burn very clean." She handed over a tall candle in a holder and a Mason jar of matches. "Anything else?"

"No, thank you. That's perfect."

In the sick room, she found Mary reading quietly at the foot of Christian's bed. "He was quite fitful, while you were gone. But he didn't seem to need any more medication."

Sadie set the tray on their ersatz table. "Thanks, Mary. It's time for your dinner, now. I'm going to pull these two chairs together and spend the night here with him."

"Very good. I will be back in the morning. You can't do this all by yourself, Sadie."

"That would be a tremendous help. Thank you so much, Mary." She embraced the frail older woman.

Sadie drank her broth and then managed a few hours of sleep, before she was awakened by Christian's delirious shouts — "No. No. Don't do it, Mr. Greim. No. No, you can't do it. Not fire. My brother..."

Sadie lit the candle.

He thrashed about and punched at the air. Sweat dripped from his brow.

"Christian. Christian wake up. You're having a bad dream. Wake up." She grasped his elbows gently.

"No. Not the barn. They are ...sick animal. Stop it. No... Mum!"

"Wake up. Let's get you some more medicine and I have broth for you. Could you eat a sandwich?"

His eyes are wild. And he's sopping wet with perspiration.

She gently wiped his face with the dry napkin. He looked around. Then he blinked and sank back onto the pillow.

"Open your mouth, please. This is to make you feel better. Good. Now, a spoonful of the sweet syrup. And, how about some of this delicious broth? It's no longer hot, but it will taste good, anyway."

She got half a cup of broth into him before he turned away and fell asleep.

Oh, I might as well eat this sandwich, before it gets stale. Come to think of it, I haven't eaten since breakfast. I guess that was yesterday.

She finished off the ham and cheese, then blew out the candle.

Crepuscular rays of bright morning sun filtered in through the window and lighted the foot of Christian's bed. Sadie sat up.

Oh, my aching neck. Oh, my back. And my eye feels swollen. It's probably purple, by now. Why am I sleeping suspended between two chairs?

"Knock, knock." Mary peeked in, then entered carrying the tray.

"I came earlier, but you were both asleep. So, I took the liberty of removing the tray, and I brought you both some breakfast... and more broth for Christian."

Smells of bacon, biscuits, and hot coffee wafted Sadie's direction. Christian opened his eyes wide and managed a faint smile.

"Bless you," Sadie said. "That smells wonderful."

"Let me feed him, while you start on this. You look like you've had a hard night."

Mary cut small bites of bacon, biscuit, and gravy for the boy. "Christian, you are looking better this morning. How do you feel?"

"H-hot and c-c-cold," he said.

"Well, let's get this down you. Maybe it'll help." Mary supported the weak young man and spoon-fed him most of what she had brought.

"I practically inhaled mine," said Sadie. "Thanks. Let me get him some more medicine."

When that was done, Christian rolled over and soon emitted a soft snore.

Mary said quietly, "Now you go away, Sadie. Put your feet up somewhere and don't come back until at least mid-afternoon. I will hold down the fort."

Sadie clasped her hands together and placed them under her chin. "Bless you, Mary. I know just the place."

CHAPTER EIGHTEEN

April 27, 1865 8:00 a.m.

AT BROCK HOUSE HOTEL

M ac walked into the dining room, where people were enjoying breakfast. *I must question Neville Beaumont and Bram Maas before they leave to go hunting again. Oh, looks like Neville is holding court at the table in the corner.* He approached the group.

"Good morning, all. Mr. Beaumont, I need your help. Will you be so kind as to accompany me to the back parlor?"

"Mr. McNally, another time, perhaps. We've engaged a guide for hunting and I am due to join him shortly. Good day." Neville wiped his mouth, patted his mustache with a napkin, and stood.

"Sir, I'm afraid I must insist. This is very important."

"Oh, all right." Neville slapped Mac on the back. "I can spare a couple of minutes to help you. Let me tell you how we shot that great buck yesterday."

In the parlor, Mac pulled out his pencil and notebook and gestured to seats at the small table. They both sat. "I've been asked to look into the recent death. Let's start with your full legal name, sir."

"Neville Beaumont, of course. Everyone knows that."

"What other names have you used in the past?"

"Other names? Why none. See here, my good man. You said you need my help."

"Yes, this helps. Where is your home?"

"Savannah, Georgia. My plantation is called Windsweep."

"Where were you born?"

"I say. Can we do this later? I really need to be off." He stood to leave.

"No, Mr. Beaumont. We need to do this now."

"Listen here, Mac. I don't know who you think you are, asking questions like this. You can't interrogate a man of my standing ... a fine upstanding citizen."

"I'm trying to untangle this Luther Greim situation, Mr. Beaumont."

"You have no authority. Questioning a member of an important Savannah political group? How dare you?"

"Mr. Beaumont. Neville, if I may."

"You may not."

"I'm the closest thing to a law man that we have in this village. We've sent for the provost marshal in Jacksonville. It would be in everyone's best interest if we can get to the bottom of this murder before he arrives."

Neville paled. "Murder? I thought Luther stumbled around in the dark and fell over-board?"

"Maybe he did. We need to know more. Now, where were you born?"

"Can't you figure out that a wealthy plantation owner from Savannah would have been born there?"

"How did you get along with Luther Greim?"

"We played cards. He was very coarse."

"How long have you known Luther?"

"Are you suggesting...? You have no jurisdiction...can't accuse a prominent member of society. How dare you even suggest such a thing? We are finished."

He jumped up, knocked the small table askew, and stomped out.

Very obstructive. Naturally pompous? or hiding something? I'm guessing Bram is probably with him again. No use looking for the trader 'till this evening.

Mac looked up and glimpsed Sadie. "Oh, Sadie. Have you written that list for me? Names of relatives whom you've nursed, dates, places?"

"Mac, I can't remember, exactly. I was back-and-forth. Let me think about it and I'll get back with you later."

"Right. Don't leave it too long." *Poor kid. Puffy. Purple. and looking pained. She has looked better. Is she also suffering from a guilty conscience?*

Mac rose. *Time to adjourn to the veranda and feed Fluffy a treat.*

There's Jacob, seated in animated conversation with Hattie and Jennie.

"We need to celebrate our return to business," Jacob said. "I'm going to offer a free excursion to Orchid Springs. That should get everybody's attention. All our hotel guests and everybody for miles, even our Brock House staff, will be invited. We can have music and dancing and free drinks."

"Well, maybe one free drink per person, Papa. You know most of our passengers are heavy drinkers, and the bar is the most popular place on the ship," said Hattie.

She has a practical head on her shoulders, thought Mac, as he pulled out a deck chair to join them. *Lean war years don't produce enough income to allow lavish entertaining.*

"True," said Jacob. "The well-stocked bar room of Brock House is a large part of its draw."

"Why don't we offer a free glass of rum punch to each guest," said Jennie. "That way we can use a lot of fruit juice, which is easier to come by than liquor. And they can pay for any extras. How many passengers, do you think?"

"From similar events in the past, I'd expect 150 whites and 100 negroes to take part in the general merriment," said Jacob.

Hattie jumped up and hugged her father. She said, "We've kept our heads down for four long years. I think everybody's ready for some fun. You set the date and we'll start the preparations."

CHAPTER NINETEEN

April 27, 1865 Late Morning

AT SNOW BIRD COTTAGE

*T*he short walk around the lakeside to Snow Bird cottage, my cottage, energized me and helped air out some of the fog in my head, thought Sadie.

Hmm. A little shed near the lakeside. A tiny wren with a giant voice warbled atop the low structure. *Let's look.*

She opened a rickety door and peered inside the musty building. *A canoe? Correction. Make that a red-cedar-log dugout canoe!*

Oh, Aunt Cora. How I love adventurous you. Why didn't I come visit earlier? I feel like you're here.

She looked around the sunny shoreline of Lake Monroe as far as she could see. *Oaks, cypress, palms, and palmettos. And a silhouette of a person.*

Tomorrow, Aunt Cora, we paddle. Remind me to ask Mac how far it is across this lake.

She started up onto the porch. *Oh, you know you're curious. Just walk all around it.* She stepped back down to investigate the flowers planted around the house.

Perfuming the air, deep green gardenia bushes snuggled against the white wooden lattice work at the base of the house.

Bright ruffled red and yellow hibiscus, against a profusion of saw-tooth green leaves, bloomed below the west windows. They made her smile.

There you are, Aunt Cora. You loved your bright colors.

She continued exploring to the back of the cottage. Well, look at that — a little red brick building with windows. The kitchen? From an enormous shade tree, she reached up and picked a fresh-crisp leaf. As she crushed it in her fingers, a slightly medicinal scent arose.

Mmm, camphor. Aunt Cora, you brought seeds from your trip to Japan! And it's so big that it protects almost all of the back veranda, which seems to wrap around the house.

I'm still amazed at the lush growth everywhere. A wooden bench. Sadie sat and surveyed her garden.

A mockingbird sang a trilling song from the top-most branch of a loblolly pine. She watched as he flew straight up and then came right straight back down again, doing pirouettes and twirls. *Showing off for his lady. Love is in the air.*

Leading off into the distance, *160 acres of distance, if I remember correctly,* a staggered line of showy small dogwood trees swayed in the light breeze. Their profusion of pinkish-white flowers danced. Between them, the grass was flattened. *A path.*

She got up and walked toward a neat rectangular vegetable garden at the back of which was a very small jasmine-covered building.

Heavens to Betsy. And there is the outhouse. Complete with the traditional half-moon on the door.

From a long waist-high trellis, she plucked a green pod and munched. *Early pole beans. Mm, sweet. I see cabbages, a row of carrots, and another of onions. But I wonder what the rest of that is?*

She walked along the path into a small glade and startled a brown rabbit with long floppy ears. Five little brown sparrows lit on the grass and started pecking, in search of breakfast.

Here. Let me help. She dug into her pockets and produced a cookie, which she crumbled and tossed to the little visitors.

The path curved and led on, but after some minutes, Sadie returned to the cottage. *Odd. A big canvas bag hanging in the sun, above head-height in the narrow space between the cottage and the brick building.*

She stepped onto a small square platform about two inches above the ground. *A spout, like a watering can with a valve, is fixed to the bottom of the bag.* She turned the valve.

Eeee. A spray of warm water in my face and all over my clothes. A Florida Bath. Ha, ha, ha. Just what I need. I'm crazy, but I'm stripping right now.

All clothes into a nice flat pile. Now, jump on top and stomp. Stomp out the dirt. Stomp out the sweat. Stomp out the anxiety. Stomp out the fear. Rub everything clean. Clean. Clean. Clean.

She frolicked until the water ran out. Then she squeezed the water out of her clothes and hair. *They should dry in no time, if I spread them over a chair in the sun. And my hairpiece, too.*

She lazed a few minutes in the sun. *How long had that water been in there? How did it get in there? Can I fill it back up?* Finally, she dressed, re-pinned her hair, and climbed up her back steps.

The door is unlocked? Again? I locked it yesterday. Or did I? I must be really tired.

Sadie found a small bedroom and a larger one. *Aunt Cora's bedroom. Oh. What a big book.* On the table beside the bed she found Cora's copy of a book by a South Carolina surgeon, Francis Peyre Porcher: *Resources of the Southern Fields and Forests, Medical, Economical, and Agricultural: Being Also a Medical Botany of the Confederate States; with Practical Information on the Useful Properties of the Trees, Plants, and Shrubs.*

She paged through the book. *This could be very useful.*

The bedsheets smell fresh. I'll just rest my eyes for a moment.

She awoke hours later. *What kind of noise was that? I'm getting hungry. It's about time to explore what might be my kitchen.*

A search in her pockets produced the house key and she proceeded to the small brick building out back. *Unlocked? What's going on here? The wood stove is warm, when it should be cold.*

I need to go back to Brock House and check on Christian right now. But tomorrow, I'll get to the bottom of this.

At Brock House Mac decided, *The only way I'm going to be able to question Bram is to stick to Ava like glue.*

When he found her on the front veranda in conversation with Martha, he picked up Fluffy and joined them. "Good afternoon, ladies."

"Oh, is that your cat?" said Ava.

"No. She just seems to like me. My animal magnetism, you know."

"We have a gray tabby cat in Eau Galliee. She's a marvelous mouser," said the talkative Merritt sister.

Ava said, "Ours is, too. She's orange, like this one. Stores in New York are dreadfully bothered with mice. But our Coco keeps them away."

"Do you enjoy living in New York? I've heard that you are plagued by more than mice - rough gangs of violent adolescents," Martha said.

"Yes, that is a problem. We have seven or eight very violent gangs who fight each other. In our neighborhood the Dead Rabbits, mostly young Irish, are always fighting with the Bowery Boys, who dress posh and usually have day jobs. They're also very political. Matter of fact, that 'swell' Neville Beaumont kind of reminds me of one of those Bowery Boys I knew. He dressed really nice and was a printer in the shop where I had my advertising bulletins made."

"What happened to him?"

"Disappeared. Probably either killed by a rival gang or graduated to higher political echelons," said Ava. "Oh, hello, Mr. Maas. Have you enjoyed your day of shooting?"

Mac said, "Bram Maas. I need 10 minutes of your time. Will you accompany me to the parlor, please?"

CHAPTER TWENTY

April 27, 28, 1865 Late Night

AT BROCK HOUSE HOTEL

When Sadie entered the sick room, Mary said, "He has been thrashing about this afternoon. I gave him some willow several hours ago, and it seemed to help a little."

"Knock, knock."

"Hello. It's just Daisy. I brought you some dinner." The busy head housekeeper carried in a metal tray and set it on their 'table.' She removed the napkin to reveal many dishes.

Oh. The smell of fresh bread.

"They are ready for you in the dining room, Miss Mary."

"Thanks. I'll be going now, but I'll be back in the morning. Have a good night."

After she left, Daisy burst out, "Please ask Mr. Lavigne again about that housekeeping job. We are run off our feet, with so many people to do for. When Christian gets better you could be a big help."

"Do you think he would consider it? He seemed pretty set against me."

"Mr. Jacob Brock has been on him to hire some more staff —'reliable,' he said. That sounds like you."

"This boy is still very sick. We'll see how much nursing he requires. He may need another round of quinine and I'm going to have to find a source for the fever bark."

"When he gets better, will you think about it?"

"Yes. I still haven't any money. I will consider it. Thank you, Daisy."

Fed, dosed, and tucked in, Christian tossed a little and finally fell asleep.

With a thankful heart, Sadie ate her dinner, pocketing a few bits to feed the birds later. She slept until the wee hours of the morning, when she was awakened by a shout.

"No.

"No.

"Noooo.

"Mr. Greim.

"Stop.

"Don't do it.

"Burn everything else, but not that.

"Not the BARN."

In the dark, Sadie felt around on the table for the candle and matches. *He's going to wake the whole hotel.*

He yelled, "You can't burn the barn, Greim, you evil, loathsome, lowdown scum. My little sister and brother are tending Matilda, our sick mule, in there. No. NO. MUM. We have to stop him. WHAT CAN WE DO? Mr. Greim. STOP. They are hiding in the hay. You can't burn the barn. It's burning. He won't listen. Luther. Luther Greim. You mean lowdown skunk. You MURDERER. You will BURN IN HELL."

The boy was sobbing uncontrollably. Sadie finally found the candle and matches. By the warm candle light, she could see the boy's shoulders heaving. "Christian. Christian. Shh. It's all right. You're safe. Shh." She finally held the shaking boy to her, in her effort to quiet him. "Shh."

When he ceased shaking, she said, "Tell me about your brother and sister."

"He, he killed them," the boy said, in a choked voice. Young Billy and little Sarah Jane were taking turns tending to our sick mule. That nasty Luther Greim torched the barn. He burned it and them with it. They were hiding from him. We were all that afraid."

"Are you sure that's what happened, Christian?"

"Yes. Mum and I were watching from behind the brush pile and saw him and his gang. They stole everything they could carry and set fire to our house and outbuildings. As soon as Greim left, we tried to rescue them." He choked. "A-all that was left was char and ashes."

"Oh, Christian. I'm so sorry. You are still shivering and flushed with fever. Let's get you some more medicine."

CHAPTER TWENTY-ONE

April 28, 1865 6:00 a.m.

AT BROCK HOUSE HOTEL

The sun had just risen when a very soft knock sounded at the sick room door. Sadie, already awake, sat up. "Come in," she said.

"Oh, good. You're awake," said Mary, who held a cup of spicy-smelling hot tea in each hand. "Breakfast preparations are just starting in the kitchen, so I made this myself."

She handed Sadie a cup and said, "You are looking better. How is our patient this morning?"

"Quiet, thankfully. He was delirious last night. Have you seen Mac this morning?"

"Yes. He was headed to the veranda with a cup of coffee."

"Will you sit with Christian, while I go talk to him for a few minutes?"

"Of course. Off you go."

She found Mac, in a bubble of inviting coffee fragrance, alone on the veranda, except for Fluffy curled in his lap. "Good morning. Beautiful day isn't it?" he said.

"Yes." She plopped down in a chair next to him. "Mac, Christian was delirious last night and gave something of a confession."

"Oh?"

"Luther Greim burned their homestead and killed his little brother and sister. That certainly gives him a motive — or would you say two big motives — to murder the man."

"Sadie, that sounds like pure fantasy to me. A bad dream from his fever, maybe the medicine, and the fact that he was very affected by this murder."

"But Mac, he..."

"Sadie, I know you are trying to help your situation by finding others with a motive to murder Luther. But sit for a moment and think. He's just a boy."

"But a very big boy...

"He is a bean pole. Luther weighed at least 250. It would take a great amount of strength to move someone that big."

"Unless he lured him outside somehow and pushed him into the lake. And do we have any evidence that Luther was dragged?"

Ava and Bram appeared on the porch. "Sadie, drop it," he said, in a low voice. He thought, *We do need to examine the Katie Asbell, though. What evidence will be there after four days?*

Ava was laughing at something Bram said. "And he has such nice manners, too. We'll tell all our Georgia friends to vote for him."

She said, "Good morning Mac, Sadie. You will never guess. Neville is going to run for governor of Georgia. We may be friends with a governor."

Kat Ashley came out the front door, with her hand over her mouth and taking large gulps of the fresh air. Ava whispered something to Bram.

"This was a bad idea. Excuse me. I'm going to get some tea — and some of the digestive medicine that Sadie gave me," Kat said. She turned around and went back in.

"She's a pretty little thing and all alone. Too bad she's so sick," said Bram.

Ava half covered her mouth and said, "Don't be a goose, Bram. She's not sick. She's pregnant, or my name isn't Ava Maas. She is not alone either. Can't you see how Buck follows her everywhere?"

"Oh. Well, good. Maybe he'll marry her."

"Don't be silly. No man wants another's castoffs. When he finds out, he will run. Then she will be alone, with a child she doesn't want. That's what is too bad. Let's go back inside."

"Does Ava have any children?" Sadie said to Mac, after the Maases left.

"She says not. And he said practically nothing last night. It was like questioning a turnip."

Sadie chuckled. "She sounds envious."

"I think you're probably right."

"Before I forget, I meant to ask you. Do you know how far it is across this lake?"

"Five miles. Why? You planning to swim across it? You know it's full of alligators, right?"

"I respect the rights of those gators. But they'll have to hunt something besides me. I won't be swimming in their lake."

"Did you write that list for me?"

"You want to know where I've worked. How far back should I go?"

"How many jobs have you had?"

"Mac. Don't you know it destroys a lady's allure when all the secrets are gone? I'll think about your list, but right now I have to check on Christian."

She stood and went to fetch some breakfast, this time for all three of the sickroom inmates. She carried it back there and was surprised to hear voices coming from inside. She knocked and entered.

"It's about time," said Christian. "I'm starving." He sat on the side of the bed, with his feet on the floor.

"Our prayers have been answered," said Mary. "His fever has broken."

"And don't forget Sadie's sweet medicine. I think it must be time for me to take some more. And some ham. And some eggs. And some biscuits," the boy said.

Sadie scooted the 'table' over in front of him. "Here. Get started on this." And she did give him more medicine, for she knew it was too early to stop.

"You'll stay here with him today, Mary?"

"Yes. I brought my book. And it looks like he might be ready for conversation."

"All right. Let's eat, then I'll take the tray back to the kitchen and be off."

Soon she was at the door of the cookhouse. "Thank you, Mrs. Weathers for a fine meal."

She headed for her cottage to find out who walked on the shores of Lake Monroe, ...and more importantly, to find out how locked doors become unlocked and supposed cold stoves become warm.

At the cottage Sadie went straight upstairs to fetch the spyglass. She pulled it out, fitted it to her eye, and searched the lakeshore. *People? No. All is quiet on the lake.*

What do I need for paddling? A hat. A long sleeve shirt. A jug of water.

She skipped back down to the closet.

"Ta-dahh." *One woven palm leaf hat. One red plaid shirt, long-sleeved. Rubber boots, one size too big. Do I need these? Maybe. Yes.*

She removed her chignon and placed it on the dressing table. *Ah, to remain pinless. Now, plop the hat on top.*

Out on the lawn several robins were searching for breakfast. "Here." She dug in her pockets and tossed the food to her hungry visitors. *I saved this especially for you.*

When she launched, sun sparkled off little wavelets. *Aunt Cora's unique dugout is easy to paddle.* She stopped momentarily to wave off a swarm of insects. *These mosquitoes are beastly.* "Smack."

Ooo, alligators. Several alligators cruised by her craft. *Yikes. They are just eye bulges and saw-tooth backs, barely visible above the surface of the water. Stealthy beasts.*

Across the lake Sadie saw two silhouettes. *Is that one a man with a shovel? Maybe he's digging for clams? Curious.*

This should be about the middle of the lake. Mmm, the breeze feels good. Less bugs. But it's blowing my hair into my eyes. Glad this hat has a tie.

"Hey, stop it." *A snout with eye bulges bumped me.* "Shoo. Leave my boat alone." She smacked the snout with the end of her paddle, tipping herself dangerously to one side.

Maybe it wasn't such a good idea to take this dugout on the lake by myself.

She looked behind her and could barely see Snow Bird Cottage. Ahead, she could see the beach.

She put on a burst of speed and shot the little craft right up onto the sand. She jumped out. *Oh, it feels good to stand up, away from the gators. Thank you, Aunt Cora for the wading boots. Please, God, don't let there be any snakes here.*

What in the Sam Hill is that? Just back from the waterline, in a deep pit partly filled with water, an animal thrashed. Closer inspection showed it to be a five-foot gator.

That must be an alligator catcher. Is there such a thing? Or maybe it's a cage for one already caught.

As she moved farther and farther from the water's edge, she saw several rectangular pits partially filled with water.

The sky turned gray. *Time to start back.* She clumped to the water's edge and hopped into the canoe.

Where did this wind come from? It's fierce. And it would have to be coming directly at me. Lot harder to paddle back against it.

"Crash." Lightning flashed in the distance. *Ahh. Just what I need. A squall while I'm still out here on the lake.*

Thunder rumbled. "Boom."

The bottom fell out of the sky. All its accumulated moisture came down at once.

"Aack. "*Cold rain sluicing down the back of my neck.*

Rain pelted sideways across her bow. It stung her bare face, harder and harder.

This miserable rain.

It sure spurs me to paddle faster.

One of those lightning flashes is going to turn me into toast.

Go, girl, go.

The lightning came faster. "Crack. Boom."

I hope I'm going in the right direction.

If this rain would let up, I could get a bearing on Snow Bird Cottage.

During a lull, she spotted it.

Go.

Dig that water. Plant, twist and pull.

Right, left, right, left.

The rain started again harder.

Almost there.

Almost.

Ahh. Soft bump of sand.

"Aaack." *Not Sand.*

An enormous gator rammed the side of the little dugout.

Great Caesar's ghost. He's twice as long as my boat.

She smacked and pounded at it.

Go away.

I refuse to be your midmorning snack.

She whacked down hard with her paddle on one big eye.

The ramming ceased.

Go, go, go.

Fear pushed her speed.

Soft bump.

Oh no.

Not again.

Her little craft slid up on shore.

Hallelujah.

Made it.

Thank you, God.

Oh, joy.

I'm exhausted, drenched, cold, and mosquito bitten, but I'm here.

She stumbled out of the craft and sank on her back on the beach.

Cold rain spat in her face.

It rolled down her neck, over her saturated clothes, and flooded into the sand below.

Maybe the cold will be good for my purple eye from Luther's slap.

I'm a mess.

She summoned the dregs of her energy and got up. *Keep moving, Sadie. Put the boat away in the shed.*

In the cottage, she rubbed her skin dry with a towel, wrapped her hair, and put on dry clothes from her bag.

I have earned a nap. Shivering, she pulled down the sheets and climbed under the warm covers.

Mid-afternoon she awoke to bright sunshine blazing through her window. *Crazy Florida weather.* She got up, hair mostly dry, and stepped outside the back door.

The sound of birdsong greeted her and she unwrapped and rubbed her toweled hair. *I have to go check on Christian... and I'm getting hungry.*

I must see to getting some supplies for here. Guess I need to earn some money first.

She went back inside and combed her hair. After it was pinned up, chignon in place, she locked the doors and walked back to Brock House.

Who dug the pits?

Chapter Twenty-Two

April 28, 29, 1865

Later at Brock House Hotel

B oth Sadie and Christian ate hearty dinners. The boy was in good spirits.

"I don't need more medicine, Sadie. I'm fine."

"Christian you have to keep this medicine in you for at least four days. Open."

He fell asleep early and they had an uneventful night. Shortly after day break he tapped her on the shoulder.

"Mmnpf. You're up. And dressed. Mary just washed and dried those clothes for you yesterday."

He said, "Where is everybody? I walked down the hall and there's no one."

"They are all asleep. That's where you should be, too." She yawned.

"I'm not sleepy."

"Christian, do you remember what you told me yesterday after your horrible nightmare?"

"You mean about Luther killing Sarah Jane and Billy? Yes, and it's all true. I'm glad I told you. He was pure evil and needed killin'. But I didn't do it."

"Mmm. I know you're feeling better, but you need to take it easy today. Noah will be back tonight and you will have to go back to your normal job."

"All right, but my stomach's growling something fierce. When do we eat?"

She laughed. "Let me go make us some tea and see if I can find anything left over in the kitchen. You stay here. If they find out you're chomping at the bit, they'll put you to work. And then you'll relapse."

"Yes, Miss. I could eat some of that oat cake, even if it's dried out."

As she walked down the shell road to her cottage, Sadie thought about her future.

Christian is getting better and Noah will be back tonight. How long do I want to stay here? At least until the hunt surrounding Lincoln's murder settles. That may take quite a while.

Maybe I could grow produce to sell. Her steps led her into the back yard.

I don't want to think about a long-term plan. I just need a way to get some income now.

Sadie, deep in thought, jumped back at the sight of a short, stout negro woman, with her black hair in a fat shiny braid atop her head, like a crown.

She also wore a two-foot-long red, yellowish-white, and black banded snake coiled around her neck.

"Great Caesar's ghost! Who are you? And what are you doing in my garden?"

The trespasser said, "I am Jane Marsh and I live here." She uncoiled the snake and held it out toward Sadie. "She's really smooth. Want to pet her?"

"Heavens to Betsy. I wouldn't think of such a thing...And who told you that you could live here?"

"I've lived here for nearly three years — ever since Mrs. Bird bought me in Cuba. Who are you?"

"I..I...I'm Sadie Snow, her niece. She left the cottage to me. But, but, she b-bought you? She wouldn't. Aunt Cora was an abolitionist...and, and a fighter for fairness and equality."

"She was fair. And she treated me equal. That sale was the best thing that ever happened to me."

"I, I can't believe it."

"My father is a rich Spanish planter in Cuba who had me educated to be a lady, so he could show me off. He used to take his whip to me, too, when he got in one of his rages." She draped the snake inside a large wooden box.

"One day I grabbed the end of that leather and pulled it away from him." Her big wide-set dark-brown eyes flashed.

Sadie now noticed long scars on Jane's bare arms and chest that showed out from under her flowing white sun dress.

Jane said, "The next day he sold my mother and me in Havana. The slave trader covered my scars with long sleeves and a floor-length skirt.

"But when I got on the block, I ripped off those sleeves and let everyone see the welts... I think Mrs. Bird bought me to save me from such again."

Sadie was shocked into silence at the tale of brutality.

Jane said, "I made lemonade. Do you want some?"

After a moment Sadie said, "Thank you. No." She looked into Jane's eyes. "I'm here now. And you are free — free to go wherever you like."

Jane pouted her full lips. "Where should I go? This is my home."

"I see. "*Aunt Cora, you're still here.* Then she said, "Jane, I'm going inside. Perhaps we could look at my new home together?"

"Yes. Let's walk and talk."

So, the two ladies toured the house and grounds. "Was it you who painted the cottage?"

"Yes. We started it together. But then she was very ill. She made me promise to finish painting the cottage, even if she died."

"Oh." *She was thinking of me, even then.* She paused, then said, "Why didn't I see you the first day?"

"I hid, of course."

"Why did you come out now?"

"I've seen how you feed the birds. You seem to like this place very much."

"Yes, I do." *She's been watching me?* "Oh, no." *The shower dance, when I was so very tired.* "You didn't see me taking a bath?"

"I confess that I did see a little of that. You were very funny." She chuckled. "But, no matter. And I'm glad you took out the canoe. You are so brave. It's been sitting ever since Mrs. Bird died."

"You don't like canoeing?"

"Mercy me. No. Not unless I have to."

"Jane, I don't see why we can't both live here. Except that I have no money for supplies."

"I haven't any, either. After Mrs. Bird died and the housekeeping money ran out, I ate out of the garden."

"Daisy, the head housekeeper at the hotel, said they need help. They have a sudden influx of new guests, due to the end of the war. I planned to go this afternoon and ask for a job as a housekeeper. You could go with me. Do you have skills?"

"I wouldn't mind a job as a cook. That was my hobby in Cuba. And Mrs. Bird really liked my cooking. I learned about making pastry, cakes, roasts, and gravies from a book in Mrs. Bird's library. She said it was the first American cookbook. The flyleaf says it was printed in 1796." She went to a shelf and took down a book. "See?"

American Cookery. Its subtitle was: "The art of dressing viands, fish, poultry and vegetables, and the best modes of making puff-pastes, pies, tarts, puddings, custards and preserves, and all kinds of cakes, from the Imperial Plumb to plain cake. Adapted to this country, and all grades of life. By Amelia Simmons, an American orphan."

"You know how to do all that?"

"Yes."

"What are we waiting for? Let's go. No, wait. First, we need to look the part. Mr. Lavigne, who does the hiring, is very particular about staff looking traditional."

Sadie costumed them from articles in the closets and her bags. She could do nothing about Jane's plump shape and big feet.

But she found that the woman's closet was full of neutral clothing that would be suitable. *White. Black. Gray. She seems to prefer neutral colors. No red, fuchsia, purple, lavender, violet. I'd die.*

She chose a simple skirt, blouse and cardigan for herself in navy blue. When she was satisfied, they closed Snow Bird Cottage, and headed for the hotel.

In the back hall of Brock House Sadie said, "Jane, come and meet my friends, Mary and Christian."

"I don't know. I haven't been around many people this last three years. What if they don't like me?"

"Nonsense. Just be your own pleasant self and they will like you fine."

"All right."

The door to the store room where she and Mary had nursed Christian stood wide-open. Christian's tenor voice came from next door and was answered by Mac's deep bass. *A heated debate about ammunition?*

Sadie looked in. *Christian seems bright eyed and fever free.* "Hello, you two. Where is Mary?"

"I told her that I don't need a nurse anymore. She just laughed and said she has some things to do. Besides I wanted to talk to Mac."

"Ah. Let me introduce you. Jane Marsh, these are my friends Mac McNally, a former Pinkerton detective, and Christian Ames, who is employed on the steamer *Katie Asbell*. Gentlemen, this is Jane, who was a great friend of my Aunt Cora." Jane didn't correct her. "Excuse us. We are on our way to see Mr. Lavigne."

Mac raised an eyebrow. He said, "Ladies," and nodded.

On the way to the manager's office, Sadie said, "I should warn you, Jane. The last time I asked Lavigne for a job he turned me down. He also looked down his nose at me. But don't let that stop you. We need this. And he needs us."

At their knock, Mr. Lavigne said, "Come."

The room reeked of his pipe smoke. He looked them up and down and seemed puzzled. "What's wrong?"

"Nothing at all," said Sadie. "Everything is right. We have come to help you with your labor shortage. Jane, this is Mr. Lavigne. Mr. Lavigne, Jane is an excellent cook and is willing to share her talents with your hotel guests."

"Hmm. We are hiring. Do you have references?"

"Yes, sir. I've cooked for Mrs. Bird for three years. I am accomplished with pastry, cakes, gravies, roasts..."

"All right. Go on out to the kitchen and show our head cook, Mrs. Flowers, what you can do. If she approves, you can start tomorrow at regular terms and wages. An evening meal in the staff dining room is included. Close the door on your way out."

Sadie said, "Wait just a minute. Christian is much better this morning and I'm here to offer my services as a housekeeper."

"I'm not so sure about that."

"Come now. Daisy says she really needs the help and that Mr. Jacob Brock has insisted you get more housekeeping staff. I've proven reliable. What do you have to lose?"

"All right. But you are on probation. Go help Daisy this afternoon. If your work is passable, you too can start tomorrow. Good day, Miss Snow." He turned away to relight his meerschaum.

Woo hoo. Jane's a cook and I will be cleaning rooms... and snooping.

But only on things out in plain sight. I'm human, after all, and can't help seeing things and drawing conclusions.

She went to find Daisy and an apron.

CHAPTER TWENTY-THREE

April 29, 1865 Late Afternoon

AT BROCK HOUSE HOTEL

When Noah's *Katie Asbell* chugged up to the dock at Brock house, Sadie was sweeping floors and changing linens in the guest rooms.

She paused to peer out the upper floor window she was cleaning. Her heart quickened at the thought of seeing the sweet man, who was also, she guessed, 200 pounds of hard muscle.

Aboard the steamer, Noah gathered Mac's newspapers himself and then hurried to the veranda to break the news. In a low voice, he said, "Mac, I'm pretty sure we found the murder weapon. Remember the hammer that was missing? We found it in Sadie Snow's cabin when we were getting them ready for new customers. It was under the bunk and was crusted with dried blood."

"You're sure that was her cabin?"

"No doubt about it. We didn't disturb anything in there. We just locked it and Luther's, too."

"I want a look at those two cabins, right now. And that of Christian Ames. Sorry, Fluffy. Let's see if Jennie Brock has an Argand lamp we can use." He stood and dislodged the tabby.

Jennie answered their knock at her door in the private area of the hotel. "Come in, Mac, Noah."

"We can't stay. We need a bright light. Do you have an Argand lamp we can borrow for a few minutes?"

"Why, yes of course. Here. Careful. It's fairly full of oil."

"Thanks. We'll bring it back when we are done."

They headed back to the steamer with a grim sense of purpose. "I don't need to tell you that this looks really bad for Sadie Snow," said Mac. They walked up the gangplank. "Greim's cabin first, I think."

"Right. Here we are. Just as it was four days ago," said Noah, opening the door. "Hmm. We didn't see those spots on the wall before." Mac held up the powerful lamp.

"I need my pocket knife," said Mac. He handed over the lamp and, after hunting among his numerous jacket pockets, he produced that useful tool. He scraped at one of the spots behind the bed and deposited the residue into an envelope that he fished from another pocket. "I'll bet my Derby hat that Mr. Greim was killed here. It's faint, but I think that is a blood splatter arc on the wall behind Luther's bunk," said Mac.

From a pocket, he pulled out a tape measure and checked the distance between each droplet. "Wait while I make a quick sketch."

They examined every inch of wall, floor, and door. Smears and a fist-sized stain on the floor looked suspicious. Mac added them to his sketch and sampled them, too.

."We're done here. Let's go to Sadie's. You are sure it was hers?"

"Absolutely certain, Mac. This is it." He unlocked and opened a door. "And this cloth bag in the corner here has the hammer that the boys found under the bunk."

"It wasn't in the bag when they found it?"

"No. I put it in the bag. It was just a claw hammer with dried blood all over it."

"I'll take that to examine in the bright daylight."

They repeated the thorough search of walls, floor, and door.

"Nothing. That's curious. No stain under the bunk, and yet the hammer is covered in dried blood. Did she clean the cabin?" Mac whipped out a magnifying glass and examined every inch of the floor. "No blood anywhere."

Noah said, "What I'm wondering is if she hit him and threw him overboard, why would she carry the hammer back to her own cabin?"

"Maybe she was dazed and not thinking clearly... just hiding the weapon."

"Then, why didn't we find any blood stain under her bunk?"

"She must've cleaned the cabin, Noah. Just because your men didn't clean it, doesn't mean that she didn't. I know you don't want it to be her. I like her, too. But we can't ignore this solid evidence."

Noah said, "She cleaned the cabin, but left a bloody hammer, which left no bloody stain on the floor, under the bunk? Mac, you really think that woman, who has been nursing Christian since we've been gone, walked into Greim's cabin and hit him with a hammer? Your theory is that she pushed, pulled, rolled, or dragged that bear of a man overboard and then carried that bloody hammer back to her own cabin and put it under the bunk? That's nuts."

"Maybe she was nuts when she did it. Or maybe she had help. Noah, we are going to have to turn her over to the provost marshal when he comes. When will he be here?"

"That arrogant so and so. He said it's not his job, he's busy with army paperwork, and it would be a few days."

"I suspected as much. We're going to have to bury that corpse. We've held off as long as we can. Could a couple of your men help with that?"

"I suppose so. You said something about Christian Ames's cabin?"

"Not much use looking now... but might as well be thorough." They found nothing out of the ordinary in the cabin he shared with Jan, the server/dishwasher.

"What are you going to do about Sadie?"

"The boy seems to be healthy again and ready to resume his duties," said Mac. "We owe Sadie Snow for that outcome. She just took a job at the hotel and doesn't look likely to be going anywhere. I think house arrest until the marshal arrives would be acceptable."

"I wouldn't want to be you when you tell her," said Noah.

"I'll choose a public place. She's less likely to make a fuss."

"I wouldn't bet on it."

"Maybe you'd like to come with me?"

"No, thanks." He gave Mac a wry smile.

"Well, it's late. Better get it over with."

Mac walked into the dining room to find that the only place available was next to Buck and Kat. He took a seat and hooked his cane over the table.

"Buck, when we talked Wednesday, you didn't say where you were the night of the murder."

"Didn't I?"

"No. Where were you?"

"Umm. Well. In my room."

"All night?"

Kat said, "It's all right, Buck. We're going to have to tell pretty soon anyway. He was…"

A guest, just arrived on the *Katie Asbell,* passed by their table and stopped. "Buck? Buck, don't you recognize me? It's Florence. We were neighbors near Mount Airy, outside of Brooksville, remember? How is Naomi? And your beautiful children, Tommy and Bethany? They are two and four now, aren't they? The same ages as my two. It's not easy living on a homestead so far from the nearest neighbors."

"I'm, I'm sorry, ma'am. You're mistaking me for someone else. Excuse me." He got up and left.

Florence stood there, mouth agape.

Well, now, Mac thought. "Good evening. I'm Mac McNally. Who did you think you were addressing, ma'am?"

"Buck. Buck Stotts, of course. Everybody knows him in West Florida. He's just, just bigger than life." Food arrived at their table and the interloper walked away.

"What were you saying, before we were interrupted, Kat? Something you and Buck are going to have to tell?"

"Oh, nothing Mac. Just that we both like tabby cats. Ha, ha, ha."

"Ahh. As do I." *Time to ask my friend in Tampa what he knows about Buck Stotts. And Kat Ashley.*

Mac finished eating, then went in search of Sadie. Jane and Mrs. Flowers were still finishing, out in the kitchen. "Ladies, thank you for a delicious dinner. What was that dish with the corn in it?"

Mrs. Flowers said, "You must mean Jane's corn soufflé."

"That was mighty good, Miss Jane. I could eat that every day."

"Thank you, Mr. MacNally, but I think we would need to get a Jersey cow and some chickens to have enough cream and eggs to make it that often. I'll see about making you some special," Jane said, with a smile.

"Thank you, and please call me Mac. Jane, have you seen Sadie?"

"Not since she ate dinner here with the staff, sir. She took some stale bread for the birds and started for the cottage. I'm headed there in a few minutes. I'll be glad to show you the way."

"Thank you. I know Snow Bird Cottage. But I'm afraid I'm not up to the walk. Would you tell her I need to talk with her? Tomorrow morning will be soon enough."

"Yes, sir. I certainly will."

Chapter Twenty-Four

April 29, 1865

After Dinner at Brock House Hotel

"**K**nock, knock."

"Go away," Kat said.

"Kat. It's me. Open the door."

"No. I don't want to talk to you."

"Kat, I love you. Please open the door."

"What did that woman mean, about your children? And who is Naomi?"

"Open the door and let me explain."

"She said everybody knows you. You are bigger than life. What does that mean?"

"Kat, all that matters is that I love you. And you love me. I will take care of you. I promise."

"You promised a lot of things — 'forsaking all others.' And in front of the preacher, too, when we both said 'I do.' I love you and I thought we were going to make a life together with this new baby. Now, I'm just confused."

"Open the door. I want to hold you tight."

"Go away. I'm tired."

"All right. I will see you first thing in the morning. Remember, I love you and our baby."

Buck shuffled out of the hotel and wandered on the shell road in the dark for a long time. *What have I done? I love them both.*

When Kat became pregnant, I did the right thing and married her. I can take care of her and the baby. Just like I take care of Naomi and Tommy and Bethany.

The moon came up.

Since Lincoln signed that new law, making bigamy illegal, I've worried. Though they don't enforce it. Lincoln winked at polygamy in Utah, so long as Brigham Young stayed out of the war.

He heard rustling and crunching noises coming from the side of the road. *If a panther eats me, I won't have to worry about it anymore.* But he walked fast back toward the hotel.

So, do I want to be convicted of murder — which could happen if Kat turns against me and won't give me an alibi for the night of the murder.

The prosecutor will drone on about my igniting that big fist fight by calling that loud-mouthed, vulgar man a cheater just hours before he was killed.

Or do I prefer to be convicted of bigamy — which may happen if I tell Mac that I was with Kat the night of the murder. Kat is sure to tell him we are married. And he knows about my marriage to Naomi.

Choose.

Would Naomi feel cheated? I've done everything for her and the kids. But still...

Chapter Twenty-Five

April 30, 1865 6:00 a.m.

At Brock House Hotel and Dock

If I don't go very early, I'll miss Noah and he'll be gone for another four days. Sadie tiptoed out of the cottage and headed for Brock house.

There he is, tall and commanding, on the dock. "Good morning," she said. "What a beautiful day."

Noah was aware of her before she even spoke. He thought, *Beautiful day...and a beautiful lady, too. Her smile sends ripples of heat down my back. Stop it.* "Ahh, Sadie. You're up early. Have you talked to Mac yet?"

"No, but I got his blasted list for him. I hope that will make him happy. You look like you're almost ready to leave again. I missed you last time you left. How can we get to know each other better if you travel all the time?"

Noah held her by her shoulders and looked into her eyes. *She is so gorgeous. Strong. Charismatic. Dignified. And those amazing green eyes...*

He sighed. "I wish things were different," he said.

Sadie leaned into him a little. "Yes. I wish you didn't have to be gone so much."

He moved closer. "No. It's not that. I just, I don't know." *She's intoxicating. Her hair is warm and smells like flowers.*

"Mmm. You smell like spearmint and something else. " *What's stopping you? Kiss him.*

"Probably the lemon, and cedar oil... that we, use, for, cleaning," he murmured, at a loss for anything else to say.

She thought, *Oh, ho. you're such a romantic one, you are, Noah Asbell.* "Why don't we stroll over to the..."

"Cap'ain. What do you want me to... Oh, excuse me. Didn't know you was busy." The deckhand hurried off, looking embarrassed.

Noah drew back and blinked. *My heart is pounding, like an infatuated school boy. But, this issue of murder is serious. Back off.*

"Oh, uh. Don't let me keep you, Sadie. If there's nothing else, I have to get on the river."

Sadie stepped away from him. *Whew. Is it hot out here?* "Um, yes. Me, too. I mean, I'll get to work." *For Heaven's sake. Is your tongue tied around your teeth? Walk away.*

The first person she saw, as she approached the hotel, was Mac, on the veranda feeding Fluffy. "Good morning, Sadie. Have you ..."

"Yes, Mac. I have your list. Keep your hair on."

"You know I don't wear a wig. Never even been to the old Bailey. But come on up here, please, and have a seat. You told me that Buck accused Luther of cheating, AFTER Luther asked him about his wife and children?"

"Yes, that's right. Why?"

"Just making sure my facts are straight. I have something to tell you."

"That sounds ominous."

"It is, rather." He patted the seat next to him and said, "Keep your voice low. You are not going to like what I have to say."

"Mac. You are scaring me."

When she was seated, he said, "The cleaning crew on the steamer found the murder weapon."

"Isn't that good news? It puts us closer to our murderer."

"A bloody hammer, which matches Luther's head wounds, was found under your bunk, in your cabin."

"WHAT? You are not serious."

"Keep your voice down. How do you account for it being there?"

"I don't. You've got the wrong cabin. I know nothing about a hammer, bloody or otherwise."

"Noah and his crew are sure it was your cabin."

"No. It can't be. They're wrong."

"You can see how this looks, Sadie. We can't ignore this evidence. I'm afraid you are under arrest, until such time as you can be turned over to the Jacksonville provost marshal. We will make it house arrest."

"WHAT? NO! I did nothing wrong. What is house arrest? You want me to stay in one room of the hotel? I just got a job cleaning in this hotel. I was hoping to get information to help solve this blasted murder."

"Yes. I know."

"And I just inherited my aunt's cottage, and met a woman who served and loved my aunt, and I'm happier than I've been in a very long time." She burst into tears, choking and gasping.

"I know that, too. Sadie, and..."

"It's not fair. I've worked so hard. Come on, Mac. I have no money. Where am I going to go? Let me keep working."

"Sadie. What if we keep this information just between us? You continue with your job and your new cottage."

"You would do that?"

"I can't imagine how you could leave here without me knowing. Walking out, you'd have scorpions and snakes falling into your hair and you'd be tripping over alligators. You would be hard put to find a horse. That leaves boats, which we've got covered. If I permit you to continue as usual, will you agree to stay here and face the marshal?"

"Oh, Mac, I don't want anything to do with any provost marshal. But I trust you. Yes, I suppose I agree. How long will that be?"

"We don't rightly know. He says it's not his job, he's tied up with army paperwork, and that he might make it in a few days."

"God help me. Heavy, heavy the ax hangs over my head, until that day."

"An explanation for how that hammer got under your bunk would go a long way toward clearing you."

"If I had one, I'd shout it from the top of the tallest Queen Palm. But you can bet your last dollar that I'm going to find out who did it. Because, I didn't."

"Then why frame you? What have you done to make someone that angry with you?"

"I don't know. But I have a lot of cleaning to do today and I can really think, while my hands are busy. You must wonder about it, too, Mac." She wiped at her eyes.

"Mmmm," he said.

"This corner of the veranda, where the wind blows and no windows are within hearing distance, makes an excellent office for you, doesn't it, Mac?"

"Yep. I keep regular office hours, if you need to find me or just want to talk."

She took his hand in hers and searched his deep blue eyes, through his rimless spectacles. "Thanks, Mac. Oh, and do you have another one of those small notebooks that I can use? Can't be a detective without a notebook."

Mac patted around his many pockets and finally produced a new pad and pencil. "As a matter of fact, I do."

He offered them to her. "Here. For your new job."

"Will I have to show you everything I write in here?"

CHAPTER TWENTY-SIX

April 30, 1865 Later Morning

AT BROCK HOUSE HOTEL

A s she and Sadie swept and tidied the back parlor, Daisy said, "Mr. Lavigne says they are burying that Greim fellow this morning. We are all to go out for a short service to show respect. They'll ring the bell when it's time."

"All of us? With the amount of work we have to do? The hotel just comes to a screeching halt while we pay respects?"

"Yes. I'm sure it will be short. He has no kin here."

"Daisy, do you know anything more about Luther Greim? Was he at the hotel before?"

"I don't remember hearing his name before now."

"What about the Maases?"

"They're rich folks from New York. They come with her brother, before the war. This parlor is ship-shape, as Mr. Brock says."

"Daisy, I'll go do the upstairs-front rooms. None of those guests was scheduled to leave this morning. Will I hear the bell up there?"

"Oh, yes. It's mighty loud. All right. I'll start down here."

They went to the linen cupboard and Sadie gathered the biggest load she could manage. *Maybe I won't have to come back down the stairs until the bell sounds.*

She carried the enormous stack to a table in the upstairs hall and plunked them down on top. From beneath it, she pulled a trolley with cleaning supplies and a wicker basket for dirty laundry.

I think the Maases asked for the end room. It's a good place to start, anyway. She placed a few sets of linens on her cart, pushed it to the door, and knocked. "Housekeeping."

"Come in," said Ava. "Why, Sadie. How nice of you to help that sweet Daisy. She was telling me just yesterday how very busy she is."

"Yes. It's just until they find some appropriate permanent staff. Where is Bram this morning?" She removed soiled towels and placed them into the basket.

"He's out shooting with Neville and Buck again. They are keeping our table well provided with fowl, pork, and venison." She chuckled.

Sadie wiped the washstand, pitcher, and basin with a clean cloth from her cart. "I'll have to thank them. I'm enjoying the fresh game. Have you vacationed here before?"

"Oh, yes. We came often before the war. My brother, Thomas, loved shooting here. Once, he insisted that we take home the head of a bear that he shot. He had it stuffed and it now hangs on his wall."

Sadie placed a stack of soft lavender scented towels on the washstand, then removed the duster from her big apron pocket and set to work with it. "He didn't want to come with you, this time?"

"Er, he's, um, he's not able."

Sadie turned and grasped Ava's hand in hers. "I'm so sorry, Ava. You mean, the war?"

"No. Not that. He fell in with some bad company and was hurt. He's now a cripple in our home."

"That must be very difficult for you. Who would do that to him?"

"It was another one of those gangs. The Dead Rabbits are mostly Irish youth, but our Thomas saw power in those boys and couldn't resist. When things went wrong, they left Thomas for dead."

"Oh, no. What did you do?"

"He crawled home to us. We got the best specialists for him. Now, he's an angry young man." Sadie released Ava and began wielding the broom.

"Is he angry with you?"

"No. I think he's angry with himself. And with the gang who betrayed him."

Sadie patted her on the back. "I'm sorry that happened to him." She paused. "Ava, I'm finished and have to go. If you need anything else, I'll be down the hall."

"Sadie, thanks for listening." Ava hugged her and Sadie hugged back.

Outside Ava's room, Sadie whipped out her notebook and wrote, "find out more about Dead Rabbits and Thomas Maas."

Next room. "Knock, knock."

"Housekeeping." After repeating the procedure and receiving no answer, she used the pass key.

A man's room. There's that red vest. Must be Neville Beaumont's room. Nothing lying open for me to read. Guess I'll just get on with cleaning.

She started by picking up all the clothes and dirty towels off the floor. *For someone with such nice manners, he certainly is sloppy.*

What about Noah? Could he have gone to check on Luther, been attacked by the drunkard, and killed him in self-defense? then thrown him overboard?

A scrap of folded paper lay under Neville Beaumont's fancy jacket. *If it's on the floor it's fair game.* She stuck the paper in her pocket. *For later.*

She absent-mindedly hung the clothes in the wardrobe and did the cleaning. *Would Noah put a bloody hammer under my bunk? Why?*

If he killed Luther, why would he go to so much trouble to retrieve the body? Answer: Once it was sighted by the crew, he had to retrieve the body, or he'd look suspicious.

But he didn't have to bring it to Enterprise.

She finished and continued with the next room.

That did focus the investigation on the passengers, rather than on Noah and his crew, who would be gone from Enterprise for four days.

Why not take it to Jacksonville?

Her hands worked through three more rooms as her mind processed. *Two days journey would deteriorate evidence along with the body and make a Jacksonville investigation more difficult. That would be to his advantage, if he did it.*

She stocked the cart with more linens from the table.

But if they took it to Jacksonville, then only he and his crew could be interrogated easily, not a good outcome for Noah, if he did it.

Did he know something about Mr. Greim that made it necessary to kill him?

To stop him from doing something?

Revenge?

Did Greim know something compromising about him?

Does that apply to the other suspects?

"Ding, ding, ding."

There's the bell, summoning us to the funeral. Whew. Six rooms done. Six more to go.

Sadie scribbled in her notebook, "How can I find out more about Luther Greim?"

Downstairs, she followed Daisy and a handful of others outside past the kitchen and laundry, and across the shell road. She approached Mac, who was leaning on his ebony cane, next to Noah and members of his crew.

The sight of Noah still made her heart race. She couldn't get rid of the fluttery feeling from their near kiss this morning.

Stop it. She took a deep breath. *Listen up, you mutinous emotions. I'm driving. Sit down in the 'back of this buggy' and be quiet.*

In a low voice, she said to Mac, "I discovered some facts this morning, but I have more questions than answers."

"Come and talk to me when you finish for the day," Mac said.

Early morning sunshine and trilling from songbirds lent their small group a holiday feeling, rather than the expected funereal somberness.

Noah stepped forward and said, "Please join me in singing, 'Amazing Grace.'"

What a wonderful baritone voice he has, she thought, as he led the song.

When the song finished, he said, "We knew Mr. Greim only two days, during our travel from Jacksonville. If any of you know of relatives we should contact, please tell Mac after the service. It's right to show our respect at this time. Please bow your heads and recite the 23rd psalm with me. The Lord is my shepherd, I shall not want..."

That was a short service. Back to work.

By the time she had finished 12 rooms, Sadie was ready to sit. In the staff dining room, the groundsman said, "Is there any more of that corn pud? Don't know as I've had it before. It's right good."

Sadie said, "That would be Jane's corn soufflé. I think that's the last of it. Everybody in the dining room asked for seconds. By the way, does anybody know anything about the man who was buried today? Did he ever come here before?"

The groundsman said, "Wadn't he head of that gang of bandits, what went aroun' during the war stealing from homesteaders 'n burning people out?"

"Surely not. Wouldn't the law catch up with people like that?"

"Nah. Wasn't no law, back in the sticks. Like here. We're gonna be a'needin' to get us a sheriff, soon. Pass the salt, Miss."

Sadie excused herself and made it to the veranda in time to see the *Darlington* thrash up to the dock. She sank into a deckchair next to Mac. "We need to know more about Luther Greim, Mac. How do we do that?"

"I'm working on it. Some of my contacts may send information. But for now, basically you listen every time someone offers to talk. You can get a great amount of information by talking with people and listening. Always listening."

"The only guest I talked to was Ava. We need to know more about her and Bram Maas, too. Did you know she has a brother named Thomas who is a cripple from some bad incident with a New York gang called the Dead Rabbits?"

"Take a breath, young lady. Yes, I did hear something about Luther and the Dead Rabbits. I agree, we need to know more about them."

"And I've been thinking about Noah. It's hard to imagine that kind of man killing someone. Furthermore, I can't believe he would put a bloody hammer under my bunk. He just wouldn't."

"Sadie, you are learning an important lesson about investigating. Listen to your intuition. Don't ignore evidence, but sometimes your gut knows more than your head."

Jacob Brock came up the front steps with two guests. He said, "Look who I brought, everyone."

"From Brunswick, Maine, meet Reverend Calvin Ellis Stowe, professor of Biblical Literature at Bowdoin College," said Jacob.

"And with him is his lovely wife Harriet, whom you might know as the author of that best-selling book, *Uncle Tom's Cabin*. Introduce yourselves, folks."

Half the inmates of Brock House had ventured out to the veranda at the approaching sound of the *Darlington*. Calvin and Harriet shook hands with Mac and Sadie, the Merritt sisters, Hattie and Jennie Brock, the Maases, and Neville Beaumont.

Mac said, "I went to hear your father Lyman, when I was working in New York, Harriet. He is a powerful speaker. It's good to have you and Calvin here."

She smiled and said, "You're very kind."

Jacob continued, "They have professed interest in buying some property on our beautiful Saint John's River. Make them welcome."

"Thank you, Jacob," Calvin said. "We look forward to conversation with you all later. Now, it's been a long journey, and we need to get settled."

As they moved inside the hotel, the whole group, with the exception of Mac and Sadie, trooped after them, amid a general buzz of conversations.

"Such is the price of fame," said Mac.

"Maybe they will get some peace, once the new wears off," said Sadie.

"Perhaps." He paused. "They have a lot of connections. We might find answers to some of our questions by listening to them." Silence, punctuated by evening sounds of waves slapping and birds going to sleep, stretched between them.

"You've done some good work today, your first day as a detective. Remember to listen to that little voice inside your head. Good night."

He dislodged Fluffy, picked up his handsome, gold-tipped, ebony cane, and followed the group inside.

Over his shoulder he said, " With all the new guests Jacob brought, tomorrow should prove to be interesting."

CHAPTER TWENTY-SEVEN

April 30, 1865 Evening

AT SNOW BIRD COTTAGE

That day Sadie told no one about her "house arrest," which had been negotiated to "community arrest." On her way home to Snow Bird Cottage, she thought about confiding in Jane.

She is cunning and well educated... and I really need an ally. Would she work against me, so she could continue to live here alone? I'm just too tired to think about it.

The pretty negro woman sat on a bench on the back porch, snapping early runner beans, and watching the sun go down. She smiled and said, "These will be so good with that piece of pork that I brought home."

If she has reason to get rid of me, she probably wouldn't say so. But, why not ask? "Jane, if you could continue to live alone at Snow Bird Cottage, would you prefer that?"

She looked up in alarm. "Oh, you're not planning on leaving, are you? You just got here. And we got jobs."

"I know. But would you prefer to be on your own?"

"No. This place is too big for one person to take care of. It's lonely, too. Even if you left and someone else in your family came, they might not like it here as much or be as kind as you."

Sadie rolled her eyes and grimaced. She said, "I can't imagine my adventurer brother out in Denver living in Enterprise. Almost anyone in my family would sell this charming cottage to the highest bidder."

"Then I would be out of my home. No, your appearance at Snow Bird Cottage was all to the good. I was lonely before you came. You are much like her -- Cora, I mean. She, too, was smart and kind."

"Thank you for the compliment. Aunt Cora was very dear to me," Sadie said.

"She loved bright colors, like you do -fuchsia, lavender, purples, reds, oranges. She planted the flowers blooming in the backyard. Always we had a vegetable garden."

"Mmm. Looks like those are some of her beans."

"They are. I especially value the fragrant cooking herbs, such as rosemary, thyme, peppermint, basil, and oregano, that she planted. We have healing herbs, too. I don't know the names of all the plants in the little side garden, but she talked of boneset, comfrey, calendula, feverfew and toothache plant, spilanthes."

A joyous chord twanged inside Sadie. "I must see that wonderful herb garden tomorrow. I had no idea. Things have been so hectic."

She sobered. "Jane, I have some terrible news. I would like to keep this our secret. They found the murder weapon under my bunk in the *Katie Asbell.*"

Her companion said, simply, "Did you kill him?"

"No. Of course not. But, if I don't find out who did, they're going to bind me over to the Jacksonville provost marshal."

"Can I help?"

"Just being my friend helps. And keep your ears open around the kitchen and during deliveries. Something connects one of the other guests to Luther. We just have to find it."

Sadie pulled out her notebook. "Let's start a list of everybody, young and old, who had a motive to kill Luther. First, Christian confessed that Luther burned his family's barn, with his brother and sister in it. That's a strong motive. Second, Martha Merritt said Luther's gang was stealing their rum. Third, Buck accused him of cheating. That started the whole thing. Fourth, Luther punched Noah, which gives him a motive, but I don't think Noah did it." She shared her previous thoughts on the subject.

Her roommate said, "This is a list of facts. Opinions don't belong on it."

"True. He stays, until I can prove otherwise. Thank you... Luther hit me, too, but I know I didn't kill him."

"Right. Leave your name off."

"Jane, do you think Mrs. Flowers or the negro boy server, Percy, would have any objections to my sitting in the dining room for my meals? I need to talk to these suspects."

"You could ask them in the morning."

"I could help Percy wash the dishes after dinner."

"He'd probably jump at that offer. But Sadie, you're going to be so tired you won't be able to do your work."

"It'd only be for a few days. I'm too tired right now to go on with this. I can think about it tomorrow. Unless they arrest me. They wouldn't dare. I'm going in."

She went inside. "Mmm. " *What is this in my pocket? Must be the note that fell from Neville's pocket.* She untied her pockets from under her grey cotton skirt and turned out the contents into her top dresser drawer. *Later.*

Sleepy.

From the drawer, she removed clothes for the next day.

Wonder how Noah is?

Chapter Twenty-Eight

May 9, 1865 Morning

At Brock House Hotel

M ac sat in his usual deck chair and looked out over Lake Monroe. *What if Buck killed Luther to keep him from spreading the word about a wife and children in Mount Airy?*

Buck has followed Kat like a lapdog, since they arrived. He sipped his morning coffee.

Harriet Beecher Stowe came out on the veranda. "Good morning, Mrs. Stowe."

"Please call me Harriet. Good morning to you, too, Mr. MacNally. Are you vacationing here?"

"No. I retired from the Pinkerton agency, visited here, and stayed. I quite like this place." He shifted the cat in his lap. "Have you already thought about where you would like your home on the St. John's?"

"We were told about orange groves for sale near Mandarin. The area looked lovely as we cruised by on our way here. We are going to arrange for a tour as soon as possible. Perhaps we can find buildings suitable for a school. I'm interested in the education of the freedmen near here."

"Worthwhile, I'm sure. Tell me, have you ever, in your travels, heard any of these names?"

He handed her his notebook opened to a list: Sadie Snow, Noah Asbell, Kat Ashley, Neville Beaumont, Luther Greim, Ava and Bram Maas, Martha and Mary Merritt, Buck Stotts.

"I thought you were retired?" She chuckled.

"Once a detective, always a detective. We buried a man yesterday and know little about him. Foul play was involved and I thought you might have information that would help. News is slow to filter to these parts."

"Well, let's start with the most obvious. Katherine Ashley, Kat, was the governess of Queen Victoria."

"Er, no. The one I need is a young woman. Perhaps she's using an alias. Go on."

"I know Ava and Bram. They are Dutch from Manhattan. She owns a big emporium and he trades up and down the Hudson. My brother, who is a minister there, worked with Ava to put a stop to those criminal youth gangs."

"Do you know anything about the Dead Rabbits?"

"Oh, they're a bad lot from the Manhattan slum, Five Points — mostly tough Irish Catholic boys and a few girls. Luther Greim is on your list. I think he is or used to be a lieutenant with them."

"Why would Greim, surely a name of south German origin, be in with a group of Catholic Irish?"

"I think he was a foundling, but gang members aren't that particular. Evidently, he is a strong leader."

"Was a strong leader. That's who we buried."

"Ahh. My brother and his parishioners tried to improve conditions in that neighborhood. But he said Luther Greim and John Morrissey continued to pull Irish youth back into thievery and murder."

"Do you know any of these other names?"

"I've heard of a couple of them. I believe Noah Asbell is a boat captain and was engaged to a debutante in Atlanta. I don't know what happened there." She tapped the notebook at the name 'Neville Beaumont.' "I don't know him, but I'm told that he has political ambitions."

"That's putting it mildly. He wants to be governor of Georgia. And I think he's already campaigning."

"Hmm. Now, let me ask you a question. Do you know anyone interested in selling a large home on the river? We want a citrus grove, too."

"Yes. Several families have been hard hit by the war. Let me give you some names and directions to the homesteads." He retrieved his notebook and began writing on an empty page.

"Can I still get breakfast? I know I'm late, but I couldn't figure out what to wear," said a pert brunette in a red dress. "Good morning, everybody." She sat down next to Neville Beaumont, who greeted her with an expansive smile.

He hailed Percy, the negro boy with tight blond curls, who was finished serving and now was needed out in the kitchen to wash the dishes. "Bring more dishes of everything for this lovely lady, my good man."

"Oh, not everything. Could I have some eggs and ham, with coffee? Please."

"I'll see what I can do, ma'am."

Instead of bowls of food and a place setting for her, he came back with a covered tray, on which he had placed a loaded plate, silverware, and napkin.

As he juggled all those things, transferring them to the table, the preoccupied young man brushed the hot plate against the girl's arm. "Ow. Oh. Aarghhh. Oh, my arm. My skin is very sensitive. Oh, I think I have a blister already. You burned me. My arm will be a mass of blisters."

"So sorry, ma'am. It was on the stove, heating."

"Well, don't just stand there, boy. Do something," said Neville.

"Yes, sir." He removed the hot plate and started back to the kitchen.

"Oh, now I'm blistered and hungry," moaned the girl."

"Bring her plate back, you miserable boy," said Neville, at top volume of his voice.

With downturned eyes, Percy returned the plate to its place in front of the woman and scurried back to his dishwashing duties.

In the kitchen, Jane asked, "Are you all right, Percy?"

"I accidentally brushed the lady's arm with a hot plate and it burned her. What can I do?"

"I'll get Sadie. She has medicine for it." She rushed to the staff dining room and explained the problem. "Where is Sadie?"

"I just saw her getting cleaning supplies to take upstairs. If you hurry you can catch her," said the caretaker.

Jane rushed to the stairs and found Sadie with an arm full of towels. After a quick explanation, she said, "Can you help her?"

"Yes, I'll get the camphor salve from my bag."

Sadie retrieved the jar and headed to the dining room. "Excuse me. Let me through, please," she said to the people crowded around the young woman, who was holding her arm and rocking back and forth.

In sympathy, several pink ruffles from her loose sleeves jiggled and flopped rhythmically.

"Hello. I'm Sadie. Show me your burn, please. I have some medicine that will help."

Now in tears, she uncovered her arm. "Oh, ow. It's as red as a piece of meat and already blisters have popped up the whole length of my forearm."

The sweet piney smell of camphor filled the air, as Sadie gently smoothed the green salve over the burn. "This is very calming. It will relieve your pain and heal the burn."

A gray-haired woman with sharp features jumped up from a seat nearby. "What is that? What are you putting on there? Are you a licensed physician?"

"In answer to your questions, camphor salve. It's made with olive oil, camphor leaves, and beeswax. And, no. It appears we do not have a physician in the room."

"Well if you aren't a physician, why in God's name are you treating her?"

"Because it's always been my view that we are all in this world together and have to look out for each other."

The lady turned to the burned girl and said, "Don't you know she could be sending you to your death? We need a real doctor."

"But it feels better already," the poor girl said.

"Nonsense. Those blisters could burst and the substance she put on there could make them go bad. Doctors would have to amputate. Or worse."

Her eyes flashed and bored into Sadie. "And you should be prosecuted for practicing medicine without a license. I would like to lay a charge against this woman and see that she is stopped immediately."

Sadie gasped. "Well, really. You are welcome to wash off the medicine, if you choose."

"No, no. The damage is done now," said the woman.

"What damage?" said Kat. "Sadie was helping her. She wouldn't hurt her. I took Sadie's medicine and now I'm cured."

I think morning sickness cures itself, thought Sadie. *But thanks, Kat.*

"She cured Christian," said Mary Merritt. "He was in a bad way with fever and now he's back to work. She may not be a doctor, but she helps people. And she doesn't ask a cent. She's good people."

"I still want her stopped. She could do serious harm."

"No. Let's leave it. I'm not hungry anymore," said the girl. She fled the room.

Sadie returned the utensils and plate of cold food to the kitchen.

"Here. Take this. Mrs. Flowers made it for you," said Jane, offering a steaming cup of tea. "That harpy had no call to jump on you like that. Go sit on the porch and have a few deep breaths."

Sadie did as she was told and sat next to Mac. "Mmm, this smells like orange spice tea. I've just been attacked for trying to help someone, Mac. That's how this whole thing with Luther started, too."

"How's that?"

"Buck called Luther a cheater and things got heated. Kat cried out for us to do something. If I had just stayed in my chair, instead of jumping between the two of them, none of that would've happened."

"You don't believe that for a minute."

"No. Buck was really angry and looked frightened, too. What if he was afraid Luther would expose some secret?"

"You might be onto something. A guest recog..."

"Aieeee. Snake."

She nearly knocked over the chair, in her haste to get away. She pointed out toward the dock. "There. In the grass. Don't just sit there."

The tea slopped over Mac's elbow. "Mmm, you're right. Jacob's private stash of orange spiced oolong..."

Back to work. These linens smell like lavender today, thought Sadie. *Up we go.* She carried a load up to her table and put a stack on her cart.

The sky looks cloudy. Maybe more of the guests will stay in on a day like today. We've already done the parlors, so that will give them a pleasant place to spend the day.

"Knock, knock."

Bram said, "Come in. Oh, Miss Snow, how nice to see you. Ava mentioned you are helping out until they can find permanent staff."

Sadie wiped at the wash stand and wracked her brain for questions to ask him. "Are you enjoying your stay in Enterprise?"

"Oh, yes. The shooting is wonderful."

"Where is the best place for shooting?"

"We've hired a guide to show us around. He takes us to ponds with lots of ducks and woodlands teeming with deer."

"Yes, thank you for sharing your game with others here in the hotel. I really appreciate the fresh food." She took her broom to the floor.

"Are Neville and Buck good shots, too?"

Bram laughed. "Buck is. He's a country boy. But Neville is terrible. You'd starve, if you depended on him."

"Is he from a big city?"

"He shoots like he is, but he says he grew up near Savannah. Maybe they don't have many squirrels and rabbits in Savannah."

"I guess not. He always seems to have rather grandiose ideas about himself. I would think your area in New York would be grand. What's the best thing about living in New York?"

"Well, it's home. I've always lived there and I'm comfortable there."

Sadie put the broom back on the cart and took out the feather duster. "In spite of the gangs? Ava said you have a Dead Rabbits gang. They sound terrible."

"The woman is a saint. She worked with Reverend Beecher to improve the situation. Many hundreds of dollars from Ava's pockets puts food on the tables for the poorest families. She and her business friends gave some of those young criminals apprenticeships and jobs, which turned them into productive citizens."

"That's wonderful," said Sadie. "Oh, Bram. I was wondering. If you don't own a gun, are there other ways of taking animals for food?"

"Of course. Old timers used clever traps and lures."

"Have you ever seen holes in the ground to hold animals?"

"Yes. The hog holes, as they are called, are pits used to capture wild hogs. Would you excuse me, please? I'm going down to see if Mac is finished with his newspaper. It may be stale news, but it's the only news we have."

That's a blessing for me. "Of course. I am just finished here."

They exited and Sadie knocked on the next door along the hall. "Housekeeping."

"Come in," Neville Beaumont said. "Well, well. If it isn't the inquisitive quick-change artist, Miss Snow. Come to check up on my campaign?" His black eyes danced with amusement.

Be calm. "I've brought you some fresh towels, but I'd love to hear about your campaign. Have you formally announced your candidacy?" *Washstand first.*

"Not formally, no, but contributors are promising their support."

"When do you expect to join the race?"

"I'll give it another month's time. By then I should have amassed a war chest sufficient to win by a landslide."

"That sounds time-consuming. Who looks after your plantation when you are gone like this?"

He laughed. "Don't worry about that. I have good managers."

"Oh, of course. Is there a Mrs. Beaumont at home?"

"No, but I expect Atlanta has some lovely belles, who would be happy for the job." He laughed. "I'll marry someone who is pleasant to look at, and well-connected -- with wealth and status to equal mine.

"Mmmhmm." She started dusting. "Tell me more about your plantation."

"Oh, Windsweep is the most beautiful property in Savannah."

"What crops do you grow?"

"We grow cotton."

"How many acres do you have under cultivation?"

"I can't help thinking I've seen you somewhere before."

"No. I'd remember you." *No chance I'd forget your devilish good looks, with that shiny, slicked-back hair, oh-so-groomed black van dyke beard, and tiny mustache.*

"That's just it. I remember you from somewhere."

"All finished. Enjoyed our conversation. Buh, bye." *What are the chances that he will remember me from the stage? Very low, I hope. He may never have been to the theater.*

She retrieved more linens from the table in the hall and started to knock on the next door, when it opened, startling her.

"Oh, hello Sadie. I thought you might be Kat. Have you seen her?"

"Not since last night. I'm helping with the housekeeping until the hotel can find permanent staff. Can I tidy your room for you?"

"Yes, thank you. Come in. Look. It's raining." His eyes stared out the window. "Where can she be?"

"I can't imagine. You seem very fond of Kat. Do you have a special relationship?" She swept his floor.

"Special relationship? Yes, you could say that."

"Tell me about your work. You said you travel? Where do you go?"

"All of West Florida, plus Saint Augustine, Jacksonville, and some of south Georgia."

She mopped. "Have you come here for a vacation before?"

"Yes, several times. Look, Sadie. I'm worried about Kat. I need to go look for her. Will you be all right here by yourself?"

"I'm just about finished, Buck. Go on out and I'll mop behind us.

"Thank you for your concern for Kat and for me. You are very kind. She's probably curled up in some nook reading."

But she wasn't. When the sleuth-in-training knocked on her door, she didn't answer. So, Sadie used the pass key and found the room empty.

Heavens to Betsy. Buck, you didn't harm her, did you? You wouldn't. But I suppose love, and maybe love rejected, makes one do strange things.

She trotted downstairs and found Daisy. "Kat Ashley isn't on the list of those checking out, yet I found her room empty."

"Sorry. I got busy and forgot to tell you. She checked out at the last minute, right before *the Darlington* left this morning. She just said she was cutting her visit short and that she had enjoyed her stay."

"That's Kat. Polite and pleasant, come hell or high water. Does Buck know? He was hunting her this morning."

"Poor guy. I didn't tell him."

"I'd better find him. He must be worried sick."

He wouldn't hurt her. Would he?

Who knows what secrets lurk beneath the surface for that couple?

She went back up and knocked on his door. No answer.

I hope he hasn't disappeared, too. If I have time when I finish this evening, I'll come back up and check on him.

That evening Sadie had her dinner in the dining room and sat between Martha Merritt and Mac. He said, "What interesting information have you listened to today?"

"Bram says that Neville shoots like a city boy, but that Buck is a good shot. He thinks he's from the country. And old timers dig deep pits around here to trap large animals."

Martha said, "Yes, they do that in our neck of the woods, too. It saves on ammunition, which was scarce during the war."

Sadie said, "Mac, about Kat and Buck. She seems to be..."

Midway through the sentence, Buck, carrying the indigo flannel shirt that Sadie had seen Kat wearing as a wrap, burst into the dining room. Water dripped from the soaked garment. He stood, scanning the room.

When he recognized Sadie, he squelched over and sank into a chair opposite her. "Have you seen her? I found this in the back garden. I waited as long as I could. Then I started searching. She was not in the gardens. She isn't sitting on a deck chair, either. I checked them all."

"Buck, Dais..."

"And I looked in every nook and cranny. All that's left is the lake or the pinewoods and marshes. Oh, what have I done?" He closed his eyes and rubbed his hands over his bald head and down his cheeks and beard.

"If anything happens to that sweet, lovely girl..."

"Buck, I'm sorry that I didn't tell you sooner. Daisy says that Kat checked out early this morning, right before the *Darlington* headed back to Jacksonville."

"Thunderation. I wish someone had told me. I've been worried sick all day. But thanks for letting me know."

Sadie said, "Buck, tell us more about Kat. Where is her home?"

"She is a governess for the family of Doctor Alvarez, south of Saint Augustine."

"Where is her family?"

"Her real name is Catherine Flanagan. And her parents are Mary and Pat Flanagan. I think they have a place near Manhattan, New York."

"Why is she using a different name?"

"We were trying to keep our marriage a secret a while longer." He rushed on, as if to avoid any more questions. "Do you think she would go to New York?"

Mac said, "I think it's likely. Buck, you know you can't go after her. We are in the middle of a murder investigation and you are a suspect."

His complexion reddened. "I didn't kill that cheater. You can't keep me here, Mac. I need to find her." He rose to go.

"If you leave now, the marshal could put out an arrest warrant for you that would follow you wherever you go."

He sank back down with his head in his hands. "How would I get away from here, anyway, without a boat?"

A big strong guy like you could go far in a dugout canoe.

I could loan you mine.

But I won't.

Probably.

It wouldn't be right.

CHAPTER TWENTY-NINE

May 1, 1865 Late Evening

AT SNOW BIRD COTTAGE

About an hour before dark, Jane held up a shiny object for inspection. She said, "I was cleaning out the tray of ashes at the bottom of the wood stove and found this knife."

Sadie looked up from reading the newspaper, which she had borrowed from the bottom of Mac's pile. "A knife, in the stove?"

"It looks like your foraging knife," she said, holding out the short sharp cutter for inspection.

"It IS my foraging knife. It's supposed to be in that basket by the back door. It is unique, Jane. My friend, Walt Whitman, gave it to me for our gathering trips. He swore the runes on the handle are protective magic and that they spell Sarah. I always figured he was just having fun with me. What in the Sam Hill was it doing out there?" She pointed toward the back door and the outside kitchen.

"Are you talking about Walt Whitman, the poet?"

"Yes. He's a joker."

"I've read some of his poems. What a talent that is. One of Miss Cora's newspapers said he was in Washington visiting his brother. Is that where you lived before coming here?"

"I can't talk about that. Maybe later I can tell you all about it. Right now, I'm concerned that neither of us knows how my knife got into the ashes tray under the stove. The handle isn't burned at all."

That's one of the really special things that I brought with me from Washington.

"When I first arrived, there were worrisome unexplained events. But that was all because of your being here. I don't believe in elves or fairies. That thing couldn't have grown limbs and walked out of this cottage. And, even if it could, why would it go under the stove, anyway? What's going on?"

A walking knife?

She put the knife away. That night, she was especially careful about locking all the doors.

CHAPTER THIRTY

May 2, 1865 Morning

AT BROCK HOUSE HOTEL

The day dawned with peach, rose, and robin's-egg blue skies. Sadie knocked on the other bedroom door. "I'm going early to talk to Mac," she said, in a low voice.

"All right," said a groggy Jane. "I'll see you there."

She trekked the shell road, which had become bright and sunny. *Listen to that warbler. Wonder if I can imitate it.* "Sweet, sweet. I'm so verySWEET. Sweet, sweet. I'm so verySWEET." *Come closer,* she thought.

I wonder if Noah listens to bird songs when he's docked for the night? Dawn and dusk are filled with a symphony of chirps and warbles here on Lake Monroe and on the St. John's River. He can probably identify most of the birds making them.

Her thoughts turned to *the Katie Asbell* and the pretty young woman, Kat.

Oh, Kat.

What are you running away from?

Or to?

Did you go so you wouldn't have to tell us that Buck killed Luther?

Do you have evidence that would point to Buck?

On the veranda, she sat next to Mac and posed those same questions. Fluffy padded around and around in a circle on Mac's lap, before she settled.

Mac said, "Sadie, you are still a suspect and I can't discuss any details with you. But I don't think it's any secret that Buck has a family north of Tampa, and that he has kept them hidden from Kat.

He continued, "Obviously he has a relationship with Kat also. Would he be willing to kill Luther Greim to keep that a secret? Your guess is as good as mine. We have no evidence for that theory. Our only solid evidence indicts you."

"Don't remind me, Mac. I'm doing my best to find out who really did it. But there's something troubling that I need to ask you about. Jane found my foraging knife in the ashes beneath our stove last night. Neither of us put it there."

"You think you've had a break in? What was taken?"

"Nothing that we could tell. I'm a little worried about our safety at the cottage. Are there any special door and window locks that would help?"

"Yes. Some of the special ones cost a king's ransom. How many doors and windows do you have? And what kind of locks are on them now?"

"We have four doors, plus the door to the kitchen outside. I'll have to count the windows. And one key opens all the doors."

"May I see your key?"

"Of course. Let me just get it out of my pocket. Here it is."

"Sadie, this is a skeleton key. It will open just about any mortise lock. That's the problem right there. Most homeowners have keys similar to this. So, almost everybody would have access to your cottage."

"Oh, no."

"We need to get you some decent locks. The ones you have now were fine when people locked their front doors, to show the neighbors that they were gone. But they left their back doors unlocked, to give friends access in case they needed to drop off anything."

"City folks certainly don't do that."

"Yes, I know. Let me see what's available. Sometimes locksmiths put ads in the newspapers."

"So, should I be putting chairs under the door knobs at night?"

"Yes, that would be a good idea. Or we can figure out some wooden wedges for you to put under the doors. But that won't do any good while you're gone."

"Jane and I will be at work all day long. We need the money. We can't sit home defending the castle."

He chuckled. "Until we can get you set up to keep out unwanted visitors, don't leave anything of value in your cottage."

"All right. Thanks, Mac. That'll be easy. I don't have anything of value to leave there."

Mac chuckled. "You have much more than you think."

"I'll need a few paychecks before I can order anything." She rubbed her forehead with her fingertips. "I guess the real question is, who would do that and why?"

"Good morning, early risers. What a beautiful day," said Calvin Stowe, as he stepped onto the veranda carrying a cup of steaming tea.

Sadie said, "Good morning, Reverend Stowe. Oh, it's getting late. Do either of you have the time?"

Mac pulled out his pocket watch. "Yes, it's six fifty-five."

"If you'll excuse me, I have to get to work. Thanks for your help, Mac. Gentlemen, enjoy your morning."

Now, who and why?

Sadie grabbed her apron from a peg in the staff closet, and started work in the front parlor. *Does that walking knife have anything to do with Luther's death? If I don't find his killer, I'm going to jail. Or worse. If I'm connected to Evangeline Bright, I could hang.*

She swept furiously. *I can't ask people, "Did you plant that hammer in my cabin on board Katie Asbell?" Or, "Did you break into my cottage to play hide and seek with my knife?"*

"Good morning," said Daisy.

"Oh, hi," Sadie said. "I've done the dusting in here, already. The windows are smudged. Shall I wipe them next?"

Daisy said, "Yes. I like that about you, Sadie. You see what needs to be done and you do it."

"You give me too much credit, Dais'. I just like looking out at the lake and the trees."

"Right. Don't think I haven't noticed that you take the upstairs rooms to keep me from having to climb up and down the stairs with all the heavy linen and porcelain pots."

"Flummediddle, to borrow a saying I heard from Bram Maas."

"What's that?"

"I don't know exactly. But I think it's something to do with silliness. I know it sounds silly."

They continued to work in the early morning quiet.

Why don't I just ask if any of them knew Luther before we all met on the Katie Asbell? That could link to a motive. I suppose they won't tell me, even if they did know him. But it would be interesting to hear what everybody has to say.

They finished the public areas. Sadie said, "All right. I'll gather a load of clean linen and do the rooms upstairs."

As she had done the last three days, she started at the end of the hall. "Knock, knock." She said, " Housekeeping."

"Good morning, Sadie. Come in. You're the perfect person to answer this question for me." In each hand Ava held a dress.

"Jacob Brock is going to have a big party on the *Darlington,* with everybody getting to go to Orchid Springs. Which dress do you like better? The blue or the purple?"

"I am hardly a fashion expert, but I do think the blue highlights your eye color famously," said Sadie, while removing used towels from the wash stand.

"Oh, good. I thought so, too. I hope they have orchids there. Several more couples from New York arrived on the *Darlington* Sunday night, and I have to keep up my fashion reputation."

"From New York? That must be nice for you. People that you knew back home?"

"No. Only marginally. We move in different circles."

Sadie took her broom and started sweeping. "I was wondering, did you know Luther Greim before we all met on the *Katie Asbell?*"

Ava gulped and turned red in the face. Then she paled, put her hand over her mouth, and said, "Oh, er, um, I um, no. I, um, no I didn't." She turned away to hang the dresses in the wardrobe.

That's an interesting reaction.

"Sadie, you won't need to mop today, because Bram and his friends didn't go out yesterday. That will be all. Thank you."

Well, I know when I'm being dismissed.

"All right. I'll see you tomorrow."

She gathered her things, hoisted her big dirty-linen basket onto the cart, pushed through to the hallway, and ran straight into Bram, Buck, and Neville. They were outfitted for hunting. "Pardon me. Hello. I thought you were out looking for our dinner."

"Our guide, Gator Simmons, never showed up," said Bram, in a tone that clearly said he was disappointed.

"There's always tomorrow," said Buck. "I wasn't feeling all that much like it, anyway."

Neville said, "We'll meet same time in the morning. And if he doesn't show up, we'll demand he give our money back."

That shows high-level thinking.

Each of them headed for his own door. Since Neville's room was next for cleaning, Sadie followed him in. "I'm sorry your guide didn't show. Has that happened before?" She started her routine cleaning.

"No. Until now, he's always been where he said he would be."

"Is he good at his job?"

"He's an excellent guide. He takes us to extraordinary places."

"Are you a good shot?" *Sweeping, now. I'm getting faster at this.*

He narrowed his eyes at her and said, "I can hold my own. Why do you ask?"

"No reason. Just making conversation. I wonder, had you ever met Luther Greim before our cruise on the St. Johns River?"

"Did anyone ever tell you that you sound like the grand inquisitor in some impossibly dull French play?" He chuckled at his own wit.

"No, Neville. No one ever did. Was your answer 'yes,' that you did know him, or 'no,' that you never saw him before our trip?"

"I don't believe that's any of your affair, but no, I never saw him before our trip."

"Are you going on Mr. Jacob Brock's excursion to Orchid Springs on the *Darlington?*"

"Excursion?"

"Yes, with dancing and music and free drinks. Sounds like fun, don't you think?"

"Hmmm. Will there be many people there, you think?"

"Oh, bound to be. It's free and people haven't had many parties during the war. Everybody's talking about it."

"It sounds like an opportunity to build my war chest."

"I am finished cleaning, Neville. Good bye."

She wheeled her cart out, filled it with fresh towels from her table, and cleaned three more rooms.

At Kat's room, she knocked. No reply. "Housekeeping."

Have they given it to someone else?

Open the door to check the condition of the room.

It looks empty and clean. Give it a quick wipe, add fresh towels, and move on.

The next room in line for cleaning was Buck's.

"Knock, knock." She said, "Housekeeping."

"Come in, Sadie," said Buck, in a sad voice. His usual brilliant smile was missing.

She carried a fresh towel and her broom into the room. "It's too bad about your hunt this morning. I suppose you don't know what happened to your guide?"

"I didn't really care, but now that you mention it, he has always done what he said he would do. He's a good guide. I hope a snake didn't get him."

"Aack. A snake?" Sadie stopped.

"He said that the first time a rattlesnake bit him it hurt like the devil. Was on his hand. Had fever, aches, and the shivers for days. His arm swole up and he couldn't breathe."

"Good Lord, a mercy." She shivered, then resumed cleaning. "How did he survive that?"

"Stayed in his bunk with his hand down low on the floor. And just kept drinking water, is what he said."

"I pray to God that isn't what kept him from leading your group today. And speaking of your group, I'm wondering if anyone knew Luther before we all met on the boat. Did you know him earlier?"

"Um, well, no, you know, I didn't. No. I didn't. Before playing cards."

Another interesting reaction.

"You're certain to be glad when the investigation into that odious man's death is finished. Kat probably deserted us to get away from all that. I'm sorry she left. I miss her."

"Me, too."

"I'm finished, for today. Cheer up, Buck. I always find that taking a walk makes me feel better. Maybe it would do that for you, too."

"Maybe I will."

Sadie cleaned four more rooms. At the last room for the day, she knocked and said, "Housekeeping."

Harriet Stowe opened the door and smiled.

Sadie said, "Good afternoon. Is this a convenient time?"

The author said, "Perfect timing. Please come in. I was about to go out for a walk. You are Mac's protégé, aren't you?"

Sadie's eyebrows shot up. "Oh. Um, he's a friend. I am learning from him and he's helping me with security at my new cottage." She gathered an arm full of damp towels. *Ask her your question before she leaves.*

"I know this is an unreasonable request, but before you leave, could you answer a question for me?"

"What's your question?"

"A man by the name of Luther Greim was murdered here a few days ago and very little is known about him. Do you know anything of him?"

"Funny that you should ask. Mac asked me the same thing. Luther was a leader in a New York street gang. I forgot to tell Mac that Greim left Ava Maas' brother for dead. The poor man has had a long road to recovery and he is still a cripple."

Ava lied! She had a grudge against Greim. That certainly gives her a motive for killing him. She and Bram together could have gotten a big burly man overboard, especially a drunken one. That's why she was so evasive. "Thank you, Mrs. Stowe."

"You are welcome. Ah, there's my hat. I'm going now. See you later."

Sadie whizzed through her cleaning and headed out to the kitchen. Jane was pulling bubbling pies from the oven.

"Ohh, meat with onion. That smells so good. And it looks like you've found another source for cream and eggs. I see you've made more corn soufflé. Mmm. Jane, I've found someone else with a very good motive for killing Luther. I'll tell you at home." *It feels right to call our cottage 'home.' Now, I have to change into a Brock House guest."*

She removed her apron, pumped fresh water to wash her hands and face, then smoothed her hair. But dinner was uneventful. She listened to conversations all around her. Not one gave her anything that could help.

Dishwashing afterward with Percy was more productive. He told her all about waiting on the three couples who had just arrived from New York.

CHAPTER THIRTY-ONE

May 2, 1865 Evening

AT SNOW BIRD COTTAGE

On their walk home Sadie said to Jane, "...and all along Ava had a great reason for wanting Luther Greim dead."

"That's good, but it won't keep you from being their main suspect, will it?"

"I guess not. But it gives us a reason to look at someone besides me. Let's hurry. I'm going to have to use the outhouse."

"Ahhh." *The cottage at last.*

"I'll be in, in a minute." She moved down the path towards the back garden. *That jasmine can be overpowering, but at least it covers the outhouse smell. When it's finished blooming, we'll be back to breathing through our mouths.*

Sadie felt the rough wood under her fingers as she gripped the door handle. *This thing tends to stick. Yank it hard.*

The door swung open.

Something smacked her in the face.

"Aaack."

What in tarnation is that?

Limp.

And furry.

And dripping?

She wiped a droplet from her face.

Red.

In the murky interior, she could just make out the shape of the dead squirrel.

Is that?

Yes, it is.

My foraging knife.

Anchoring this poor dead thing to the inside of the door.

That's...

Horrible.

How dare somebody do this to that poor creature?

Her breath came quicker.

Her voice trumpeted into the quiet evening.

"And for what?

To spite me?

To run me off?

Well, it won't work.

I'm here and here I'm staying.

So, get used to it."

Her voice rose to top volume.

"I'll hunt you down.

You good-for-nothing,

stinking,

ROTTEN

WEASEL."

Jane came running. "What's all the noise? Are you hurt?"

Calmer now, Sadie said, "No, but somebody's going to be, when I catch him. Look what I found." She pointed at the door.

Jane reached up and pulled out the knife. She held it out to Sadie.

"And it's dulled my knife, too," said Sadie, with a scowl. She took the knife and plunged the blade into the dirt at her feet to remove the blood. Then she wiped it clean on a handful of hibiscus leaves.

The calm, experienced cook picked up the dead animal. "I'll just skin this creature. Fried squirrel is good for breakfast."

"Thank you, Jane." She looked down at the foraging knife. "That dirty,   despicable, devil won't be able to find this again. Let him look until he's blue in the face. I'm taking this knife with me, tomorrow."

"You put three women on the suspect list. What makes you so sure it's a 'he'? Can you account for their whereabouts all day yesterday and today?"

"No, of course not. It just seems like something a man would do."

"Sadie, you say women should have equality with men, should have the vote. It's true, you know, that we are equally able to kill."

"Yes, I suppose you're right."

"And what makes you so sure that this has some connection to Mr. Greim's death? Perhaps it's about this house or your aunt. Maybe it's about you. Did you bring some conflict along with you?"

"I don't know, Jane." She shook her head. "The solicitor said this cottage is legally mine, so I don't see a conflict there. Maybe it is about something that happened before I came... with Aunt Cora or this house, but it feels mighty personal."

"It looks like your questions have upset somebody. That person wants you to go away."

"I won't be scared off and I won't stop investigating. I'm going to hunt down the person who did this. And, if I can, I'm going to find Luther Greim's killer."

"What if this person with the knife fetish and the one who killed Mr. Greim are one and the same? That is a dangerous person."

"I'm not afraid of him. He should be afraid of me."

CHAPTER THIRTY-TWO

May 3, 1865 Early Morning

AT BROCK HOUSE HOTEL

"I have so much news for you. I don't know where to start." Sadie sank into a deck chair beside Mac.

"First, Mrs. Stowe told me that Luther was the one who left Ava Maas' brother for dead. That would give her an excellent motive for murder. She and Bram together could move a hulking big drunk like Luther."

"Mmmm."

"When I asked Ava if she had ever met Luther before our cruise, she turned red, then she turned white. Then she stammered, said 'no,' and kicked me out. I asked Neville the same question and he just said I'm nosy, but he also answered, 'no.'"

"You are making people nervous with your questions."

"Yes. But, if I don't ask questions, I'll never find out who killed him, Mac. When I asked Buck if he knew Luther before our two days on the Saint John's River, he hemmed and hawed. Finally, he said, 'no,' too."

"It comes down to the age-old question of 'who's lying?'"

"I'm wondering if he's a bigamist, Mac. He sounds guilty of something. Maybe Kat left because she knows that Buck killed Luther and she wanted to put distance between herself and the killer."

"We have no evidence of that, Sadie."

"True, and you do have evidence against me. But I'm not so stupid that I would kill someone with a hammer and then carry the heavy, gruesome thing back to my cabin. It would be much easier to drop it into the lake."

"Yes…"

"And last night I was smacked in the face by a bloody, dead squirrel, pinned by my foraging knife inside the door of our privy. That's the same knife that was put into the ashes under our cooking stove by an intruder, two days ago."

"Someone's trying to scare you, Sadie. This could be a very dangerous individual. I want you to stop asking questions."

"Mac, no. I'm more determined than ever to find whoever did it and to expose Greim's killer. Lots of others have motives for killing Luther. Number one, Christian, because Luther killed his brother and sister."

"He's a boy. That's very unlikely."

"You can't rule him out just because he's young. Number two, Buck, because Luther knew about his wife and children. He had to figure that sooner or later Luther'd shoot his mouth off and get Buck into trouble, and not just with Kat. Also, he's strong enough to move a big man like Luther."

"He is, indeed."

"Number three, the Merritt sisters had reason to get rid of him, because he was robbing them of their rum, which is a big part of their income."

"They are…"

"Don't tell me they are old and frail. Those ladies are tough as nails. The two of them could move him, but it's more likely that they outsmarted him, instead. They probably talked him into jumping into the lake."

Mac chuckled. "Sorry. It's no laughing matter. Who else has a motive, according to you?"

"Ava and Bram, because Luther led her brother into crime, then got him almost killed." She paused. "I didn't know any of these suspects before I got onto the *Katie Asbell*. The question is, would any of them try to frame me by putting that hammer in my cabin?"

"If you are really determined to investigate, I think the question is, do you know how to shoot?"

"SHOOT? No. I'm not interested in shooting things."

"Every other person in this hotel has at least one gun, if not more, and bags of ammunition. If one of them has killed a person, they probably wouldn't hesitate to kill you, if you get in their way. Again, I'll ask. Do you have any experience with guns?"

Sadie gulped. "My father took my brother and me out a few times to get the feel of his new pride and joy, a Colt 1851 Navy revolver, and my grandfather's old muzzle-loader shotgun. He told me about the early shotguns with long rectangular barrels. You know, they shot iron cubes called 'dice.' But I don't like any guns. They're loud."

"I don't think you have much choice, young lady. Until we can get some proper locks for your cottage, you are in danger. You are prying into peoples' business and somebody doesn't like that. You say you didn't do it. I'm inclined to believe you. Chalk that up to my listening to my intuition. That leaves us with a killer on the loose. I'd feel much better if you had some protection."

"Now listen here, Mac. I can take care of myself."

"Not against a shooter, you can't. This morning is as good a time as any for me to teach you how to shoot. Wait right here."

"No. I can't. I have a job to do."

"Leave all that to me. It won't affect your pay packet."

Later when the groundsman stopped the cart in front of Snow Bird Cottage, Sadie climbed down and said, "It will only take me a moment to change. I still wish you would tell me where we are going."

Mac said, "It's faster to show you. Just go get ready."

Sadie inserted her key into the lock of the front door and it swung open noiselessly. *Ahh. Everything is in order. And Jane left a bouquet of gardenias in here. Smells good.*

She closed the door behind her and hurried to her bedroom. *Now let's get out of this long skirt.* She untied the drawstring around her waist and the skirt puddled on the floor around her feet. Next, two tie-on pockets were loosed and fell on top.

I guess I'll need these again when I change back into a hotel cleaner. She gathered the skirt and pockets and folded them into a square temporary pillow for the rough board seat of the cart.

Rummaging in a dresser drawer, she found what she needed. *All right. Trousers. And a shirt with pockets.*

She dressed quickly and then rushed back out the front door, locking it behind her. The mule was munching grass beside the shell road.

Mac offered her his hand, from where he was waiting in the cart. "It's not far from here," he said.

Good. No comment from him about my 'manly' clothing. "This is all new territory to me," she said as they traveled on from the cottage.

"It's a safe place to learn shooting, as the bullets are stopped by the mound. We can't shoot anyone accidentally. In the scrub, bullets can travel a long way past a missed target."

A few minutes later they approached a large shell midden. "My goodness. That pile of shell is taller than the Brock House Hotel," said Sadie. "It's a lovely spot, with all those tall queen palms framing it. But what is that strange smell?"

Mac climbed down from the cart and handed the groundsman a coin. "Thank you. There's another in it for you, when you return at one o'clock."

"Thank ye. Ye allers did trade far with me and was up to yer word. I'll be back, right sharp, like. Yes, sartin, sir."

Mac retrieved his cane, a wooden box, and two folded chairs from the seat. Sadie patted the old gray mule, whose hair felt course under her fingers. Then she took charge of the camp chairs and box. The driver left his passengers in the clearing, where blue jays fussed at them.

"You are smelling that sulphur spring, Sadie."

Mac limped closer to the tall shell mound. "I've been told that 20 years ago, actually 24 years ago - it was in 1841, Cornelius Taylor built a hotel near where the run-off from the spring empties into the lake. It was up there, right on top."

"A hotel? Where is it?"

"I guess a pile of shell isn't a very stable foundation for a hotel. It seems to be gone. He called it Green Springs and told everyone that the sulfur water down here has healing properties."

"Mmm. Consumption cure?"

"Yes. Bring the camp chairs and unfold them, please. Put the box on top of one. Thank you." He opened the box and removed an elegant shiny handgun.

"This is a .36 caliber Lemat nine-shot ball and cap revolver. It has an unusual secondary .28 gauge smooth-bore barrel, capable of firing buckshot."

"A revolver and a shotgun, all in one?"

"Yes. It's fondly known as a grape shot revolver. Grape shot is metal balls larger..."

"I know what grape shot is."

"Right. Take it out and hold it in two hands, like this, for shooting. Place your dominant index finger along the cylinder, never in the trigger guard, until you're ready to shoot. Don't aim it at any person, including yourself, unless you intend to fire."

"I'm not planning to shoot anyone."

"Think on this, city girl. If someone or something threatens your life or the life of someone you love, can you pull the trigger?"

If Aunt Cora were standing here and some varmint had a knife to her throat, could I shoot him? "Um, I think so, yes."

"Not good enough. You must know for sure. Stay with that question until you decide if you can or not."

"All right. I will." She looked down. "It's beautiful, for a deadly weapon."

"It isn't as pretty as the earlier models carried by many of the senior confederate officers, but this one will shoot standard ammunition. That means you won't have to cast your own bullets, which entails melting lead and pouring the resulting liquid into a mold."

"Ahhh, good. And what is this leather box?"

He opened the box to show three rows of 10 brownish cylinders each and a row of five bigger cylinders. "This is a cartridge box with a tin liner to protect the cartridges from sparks that could set off an explosion."

"An explosion? Aww, I don't know about this, Mac. It's the explosion part I don't like."

He faced her. "Sadie, I've been watching you for a week. You are smart, capable, and methodical. Many people of lesser abilities carry and shoot guns. You will have no trouble."

"I still haven't decided that I will be one of those people. But I'm interested in learning... and curious about this gun."

"Good. Now, these paper tubes are your cartridges. Each one is filled with a measured amount of black powder and a minié ball. Well, it isn't a ball. The bullet's actually a long hollow cone of soft lead with several grooves at the base. It's smaller in diameter than the inside of the cylinder, which makes it easier to load."

"When my father took us shooting, we used balls, and they had to be rammed down really hard with a ramrod. I wasn't quite big enough to do that."

"Traditional spherical bullets, balls, have to be bigger than the cylinder, which is why you have to pound them in so hard."

"Like jamming a fat purple muscadine down the end of a little fife?"

"Exactly. The Miniés still have to be rammed down, but not as much. Go ahead and take out a cartridge. Hold it at the base and bite off or tear off the top end just above the bullet. "

"Blech, Fthewy," she said. "It tastes like it has a gob of fat on it."

"That's because it has a gob of fat on it, to provide water resistance and lubrication." He laughed. "You should see your sour face. The manufacturers use fat from hogs or cows. It does cause problems for people with strict dietary restrictions."

"I'm sure not going to eat this stuff."

"No, but you're handling it. In 1857 new cartridges greased with tallow helped start the Indian Rebellion. The Brits employed native Hindu or Muslim soldiers, who were insulted by being required to use the tainted ammo."

"You mean they went to war solely because their religions forbade them from touching anything to do with those animals?"

"Yes. That was a sticking point. They had other complaints, too. But we digress. Point the gun up at the sky, then drop the cartridge, torn end up, into one of those nine cylinders."

"Like this?"

"Yes. Now unlatch the jointed ramrod, which is attached to the left side of the gun here. Line up the filled cylinder under it. Grab the top of the ramrod and pull back hard to seat the bullet. Perfect. Now do that eight more times."

"Whew. It's time consuming."

"Not compared to the time it would take you to cast your own bullets, soak paper in saltpeter for creating your own paper cartridges, and measure black powder for each shot."

"Yes, I can imagine. Am I done?"

"Not quite. Fill each cylinder to the top with this lard and beeswax mixture." He pulled a tin of the fat and a small wooden spatula from one of his voluminous pockets.

She did as instructed and wiped a little excess off around the edges with her finger. "It feels somewhat stiff and creamy."

"Yes. I usually just use my fingers. I mix this myself. It's good on chapped hands, too."

She bent double and let out a peal of laughter. "Haaa. Ha. Ha."

"What?"

"We are loading your gun with hand cream. Ah, ha, ha."

"Ha, ha, Sadie. Funnier than a rifle with a curved barrel for shooting around corners... Where were we? Oh, yes. The ramrod for the larger barrel is inside this ramrod that you just used. Pull it out, like this."

"That's a good way to carry it."

"It is. Load the grape shot, next. Take out one of those larger paper cartridges, which is actually two bags in one, and carefully unwind the top end.

"Now pull out the bag inside, which has your measured powder and pour it into the large smooth bore barrel."

"This?"

"Yes. Wad the paper, push it down on top, and pack it down tight with the ramrod. Then pour in the grape shot from the remaining bag, crumple that bag, too, and stuff it into the barrel. Pound all those elements down hard."

"Does it need hand cream, now, to hold it in place?"

He rolled his eyes at her. "No, the paper does that. I prefer the term 'bore butter.' And the last step is to add the percussion caps ever so carefully." From another of his pockets he pulled a small leather pouch and pulled open the flap.

"Pull up that inside wool flap and pick out a foil cap. Now push it onto the nipple at the back of one of the cylinders, back here by the hammer."

"That's fiddly."

"Take your time. Do that for all nine cylinders and inside the leather pouch you'll find a packet of larger percussion caps. You will need one of those for the shotgun load."

After a few minutes Mac examined the gun. "Perfect. Are you ready?"

She nodded. *Not sure my ears are ready.*

"Pull back the hammer. At the top of the hammer is a lever. When it is up, you can shoot the .36 caliber. Flip it down to shoot the shotgun.

"Both eyes open.

"Hold it in front of you like I showed you, trigger finger straight.

"Line up the center of the hammer with the tip of your gun and aim at that big oyster shell over there.

"Squeeze the trigger slowly."

"BANG." Twenty yards away shards of bone and shell jumped.

"I missed."

"Try again and this time take a full breath, then blow out slowly as you squeeze the trigger. Stay very still."

"BANG." Her eyebrows shot up. "I hit it."

"Sadie, I think you will become quite the marksman. Excuse me. I mean markswoman. Pull the lever down on the hammer to try the shotgun. And before you go on, I want you to know that I'm prepared to loan this to you until your cottage is secure."

"That's awfully kind of you, Mac, but what about you? Won't you need it for your safety?"

"Don't worry about me, young lady. This is just my latest addition to my collection of weapons."

"Where did you get it?"

"Bought it off one of the few blockade runners who got through last year. It's a little heavy, but it's a brilliant concept."

Sadie heaved a sigh. "I appreciate your thoughtfulness and generosity, Mac, but I'm not sure I want it."

"All right. You think on it. The offer is always there. Now see how you like shooting the smooth bore."

CHAPTER THIRTY-THREE

May 3, 1865 Evening

AT BROCK HOUSE HOTEL

I wonder how Mac talked young Percy into doing some of my rooms this morning, while we went to the shell mound. That boy was really pleased with himself when we got back. What a kind-hearted fellow.

Sadie still had six more rooms to clean at the Brock House Hotel when she heard the clatter of *the Katie Asbell* docking. *Noah's back. I hope he's all right. Please God, don't let him be bringing the provost marshal from Jacksonville. I need more time.*

She swept furiously as she watched Gator Simmons through an upstairs window. *He looks healthy enough.*

The hunters' missing guide met the boat with skins to sell. *That's typical, I suppose. The last time I saw him he was selling a gator lashed to a board. I'm glad he's not suffering from snakebite.*

Harriet Beecher Stowe approached him. *She must want him to guide them to some of the homesteads that are for sale.*

More new guests trooped off the boat. *Hurry. Mop faster. They'll be wanting their rooms. You need to finish. Before it gets dark.*

She stepped out of the room and almost bumped into Daisy. "I'm finished downstairs and thought you might want some help up here, mopping or carrying chamber pots."

"Bless you. If you can deal with sweeping, I'll empty chamber pots," said Sadie. "I think there are only three clean ones left in the cupboard."

"We've had a lot of breakage, lately. I'll ask Lavigne to order some more."

Sadie gave a weary smile. She made several trips to the privies with chamber pots, which she emptied, scrubbed with washing soda at the back-yard pump, and hauled back up to the storage cabinet. *Whew.*

The last clean towel's in place. Now, to carry this heavy basketful of wet ones downstairs and out to the laundry. Finally, back up again for mopping.

"Well, everything's sparkling and fresh up here," said Daisy, at last.

"Thanks for your help, Daisy. I'm going to the dining room to do some detecting, now." She went to the dining room, only to be surprised.

"Where is everybody? This place is deserted. Oh. I guess it's too late for dinner."

She grabbed a fast supper in the staff dining room and helped Percy wash the dishes and clean. "Thank you again, Percy, for cleaning for me this morning. I appreciate it."

The shy boy said, "You're welcome. Glad to help you, Sadie. I'll see you tomorrow."

She found Mac on the veranda and sagged into a chair next to him.

"Have you decided yet?"

"I'm still thinking about it, Mac. What news of the Lincoln assassination plot?"

Noah came striding up the front steps. "Good evening, Mac, Sadie."

Sadie's heart beat faster and she nodded in his direction.

"Here are your newspapers, Mac, and a letter that looks important."

"Evening, Noah. Thanks." Mac opened the *Charleston Daily News.* Sadie leaned closer to read along with him.

Mac read aloud, "ARRESTS IN LINCOLN CONSPIRACY. Death Penalty Sought."

Sadie sucked in a big breath as he continued.

"Mary Surratt, owner of the boarding house where confederate conspirators plotted to overthrow the United States government, was arrested with Louis Payne and trial is set for May 12, before a nine-man military commission. This brings to eight the total of defendants, who are in custody, accused... etcetera."

"Booth is dead. It looks like they've got all of the traitors," said Noah.

And I fervently hope that will be the end of it, she thought.

Mac opened the dispatch and raised his eyebrows behind his rimless spectacles. "This confirms that Luther Greim was a leader of a street gang called the Dead Rabbits in Manhattan, before graduating to crime in southern climes during the war."

"I told you what Ava said about the gangs."

"Hmm. Dossiers on William 'Bill the Butcher' Poole and Mike Walsh, leaders of the main rival gang, the Bowery Boys. Not much on Buck Stotts. Seems like he's quite the ladies' man."

Noah said, "Don't get so tied up in your fascinating report that you miss this colorful sunset, Mac."

Sadie said, "Ooo. The sun dipped into the lake already and that big wide sky is glowing purple and pink, along with the blue. Look at that reflection on the lake."

"I never get tired of it," said Noah.

"By the way, Jane asked me to tell you that she is going on to the cottage, Sadie," Mac said.

"Oh, no. I worked late and now I'm going to be walking home in the dark."

"Why don't you accompany her Noah? It's a nice evening and you probably need to stretch your legs after being cooped up on that little eggbeater of yours."

"Ho. Watch what you say about my precious 80-foot, iron-hull stern-wheeler." He laughed, then turned to her and said, "I would love a walk, Sadie. Bye, Mac." He offered his arm.

Oh, good. I can ask him about his involvement in Luther's murder. "Bye, Mac. Thanks for everything," Sadie said.

Noah breathed in deeply. "It's a beautiful evening. I see a full moon coming up over there." They started along the shell road.

He said, "I've missed you." *And wondered what you were doing and who you were doing it with.*

"Who, Who wh, Whoooo."

Sadie gripped his arm tighter. "Hey, relax. That's just a barred owl."

A potential mate answered from a distance. "Who, Who wh, Whoooo."

"Love's in the air," he said.

Sadie thought, *It certainly is, if my pounding heart is any sign.* "It just raises the hair on the back of my neck." A shudder rippled up her back.

She tripped on a root in the road. "Oops, sorry," she said, as she fell against him.

He held her closer, to steady her against his side. When she shivered, he draped his muscular, warm arm around her shoulders and pulled her close. "Do you have a boyfriend, back where you came from?"

"I did, but we broke up. He was cheating on me with another..." *I almost said, 'another actress in the troop.'* "...a friend. That's one reason I came. What about you? Any special lady in your life?"

"Do you promise not to laugh, if I tell you?"

"No, I won't."

"All right. I was engaged to an Atlanta debutante before the war ended. Then we both woke up and realized that I am not cut out for that kind of life — dressing in fancy clothes and attending elegant soirées."

She pressed her lips together and stifled a laugh.

"You promised."

"Yes, I'm sorry. I just can't picture you in formalwear doing the Virginia Reel."

"No. That's not me."

"Look at that shimmering silver moon, reflected in the lake. It's almost like daylight out here," she said. A slight breeze felt warm on her cheek. She gazed up into his eyes and then looked away. "I can see the gray-green of the moss swaying in the trees. And the texture of the bark. *"And feel chills running up my spine. Even enfolded in your warm arm. Especially enfolded in your warm arm.*

He said, "It's magical here by moonlight." *And your green eyes are like two enormous emeralds. Aaa. The shape of her upper lip is making me lose all reason.*

Struggling for conversation, she said, "Mmm. I smell gardenias. And look. The tall glittery moon reflection seems to be dancing across the wavelets. It's like a pathway leading right up to heaven."

"My, aren't you poetic."

"It must be the moonbeams. I feel giddy this evening. *"And I forgot all my previous questions regarding your possible involvement in the murder.* She looked over at him in the soft moonlight.

His brown eyes look bigger than ever, with the black pupils wide-open.

They were almost to Snow Bird Cottage. *I don't want to go in yet. I want to kiss him.* She moved closer. *I never really suspected him, anyway. All that was just an exercise in thinking, wasn't it? My intuition tells me that he would never do such a thing. And Mac said to listen to your intuition, right?*

"Noah, I missed you, too. I watched you leave last time and counted the days until you would be back. *"I'm tingling all over.*

She moved to face him and looked deep into his eyes. *Oh, I can feel his breath. coming faster on my hair.*

His hot lips brushed softly over her forehead and lingered, before moving down to kiss her eyelids.

She breathed deeply and let out a slow contented sigh.

Then, he jerked back, as if a bee had stung him. "Oh, Sadie. I'm sorry. This is a mistake. I should not be doing this."

"Mistake?" she said in a dreamy voice.

"Yes," he said, as he pulled away. "Sadie, you are the prime suspect in the murder investigation. If you did such a thing…"

"WHAT? Do you actually imagine I KILLED somebody? How could you think that? I had questions for you, too, about your involvement in the murder. You had as much motive, means, and opportunity as I did." She whacked him on the chest with her fist.

"Yes, but they didn't find the murder weapon in my cabin."

"Pft." She spluttered. "Just go, Noah Asbell. Go back to your precious stern-wheeler, and take your judgmental attitude with you." As his tall silhouette receded in the moonlight, she stood with tears streaming down her face. *I feel so angry and frustrated.*

And here I was, thinking that you were the one.

CHAPTER THIRTY-FOUR

May 4, 1865

AT BROCK HOUSE HOTEL

E nterprise Florida was just waking up as Sadie made her way to Brock house. She
breathed deeply. *"Ahhh."*

I smell lemony magnolia flowers. Soft bird twitters were beginning. *I think walking to
work under this big beautiful purple and pink sunrise-sky is doing me good.*

*And a 'thank you' to Percy will do me good, too. I'm going to fold all the napkins and set
the dining room tables. Won't he be surprised when he comes in and finds them all done.
Maybe he will think an elf did it.* She chuckled to herself.

She found the stack of clean napkins in the laundry, next door to the kitchen behind
Brock House. *Mmm, lavender again.*

Humming in a quiet voice to herself, she carried them to the dining room. *I'll use Aunt
Cora's napkin-fold.* Soon the dining room looked festive with shiny plates, each topped by
a napkin folded into the shape of a perfect lotus flower.

Now, I'll get started cleaning the back parlor. While dusting a dimly lit corner, two ladies
with 'New Yauk' accents entered and made themselves comfortable on the couch with
their knitting.

"I tell you, Ruth, it's a small world. Imagine Martha Merritt here. How long has it been
since we saw her undercover report about that women's lunatic asylum in the *New York
World?*"

"Oh, ages darling. She made a sensation with that piece, but it made her some enemies. I heard rumors that she was harassed after that by other reporters, those men that she bested."

"It's no wonder that she and her sister moved back to their plantation, after their daddy died and left it to them."

"Well, I heard that 'daddy' was a smuggler in his day. I wonder if they're keeping up that tradition?"

I think I just found a couple of Percy's New York guests.

Sadie dusted closer to them and their conversation abruptly stopped. "Good morning, ladies. I'm Sadie. Welcome to Brock House. Don't tell me, let me guess. You are from New York?"

The two exclaimed, "Why, yes. How did you know?"

"Just a guess. I hear you have terrible trouble there with gangs like the Dead Rabbits and the Bowery Boys."

"The Bowery Boys, where we live, dress like dandies, in top hats, red shirts, and dark trousers tucked into boots. But they have respectable day jobs."

"They can be vicious at night, Ruth. Georgie and I witnessed a fight one evening from our carriage on our way to the theater. It was brutal, like the war."

We used to have a printer, Nate Poole, who was a Bowery Boy. He used to do my husband's pamphlets. I saw a fellow here who reminds me of him. It wasn't him, though. This fellow is much darker skinned and his hair is different."

"They say everybody has a double somewhere, Ruth."

"Oh, I'd love to find my double. Ladies, would you excuse me, please. I finished this sleeve and I need another ball of wool."

"Wait just a moment. Let me get to the end of this row and I'll go up with you, dear."

Sadie said, "What's the name of the person you thought you recognized?"

"I'm terrible with names, my dear."

That doesn't help much. "Have a lovely time today, ladies." Sadie finished cleaning the parlor and started on the upstairs rooms."

At Buck's room, she knocked and got no answer. *They must've all gone shooting, again. Time for the pass key.* She knocked again, then went in.

That's strange. All his personal belongings are gone. She cleaned his room.

He couldn't leave. Mac told him to stay until the murder inquiry is finished. And he paid for his room through the end of the week. I saw it on the list. Surely, he wouldn't have gone after Kat.

Ye gods. Doesn't he know that disappearing makes him look guilty of murder. He might as well confess.

She carried the basket of wet towels downstairs and on the way to the outdoor laundry she met Daisy. "Daisy, Buck's room is empty, with all his personal possessions gone. Did he check out? He's not on the list."

"Really? His room is still listed as 'reserved.' Isn't he a suspect in that murder?"

"Yes. If he has gone, he will be in trouble. But, how could he go? I don't think Noah would sell him a ticket. He would get himself in trouble for transporting a suspect. Could he walk out through the palmettos and snakes? With a suitcase? And no guide?"

"All good questions, I'm sure. Sadie, would you go tell Mr. Lavigne, please?"

"All right. *"Hmm. Would Noah help Buck?*

Sadie knocked on Lavigne's office door. *He's smoking that pipe again.* She waved her hand in the air. "Whew. I'll just open the window for you."

"Leave it, Miss Snow," he said in a loud baritone. "What was it you wanted?"

"I was just up cleaning Buck Stotts' room. All his things are missing, but he is not on the list of those checking out. He has reserved through the end of the week."

He looked down his judgmental nose at her. "Are you causing trouble again, Miss Snow? I give you a simple job — clean a man's room. What do you do? Run the man off. I won't have it."

"Now, just you wait a minute. First of all, we don't know that he has run off. And second, it's nothing to do with me, Mr. Lavigne. I'm just telling you that his room is empty."

"You're treading on thin ice, Missy."

Oh, for goodness sake. "Thank you for your time, sir. Goodbye. *" You irritating man.*

That evening she went for dinner in the staff dining room. *I can't stand the thought of polite conversation with more guests. I don't know, anymore, who I can trust.*

Percy stuck his head in. "I know it was you what folded those napkins so purty and set the tables this morning. Thank you."

Sadie smiled at him. "Don't expect me to do that every day. It was just a 'thank you' for your help yesterday. I'll come out and do dishes with you in a minute."

His rough chapped hand felt scratchy as it clutched at hers. "An' I want to know how to fold them napkins that-a-way."

"Of course."

When she was finished for the day, she found Mac on the veranda, as usual. She told him the gossip of the morning. "...and the other one said she heard that the Merritt patriarch was a smuggler. Could those sisters be smuggling and have run afoul of Luther and his gang?"

"That area is full of fast boats. It's possible, but they would have other people doing all the dirty work for them. They wouldn't be directly involved."

"What if they hired Luther and his gang, had an argument over money, and decided to get rid of him? No. It doesn't seem possible. Those nice little old ladies?"

"Remember how your opinion of Martha changed after a conversation about her plantation?"

"True. The more I find out, the more confused I am, Mac." She paused. "I've decided. I would like to borrow the LeMat gun, until I get new locks and this murder investigation is finished. I think Jane and I will be safer."

"I thought you would. You are smart and principled, like your Aunt Cora. I came to know her and her husband well. After he died, we spent a lot of time together. She was kind, compassionate, and powerful. She could also be hilariously funny and very brave."

Sadie stood with her mouth open. *Maybe 'spy,' not 'birdwatcher.'*

"I'll go get it for you. Be right back." He got up and headed for the door.

And that, Sadie, as all actors know, is the stage direction called "exit stage right." Great Caesar's ghost. They were good friends, or more, and he never told me. That's why he's so nice to me.

That evening as Sadie walked home to Snow Bird Cottage, she handled the LeMat gun box carefully. *I needed both of my deep tie-on pockets under the slits in my long 'suitable-for-Lavigne' skirt today.*

The weight of the heavy leather cartridge box, Mac's beeswax 'bore butter,' the foil percussion cap pouch, and the extra black powder and grape shot caused those pockets to sag a bit, but they held.

'It's fully loaded and ready to go,' he told me. I guess that's reassuring.

In the twilight, a doe and two fawns bounded across the road in front of her. *Take your time. You have nothing to fear from me.*

She looked at her cottage up ahead. *Jane is home before me again. This is getting to be a habit. I hear her voice. Singing? No. Reciting dramatic poetry? I wouldn't put it past her.*

She stopped with her hand on the front door knob. *What's going on? What is she doing? Thumping and crashing?* "Jane?"

Now it's louder. A sort of whining.

"Jane. Is that you? Who are you talking to?"

"Ahhh. It's. Knocking...

"Mfptfpt...

"...Table. HELP."

"Jane. What's happening in there?" Sadie set the LeMat gun box on the porch and snatched open the lid. She pulled out the shiny weapon as Mac had shown her.

Pull back the hammer and check that the lever is up. As soon as the door is open, both hands on the gun.

Sadie threw open the front door.

"Wham. Crash."

This is chaos.

Pieces of sturdy wooden furniture lay broken on the floor. *Dishes smashed? with shards everywhere.*

Her hands cradled the gun the way she practiced. *What in tarnation?*

"Wham. Kerwham."

"Jane. I hear you. Where are you?"

"Sadie. Help..."

She saw the tableau in seven seconds.

At the far end of the dining room.

Up against the wall.

Jane, cowering and whimpering.

Atop the wobbling dining table.

The legs of which were being turned into kindling.

By half a ton of muscular, thrashing, gray GATOR.

"Do something."

"Great Caesar's ghost. "*He stretches half the way across the dining room.*

At the sound of Sadie's voice, the 13-foot saurian turned in her direction.

Jane kept shaking her head. "...came home. Saw mess."

"And, what? You came in to clean it up?"

"Saw him too late. Charged me... 300 teeth clashing. Tail knocking everything to bits. Do something."

"Stay there."

"What else can I do?"

The gator charged straight for Sadie.

She thrust the LeMat in front of her.

Aimed.

And fired.

"BANG."

Ears ringing. I'm sure I hit it.

It kept coming. Almost on top of her.

Get up. Onto the sideboard. Up she went.

She aimed and fired.

"BANG."

Too loud. Didn't slow it down.

Still, it came.

Launched itself up.

Onto the sideboard.

Snapping.

Danger of tipping over.

"Great Jehoshaphat. What does it take?"

Wait. Wait.

What did Mac say?

Flip the lever.

The gator scrabbled.

"Scritch. Scratch."

Front and back claws.

Trying to get a grip.

She pulled back the hammer a third time and flipped the lever down.

The gator came.

Strong jaws snapped, then opened wide, threatening her with staggered rows of big teeth. "Hissssssssss."

Ready to chomp.

"BOOM."

Whoa, Nellie. Recoil knocked me back from the huge carnivore.

"Crunch. Crash."

No. No. No.

I'm sliding. Toward him. He's smashed the leg off the side table.

"Aaahhh."

Careful of the gun.

She fell in a heap.

Ow, ow.

Go to the side.

Ow, *ow, ow.*

Get away from the violently pounding beast.

Ow, my hand, my knee. Broken glass everywhere.

Go.

She scuttled away. Gun aimed down.

He's going back towards Jane.

Pull back the hammer.

Flip the lever up.

Aim at his head.

Squeeze trigger slowly.

"BANG."

The gator finally slowed.

Here he comes at me again.

He flailed.

"Wham. Whack, whack, whack."

Ow. Blood from my left hand is dripping everywhere. The tangy earthy smell of blood filled her nostrils.

The ferocious animal soon turned the sideboard into a pile of sticks.

He's slowing. Aimless flopping.

She found herself crouched in the hall, facing into the dining room, gun at the ready.

Ow. My knee hurts. Must've bumped it when I fell off the sideboard.

Don't get any blood on those percussion caps.

Shouldn't he be dead by now?

I can hear Jane breathing faster than the ticking of the hall clock.

The sour taste in my mouth is probably from my fear.

She watched and waited.

The flopping is giving way to twitching. I think I've finally stopped him.

Jane said in a small voice, "Is he dead?"

Jane's breathing is slower now. "He must be. He's wearing three .36 caliber hunks of lead and a charge from a .28-gauge shotgun."

"Where in the world did you get that thing?"

"This 'thing' is a nine shot LeMat revolver with an auxiliary smooth bore shotgun. I borrowed it from Mac. He thought we needed protection."

"Well, thank God for Mac. I'm awfully glad you showed up when you did. As soon as I stop being scared spitless, we'll pick the glass out of your hand and rinse the blood from your clothes. "

"I'm not worried about that. Are you all right?"

"Yes, indeed." Her eyes flashed. "I'm going to skin this behemoth and cut up his tail for breakfast."

She's joking?

"We finally have something to share at Brock House. Crispy. Fried. Gator."

Not joking.

Jane chortled, a high-pitched, almost-hysterical sound. "We'll need that coil of rope from the kitchen cupboard to drag him outside. A sharp knife and our biggest pots. We have to hurry. It'll be dark soon."

"Well, I think I just glimpsed the Havana lady who tore off her sleeves. Do your friends at Brock House know you are so funny?"

"Funny?"

"You've been menaced by one of the biggest, most ferocious gators in Lake Monroe and, when all the excitement is over, all you want to do is **cook** him."

It was a relief to laugh together.

"I wonder if anyone would buy the hide with all those bullet holes in?" said practical-minded Sadie.

"I know we need the money, Sadie, but I am planning to make you some shoes with this skin."

"You know how to make shoes?"

"I am a Cuban lady. I know how to make many beautiful things. And right now, you need something beautiful. The part with the bullet holes will be used to make decorative flowers on the toes. Everyone will know that you have killed this gator. They may be less interested in threatening us."

Tears sprang to Sadie's eyes, but she chuckled and shook her head. *I have to laugh, or I'll cry.*

"How did that critter get in here? He couldn't have crawled up the steps, Jane. Well, he might have, but it's unlikely. Somebody brought him in here. Who can handle live gators? The same 'somebody' who used my knife to scare us? I have a bad feeling about this."

CHAPTER THIRTY-FIVE

May 4, 1865 Evening

AT BROCK HOUSE HOTEL

"I was halfway back to Manhattan. I thought about Buck the whole way. And, I suppose it's not a secret anymore. I thought about this baby and our future together. Isn't there anyone I can ask to find out where he was going?" said Kat.

Mac thought, *Did Buck send her to play this role? Did he think he could escape a murder charge by looking like a love-sick Don Juan? A good man driven to the brink by love. Interesting that she should show up back here now.*

He said, "I'm sorry, Kat. Buck and his belongings seem to have vanished into thin air this morning. A tracker checked the area around the hotel and he doesn't seem to be walking or paddling a small boat out. He couldn't have purchased a ticket on Noah's steamer."

"Why would he leave? He was supposed to stay here, until the investigation is finished."

"Yes, and you do understand that this makes him look very bad. The marshal will jump to the conclusion that he's guilty and issue a warrant for his arrest. If you know where he's hiding, you must tell him to come back."

"I don't know. I thought you would know. I was the one who was running away. He was supposed to stay here. When I was headed for New York, I thought, ' What are you doing? You want a life with this good man who has promised to protect you and the baby and provide for you.'"

"Kat, why did you leave? Did he refuse to marry you?" *Because he's already married.*

"What? No. We are married. It just has to be a secret, because his boss at Guaranteed Mutual wanted Buck to marry his daughter. That would be a difficult position for anyone. Buck didn't want to lose his job."

Is it my place to tell this young woman that her new husband already has a wife and family? That he may have killed somebody to keep that secret?

"Kat, tell me what you did the night *Katie Asbell* docked at Brock House."

"I unpacked and freshened up. Then we, Buck and I, went to dinner in the dining room. We were tired from our travels, so we went to bed."

"You booked separate rooms. In view of the fact that you are newlyweds, I assume you did not sleep in those individual rooms apart."

"No. That was just to keep our secret. Buck came to my room."

"What time was that?"

"It was dark. We had to use candles. That was probably seven-thirty."

"Did you see anyone moving about between the hotel and the steamer that night or anything suspicious?"

"No."

"When did he leave?"

"I don't know. He was gone when I woke."

"When was that?"

"The sun comes up about seven. It was sometime after that. Mac, Buck didn't kill that awful man. He isn't like that. I came back because I realized I can trust him. It doesn't matter what he has done — robbed a bank or a train, stolen money from his employers, or married someone else before me. He can tell me and we'll work it out."

"So, you would accept Buck as a husband, even if he had another wife and family elsewhere?"

"Yes. Yes, I would. Whatever time he chooses to give me and this child of ours, we'll use it and have a happy family."

"Do you realize you're talking about bigamy, which is now illegal and could land Buck in jail?"

"Yes. He loves me and I'm sure nothing bad will happen while he's around."

"And if he killed someone to keep that a secret from you and the world?"

"No. He would never do that. Listen, Mr. MacNally. I work as a governess, teaching the children of others. And I'm good at it. But I don't want to raise someone else's children.

I want to raise my own... with Buck. I just have to find him to tell him that. I've paid for my room through the end of the week. If I haven't found him by then, I'm leaving."

CHAPTER THIRTY-SIX

May 5, 1865 Early Morning

AN INVITATION AT BROCK HOUSE HOTEL

"Mac, how many people do you know who can handle live alligators?"

"Several of the old settlers dealt in gator skins, when they were in need of money. Why? You going to give up your job and become a gator wrestler?"

"It's no joke. Somebody deposited a 13-foot gator in our cottage yesterday. I returned home to find Jane trembling atop the table, in the dining room. That beast had already knocked one leg off the table and was working on the others."

"Oh, no. Is she all right?"

"Yes. She's fine."

"Did you see anyone around?"

"No. Only a doe, plus some birds, rabbits, and bats."

"What did you do?"

"I shot him with the Lemat. Thank God I took you up on your offer when I did."

"Good. Who do you think did it?"

"I don't know, Mac, but I intend to find out pretty sharpish. If I don't, you will be investigating another murder, either mine or that of the intruder who's been doing this."

"Promise me you won't shoot anyone, Sadie, unless they threaten your life."

"I promise."

"We are going to figure this out and we might have some help, for a day or two. Another detective friend of mine came in on the *Darlington* last night, just for a bit of rest and some warmer weather."

"Another Pinkerton detective?" *who might find out that I'm from Washington and knew John Booth.*

"Yes, that's right… just finished a case and needed a break… four nights, then back to Chicago."

She breathed deeply. "That's wonderful. But right now, I have to go to work. I'll be back this afternoon. Maybe you and your friend will crack the case, or cases, while I'm gone." With her bandaged hand to her side, she moved to the door with a slight limp.

Daisy greeted her. "Sadie, what happened to you?"

"Let's start on the front parlor and I'll tell you."

In the parlor a slender, brown-haired woman sat at the desk by the window, writing with pen and ink on a pad of paper. She looked up and greeted them. "Good morning. I'm Kate. I came in here because the light is so good Do you need this room to yourselves?"

"Hello. I'm Sadie and this is Daisy. We need to sweep and dust, but we don't want to disturb you. We'll come back later."

"Nonsense. I get the flow going and ignore everything else. You won't bother me a bit. Please go ahead."

"Thank you. We'll start in the back."

As she swept, Daisy said, "All right. Why are you limping and what happened to your hand?"

"An intruder's been trying to scare me. I didn't want to believe it, but it's gotten progressively worse." She added the long stick to her duster and swooshed dust off the trophy animal heads hanging on the walls.

"Someone was trespassing at Snow Bird cottage?"

"Yes, several times. Mac says our mortise locks can be opened with almost any skeleton key. I don't have money to buy new locks, yet. So, every day, while we're working, our cottage is open to anyone with a skeleton key. Yesterday I returned from work to find Jane cowering atop the dining table. An enormous alligator was filling up my dining room and trying his best to reduce the table legs to matchsticks."

"A gator? In your cottage? That's dreadful. Were you afraid? What happened?"

They worked their way around the room as the story came out. "... and I shudder to think what would have happened if I hadn't borrowed the LeMat gun from Mac yesterday."

"You could have been killed."

"I'm lucky. My knee has swollen alarmingly, to the size of a round bread loaf, and we removed a dozen pieces of glass from my hand, but I'm going to get a new pair of shoes out of it." She chuckled.

Daisy's eyebrows shot up in surprise.

"When the drama was over, Jane was furious. She's on a mission to make that critter a contribution to us. We dragged it out into the yard and dressed it. Everybody in Brock House will get to taste her crispy fried gator tail this morning at breakfast."

"And shoes?"

"She's already gathering oak ashes for lye and oak bark for tanning solution to turn the 13-foot hide into leather for a pair of shoes. She insists on using the bullet-riddled parts as decoration to advertise the fact that we killed that gator, which was supposed to kill us."

"Ye gods. And you walked to work today?"

"Yes, indeed. We even pulled a wagon load of meat behind us. I'm fine. We need the money and you can't clean all those rooms by yourself." She paused. "I did bring some of my willow bark pain tincture."

"You clean downstairs today. I'll take the upstairs."

"Thanks, Dais'. I won't argue with you."

"Stay here. I'll get a pile of clean linens for the downstairs cleaning trolley."

Moments later, Sadie took the loaded trolley and began her rounds.

In early afternoon, Sadie helped a lady in the hall to 'right' an inverted parasol.

"I lost my hat. That beastly wind blew it into the lake. If I hadn't been holding my parasol in both hands, it would be gone, too," she said. "It's a gale, picking up handfuls of sand and swirling it sideways. I had to shield my eyes and it stung my hands and face."

As Sadie cleaned the next room, she looked out the window. *Whew. The hanging moss is blowing sideways.*

She finished that room and stepped into the hall. *Time to take pain medication.*

"There you are," said Jane. "The sky is very dark outside and Mrs. Weathers said for me to go home early. Old timers are saying the storm will be a bad one. Do you think Lavigne will let you leave early?"

"Daisy really needs me and I don't want to give him the satisfaction of saying 'no.' I'll finish and be home as soon as possible."

"All right. I have to go scrape our alligator hide some more and salt him down."

Sadie knocked on the next door. "Housekeeping."

"Oh, hello Sadie. Come in."

Sadie blinked. *The brown-haired woman from the parlor. Kate. She's quite a commanding person. Self-possessed...* "Hello again, Kate. I'm here to give your room a brush up."

"Brush away," she said, with a smile. She stood up from her chair and gathered a stack of papers.

Sadie wiped down the basin and wash stand. *Where is she going with the papers? Oh. Very handsome. She put them in a brown leather accordion-style case, resting on the floor.*

"Do you like your work here, Sadie?"

"Yes, I do. It's exactly what I need, right now."

Sadie dusted and noticed the other woman. *Graceful in her movements, too.*

"Have you ever thought of doing any other kind of work?" said Kate.

Every day. But you aren't to know that. "Like what kind of work?"

"Well, clerical workers are in great demand nowadays. Record keeping and nursing are steady professions. Someone mentioned that you nursed a crew member from the steamer, and even compounded the medication yourself."

Who is this? Checking up on me? "None of those jobs appeal to me, Kate. I nursed Christian, because I learned about it during the war and no one else was available. And you? Are you enjoying your vacation?"

She was reaching for a fresh towel, when a flash of lightning lit the room and a rumble sounded overhead. "Ooo. It doesn't look good for walking home."

"Oh, my. It certainly doesn't. Could you stay here at Brock House overnight?"

"No. I really need to go to the cottage. A little rain won't hurt me." *Get on with your cleaning, Sadie.* "I'll just finish your floor." She removed the mop from her cart.

"No need for that, today. I'm sure it's clean enough."

"All right. Thanks. Then I'm finished here." Sadie opened the door into the hallway.

"Sadie, I've been looking for you. My don't you look pretty today," said Neville.

Oh, Neville, not right now. "Hello, Neville. I'm in a bit of a hurry at the moment."

"Everyone's talking about our breakfast. I hear we have you to thank for our delicious fried gator. You are incredible — shooting that huge beast. Who would expect you to confront that thing with a gun... and cut it up for breakfast?"

Why is he turning on the charm? charm that has heretofore been missing in his dealings with me. "I just did what I had to do, Neville. Would you excuse me, please."

"Don't leave yet. I was wondering if you would go on Jacob Brock's excursion to Orchid Springs with me? I thought we might get to know each other better."

Oh, folly, fudge, and flummediddle. What am I supposed to say to that? Since the green and purple of my bruised eye, inflicted by Luther Greim, has disappeared, I look presentable. Maybe he thinks having me on his arm will help him attract more donations to his political campaign.

"I can't think about it right now, Neville."

"There will be a lot of people on that excursion, many politicians and industrialists, who have connections and money. It will be a great place for us to meet people and dance. We'll have fun."

And, there it is. I'm to be his path to people with connections and money. "Neville, a really big storm is coming and I must hurry. I can't stop to talk now. Let's discuss it later."

"All right."

She cleaned and thought. *He is a very handsome fellow and quite persuasive. Watch yourself. His ambition is bigger than Georgia, I think. And he wants a debutante wife and life in the limelight. You, on the other hand, are happy creating a quiet life here, at least for now.*

Sadie finished her last room. *I better go now.*

Daisy came down the hall. "Sadie, Mrs. Weathers sent you this plate of dinner and said she and Percy don't need help tonight. She said you should go home."

"Thank you. I will."

She sat in the back parlor and hurriedly ate her dinner. *Is it safe to carry the Lemat gun box in this rain?*

When she was done, she stepped to the veranda to gauge the strength of the storm. Mac and Kate were sitting sheltered, close to the building. The tough ex-Pinkerton man held a nervous Fluffy on his chest, so she could hear his calming heartbeat.

"Hello, Sadie. We were just talking about you. Have a seat."

"I can't stop. I..."

"Flash. Crash. Boom."

"Please sit. I want you to meet my friend and colleague, Kate Warne. I mentioned her this morning. When Alan Pinkerton hired her, over the objections of his brother and business partner, she was the first Pinkerton woman detective."

Sadie sat.

"I hope you don't mind, Sadie," said Mac. "I wrote to Kate to see if she might have time to come help us with this investigation."

"You came specially to find Greim's killer?"

"I can't stay long enough to complete an investigation. But Mac told me what you have so far and I can offer techniques and insights that might help. Mac is 100 percent sure you are innocent. I agree that it looks like the evidence against you was planted."

"Thank you for that sensible conclusion."

Mac said, "Pinkerton agents are known for sensible conclusions, Sadie. The hammer found under your bunk was covered in dried blood, yet there was no blood stain on the floor where it was found. I examined the floor of your cabin with a magnifying glass. That rough wood floor would have held stains deep in the fiber, but it showed no trace of blood."

"I heard what you told Daisy about your encounter with the alligator. That shows grace under fire, Sadie," said Kate. "It also seems that you are making someone very nervous with your questions. That's good for the investigation, but dangerous for you personally."

Mac said, "Let's look at who had an opportunity to plant that murder weapon in your cabin. You removed everything out of your cabin before you went to Brock House?"

"Yes."

"Did you check thoroughly under your bunk at that time?"

"Yes. I stored my bags there and had to remove them to pack."

Kate said, "Mac, your blood spatter evidence on the wall of Greim's cabin shows that he was killed there. If the hammer was dropped by the attacker at the time of the murder, the blood must have dried while the hammer was in the victim's cabin."

"Yes. I found blood stains on the floor in his cabin."

"Some time later that night or early the next morning the murderer went back and put it into Sadie's..."

"Flash. Crash. Boom."

Sadie said, "He must have been killed after dark the night we arrived, probably late when everybody was asleep. We could ask if anyone was seen lurking near the steamer after we all disembarked."

Mac said, "You would have been identifiable by your clothing, which was unique then, Sadie. You wore trousers and a knee-length skirt."

"Marvelous. That can help rule you out."

"I thought I was already ruled out."

"Only on the murder weapon. You could still have lured him out of his cabin and pushed him overboard," said Kate. "But the others could have, too."

Mac said, "And nothing tells us so far that it was not done by a deckhand."

"Flash."

"What is the possible motive? You said he was rude to everyone. Would any of your suspects murder him for revenge? Hate? Jealousy?"

Mac said, "All the witnesses told me that Luther was coarse, rude, and thoroughly loathsome. But do you murder somebody you can't stand? Not without another motive stacked on top. Revenge is a motive for Ava to kill him."

Kate said, "Money is a strong motive. Did he have money issues with any of your suspects?"

Sadie said, "Bram? Ava? Neville? Buck? He was stealing rum from the Merritt sisters."

Mac said, "They are the tough and wily daughters of a pirate, not 'sweet little old ladies.' They could have hired someone to kill him. If it came right down to it, they could probably kill him themselves. That would put a stop to his thieving."

"Flash. FLASH. BOOM." Sadie saw Fluffy's claws dig in, as if for traction, preparatory to flight.

"That was close. We need to get off this veranda. Let's adjourn to the back parlor and find a blanket and pillow for you, Sadie. It would be dangerous to go out in this weather."

"I can go, but I should hurry. May I have an old newspaper to hold over my head?"

Mac said, "That is not a good idea. You might get struck by lightning."

"Or lose your footing on the flooded road, and fall. You could break a limb," said Kate.

"Or be struck by flying debris," said Mac.

"Or have an overhanging tree branch fall on you."

"All right. All right. You convinced me. The rain is blowing sideways, almost up to my chair. And I can hardly hear you, because it's howling so... Plus my knee is throbbing."

Sadie carried extra linens, blanket, and a pillow from the hall cupboard to the back parlor, where the three settled comfortably. The cat pounced on the arm of Sadie's chair, walked around her lap, then snuggled herself down into a tight ball, as if trying to disappear. "Would you look at that," she said, with a smile, as she petted the soft animal. "Where is everybody?"

"The hotel guests are probably cozy, all cuddled up in their rooms," said Kate. "Stormy weather does that."

"Kate, tell Sadie about your first big case, saving Lincoln," said Mac.

"Oh, that was four years ago, before the inauguration. I was a young widow, 23 at the time, and I had been working at Pinkerton's a few months. Mac was on the team investigating secessionist activity in Maryland for Sam Felton's railroad, weren't you, Mac?"

"Yes. Felton is president of the Philadelphia, Wilmington, and Baltimore Railroad. He was concerned about threats of damage to the railroad and we found information about that. We also got wind of an assassination plot."

She said, "Alan sent me to Baltimore. I used the alias 'Mrs. Cherry,' and took a trunk of fancy ball gowns. I infiltrated secessionist social gatherings, posing as a flirting Southern belle. A thick Southern accent and a lot of giggling made me welcome in places such as the classy Barnum Hotel. It seemed a lark at the time, but I changed my mind after one of our agents was later hanged as a spy."

"You played a part to get close to a particular group." *Like what I do on the stage, only the stakes are higher. Investigating is serious business.* "Did it work?"

"I discovered how they planned to assassinate Lincoln. I also found out the exact time and place where it was to be carried out."

"Partygoers told you all that?"

"Yes. They boasted about their plot to kill the president-elect. They were going to stage a fight to draw away the few policemen at Calvert Street Station in Baltimore. Then secessionists would surround his train and shoot him. They said that he would never be president."

"Couldn't he just take another route to Washington?"

"No. Whatever route you choose, all the trains going to Washington have to go through Baltimore. Alan told Lincoln about the plot and we were hired by the railroad to get him safely to his inauguration."

Mac said, "Kate is being modest. She made almost all the arrangements to smuggle Lincoln into Washington."

Kate said, "Rather than ride publicly in an open car through the city streets between train stations in Baltimore, as planned, I arranged for him to take a midnight train straight through to the capital, not stopping in Baltimore to make a speech."

"I bet that surprised a lot of people. Politicians like publicity. Don't they have to shake hands and kiss babies?" said Sadie.

"His confidence in the people was unbounded. He previously refused the usual army escort, because he didn't fear any violent outbreak. We heard a great deal about 'not greeting my public.'"

"Did you use a private train?"

"No. I thought that would make him even more of a target. He let us disguise him. In Philadelphia I reserved four double berths in the sleeper car at the back of the train for my 'family,' and gave big tips to the conductors. I told them my invalid brother would be accompanying me, that he would retire immediately to his compartment behind closed curtains, and that he was not to be disturbed."

"Lincoln traveled incognito as your brother? Good heavens. This is beginning to sound like a dime novel."

Kate laughed. "We couldn't disguise his height, so we had him hunch over. We replaced his signature stove-pipe hat with a soft felt cap. And wrapped up that strong jaw in a shawl."

"What a picture that brings to mind. Oh, my."

"Alan came to Philadelphia to escort Lincoln onto the train. We pulled out of the Quaker city just before eleven that night and arrived at Baltimore at three-thirty the next morning, hours ahead of the original schedule. They didn't need me to be the 'sister' anymore, so I got off in Baltimore. Their car was to be transferred to the night express to Washington, but that train was late getting in to Baltimore. They waited in the terminal some nervous minutes."

"Wasn't that very dangerous?"

"It was. We were three agents and Lincoln in a car with all those members of the public, stuck in the very spot that assassins were supposed to strike. At that point the president-elect had little protection, idling there in the Baltimore station. The possibility that someone might have leaked our plan to the rabid secessionists loomed large."

"What did you do?"

"Eventually the sleeping cars with Lincoln on board were shifted to the other engine and off they went. We had Pinkerton operatives standing watch at every switch, bridge and crossing."

"That was prudent."

"They had orders to signal — two light flashes, a short pause, then two more flashes — that all was well as Lincoln's train approached. Those signals continued to shine throughout the night. His express train arrived safely in Washington around six in the morning."

Sadie covered a yawn. "I'm sure he was very grateful. At least he had a chance to sleep."

"On the contrary, the poor man didn't get much rest at all that night. He was so very tall that he couldn't lie straight in his berth. His was a rare good humor, though. He joked all the way to Baltimore."

"I'm curious about how you agents disguise yourselves and how many accents or dialects you must know. And have you learned defense techniques that don't use weapons?"

Mac said, "As much as I would like to stay up talking about unarmed combat and disguises..." Yawn. "I'm afraid I have to go to bed now. Good night, ladies."

Sadie said, "I do want to talk about unarmed combat and disguises. Perhaps tomorrow?"

"Yes, Sadie. I'll leave you to your couch...and your cat." She chuckled. "By the way, I heard Neville Beaumont's invitation. He's a suspect. Never pass up a chance to get closer to a suspect."

"But I don't like him."

CHAPTER THIRTY-SEVEN

May 6, 1865 Early Morning

AT BROCK HOUSE HOTEL

"Pssst. Sadie."

Sadie opened her eyes to weak rays of sunshine from the window. *Where in the world am I? Oh, yes. Brock House back parlor.*

Jane stood beside the couch with a parcel. "I thought you might need these."

"What is it?"

"A change of clothes. The storm last night was extraordinary. That big old oak next to the boat shed came down and I climbed over three pine trees snapped off and blocking the road this morning. Frogs are swimming in the puddles.'"

Huh. "Thank you. It's awfully quiet in Brock House this morning."

"Yes. It's early. We have to start the punch and make cakes for the excursion, which is the day after tomorrow. Mr. Brock will be back tomorrow night."

"But that's only the sixth. He's not due 'til the eighth."

"I guess he won't start regular advertised service until after this party, to celebrate his return."

"What are you putting in the punch?"

"It'll be rum punch with orange, pineapple, and lime. I have to get out to the kitchen, now. See you at dinner."

"Would you mind if I invited a guest some evening?"

She laughed. "Noah's always welcome."

"No. Not him," she said with a sharp edge to her voice. "A friend of Mac's."

Jane's eyebrows went up as she left. "Yes. Fine."

Sadie put on her shoes, grabbed an extra pitcher and basin from the storage shelf, and hurried out back to pump some water.

In a vacant room, ablutions complete, Sadie donned her fresh clothes. Then she stepped to the veranda. *Air is damp. Everything washed clean.*

"Oh, good morning, Fluffy." *Wildlife is very subdued. Birds singing softly. Little clucks, instead of full-blown songs. No Mac.* She sat.

The cat jumped lightly into her lap. *Aww.* She felt the pat, pat of one soft paw on her face. Soon a feline rumble sounded from the curled fuzzy ball warming her knee.

Guests, wide-eyed and talking about the power of the storm, trickled out of Brock House. They all carried steaming cups, which perfumed the air with smells of cinnamon, chocolate, and coffee. *I could use the comfort of a hot tea, before I go to work.*

She made her way out to the kitchen where she found Jane making pastries. Kate stood there with a small plate of ginger bread. "Good morning, Sadie. Mrs. Weathers kindly gave me a sample of her party fare, but don't tell anybody. It's a secret."

"That smells spicy. If you're sharing, I'll brew us a cup of tea and we can eat in the side garden."

"Perfect. I'll go on out there."

They ate and talked. "I have to go to work now. We could continue this conversation at the cottage this evening when I finish."

"Oh, I've heard a lot about that place. I'd love to see it."

"Good I'll meet you on the veranda after dinner."

"How far away is it?"

"Only a ten-minute walk south on the shell road."

"I need some exercise. I might walk over there after breakfast. Would it be all right if I sit on your porch a while?"

"Of course. And since any old skeleton key or hairpin will open the door, feel free to have full run of the place."

"I won't do that, but I've heard the garden is interesting. And Mac said you have a dugout canoe."

"Yes. Feel free to take it out and explore. But watch that the weather doesn't sneak up on you. I got caught in a storm out in the middle of the lake and it was all I could do to get home."

"All right. I might do that."

"See you later." Sadie hurried inside.

She caught sight of Neville in the hall. He strode up and said, "Good morning, Sadie. You are looking particularly lovely this morning. You will come to Orchid Springs with me, won't you, dear lady? It will be so much more pleasant with you by my side."

"Good morning, Neville. Yes, I'd like that. It sounds like a splendid party."

"Jacob is planning music and good food."

"Goodness knows, we all need to dance and have a good time, after four years of this terrible war. Excuse me, now, please. I have things to do."

Sadie did her work automatically. *How much do I dare tell Kate Warne? It might help her, in her line of work, to know some of the techniques I learned in New York for self-defense. I could share that. It's Washington and the Booth family that I need to be quiet about. I wonder what I can learn from her?*

Sadie dined in the dining room, where Bram and Neville told a story about shooting deer at Salt Springs. She learned about a guest being cured of his rheumatism in the sulfur spring, and she listened to a new recipe for cornbread. But she didn't get any further in her investigation of the murder.

Out in the kitchen she helped Percy wash dishes. In an effort to lighten the mood of the overworked kitchen staff, she flicked a finger full of the slippery soft soap suds at the boy. "Ha. Got you," she said, with a laugh.

He retaliated. By the time they finished, they were both sodden, but everyone, including Mrs. Weathers, was smiling.

Time to meet Kate on the veranda. But her new friend was not there yet.

Sadie chatted with Mac, accepted the gun box from him, and went to the staff room for privacy to stow it under her skirts.

She started back to the veranda. "Oh, hello, Kate. Let's go to the kitchen. You will want to meet the other person who lives in the cottage."

The kitchen was hot, but it smelled wonderful — of roasted meat, ginger, cloves, and cinnamon. Jane was brushing ashes from one of the big wood-burning stoves into a large pail.

"Jane, this is the friend of Mac's that I was telling you about. Kate, this is Jane."

Kate said, "I'll bet you will be glad when this excursion is finished. I'm sure they don't realize how much extra work it is for you. Let us help you take those to the trash pit, Jane."

Jane said, "I want to take this lot home to make lye for tanning our alligator hide, but it's very heavy. You could help me carry it. I'm afraid it'll slow us down."

"Yes. All right."

"And I will, too."

The three walked, talked, and took it in turn to lug ashes to Snow Bird Cottage.

"I saw your rifle-toting friends Bram and Neville with Gator Simmons today. They all introduced themselves when we ran into each other on the road near your cottage," said Kate.

Sadie said, "Gator is their guide and takes them to his favorite hunting grounds. They have contributed a great amount of fresh game to the Brock House dining room tables."

"I hope they didn't disturb that salted alligator hide I left out back in the big bucket," said Jane.

"I expect they were just going hunting again," said Sadie. "It's good to know that a good hunting ground is close to our cottage."

"I took out your canoe and saw them again, continuing down the road. I followed their progress for more than a mile, before they ducked into the pine woods. Have you seen that great midden mound of shell and bone?" said Kate.

"Yes. That's where Mac and I shot the LeMat gun. Can you believe someone built a hotel on top of it?"

"Really? There's no sign of one now." Kate turned to Sadie. "I sure would like to see that gun. I've heard a lot about them, but I've never seen one. Where is it now?"

"The box is in a large pocket suspended from my waist and strapped to my leg. It doesn't show under this skirt. It is somewhat awkward to carry."

"It will take a long time to get to it, if you have trouble on your journey to and from your cottage and need it."

"True, but I also won't accidentally get a load of grape shot in my leg."

"When I get back to Chicago, I'll see if I can find a better way for you to carry it. You need good protection for the trigger guard and the foil percussion caps."

"Maybe I won't need it much longer, but for now I can't leave it at home, so I tote it to work and leave it with Mac during the day. Then I take it home, remove it from the box, and keep it handy, so we'll be safe from any more alligator deliveries."

Jane said, "Or worse."

"Sadie, you said you want to talk about defense techniques. I heard from Mac that some onlookers thought you threw Luther Greim to the deck, after he punched you. Others dismissed it as impossible."

"That's one of the reasons I invited you this evening. When I was in New York, a friend showed me some ways to defend myself and I thought they might be useful to you. And perhaps Jane and I could learn from you."

"Ah. Thank you. I have learned only rudimentary methods. I am always ready to add new tools to my arsenal."

Jane said, "There's the cottage. While you two do that, I'm going to check on my alligator hide."

The three women trudged around to the back of the cottage.

Sadie said, "Where do you want this bucket, Jane?"

"Put it in front of the kitchen door. Thanks."

"What smells so... so sweet?" said Kate, inhaling deeply.

"The datura is blooming. Some call them angel trumpets." Sadie pointed to a spot in the garden. "They are pretty, just tall bushes, really. We have a purple and white variety and one that blooms peach-colored. They are poisonous when boiled in a liquid and the smoke is poison, too. But their fragrance is perfectly safe and they all smell so good" She took a big breath.

From a large bucket Jane removed a salt-encrusted, dripping roll of alligator skin, tied with string. Inspecting it, she said, "I'm going to take this down to the lake for a good wash. It needs to be scrubbed two or three times, before I put it in the lye."

"All right. We'll be inside."

Sadie showed Kate to the living room and then said, "Excuse me a moment." In her bedroom, she untied the thigh and waist ties of her pocket, and released the bulky box. She carried the gun to the living room and handed it over for inspection. "Isn't it a beauty?"

Kate took the weapon, aiming away from them. "Yes, indeed. And you stopped a gator with it?"

"I did, and I hope never to have to do it again. But I am certainly glad I had it that night. You can see our furniture situation. That gator smashed several pieces into kindling...chairs, the sideboard, the dining table. Look at this lever on the hammer. When it's up, it shoots the nine .36 caliber rounds like a revolver. When you pull it down, it turns into a .28-gauge shotgun."

"What a concept. LeMat is a genius. But let's put this away and you can show me how you defend yourself without this gun."

"Right. I'll go and change clothes." Sadie took the gun to the drawer in her bedside table. She traded her skirt for trousers and returned to the living room.

"I see you're in men's clothing. It's so much easier to move around when dressed as a man, isn't it?"

"This isn't men's clothing. It's my clothing. I choose to be unrestricted in my movements right now. You would do well to tie up your skirts. Though, you'll look like someone out *of The Arabian Nights.*"

"Yes, I see." She bent forward, grasped her skirt front and back, and tied it in a square knot between her legs. "Ahh. Better. Now we can get on with it."

Sadie laughed and said, "First, Aladdin, help me pull my mattress and featherbed into the middle of this room. It will be much softer to land on. Or you could rub your lamp and ask the genie to put a thick soft cloud all over the floor."

"Very funny," Kate said. "Right. Mattress into living room. Good idea."

Sadie said, "A most useful technique is the hip throw. I am face-to-face with my opponent — that's you. Then I do what looks like a hug, with my body at a right angle to yours, and my head leaning against your left shoulder. Like this."

"Yes?"

"I put my left hand on your right arm, then I grab tight behind your right elbow and scoop your right arm up to pin your wrist under my left arm pit. This way."

"And this all happens fast. Right?"

"Yes. Now I bend my right knee slightly and step my left foot about 12 to 18 inches in front of yours. My two feet now form a V with yours. I pull down hard on your right elbow and push hard on your back with my right hand to tilt you forward. Both my feet now step directly in front of yours, all four facing the same direction."

"That's awkward."

"Yes, but only for a moment. My left heel steps between your feet and on the line made between your two big toes. My right arm is reaching around the back of your waist. My tailbone moves over in front of your right thigh. I look over my left shoulder and pull you around in front of me, pushing with my right hand against your back to topple you over."

"AAagh. Glad you thought to put the mattress there."

"Mmm. Now you try it."

After a few minutes, Kate said, "That's work. I'm going to feel this tomorrow."

"You are doing very well."

"Do you practice it?"

"Huh. Can you imagine practicing this at Brock House? In the parlor? Ha, ha. Seriously, I haven't had anyone to practice with in a long time. I go over it in my mind and move my body in a sort of simulation. Other ways to defend yourself...you can choke an attacker, poke his eyes, or apply pressure to joints -- anything that bends, such as fingers, wrists, elbows, shoulders, or knees."

Jane came to the door. "Kate, come see our alligator hide before it gets dark."

Outside, the ladies joined Jane, who examined the gator hide, suspended over a rope stretched between two trees.

"Oh, my. It really is long, isn't it?"

"Yes. Feel it. You, too, Sadie. It's rough," said Jane.

They felt the drippy, bumpy skin. "Ugh. I don't like to think about this thing," said Sadie.

Kate said, "If our skin were that thick and had soaked in salt water, it probably would feel like that, too."

"Speaking of skin, Kate, do you like snakes?"

"I don't exactly like them. But some are very pretty and have colorful patterns. Why do you ask?"

"I want to show you my snake before it gets dark,"

Kate said, "Ooo, is it venomous?"

"No. She's a sweet scarlet king snake."

Jane disappeared for a moment and returned wearing a two-foot long red, yellowish-white, and black banded snake around her shoulders and neck.

Kate gasped and jumped back. "Jane, that looks like a coral snake, which is deadly."

"No, there is an old rhyme, which helps you tell the difference. 'Red on yellow, kill a fellow. Red on black, friend of Jack.' See, her bands are red, black, yellow, black. No red, yellow. She is smooth. Want to hold her?"

"Hmm. Okay."

Jane handed her over and Kate said, "She does feel smooth... and cool under my fingers. Ooo, I can feel her muscles as she writhes. How do you know it's a 'she'?"

"She laid eggs last year."

"How interesting."

Sadie shuddered. "Great. Now I have two friends who play with snakes. Oh. Look. Lightning bugs."

In the undisturbed areas of the garden, two little beetles turned on their lights.

"I see five, blinking and flying into the treetops," said Jane.

Soon, the whole glade was filled with tiny floating lights that flickered on and off.

"More are coming out every minute. It feels like fairyland," said Kate. "I've never seen so many."

"Maybe you've never been in such a wild place."

"Oh, it's so beautiful. I hate to leave. But I'm going to have to go back soon. May I borrow an oil lamp?"

"Wait. I haven't learned how you Pinkerton agents disguise yourselves," says Sadie.

"Perhaps we can do that tomorrow," said Kate. "Also, you mentioned regional dialects and accents. That conversation could take all day. Maybe you have a break during the day?"

"No. Lavigne is very stodgy about staff hours. But we can certainly look at those things tomorrow night after work."

After Sadie brought the lighted oil lamp, they said their 'good nights.'

Jane drew water and poured it into the bucket of ashes. "Those lightning bugs are really pretty, but it's getting almost too dark to see what I'm doing. Will you help me get this hide off the line and into the lye, please?"

"Of course."

"I need to weigh it down with some of these rocks to keep it fully submerged." She stopped. "Listen. Did you hear that branch crack?"

"Mfpttchooo."

"That sounded like a sneeze coming from over there... Who's there? Come out."

"OK. You asked for it." Sadie hurled one of Jane's fist-sized rocks in the direction of the noise.

"Yeeoouwch."

"SCRUNCH, crunch, crunch, crunch."

And then all was silent.

CHAPTER THIRTY-EIGHT

May 7, 1865 Early Morning

AT BROCK HOUSE HOTEL

Mac and Kate were already on the veranda when Sadie arrived the next morning. Mac dangled a short length of pink yarn with the end wadded into a small ball. Fluffy danced around it, pounced, and caught the tiny lump in her teeth. She 'killed' it, with shakes of her head.

Sadie bent to pat the cat. "Good girl, Fluffy. Practicing for a mouse, are you?" She inhaled deeply. "Mmm, the air is crisp and cool this morning. Kate, did you have any trouble getting back to Brock House last night?"

"No. Why?"

"Right after you left, we scared off someone who was skulking in the bushes."

"Did you get a look at him or her?"

"We didn't. It could've been anybody."

Mac said, "Hmm. A mischief maker or the killer? Is there any reason, besides the fact that you've been asking a lot of questions about the Greim murder, that would cause someone to target you like this?"

"None that I can think of, Mac. Unless it has to do with Aunt Cora's cottage. It can't be about Jane. She was here years before I came. I've only been here a week and a half."

"Sadie, I told you that I knew Cora very well. I've been meaning to tell you that she told me a great deal about you..."

Sadie gulped.

"She said she had you under her wing as a youngster. You spent summers and vacations with her before she moved here. She told me that you lived with her at one point and that she adored you. I know all about your acting career and your whereabouts for the last six years — your work in New York, Baltimore, and Washington. She shared everything and was very proud of you."

Her face flushed. "Oh, no. You mean all this time..."

"Yes, and while these incidents could be about the cottage, because she did help me on many investigations, I'm pretty sure it has to do with the Luther Greim murder. You are causing someone to become alarmed."

"What should I do?"

"Until we catch this killer, don't go out alone. And keep that Lemat close by, at home."

"All right."

"Cora used to say you can do anything you want, Sadie, but that there are gaps in your knowledge --science, math, physics, philosophy, biology, astronomy, classic literature. I've noticed that you are a fast learner. How do you feel about filling those gaps? Does the thought of learning more about those topics appeal to you?"

"Yes. I'd love it, but how can it be done?"

"Kate has brought the most up-to-date books in all these subjects. I think Guillaume Lavigne will give you an hour each day to study with me here on the veranda. And you can read lessons at home."

"Oh, Mac, you've been scheming, haven't you? But it'll never work. You're dreaming."

"No, leave it to me. He owes me. Furthermore, you need, without a cut in pay, a day off from work each week. I understand he has hired, at Jacob's urging, more housekeeping and kitchen help to start next week. That should give you and Daisy some free time."

"I, I don't know what to say."

"Your end of the bargain is to study to the best of your ability, which is considerable. My goal is that you equal or surpass the education of most gentlemen. And say that you will be careful, until this killer is caught."

"'Equal or surpass.' Pinch me. This can't be real."

He sat, with arms crossed, waiting.

"Eeeeeee."

A hawk screamed. Fluffy went into alert hunting mode, skulking along the banister and out into the yard.

"...Yes, of course. Yes. If you arrange it, I will do my best and be careful. Thank you. Thank you both. I realized you were checking me out, Kate. The questions about other employment..."

"You weren't cut out to be a nurse, Sadie. And thanks for sharing your knowledge - showing me how to do a hip throw. It will be very useful."

"Oh, my. I have to go to work. Again, thank you both, for seeing possibilities for me."

Guillaume Lavigne said," Great Caesar's ghost. Why would you want to do that, Mac? Girls don't need math or science. How is knowing about the colors of Mendel's pea pods going to improve her cleaning abilities?"

"She won't be a cleaner for long. I agree with Plato, who said, " A state that does not educate and train women is like a man who only trains his right arm."

"Bah. No girl has the brains to understand Philosophy."

"This one does, Guillaume. And she's already a philosopher."

"That's nuts, Mac."

"A philosopher is a person who is curious. Your cleaner wants to know how everything works and how to live a good life. She's full of questions. John Locke compared the mind to an unfinished room. Her mind will benefit from reading about the ideas and conflicts of the past 3,000 years, Guillaume."

"I'll give it one week. She'll give up, when it gets complicated."

"I don't think so. It will be interesting to see her weigh the ideas of the Sophists."

"Who?"

"They were teachers in ancient Greece who taught that right and wrong varied from place to place and from one generation to the next. Socrates disagreed. He believed in eternal and absolute rules for what is right and wrong. He taught this and, for his efforts, he was sentenced to drink hemlock. Pondering our history of great thinkers teaches us to think."

"If you say so. Have it your way. But now we are even..

Sadie moved through her cleaning without really having to think about it. *Science, math, physics, astronomy. All things I've wondered about and never had the chance to study. Imagine. Classical literature. Beyond 'Hamlet' and 'Midsummer Night's Dream.' Thanks again, Aunt Cora.*

She knocked on Kat's door. "Housekeeping."

"Come in, Sadie. I am almost ready."

Sadie pushed her cart with laundry basket and fresh towels into the room. "Ready for what?" She started her cleaning routine.

"To go with Gator Simmons in his dugout canoe. There is no sign of Buck and I'm going back to New York to stay with my parents."

"Heavens to Betsy. Why don't you wait for a steamer? And I thought you paid for your room through the eighth."

"Yes, I did. But I'm tired of waiting."

"Have you seen Gator's boat, Kat?"

"No, but Bram Maas says he takes people up and down the river, for a fee. He took Harriet and Rev. Stowe to look for real estate."

"His boat is not much bigger than a bathtub, Kat. Yes, he took them to look for real estate. But they put his tiny boat onto a steamer and it took them all to Mandarin. The Stowes spent the night as guests of someone in Mandarin and the steamer picked them up on its way back to Enterprise. He only paddles people a short distance, not over 100 miles."

"Blast it all, Sadie. I'm just so tired of trying to find Buck. I quit my job. I want to be with him, but if I can't find him, I need to go home."

Sadie offered a quick hug then resumed her dusting. "I hear you, Kat. Why don't you go to Orchid Springs tomorrow on the excursion? It will lift your spirits. I'll bet it's been a long time since you've been to a good party. The food is going to be extra special. Then you can take the *Darlington* the next morning."

"That does sound like a more sensible plan. I guess I can wait a little longer. Thanks, Sadie."

That evening on the veranda Mac said, "It's all set, Sadie. We begin next week. The new help starts then. We will meet very early in the morning out here and you will bring all your questions for discussion. You must read your lessons in your own time. Here are the books Kate bought for you with your reading assignments." He handed her a large heavy leather bag."

"And Mr. Lavigne agreed?"

"Whoo-oo." The distinctive whistle of the *Darlington* sounded in the distance.

"He did. Sadie, our studies will sharpen your skills for dealing with deadly situations. But he is slow to see that. He says you are getting 'hoity-toity,' doing schooling. I heard some moaning about 'females don't need education' and how 'women should know that their place is in the home,'" said Mac, with a hearty laugh.

"And the day off?"

"Your first one is this coming Monday, and weekly on Wednesdays thereafter. The day is yours. You can do whatever you choose."

"Oh, Mac. Thank you... Good Heavens. Isn't that Buck, coming off the *Darlington?*"

"Yes. I'd know that bald pate, enormous handlebar mustache, and giant smile anywhere."

Buck bounded toward them and up the steps. "Mac, Sadie. It's good to see you. I know I've ruined everything by running away. But I'm back. Jacob told me that he brought Kat here on the *Darlington*. Is it true? Is she here?"

"Yes, she's here and she's frantic to find you," said Sadie. "This morning, she was so frustrated that she was ready to leave in Gator Simmons's dugout canoe."

"Great Caesar's ghost. I have to go find her. "I'll be back, Mac. We'll be back. I'm not going to let that girl out of my sight."

Buck practically ran to Kat's room. He set his bags next to the door and knocked. "Kat. Open the door. It's me, Buck."

The door flew open. "Buck. I've been so worried. Where were you?" said Kat, as he enfolded her in his strong arms.

"I went looking for you. I like to never found you. If Jacob Brock hadn't told me that he brought you back to Enterprise on the *Darlington,* I might be in Timbuktu by now. Why did you run away?" he said, hugging tighter and tighter.

"Buck. I can't breathe."

"Oh. Sorry. May I come in?"

She held the door open. "Of course."

He set his bags inside the room. "Will you come with me to see Mac? I'm going to tell him everything and I want you by my side when I do it."

"All right."

He took her hand and they made their way out to the veranda, where the early evening sky was a brilliant display of gold, purple, peach, and red.

Sadie sat with Kate and Mac.

"Mac, I have to tell you. I never murdered that man. I wanted to, but I didn't. I could have done it at our homestead, but I didn't shoot him then either... I just ran him off with a double-barreled shotgun. He and his gang came to our homestead near Brooksville and bullied my wife and children."

Kat gasped. "So, it's true. You were already married when you married me?"

"I was, my love. I'm sorry. I thought it could remain a secret and that both of my families would be happy. But I was wrong. I have hurt the people I love the most. And I committed bigamy, which just became illegal. So, I may have to go to jail."

Kat said, "Oh, no, no. This baby needs a father." She stopped and squeezed her eyes closed tight. Then she opened them and said, "What will happen to him now, Mac?"

"Bigamy is illegal, but no money for enforcement has been appropriated. You will have to sort that between yourselves. However, the murder investigation is still ongoing and your traveling salesman will have to stay here until it is finished."

Buck wiped droplets of perspiration from his brow. "Thank you, Mac."

Sadie said, "Why don't you both go on the excursion to Orchid Springs tomorrow. You need a day of fun and relaxation, before you begin your 'sorting.' Jennie Brock said Jacob is bringing a fiddler to play for dancing tomorrow. Some happy music will raise our spirits."

"That sounds wonderful," said Kat. "And perhaps I can then do as you suggested earlier, Sadie — get a steamer back to New York. I'll stay with my parents there, until Buck is released and can join us."

Jane Marsh opened the front door of Brock House and emerged into the fresh breeze of the evening. She joined the small group on the veranda.

After a nod to them all, she said, in a quiet voice, "Whew. The extra baking for tomorrow's party is done. And you are going to love the special food, if I do say so myself."

She chuckled and turned to Sadie and Kate. "Are you ready for our walk to the cottage? You are coming, aren't you, Kate?"

"I wonder what his other wife will think about all this?" said Sadie.

"You might be surprised," said Kate. She set the oil lamp from last night's trip swinging on her arm for their walk to the cottage. "Many women would be happy to be supported, but not have a 'Lord and Master' around to 'do for' all the time."

Jane said, "But raising children on a homestead property would be much more difficult without a partner or close neighbors."

Kate said, "Mormon men have multiple wives, who support each other and join together in raising the children."

"I understand that Lincoln told the authorities in Utah to look the other way concerning polygamy, as long as the Mormons didn't join in the war," said Sadie. "Would either of you stay in a marriage like that?"

"No," said Jane.

"My husband died, leaving me to fend for myself. I'm not sure I want another marriage, of any kind," said Kate. "I like my freedom."

"Ah, here we are. I'm going around back and see if the scales on the gator hide are ready to release," said Jane. "I'll be in, in a minute."

Inside, the two ladies lit candles. Sadie put the Lemat gun on the table. And they turned their thoughts to investigation.

Kate said, "In the city, we take photos of the crime scene and have a medical examiner or coroner investigate. They autopsy the bodies in murder cases like yours. I think you could do that here, too, in future."

"Really? But for that we'd need a photographer and a coroner."

"You could easily learn photography."

"Hmm. That leaves the coroner."

"Yes. Other than that, you've done most of the things that we do - take witness statements, canvas the neighborhood and interview people, and investigate in plain clothes. I think you could investigate in disguise for undercover work, like I did in Baltimore."

"How do you go about disguise?"

"When Alan went to Baltimore, he went as a wealthy midwestern stockbroker. He researched the character in advance to make sure his clothing was just right and his accent was authentic. This disguise allowed him to mix with rich Baltimore businessmen."

"So, you study characters, like an actress would. And practice your accents and dialects?"

"Absolutely. And, during free times, we prepare several different kinds of characters in advance."

Jane came in. She said, "Tomorrow is the excursion to Orchid Springs. We should try on our party dresses." She gave a wry smile. "I get to serve punch all day."

"When you get a break, we'll sit together and enjoy your delicious food. You must come, too, Kate. It will give me someone interesting to talk to. I'm going to be stuck next to 'the-very-important-next-governor-of-Georgia' Neville Beaumont."

"Your job tomorrow, Sadie, is to circulate around the crowd and speak to as many people as you can. Be lively. Flirt. And listen. You, too, Jane. You will be in the perfect position to hear conversations around you. That's how we find information, connections between people, and their secrets."

Jane said, "That makes me feel better about my job for tomorrow."

"And the well-stocked bar, with a great deal of extra liquor available, will be very popular," said Sadie. "Guests can buy more drinks after their first free rum punch. They may let down their guards."

"Good. It's settled then. You are both investigating, while on the *Darlington* outing. Let's hope the rum punch loosens tongues as people dance, eat, and gossip. I may not go. I didn't bring anything suitable to wear."

"Wait. I have something that would be just right for you," said Sadie. She grabbed a candle. "Get that other light, Jane, and come with me, both of you." They went to the wardrobe in her bedroom. "Here it is. Try on this robin's-egg blue silk."

Kate held her arms in the air as her two friends slid the shiny silky dress over her shoulders. "Ooo. That feels lovely. It's soft and slippery."

"And it fits you perfectly," said Jane. "That is much prettier than any bubble skirt."

Sadie said, "You shall have it. Aunt Cora would be delighted. Wear it in good health."

They helped Kate shrug out of the party dress and fold it into a smooth parcel.

"Thank you, Sadie. It is beautiful. This is most generous. And now I have something for you, Sadie." She reached down and lifted her petticoats a couple of inches to reveal a firm leather pouch, which she unstrapped from her ankle. "This is my Colt Pocket 'five-shooter. It's a light .31 caliber cap and ball five shot revolver. And here's a snug leather ankle holster for you. I think you'll find this is comfortable to wear for long periods."

"Oh, I couldn't possibly accept such a gift. And I'm not sure I want to carry a gun at all, let alone 'for long periods.'"

"I have only carried it when I deem myself to be in great danger. That is your situation this very minute. Your questions have made someone try to get rid of you. You need it. And I want you to have it. I can easily replace it when I return to the city, but you really must wear it right now."

Jane chimed in. "Sadie, I think you have to. You are brave and fierce, but this killer probably is always armed. I can't bear to think of him hurting you."

"If you are sure, Kate..."

"I'm sure. Now, I must be going. I'll take your oil lamp again, please, and we'll meet on the steamer tomorrow."

Jane said, "In the morning, we will bring you some blue or yellow flowers for your hair. Something fragrant, perhaps verbena or roses."

Chapter Thirty-Nine

May 8, 1865 Early Morning

At Snow Bird Cottage, Brock House Hotel, "Darlington"

Delicate yellow rays of morning light filtered through the trees in the back of the cottage as Jane, with a basket over each arm, started out the rear door of Snow Bird Cottage.

She said to Sadie, "I know we are supposed to be there early, but I promised to gather some blossoms for Jennie. She and Hattie are decorating the *Darlington* with garlands and flowers. Will you help me gather some?"

"Yes, but won't they just wilt and seem sad?"

"Not if you look for woody stems and waxy leaves. Waxy magnolia blossoms and leaves are good. We have some lilies and gladioluses that would look pretty."

"I'll grab a basket and clip the yellow and red roses. She will want something colorful."

They circled the house and grounds with their baskets and clippers. "How about sweet Williams and strawflowers?" said Sadie.

"Yes, and verbena." Jane pointed. "Those small shiny red peppers will add color and we can use them for meals tomorrow."

When the baskets were full to overflowing, they went inside to put on their party dresses.

I haven't had this green silk dress on since I wore it on stage in Washington. I shudder to think about that place.

Jane came in. Sadie said, "That beige linen dress is lovely, Jane, but it's a little loose."

"Yes, I noticed. I have lost some flesh since we both started walking back-and-forth to Brock House. Here, I brought you a spider lily for your hair. Let me weave the stem in near your chignon. And these sweet Williams will look pretty on your shoulder against the green silk. There. You look festive."

"Thanks. Now you. Turn-about is fair play. Zephyr lilies, I think, for your braid. Hold still. Mmm. Stunning. They look like white stars blazing in your jet-black crown. You are party-perfect. Are we ready to go?"

"Yes."

At Brock house they carried their baskets down the dock and boarded the *Darlington*. "Jennie and Hattie have been busy already. Look at the pretty garlands. Let's take these flowers to the big salon."

Hattie looked up and said, "Wonderful. More flowers. Good morning, Sadie, Jane. Looks like it will be a beautiful day for it. Thanks for raiding your garden."

"We are glad to contribute. I have to go and see to the cleaning that Mr. Lavigne thinks is essential before we leave. And Jane is going to the kitchen, but we'll see you at castoff time."

"All right. I can't wait to taste your culinary specialties, Jane."

Brock House was full to overflowing with guests, who were mingling their perfumes and rustling their silks and satins in the halls. *Excitement is in the air, and there is Neville, decked out in splendor. He could already be governor.*

"Good morning, Sadie," he said, with his eyes glowing as he took in her appearance. "You look as regal as a queen. We are going to have an enchanted day. Come and let me introduce you to some guests, who are almost royalty, the Vanderbilts, from Staten Island."

"Neville, I have some things to attend to. I'll meet you here just prior to cast off."

Oh, my. He wasn't expecting that and his momentary frown looked daggers at me — a little scary.

"Why, yes, my dear, though what could be so important on a day of fun and frolic, I can't begin to guess."

We are displeased.

He recovered quickly, though. She gave a little wave and then went on to attend to business.

Sadie finished and whipped off her apron, just as the guests were beginning to stream out to the flower-bedecked steamer. "There you are, Neville. You do look extremely handsome today," she said, as she took his arm. *A little oil on troubled waters never hurts.*

Mac and Kate approached. In a low voice, Mac said, "Thank you, Sadie, for your gift to Kate. Cora would be pleased."

She smiled at him and turned to Kate. "Here. I saved these yellow rosebuds for your hair. Let me weave them in for you. Ooo, you look pretty."

"Thank you, Sadie. I feel very elegant."

As they boarded the steamer, she turned and noticed that Kat and Buck came aboard right behind them. *They look like they're in a world of their own.*

Sadie looked forward and saw Ava in yet another bubble skirt. *Does the woman never learn? Oh, well. It will probably be so crowded that she can't possibly fall down the companionway.*

During the first part of the trip, Sadie dutifully accompanied Neville, while he wandered about and introduced himself to many influential people. They were on the stern, when she caught sight of Mac and Kate. *Salvation.* "Excuse me just a moment."

"Have you learned anything interesting?" said Kate, under the noise of the crowd and the paddlewheels.

"No, but Neville's eyes reflect dollar signs every time he meets another rich possible donor."

The Merritt sisters moved close to the trio of investigators. Martha said, "Seeing you like this on the steamer, Sadie, reminds me of that night, the night we docked in Enterprise. Everyone had gone to bed and it was very quiet. It may have been early morning, perhaps. I couldn't sleep and I felt my way down to the veranda, where I sat in a corner deck chair. I was enjoying hearing the night sounds, owls and frogs and so forth, when someone crept out the front door and walked right past me."

Mac said, "Did you see who it was?"

"No, sorry."

"They didn't see you?"

"It was new moon that night and very dark, so I guess he didn't see me. I think it was a he, because I got the impression of trousers and a man's top hat."

"Unfortunately, three quarters of the men on this excursion are wearing top hats. But, that's good, Martha. Then what happened?"

"After a while, I heard a big splash. It was like a gator hit the surface of the water with his big ol' muscular tail. It is mating season for them and I heard some males bellowing. Maybe that's what it was."

Or maybe it was a person falling into the water, thought Sadie.

"Then what?"

"He came back from the steamer very fast and took care to close the door quietly, when he went back in."

"Anything else?"

"What I remember most is the perfume that wafted in a stream along behind him. It was a distinctive smell, like cedar trees, with lavender and oranges. I smelled it again here tonight and it brought all that back. I thought you should know, that's all."

"Who smelled like that, Martha? Who smelled like the man you saw?"

"I don't know, Mac. There are so many people milling around and the breeze is carrying perfume away."

Neville appeared at Sadie's side. "There you are. Let's go to the big salon and see what kind of food they put out for us," said Neville, taking her arm. "And I understand that the little salon is generously stocked like a bar, for this trip. I need more than that glass of rum punch."

Jane was circulating in the large salon, with her tray of glasses.

Sadie said, "Look, Neville. Isn't that James Rockefeller over there? He seems to want to talk to you. I won't have any more to drink, but you go ahead. I'll join you in a minute."

Jane said, "I saved a couple of plates for us, Sadie. This crowd is like vultures. As soon as we opened the door, they fell upon the food as if they hadn't eaten in a week."

"They just haven't seen the likes of your spectacular party food and have been eating plain for the last four years, Jane. It all looks marvelous. Put down that tray and let's go someplace quieter."

They carried their plates up to the hurricane deck, which was much less crowded. "I see no bubble skirts made it up this far," said Sadie.

They settled out of the wind. Sadie tasted a tartlet. "Mmm, a smoky flavor on my tongue."

"Yes. Smoked bass from our smokehouse paired with crisp cress, from the bank of the lake. Do you like it? I used lime in the mayonnaise."

"It's wonderful." Her next choice also pleased her palette.

They shared delicate pastries, cakes, and information. "... if one can believe her, and I think we can, it tells us the killer is a man who wears perfume and a top hat, so it probably isn't a deckhand."

Jane said, "Or she's lying and it is her sister, or Martha herself...or both of them, who killed Mr. Greim." She sighed. "Jane, I just don't know who to believe, anymore." She sighed. "But, I suppose, I need to go dance with my knight in shining armor. They've cleared the whole cargo deck for dancing. Can you hear the fiddler from the salon? He played some frisky tunes while we were circulating on the stern. "

"The fiddler is okay, but I would prefer to hear some Congo drums and a good rumba. I suppose it's time to pass around trays of cheese straws."

When the *Darlington* arrived back in Lake Monroe, everyone, including Neville, declared that the excursion was a big success. "I am a little disappointed, though, Sadie. I heard that General William Sherman was going to be on this trip," said Neville, tucking her hand firmly under his.

Jacob tooted the distinctive whistle, to let anyone left in the town of Enterprise know that they were docking. Kate appeared next to Sadie. "I am going to say goodbye now, because I'm leaving early in the morning and you won't be at Brock house. It's your day off. Good luck with your investigation and your new lessons. May I give you a hug?"

Sadie answered in a low voice, "If you won't throw me." And they both laughed.

The *Katie Asbell* was already at the dock. Christian waved from the bow of the steamer. *That boy has made a full recovery. Something looks different about him, though. What is it?* She waved back.

Then she saw the captain of the *Katie Asbell*. Noah stood greeting many friends as they disembarked from the *Darlington*.

Be quiet, heart. Did you really have to stop a beat at the sight of him?
He is such a handsome fellow. Too bad he thinks you could be a murderer.
But enough of that.
Relax and be casual. Tomorrow's a day off.
What will I do?

CHAPTER FORTY

May 9, 1865 Morning

AT SNOW BIRD COTTAGE

T he day dawned bright and cloudless. Sadie yawned. *What was different about Christian, yesterday? His clothing?* She sat up.

Eureka. I've got it. "Jane, I know what was peculiar about Christian at the dock after the excursion." Sadie sat on the edge of her bed.

"What's that?" said Jane, as she came in.

"He was wearing Luther's ace-of-spades, silver belt buckle."

"The ace of spades? That's a powerful symbol of death, or at least bad luck. Why would Christian wear such a thing?"

"More important questions are, where did he get it? Is he the killer? Did he take it off the dead Luther, before he chucked him in the lake?"

"Oh, mercy."

"But to answer your question, some people laugh at that superstition and use it to frighten others. They fashion themselves as the bringer of bad luck or death. It gives them power over those who are superstitious."

"But Christian is just a boy. He probably doesn't even know that it's supposed to be bad luck."

"Maybe. Or maybe he's trying to use some of Luther's power for himself. We know he hated Luther."

"I would too, if he had killed my brother and sister," said Jane.

"Mac says Christian's too young to have killed Luther. He sees him as too small to have pitched that heavyweight overboard. But he might have lured him out of his cabin."

"He could have had help."

"True. Luther was well-liquored. And I can see a boy like Christian not wanting to let a shiny belt buckle go to the alligators. Whichever way it is, will you be sure, Jane, to go tell Mac our suspicions?"

"Yes, I will."

"I mean, first thing, before you do anything else. Mac needs to know, so he can investigate while the *Katie Asbell* is still in Enterprise."

"All right. Yes, I'll tell him as soon as I get there. I'm going now. Enjoy your day."

"Thank you. Have a pleasant walk."

After Jane left for work, Sadie sat with her thoughts bouncing from one topic to another. *Can that boy really be a murderer?* And then...*This isn't fair. Everybody needs a day to rest and to do as they choose. I can't be happy until everyone else has a day off, too. I'm going to talk to Jacob Brock about it. Tomorrow.*

On her bedside table sat a bowl of porridge with fruit. *Jane's so thoughtful.*

She munched and thought. *I'm completely out of fever bark and willow. The woods behind the cottage are right for growing those. This can be a day of exploration. I'll take the biggest basket and the knife gifted to me by Walt Whitman.*

Sadie prepared for her walk. *Ahh. I probably should carry Aunt Cora's small hatchet for boneset and knotgrass. Now where is my broad-brimmed hat?*

While rummaging in the wardrobe, she came upon a ball of bright red yarn. *Hmm. Hansel and Gretel left breadcrumbs. Perhaps I can leave snippets of yarn.*

She spied the LeMat on her bedside table behind the oil lamp. *That gun is heavy and cumbersome for carrying in the woods. I don't expect many alligators there. I'm just going to hunt some bark and leaves. Why would I need it? I could take Kate's Colt pocket five-shooter, which is under my pillow. But I can just imagine getting it tangled in some briar patch. I don't need it either. I'll leave them here.*

In her exuberance for the task, she set out without regard for her promise to Mac, that she wouldn't go anywhere alone.

It's a good thing I brought that red yarn. All these palmettos look alike. She pulled out her foraging knife, cut off a length of yarn, and tied red fluff to a spear-like, pointed, gray-green frond.

This undergrowth is dense, dense, dense. What folly it would be to try moving about here in a long skirt. Thank God for trousers.

Rippling waves of wispy white cloud spread across the brilliant blue sky overhead. *I could be in a Monet painting, like the one I saw in New York. I wonder if Monet hears birds and crickets and frogs while he paints? He probably doesn't have to kick through the underbrush to set up his easel.*

Oh, that marshy area ahead is covered with fresh green willow. I could fill my basket right there. Better leave some room in the basket, though, in case I find a fever-bark tree.

She cut willow and did a bit of daydreaming. *I remember Dr. Mary Walker's words... "Willow will never be as effective as opium, but it's available. We can't always say that about opium."*

She was a good teacher. "Evangeline, be careful of the proportions you use when preparing the fever bark or willow tinctures."

Is that a fever-bark tree? Sweet little tree growing in the swamp. Much like the ones in Washington. Oh, joy. And it's blooming. Very showy flowers, white, tinted with red.

Yay. In my own backyard, so to speak. Or somewhere in the 160 acres behind the cottage. I can brave this thicket, if it means I'll get some bark from that tree. And off she went. Kick. Step ahead. Stump. Another step ahead. "Whew." At a clearing, she stopped for a rest.

Something made noise behind her.

"Rustle. Rustle. Rustle."

She turned to look.

Nothing.

The commotion stopped.

It's probably just squirrels chasing each other through the leaves. The pretty redhead trudged ahead toward the tree. When she stopped for a breath, she heard it again.

"Rustle. Rustle. Rustle."

She froze... listened.

What in the Sam Hill? The sounds, at a distance, stopped.

She walked across a small clearing and into the brush.

Behind her she heard small sounds. "Swish. Scrunch."

A deer? Stepping on a branch?

She stopped.

The sounds stopped, too.

Some hunter? Who thinks I'm a deer?

Silence.

My weathered beige palm-frond hat...

Is not shaped like a deer.

What's following me? Deer would run away. A predator of some kind? Which makes me what? Prey?

A small knot of fear clinched her stomach. Moving toward the fever tree again, she thought, *Big black bears live here. They think I'm stealing their berries?*

Oh, folly, fudge, and flummediddle.

It's not funny, Sadie. Bears and panthers and wild boars are at home here. They all have big sharp teeth.

Don't panic. Just turn around and go back. Do not run. Go slowly and make a lot of noise. Maybe you can scare it away.

I already made noise with my kicking and stomping. What else can I do?

The Magic Flute! She opened up her mouth and sang the *'Queen of the Night'* aria, at the top of her lungs.

...Silence. No birdsong. No bees. No crickets. No predators.

Mozart to the rescue. It's been months since I sang that every night in front of the stage curtain, during the scene change. That did the trick, though.

She continued to the tree. *All right. Chop small branches. Fill the basket.*

Now, three pieces of red yarn for the fever tree. That will make it easy to see it next time, when it won't be in bloom. If I leave other snippets of yarn on the path, I can find my way back here.

I would like to find some boneset.

More exploring rewarded her with an overflowing basket of medicinal herbs. Tired, but feeling successful, she began to retrace her steps.

Where is the red yarn? Maybe it was over there. She looked. And looked.

It's gone.

Where did it go?

Maybe somebody is following you. The same somebody who plays games with knives and alligators. This could be their 'red yarn' game. Now you see it, now you don't.

A wave of fear made her shudder.

Okay. I am scared. That's all right. I am lost. That's all right, too.

How can I find my way back to the cottage?

Is that the trickling of a stream I hear? She walked toward the sound. *A stream! I don't remember this.*

Can I follow it? To the river?

No! Streams run all over the swamp.

Well, I am truly lost. At least there are not many snakes. Maybe the gators ate all of 'em. It's more likely that my kicking and stomping scared them away.

Loud powerful drumming on wood slashed through the quiet of the forest. Her nerves jangled. A raucous rattling call followed.

Then came a cry of "cuk, cuk, cuk."

Her heart thumped in her chest. *What? A pileated woodpecker.* Silly girl. *Symbol of new possibilities and courage.*

Oh, don't fly away. I need both of those things. She watched him soar through the canopy.

I was feeling alone. Now I'm really alone.

"Snap."

Or am I?

What was that?

Did somebody remove the red yarn in the hope that I'd get lost and perish?

Dreadful thought.

Maybe I just got turned around.

If I walk in ever larger circles, I might find the yarn path.

She looked up at the sun, and then walked through underbrush north ten steps. She poked a crooked stick upright into the ground. Sadie walked west ten steps, south twenty steps, east twenty, north twenty, and west again ten, where she found her stick.

No yarn.

And I don't recognize anything.

Okay, make the search area bigger by ten steps...

What the Sam Hill? I must be dreaming. Is that...? It was just a glimpse.

She squinted against the sun and looked hard in distant deep shadows.

A somewhat hunched, barefooted person with leathery wrinkled skin, hooded eyes under craggy brows, drooping salt and pepper mustache, and wearing frayed pants with rope belt and his battered, four-inch-brimmed, palmetto hat. It is! Gator Simmons.

Oh, joyful dream... The red yarn is back. But can I follow it home?

Or did someone put it in a different place to lead me farther into the swamp?

CHAPTER FORTY-ONE

May 9, 1865 Very Early Morning

AT BROCK HOUSE HOTEL DOCK

T he smell of lemon scented cleanser floated up to Noah as he leaned over the side of *Katie Asbell* to get some leverage on the long-handled mop, with which he was cleaning the side of the paddle wheeler. Movement over by the hotel entrance caught his eye. *Here comes Jacob with two other fellows. I guess he's getting ready to leave this morning, too.*

Heels clicked on the deck in the early morning fog, as the men strode down the dock towards him. "Good morning Noah. Don't you have deck hands to do that for you?" said Jacob, in a joking manner.

"Oh, I do, but they are all busy with something else. Introduce your friends, Jacob. They must be friends or they wouldn't be here just at the crack of dawn with you. What brings you all here this early?"

"Zebulon Greene, Simon Donald meet Noah Asbell, owner and captain of this pretty steamer. Permission to come aboard, Captain. We would like to talk with you."

"Permission granted. Come around this way. We'll go to the salon."

Christian sat chatting with Cookie in the salon. "Here, Christian. Carry on the cleaning I started." Noah handed him the mop with directions on the cleaning. "Now, then. Have a seat, gentlemen, and tell me what's on your mind."

"Zeb is planning to reopen the small boarding house on Thayer Street and Simon, who owns the Mercantile store on Taylor Street, is going to add souvenirs and other items to appeal to tourists. They came to me this morning with an idea that sounds good."

"What does it have to do with me?"

"We think steamer service to Enterprise every two days would better serve the tourists and help us, too," said Mr. Donald.

Jacob said, "I could leave for the four-day round trip today. In two days' time, you could leave for that same route: here to Palatka and up to Jacksonville, then turn around and travel Jacksonville back to Palatka and back here to Enterprise. Staggering the trips by two days will give tourists more flexibility."

"But, if you leave today, then I would have to stay here today and tomorrow at your dock. Eight passengers are planning to leave with me this morning to go back to Jacksonville. What happens to them?"

"To offer what I think is better service, I am willing to take your eight passengers at no cost to you or them. You will have two days to relax. And while we're talking, I have never mentioned docking fees to you, because none of us were making any money.

"You're right."

"I anticipate that soon we will be making money by the bushels. Members of the public have four years' worth of pent-up desire to get away, have fun, and see new landscapes. I think this switch will be good for business. We can talk about docking fees next year."

"Meanwhile, you could take your steamer across the lake to Mellonville and see if there's any interest in ferry service between our two towns," said Zeb. "I have a small property there. It could become a boarding house, if all things work to the good."

Jacob said, "When I get my other boat back, we can even talk about each of us having time off. But we have to start making money first. Can we shake on it, Noah? To stagger our trips by two days so that we have a steamer docking at Brock House every other day?

"I think tourists will be well pleased to have a boat available three times a week. Yes, gentlemen, I agree. I will leave on the 10th." They shook hands all around. "Zeb, do you want a ride to Mellonville today, if my crew is amenable?"

Chapter Forty-Two

May 9, 1865

In the Woods and Swamp Northeast of Snow Bird Cottage

*W*hat are the possibilities?

    I can think of three. This could be yarn I placed here, which will lead me home.

  Or somebody moved my yarn and placed it here, so I will go further into the swamp. It will not lead me home.

  Or the mean person removed it and discarded it to get me lost. And somebody else picked it up and put it back on the right path to help me. It will lead me home.

  Two of the three possibilities say follow it to the cottage. I'll not try to think of any more. It would complicate my odds.

  Go with the yarn.

CHAPTER FORTY-THREE

May 9, 1865 Early

AT BROCK HOUSE HOTEL

Jacob came up the front steps of the veranda with Zeb and Simon after their meeting with Noah. "Good morning, Mac," chorused the three smiling businessmen.

Mac nodded. "Gentlemen. What brings you out so early?"

"Good news Mac," said Zeb.

Simon said, "It is a great morning for business, Mac. We have a new agreement that will be profitable for everybody."

"A steamer will be docking at Brock house every other day starting today," said Jacob. "Noah and I plan to stick to our four-day round trips, but stagger our arrivals by two days."

"That'll certainly please travelers," said Mac.

"It will make Enterprise seem more accessible," said Simon.

"We will see you later, Mac. Work to do, you know. *Darlington* will be leaving this morning, while Noah will stay here another couple of days." They hurried off.

Moments later, Jane appeared and headed toward Mac's deck chair.

When he saw the plump cook step onto the veranda, he thought, *I hope Sadie hasn't changed her mind about keeping the LeMat close by at the cottage today.*

"Good morning, Jane. Have a seat. You're out early today."

"Yes. Thank you, but I'm only going to stay a minute or two. I have an urgent message from Sadie. She saw Christian wearing a silver ace-of-spades belt buckle yesterday and she thinks it belonged to Luther Greim."

"That is an interesting piece of information, Jane. Thanks for letting me know."

"You're welcome. I promised Sadie I'd tell you, before the *Katie Asbell* leaves for Jacksonville this morning. I have to go to work now. Goodbye." With that, she hurried away.

Oh, ho. I can think of a host of stories to explain that circumstance. He killed Luther and took it off of him, before pitching him overboard. He found it in the woods or next to the river. Somebody gave it to him, trying to implicate him in the murder. Luther gave it to him, in exchange for something. It isn't Luther's, after all.

No sooner had Jane gone, than Christian left the *Katie Asbell* and trotted up the dock.

"Good morning, Christian," said Mac, from his perch on the veranda. "I hear that you get to stay in Enterprise a while longer."

"Yes. The captain has a new agreement. We are staying here until the 10th."

"Mighty hard to make a living with a steamer, when you are docked."

"Yes, but he said he's paying us just the same. Something about better service for the customers and having a steamer dock at Brock House every other day. He and Jacob Brock shook hands on it."

"I heard. Say, that's a mighty fine silver belt buckle you have there. Is that new? I don't remember seeing you wear it before."

"It's new to me. I got it from Curly, at the Palatka General store. 'Twas the funniest thing. I went in to get some sugarcane and he practically gave this to me. It is a pretty buckle, isn't it? He said it's real silver. It has a card on it, too. I don't play poker, but I've seen the cards they use."

"It is an excellent buckle. May I look at it up-close? We might find out who made it. You would have to take it off first. "

"Okay, Mac."

The boy removed his belt and offered it to Mac for inspection.

Ahh. There are his initials, L.G., scratched on the inside.

"No makers mark. But see these initials here. They tell me that this buckle belonged to Luther Greim."

"Aaack. That slimeball? Ick. I don't want it. Keep it. Throw it away. Bleck. How could I have ever worn such a thing?" He shuddered.

"It's all right, Christian. You didn't know." He patted the young man's shoulder. "Would you do me a favor?"

"Sure, Mac. Just say."

"Then run down to *the Darlington* and find Jacob. Tell him I said to hold up a couple of minutes while I get a bag. I'm going with him. And leave a message for Miss Sadie. Tell her I won't be available for lessons for a couple of days."

"Okay. Then I'll run back to get your bag for you. That dock has gotten rickety. What room are you in?"

CHAPTER FORTY-FOUR

May 9, 1865 Evening

AT SNOW BIRD COTTAGE

*N*ext time I go foraging, I'll take a friend with me into the woods. She trudged up the back path.

Jane came running out of the cottage. "Thank goodness. Where have you been? I've been that worried."

"Foraging. Look at all my materials."

"You spent a whole day in the woods alone?"

"I don't know."

"If you don't know, who does?"

"Well, I spent the day in the woods, but I don't know about the 'alone' part. I need to catch my breath. I'll sit on the back porch and strip the biggest of these branches."

"And I have to de-scale our alligator hide some more. So why don't you tell me, while we both work? And the big news in town is that the *Katie Asbell* is going to be docked at Brock House until the day after tomorrow."

"Oh, no. Did the marshal finally make an appearance? Am I going to have to go to Jacksonville or somewhere?" *AAAhhhh. No, no, no.* "I haven't found the killer yet."

"Nothing like that. No, Jacob Brock made a new agreement with Noah. They are going to separate their trips by two days. Jacob thinks it will provide better service."

Noah will be in Enterprise tomorrow. There goes my heart again. It jumps, when I think about him. What's wrong with me? Stop it. "Speaking of service, everyone who works at the Brock house is excellent at what they do. I think we all deserve a day off once a week and I'm going to talk to Jacob about it."

"He left this morning. He won't be back for three days."

"Oh. I guess three days won't matter, in the great scheme of things."

"We do all work together to create a pleasant place for visitors to relax. It would be only fair for us to have a day to rest. Excuse me, while I go get that skin out of the lye and run it down to the lake for a quick wash. Then you can tell me all about your day of foraging."

Chapter Forty-Five

May 9, 1865

Evening at Palatka

After the *Darlington* docked at Palatka for the night, Mac, with the aid of his gold-headed ebony cane, made his way to the general store.

"Good evening, Mac. It's been too long since you've graced our humble store with your presence," said the proprietress.

Momentarily taking her hand in his, he said, "Fiona, it has at that. It is great to see you looking fit and happy. How are you and Curly getting on?"

"Well, business has certainly improved since the war ended. And Curly is as ornery as ever." She laughed.

"I need to talk to him about a belt buckle that he sold recently."

"Oh, I'm sorry. You just missed him. He went with another fellow to check their 'ham holes.' That's what I call the pig traps they dug all over these woods after the war blockades cut off all our supplies. It's one of the things that kept us going. We smoke whatever they catch and sell to the settlers in these parts."

"Ahh, when do you expect him back?"

"He should be back by tomorrow night. I'm sorry you came all this way. It must be important."

Mac pulled the belt buckle from a pocket of his vest. "Have you seen this before, Fiona?"

"Great Caesar's ghost. Not that again. I told him it was going to be trouble."

"Then, you have seen it?"

"Yes. That simpleton bought it off of somebody for a song and was planning to make a big profit. I told him he had to get rid of it. I thought it was gone."

"When exactly did he buy it?"

"You would have to ask him. I found it three or four days ago and hit the roof."

"Do you know who he bought it from?"

"No, sireee. Ask him. That evil thing caused a giant blowup between us. I was furious. The ace of spades is the mother of all bad luck."

Mac said, "Fiona, I'm spending the night on the *Darlington*, but they're going on to Jacksonville tomorrow. May I spend tomorrow night with you and Curly? I need to find out who sold this buckle to him. And try to get him to come back to Enterprise with me."

"Aww, Mac. That means more days that he won't be getting anything done around here. I told him that buckle is bad luck." Grudgingly, she said, "All right. We'd love to have you for company. It's that buckle I don't want in here."

CHAPTER FORTY-SIX

May 10, 1865

MORNING AT BROCK HOUSE HOTEL

Sadie stepped onto the veranda and looked around for Mac. *He isn't here yet. Oh folly, fudge, and flummediddle. I guess I'll see him at noon, for my lesson.*

She took a last big breath of fresh morning outdoor air and dove back inside. The lemon and lavender scents of the cleaning supplies seemed a little claustrophobic, after the great outdoors.

I read five assignments. I wonder which we'll discuss first? Biology would be interesting.

The hall clock struck twelve and she finished the room she was cleaning. *I'm coming.* When she arrived at the veranda, she found Noah in Mac's chair. Her heart started pounding. "What are you doing here? And where is Mac?"

"Well, hello to you, too," said Noah. "I was waiting for you. Mac said you are supposed to have lessons at noon."

"Noah Asbell, that is none of your business." *How can I be angry with him and attracted to him at the same time?* "And where is Mac?"

"Come and sit. I am trying to tell you."

She sat next to him.

"He's following up that information you gave him yesterday. Mac told me the buckle is definitely Luther's. Christian says that he bought the buckle from Curly at the general store in Palatka. Mac went to Palatka to bring Curly back here, in hopes he can identify the person who sold him the buckle."

Sadie gasped and grabbed his arm. "Noah, that could do it. We could identify the killer. I would be off the hook. You would be off the hook."

"Me? Now see here."

"Mac says that until we catch this killer, it is only prudent to suspect everybody." She paused and released her grasp. "And you think it could be me."

"No. I don't think that, Sadie. I-I I apologize for the other night." He laid his hand atop hers. "May I walk you home tonight?"

Oh, my. Maybe... if I could figure out how I feel. A warm tingle is running up my arm, and my heart is dancing a wild rhythm. But I ought to stop this now. "No, I don't think so. I have to help Jane cut bark from some oak limbs that came down in the storm. She needs at least a bushel to tan that gator hide. It's a big hide. Jane says it may take more. Maybe two bushels." *Stop babbling.*

"Well, then. You ladies need help. I'll just come along and help you chip."

"Oh, Noah. Why would you want to do that?"

His deep brown eyes searched her green ones. He said, "Sadie, I thought you might have figured that out, by now. I would like to see more of you. When I'm away from Enterprise, I miss you. And sometimes I'm afraid for you. I've heard about threats you have received." *There, now. I've said it.*

"How do I know that it isn't you, doing those nefarious things to make me stop investigating?"

He closed his eyes. "Ouch." *It feels like she slapped me.* A long sigh escaped from him. "Is that what you really think? Can you imagine I would do that to you?"

Since I've known you, you've been nothing but kind to everybody in sight. "No. Not really."

"Good. Then let's call a truce. I'll walk you home and help chip bark. You won't accuse me of being a morally reprehensible person."

She stifled a laugh. "All right. Deal."

CHAPTER FORTY-SEVEN

May 10, 1865

EVENING AT PALATKA

"Thank you for your help today, Mac," said Fiona. "I hear Curly coming in the back. And smell that?" She took a deep breath. "He's already started some ham smoking out in the smoke house."

Curly came in and laid a cloth bag on the counter. Fiona gave him a peck on the cheek. "Whooee. We liked'ta got more than we could carry back. And one of our traps had an escape tunnel out the side. Haven't figured out that one."

"A bunny?" said Fiona.

"Yeah. Mebbe. My buddy says they are top rate burrowers. Mac. Good to see you. What brings you to these parts?"

"I came on the *Darlington* yesterday, hoping to talk to you. I've been helping Fee today. She has graciously offered me a bed for the night."

"All right. Give me a minute to rinse my face and hands and we'll start this duck roasting." He pointed at the bag. While he washed, he said, "I already plucked and washed it, Fee. And it's stuffed with wild celery and little onions. It should make a good supper, along with some dandelion greens."

"Mmm. I can hardly wait," said Mac.

Fiona said, "I'll go pick the greens."

"What was it you wanted to see me about, Mac?"

Mac pulled the belt and buckle from a pocket. "What do you know about this?"

"Laws a mercy, not that again."

"Then, you remember it?"

"I remember it, all right. A few days ago, must've been the fourth, I bought it off a hunter. He come in with Gator Simmons, who had saddles of venison to sell."

"Did anyone besides Gator see the transaction? Somebody who would be able to identify the seller?"

Curly scratched his head. "Yep. Big Keller Oates stood there, a-waitin' his turn. I reckon he saw the feller close up."

"Can you describe the hunter?"

"Sure. Black shiny hair and one of those little pointy beards with a skinny mustache. His clothes were nice — too nice for hunting, and he had good manners."

"You have an excellent memory," said Mac.

"Yes, I remember the fellow who sold it to me. I also remember Fiona's reaction to the ace of spades on it."

Earlier in the Palatka Mercantile

"Curly, what in the world are you doing with this ace of spades on display?"

"Now, Fee. Don't get on your high horse. I bought that buckle off a feller for a cheap price. It's silver and I'm gonna sell it for five times what I paid."

"It's an ace of spades, Curly. A symbol of death... and destruction. At least bad luck. It'll bring us bad luck by scaring off all our customers. I am telling you, get rid of that thing fast. Sell it to the next person who walks in."

"What if they don't want to buy it?"

"Then give it away. I don't care. As long as it's out of here."

"Fiona, be reasonable. I can make a good profit. People who aren't superstitious use these symbols to scare other people who are. It gives them power. Somebody will pay a good price for it."

"In the meantime, we won't sell a thing. Every one of our customers will take one look and run out of here as fast as they can go. Curly, listen to me. If you don't sell it today,

I'm going to take it to the wharf and throw it as far as I can. It can't do much harm in the river."

"Blast it, Fee."

Mac said, "What did you do with it?"

"I sold it to Christian Ames for ten cents. Blast it all. I hated to do that. I could've made a good profit on it, if I'd waited for the right person to come along. But it did make the boy happy."

"Curly, how would you like a nice trip on the *Darlington* down to Enterprise? Jacob will be back tomorrow night and he'll head on to Brock House the next day. If you come with me then, to identify the man who sold you the buckle, I will help you around here all I can until then and I'll guarantee the trip won't cost you a cent."

"What is this all about, Mac? Why is this buckle so important, anyway? Fee won't talk to me for a week if I go off gallivanting again so soon."

"It belonged to a blackguard who got himself killed a couple of weeks ago in Enterprise. We think the killer took it off his body, before tossing him into Lake Monroe."

"Great Caesar's ghost. Fiona told me that buckle would be trouble."

"Will you come?"

"All right. But if Fiona stops talking to me, it will be your fault."

Chapter Forty-Eight

May 10, 1865 Evening

Snow Bird Cottage

Sadie and Noah looked up at the blue sky. Their feet crunched along on the shells of the road. A bright red cardinal zinged across their path. "He's in a hurry," said Sadie. *The sun feels warm on my shoulders this evening.* "Mmm. Smell that lemony magnolia."

He took an appreciative deep breath. *Wonderful,* he thought. "Ahh. Did you ever think you would end up in a place of such beauty... and balmy weather?" said Noah, as they walked to Snow Bird Cottage.

Sadie said, "I guess I never thought about it."

"When I was a boy in upstate New York, I liked the cold weather, with snow and ice. But as I grew older and had to work under those conditions, I came to appreciate warmer climates."

He has a musical voice. "I know what you mean. I lived for a short while with my Aunt Cora in Ohio, when I was in my late teens. I love the outdoors, but I don't love having my hands so frozen that I can't open a door. She felt the cold, too. That must be why she moved here."

A long wisp of that beautiful auburn hair is trailing behind her in the wind. I have this intense desire to reach out and tuck it behind her ear. Oh. Have to stop these rogue thoughts. "What was your favorite thing about Ohio?"

"I loved the time I spent with my aunt. She was interested in so many things. But especially I liked working in her garden and using plants, not just for food, but for medicine, too. *I can feel my heart thumping.*

"Is that how you got started making medicine and sharing it?" *She has helped a lot of people with her medicine. I admire that about her. That, and her spirit and beauty. It's like she's a magnet and I'm metal filings. I can't stay away from her.*

"Yes, and then I met Dr. Mary Walker. You've probably heard of her. She was a kind of mentor to me for a while. My parents taught me to be independent and to think for myself. Dr. Walker just built on that notion, with her ideas of equality and clothing practicality. I learned some science from her, too." *But, not the science of why my heart is jumping around like this.*

"I heard you're going to be learning more science from Mac." *Lucky fellow.*

"Yes. That is the plan. But what about you? What did you dream of, as a boy?"

"My parents expected me to study law, but my heart wasn't there. I always liked messing about in boats on the lake behind our house." He laughed. "I guess I'm still messing about in boats, aren't I?" He smiled and held her gaze.

Those deep dark eyes are so attractive. I'm almost dizzy from that look. "Uh, so, are you saying that you're just a great big boy playing with boats and you plan to keep on?"

Ouch. Pretty much. "Yes. I disappointed my parents. They still hope that I will give it up and become a lawyer. Are your parents happy with you living here?"

Nobody cares. "My father, sister, and brother are all seeking their fortunes out west. I doubt they even know I'm here. My sweet mother died when I was in my teens. And now, Aunt Cora, my kindred spirit and anchor for so long, has died. I feel very alone in the world. Sometimes, I am lonely."

He took her hand in his. *Her skin is so soft. Her fingers feel wonderful next to mine.* The peace of the afternoon and mutual sharing joined them. She shivered. "You need never feel lonely, while I'm around." He pressed her hand lightly, then leaned over and swiped a feathery kiss against her forehead. "Do you think you will settle in Enterprise?"

She gulped in air. "I already am settled in Enterprise."

"Permanently, I mean. Will you marry and have a family here?"

Whoa, boy. Go slow. I have to figure out my mixed-up feelings, before I go making any long-term commitments. "I'm perfectly happy single. My last boyfriend cheated on me. And I look at men like Buck, who aren't satisfied with one marriage. The more the merrier, according to them. They would explode, though, if one of their women committed bigamy. No. I'm not sure I want to marry. And you? Will you marry, or are you already married?"

She is beautiful when those green eyes flash. "No. You know I was engaged. Luckily, we realized that we want different things. I wouldn't be happy in the city, and she wasn't going to be happy married to an absentee husband. I'm a boat captain, who, by definition, is gone from home much of the time."

I admire his honesty and knowledge of himself. "Good that you figured that out before tying the knot. Did you have to buy off an angry father, or brothers?"

"Nothing like that. Money never entered into it. We agreed to be friends. Besides, I don't have money. I have debt — for my boat. *And at the rate I'm going, it will be a long time before the boat is mine.*

"I have neither debt nor money. I think of money as just a tool to get what I want or need. I am all right, for now. Ahh, there's Jane, sitting on the front porch. It looks like she is sharpening the hatchet and some knives."

Jane set aside the whetstone and said, "Hello, you two. Have you come to help us chip bark, Noah?"

"Yes, indeed."

She drew her thumb lightly across a blade. "These are sharp enough to start with. Let's chip some bark."

She handed a large butcher knife to Noah, the foraging knife to Sadie, and she hefted the hatchet herself. "The downed oak branches are in the backyard. I put some chairs next to them, so we won't have to hunch over. You go on back. I need to put some water into the cauldron to boil."

"I didn't know we have a cauldron," said Sadie.

"We don't. I'm using our laundry tub. I just thought you would appreciate the Shakespearian aspect of a great tub of boiling oak bark, and the tossing in of an alligator skin... after the 'eye of newt.'"

Sadie chortled with glee. "Double, double toil and trouble...

Jane and Noah joined in. "Fire burn and cauldron bubble." They all three chanted together. Sadie bent over laughing.

"No, Jane. I refuse to be labeled a 'witch.'"

"All right. And to be clear, the cauldron can't be boiling when we put the alligator in."

"You both know Shakespeare," said Noah.

"Yes. Now let's get this bark chipped. Fill up those baskets while I start the fire in the stove and fill up our 'cauldron.'" She turned and headed to the kitchen.

After completing her tasks, she returned to their trio of chairs and took up the hatchet. Soon they had filled two baskets with oak bark. Jane and Noah carried the heavy loads to the kitchen and dumped them into the hot water.

Sadie said, "I'll just sharpen these utensils while you're gone." She retrieved the whetstone and applied it to the dulled edges.

They repeated the process until Jane said, "Enough. I will let the fire go out so the oak tea can cool. I have washed the hide several times to get rid of the ashes. Will you help me check for scales I might have missed earlier?"

"How do we do that?"

"Spread it over that rope between the two trees. We'll move our chairs close and check it with our fingers. It's probably the small ones that I missed. We can squeeze the hide, too. It absorbs things. All the scales, which will feel somewhat hard, must come off, before it's tanned."

They sat in the middle of the backyard. Jane pulled the hide from her big bucket and presented each of them with an end to toss over the rope.

"Ooo. It feels like jelly."

"I suggest we work from the edges to the center. If you feel a scale, rub it gently with your fingers until it releases easily."

They flipped it over once and when they finished, they carried the dripping hide to the kitchen and immersed it in the tanning solution. "Put more bark chunks on the top to hold it down," said Jane.

"Good. Now, your reward is to sit in the twilight and enjoy the lightning bugs. I made limeade and roasted some of what Georgia boys call 'goober peas.' In Cuba they are very popular and we call them 'mani.' Who would like some?"

"If you fixed them, I'll have some," said Noah.

"Me, too."

They snacked on peanuts, sipped, and watched the lightning bugs at the back of the garden. "This reminds me of the song "Goober Peas," said Noah, and he began to sing.

"Sitting by the roadside on a summer's day,

Chatting with my mess-mates, passing time away.

Lying in the shadows underneath the trees,

Goodness, how delicious, eating goober peas."

Sadie added her soprano to his baritone and Jane contributed, in her alto voice.

"Peas, peas, peas, peas, eating goober peas,

Goodness, how delicious, Eating goober peas." They finished in a fit of giggles.

Then Jane started them all singing "Dixie." Sadie gave them the "Battle Hymn of the Republic."

What a beautiful voice she has.

"I am so thankful that this terrible war is finished. I like this song," Sadie said. She sang the first strains of "Ave Maria" by Camille Saint-Saëns. Jane joined her and their duet surrounded the three of them in peace and floated up through the trees, now dark silhouettes against an evening sky.

Mesmerizing. I feel like I'm in church. I, too, am thankful for peace and a slow return to prosperity. And I'm thankful for the possibility of having this woman in my life. He sighed and finally broke the magic spell. "I have an early departure tomorrow. I should be going. Thank you for inviting me. I've had a wonderful time."

"We appreciate your help," said Sadie. "I'll walk you to the road."

Jane said, "Bye. Come back soon. I'm going to give that gator hide a stir."

Noah tucked her hand into his, as they made their way around to the road. "I never knew tanning an alligator hide could be so much fun," he said."

"We are not expecting any more alligator deliveries, so you'll have to think of something else for fun," said Sadie, with a laugh.

I can think of a few things, but there is no way I'm responding to that. "Good night, Sadie." An owl swooped silently in front of them.

"Wisdom and prophecy, I think. Owls, I mean. They symbolize wisdom and often bring prophecies." *Do I see happiness in our future?*

He squeezed her hand and said, "I predict long life and good health for you." He released her.

"And what about you?" she said.

But he was gone into the night.

CHAPTER FORTY-NINE

May 10, 1865 Midnight

AT BROCK HOUSE HOTEL

M artha Merritt sat in a lounge chair on the veranda with her feet up in the moon-light. *The breeze is lovely and cool at this time of night. The air was a little stale in our room.*

I wonder why I can't sleep? This is getting to be a habit. But it's pretty comfortable.

A low rumble sounded from the lake. *The gators at it again,* thought Martha. She closed her eyes and relaxed completely. Her breathing became shallower.

What in the world? She opened her eyes but could see nothing. *Where is the moonlight? Is the pillowcase over my head? No. It's too rough. A stinky burlap bag. Am I dreaming? Pinch me. This is a terrible dream.*

Someone wrenched her hands behind her back. And she could feel cord wrapping around them.

"Spying on me, are you? I'll soon fix that. You're going to be my golden girl."

"Aa," she started to scream. It changed to, "Mpfh," as the burlap was mashed into her mouth and then lifted. "Pfpt. Yeck." A small cloth was stuffed into her mouth and tied there with another one, secured around her head.

Ugh. That foul-smelling bag is back, thought Martha. *How dare he?*

"Up." Her captor jerked her to her feet. He lifted her elbows. She felt a rope tighten around her chest and she got the sense that he tied it in front of her. "Walk."

She writhed and kicked at the place she thought was the source of the voice.

"Thud." She landed a kick.

"Ooof. For that, you get nothing to eat or drink. Down the steps. Now move."

He yanked her along so fast she lurched, trying to stay on her feet over the uneven ground. *He's pulling me into the woods. But I can't fight at this pace. It's all I can do to stand up. My poor house shoes are going to be ruined, traipsing around out here. And this nightgown keeps getting caught on brambles.*

Nightgown. With small ribbon bows. Rows and rows of them. All over the hem and sleeves. Can I rip one off? Yes. Drop it behind you. He'll never notice in the dark. And another.

How many can I reach? Doesn't matter. I'll pull them off and drop them every few minutes until I can't reach any more.

Martha, think.

I must try to make a mental map of where I am. Listen for noises. Count steps. One, two, three, four...twenty. Drop a bow.

She suddenly remembered the perfume of her captor. *That's the same perfume I smelled the night Luther was killed, when I saw someone go out to the steamer in the middle of the night. I think this man is very dangerous.*

She struggled and stumbled along. At 4,032 steps her captor stopped pulling.

"Scree."

A door opening on rusty hinges. Where are we?

He grabbed her upper arm and pushed her sideways. "Sit."

She bent her knees and slumped backwards, breaking her fall with her bound hands. *The dirt feels gritty against my hands, but it's relatively smooth. Tired. Need water.* "Mmm mffmf."

"Save it."

"Scree."

Is he gone? I don't hear anything. What can I do to get myself out of this? Will he come back and be angry that I'm moving around?

Who cares?

Oh, I'm so thirsty.

I'll scoot until I find a wall and something sharp to cut through these cords on my wrists. Maybe a nail.

Time to explore my surroundings.

CHAPTER FIFTY

May 11, 1865

AT BROCK HOUSE HOTEL

It's a beautiful morning for a walk, thought Sadie. *If I get to Brock House early, maybe Noah will still be there.* Her attention was momentarily drawn by a bright, jewel-like, ruby-throated hummingbird, which zipped and hovered near the red turk's cap flowers. *He's so tiny. And his brilliant red and green feathers seem to sparkle in the sunshine.*

"Zooooop."

He's gone. Already slurped up all the nectar.

Noah waved to her from the dock when she got there. "Good morning."

Her heart skipped a beat. *That tight shirt shows off his rippling muscles.* "And a good morning it is, too. I saw a hummingbird."

"Well done. They are beautiful."

"I just came down to say goodbye."

Well, now I rather wish I had taken my father's advice and become a lawyer, thought Noah. *Then I wouldn't have to leave this lovely lady. That would certainly be a more settled life.* He reached for her hand. "I'm glad you did. I had a wonderful time last night. Sorry my job keeps me away so long."

"Don't apologize. It's what you do and you love it," she said. "We'll just appreciate the time we have together."

"Thanks." He gave her hand a little squeeze. "Goodbye. See you in four days."

"Bye." She turned and strode up the dock to Brock House.

"Meow. Meow." When Sadie stepped onto the veranda, she scooped up the plaintive Fluffy. "I know. I miss him, too. It doesn't feel right, does it?"

I want to talk to Mac. I have questions about Physics and Biology. He is such a fixture here. Both of my favorite men have gone off in boats. There's that lonely feeling again.

She stroked the scrappy mouser. "Guess I will go inside and get started." As if she understood, Fluffy twisted from Sadie's arms and bounded away around the corner.

The lonely cleaner donned her apron and gathered her things. "Knock, knock."

"Housekeeping." Mary Merritt opened the door, with a frown on her face. "Oh, Sadie. Thank goodness. Come in."

"Good morning, Mary. Is something wrong?"

"I don't know. Have you seen Martha? She was gone when I got up this morning. There is no note, telling me where she is. I can't think what to do." A tone of alarm in her voice revealed her fear.

She sounds very worried. Sadie bent forward and gave a quick hug to the older woman, who had been such a help when Christian was ill. "I wouldn't worry. She probably just went out for an early morning walk and stayed longer than usual. It is a beautiful day."

"You think so? I hope you're right."

"Yes. Now I will get this room shipshape before she gets back," said the redhead and she started whisking her broom across the floor.

A few minutes later, Mary was back to her cheerful self. *It's amazing what a little small talk and a sparkling clean room will do for a person's outlook.* "Bye, Mary. I'm sure Martha will be back soon."

She cleaned several quiet empty rooms and then she came to Neville's. "Hello Sadie. Come right in."

"You sound out of breath, Neville. Are you all right?"

"Oh, yes. Quite all right, my dear girl. Just ran up those stairs too fast this morning."

She started her cleaning routine. "I'm surprised you aren't out hunting. Aren't Bram and Buck out with Gator Simmons?"

"Yes, they are. I decided to go on my own and stay closer to the hotel. I may put my feet up and take it easy today."

"That sounds like a perfect plan for a vacation."

"I've been thinking about investment along the Saint John's River. You would like that, wouldn't you, Sadie, if I moved part of my operations here?"

"Um, that would be nice for you. Neville." *And how long before you have everybody bowing to you?*

"It looks like the whole world is coming here to Enterprise. I may not have to travel for my campaign much at all," Neville said, with a laugh. "But, seriously, I have to go to New York. Will you come with me, Sadie?"

"What?" *Whatever made you think I would say 'yes' to such a question, Neville?*

"I need a personal assistant and you would be perfect. Think about it. I'm sure I can pay you more than you're earning here."

He can't entice me and now he thinks he can buy me? "No, I can't possibly do that, Neville, but thank you for the offer. It's very generous of you." *This room looks clean. I pronounce you 'finished.'* "I'm done for today. Bye."

Late in the afternoon the energetic cleaner came upon Mary Merritt in the hall. "Thank heavens, I found you. When I awoke from my nap, I found this under the door."

She produced a paper printed with these words: **IF YOU WANT TO SEE MARTHA AGAINf, LEAVE $2000 IN CASH ON THE BENCH IN THE SOUTH GARDEN BY SUNSET TOMORROW.**

"Great Caesar's Ghost. What do we do now?" said Sadie.

"Don't say that. I thought you would know how to fix this. We don't keep cash. All of our money is in property and buildings. How can we get that much by tomorrow?"

"Don't panic, Mary. Let's go to your room and discuss it."

"All right," said the older woman. She turned and marched away with purpose.

Sadie called after her, "It's quitting time. I want to go to the kitchen and get Jane. We can trust her to help us. I'll meet you in your room."

"Whatever you think is best."

In the kitchen Jane said, "Have you had dinner?"

"Jane! Martha's been kidnapped. Mary and I need your help to figure out what to do."

"Well, help me dish up three plates of this smoked ham and we'll carry them to Mary's room. She must be worried sick. This is a terrible thing, but she will do much better on a full stomach."

Mary sat in a chair by the window and looked out, as if she might see her sister walking toward the building. "You came."

"We brought food. You must eat," said Sadie.

"Thank you. I've been trying to think who would do such a thing and I've come up with nothing. We have no enemies. We do have some business rivals, but they would not do such a thing. This sounds like a desperate person, with little or no money, who sees us as rich."

Jane said, "When did you see her last?"

"Last night at bedtime," said Mary.

"Then she's been gone the better part of a day," said Sadie. "Is everything all right between the two of you?"

"Yes, of course. We were enjoying riding the steamer up and down the Saint John's River."

"Any harsh words or arguments lately with anyone? Something that would make a person angry with her or you?"

"No. And before you ask, we don't flash large amounts of banknotes around. We use very little cash. If someone knows our history, they might think we are rich. That would be right after we have sold our rum. But almost all the proceeds have to go back into the business."

"Jane and I don't have any money to help you. Do you have any friends here who would be able to raise that amount of cash by tomorrow?"

"No, probably not. We have friends here, but none that I would ask to hand over $2000."

"Then it isn't likely that we will be able to pay the ransom. Our alternative is to find Martha. If we were kidnappers, where would we hide a lady for a day or two?"

Jane said, "I've heard them tell, in the staff room, about a couple of small huts, hunting blinds, really, and some smoke houses that are back in those woods behind the hotel. Maybe we could find out more about them."

"If we start looking in there, we could end up in Saint Augustine," said Sadie.

"Our veteran hunters would know. Let's get Bram, Neville, and Buck to help us find them," said Mary.

Sadie said, "They probably would know, but what if one of them is the kidnapper? They all know you and the reputation of your plantation, Mary."

"She's right. We need somebody who doesn't think of you as owners of a prosperous plantation," said Jane.

"Gator Simmons. He takes people hunting all around here and he's probably never heard of you. He keeps to himself. He would know."

"Would he talk to us?" said Mary.

"The real question is, can we find him in time?" said Sadie.

CHAPTER FIFTY-ONE

May 11, 1865 Before Sunrise

IN AN OLD SMOKEHOUSE

*C*ome on, come on. I've been sawing at this rope for hours. She sighed. Be patient. Don't give up.

Finally, the rusty nail cut through the cord and Martha freed her hands from behind her back.

"Whoooo."

What a relief. Now to take this stinking bag off my head and get rid of this stuff in my mouth.

She stood and flexed her arms, after hours in a cramped position on the floor. *I know it's locked, but I might as well try the door.*

It opened.

He must've been pretty sure that I would just lie there cowering, or go to sleep. What kind of kidnapper leaves the door unlocked? Does he want me to get out?

Oh. No lock.

She heaved the door open all the way and looked out into the dark night. *Where am I?* A deep breath of the fresh air cleared her head.

Hmm. It smells smoky inside. This must be an old smokehouse. That would explain the nails and hooks around the wall for hanging things. At first light I'm going to find a spring. I need a drink of water.

Wait. I'm in the middle of the bush. Getting lost might be considerably worse than staying here. Maybe I could draw other people here. A fire, with damp leaves or moss for smoke?

How do I build a fire without matches? Hmm.

And what if the kidnapper comes back and catches me?

It's beginning to get light. I better do something.

She walked all around the outside of the building. *Ah. An old jar of... what? Water? That gives me an idea.*

Here is a ring of charred stones. For a fire?

To scare off panthers, when hunters don't have spare ammunition? That would apply to almost everybody in these parts during the last four years.

The clever lady gathered the bottom of her nightgown into a sling. *Right. Let's see how many of these brittle dried leaves will fit in* here. She filled it and dumped her crunchy load in the ring.

Thank you, God for this big old avocado tree. These large leaves should burn beautifully.

Next I'll need twigs, sticks, and branches, in a pile, to add after the leaves catch. And moss for smoke.

I wish I could find something to eat and drink.

The sun rose higher.

Now to concentrate this sunlight onto my leaves. She held the bottle up and moved it around until the sun was focused into a fine hot finger of light. In a short while the leaves smoldered, then flared up and burned.

She built her fire. As it burned, she cast around in a circle ever widening out from the building. *I hope I can find one of those bows that I dropped yesterday. That'd start me in the right direction to walk out of here. They must be here somewhere. Unless the wind blew them away or my captor discovered them.*

I don't want to be lost in these woods. I don't want to be here when my kidnapper comes back either.

Oh, I am thirsty. Can I drink this jar of water? Better not. It's a little bit green.

Poor Mary. She must be frantic by now. Heaven only knows what she is thinking.

Blast it. Where are the ribbons? They aren't that small.

Martha added moss to her fire and grey smoke billowed out. *Hello, hunters. Where are you today? Come investigate my fire. I better find a place to hide, in case my kidnapper returns.*

A hollow tree trunk. Perfect. Far enough away that I can watch my fire and the door of my former prison.

Martha fed her fire all day, alternating moss and branches.

Please, God. All I need is one woodsman. Somebody must use the smokehouse. Unless they have a newer more convenient one elsewhere. Don't let it belong to my kidnapper.

She watched her blaze from a safe distance, but her perfumed captor did not come. Nor did a Savior.

This smoke has kept all the animals, including people, away from here.

No. That's not right. People would want to find the source of the smoke, wouldn't they? They better hurry up. The sun is going down. It'll be dark soon.

If I kick these leaves a bit, perhaps I can find a pretty blue bow and the trail. She looked and looked for, but couldn't find, the ribbon trail she had left.

Hungry. I would give my half of the plantation for a decent meal. With a cold jug. Of sweet lemonade. So. Thirsty. Exhausted.

Stop it. Straighten your backbone, Mattie.

I am alive. I am unhurt and I am free.

Now what? I can't sleep outside tonight. The best I can do is booby trap the door.

She gathered dried grass for a bed and put it in the corner of the smokehouse. For weapons, she nestled three of the larger rocks beside the grass.

Before going to sleep for the night, she retrieved the glass jar of water and propped it and a handful of pebbles on top of the door. *At least that will give me some warning if he comes back.*

Mary, don't worry. I'm not giving up.

CHAPTER FIFTY-TWO

May 11, 12, 1865

AT BROCK HOUSE HOTEL

"Mac might know how to find Gator Simmons without asking our resident hunters, but he is not here. We're going to have to ask one of them. Let's question Neville. He's so busy working on his political campaign, that he probably doesn't have energy enough to be the kidnapper," said Sadie.

"Wouldn't he be happy to have $2000 to add to his campaign funds?" said Jane.

Mary said, "Anybody could use that money, but Neville has his own plantation. He's rich in his own right."

They trooped out of Mary's room to confront Neville, but found his room empty. "It's dinner time. We need to go to the dining room to find these fellows," said Jane.

Bram and Ava were sitting at a dining table with some guests whom Sadie had never met, but Neville was nowhere to be seen.

The ladies looked at one another. "Bram it is," said Sadie.

"Good evening, Bram, Ava. We are wondering if you are going out with Gator Simmons tomorrow, Mr. Maas? We'd like to talk to him about an excursion," said Sadie.

"Oh, an excursion for ladies. Can I come too?" said Ava.

"Um, when we get it arranged, we'll let you know. About Gator..."

"He isn't meeting us tomorrow, Sadie. We are going fishing on our own. But when we see him, we'll tell him you're looking for him."

Groan. "Do you have any way to contact him?"

"No. He just shows up as prearranged."

Was I wrong? Could Gator be the kidnapper? Surely not. What would he do with $2000?

"Are there any trails into the woods near here? Or any interesting huts that we might use to watch wildlife?"

"Yes, actually we have used the little animal track behind the hotel several days, when hunting with Gator."

Will you meet us in the morning and show us?"

"All right. How about ten o' clock?"

"Could you make it sunrise? We'd like to see the sky all purple and pink."

"All right. If you insist."

Ava said, "I'm all for an excursion, but not tramping through the woods, like Bram and his friends. And sunrise? Out of the question."

Thank you, Lord. "Very good, Ava. We'll tell you about it when we get back," said Sadie. "We have to go. Thanks, Bram. See you bright and early."

The ladies filed out. "Let's go to Mary's room and make our plans," said Sadie.

En route, Mary said, "Do you think the kidnapper would hurt Martha? I mean, if we don't produce the money."

"He wouldn't dare," said Jane. "Besides, we're going to find her before he can do anything foolish."

What are the chances for three ladies floundering around in the woods? Make that two-we can't possibly take Mary with us.

When they reached her room, Mary said, "I know you want me to stay here tomorrow, but I'm pretty good out in the woods. I want to go."

Is she reading my mind? "Are you sure? Why don't you stay here in case she shows up. Jane and I will scour the woods. If she's there, we'll find her," said Sadie.

"No, I'm going. How shall we dress?"

So, that's that. "Hmm. Brimmed hats, trousers, and sturdy shoes. Do you happen to have those articles of your own, Mary?"

"Oh, yes. I, too, am a feminist and have read tracts by Dr. Mary Walker."

"We have some clothes in auntie's closet at the cottage that would work for you, Jane."

"Good. In the morning, I'll get food and drink for us to carry," said Jane.

"Excellent. In the morning, let's meet in the kitchen before daybreak. We'll eat a bite before we go out to connect with Bram."

"Eat breakfast in the dark?"

"Why not? Who knows what we'll run into later?"

"All right. We'll use a lamp. I'll cook."

"Right now, Jane, we need to go talk to Mr. Lavigne about covering our jobs for tomorrow. Let's hope he's in."

"I forgot all about that," said Jane.

"Let me come, too," said Mary. "I'll show him our ransom note. He will want to avoid bad publicity for *his* hotel."

They trooped down to the manager's office and Sadie knocked. "Come in," he said. "Ah. Miss Merritt. It's a bit late, but I am always available to a good customer like you. What can I do for you?" He eyed Sadie and Jane suspiciously.

Mary said, "My sister is missing and we came to show you this ransom note." She handed him the paper.

"Good heavens. This is not the fault of Brock House. We've never had anything like this happen. If guests find out about it they'll think this is a dangerous place and we could have a mass exodus."

Sadie said, "I know you don't want hotel guests upset by this, sir. " *Your guests.*

Mary said, "As a service to the hotel and to me, Miss Snow and Miss Marsh have offered to help me find my sister. It's reasonable to think that she is being held somewhere close by. In order that they may be engaged on this valuable service to you, will you contact the extra food service and housekeeping employees you hired last week and put them to work tomorrow?"

"No, uh, I don't think I can do that. It would cost money to replace Sadie and Jane. Besides, Sadie already had her day off this week."

"Think what it will cost in lost revenue if Miss Merritt isn't found right away. Let us get her back before word gets out about the kidnapping," Sadie said.

"True. Well, all right. But not a word to anyone."

I guess this is not a good time to bring up the topic of all Brock House employees having a day off.

By daybreak they all stood facing the woods and swamps at the back of the hotel. Their pockets were stuffed with slabs of smoked meat, biscuits, dried fruit, and pint jars of water.

"Good heavens. You look like three gents," said Bram.

"Never mind. Where is this track you mentioned?" said Mary.

"Well the light is faint. I think it starts over here. Yes. Just there, he said, pointing to a thinning of the brush. "See here. You're not going out to the hut on your own, are you? I mean, who's your guide?"

"We'll probably just walk the track a little and turn back. I'm sure we don't need a man to show us the way."

"If you want to wait, while I get my gear, I'll lead you."

"No, thanks. We appreciate your kind offer, but we'll be going now," said Sadie.

"Okay. You feminists have some peculiar ideas of fun."

"Well, it was fun for you men, when you went out there, wasn't it?"

"Yes, but..."

"...that's different? Right. Let's go, ladies," said Sadie. She trotted off down the track and the other two ladies followed after her.

"Are you sure that was entirely wise?" said Mary. "He's been there multiple times and offered to show us the way."

"And if he is the kidnapper, he could lead us around in circles until we are exhausted. We would never find Martha, then," said Sadie. "I have faith in us. At least, I'm going to give it my best."

"Me, too," said Jane.

"We have to find her," said Mary.

For 30 minutes they kicked and stomped their way along the barely discernible trail. "Let's stop for a drink of water," said Sadie. They forged ahead to a clearing and sat on tree stumps to rest.

"Great Caesar's ghost. There's a ribbon from Mattie's nightgown," said Mary, moving a leaf and retrieving a blue ribbon bow. She held it out in front of her and burst into tears. "Walking here felt like a futile exercise and I worried we would never find her. This is proof that she has been here."

"Hallelujah," said Sadie. "Let's go."

"Where is the trail?" said Jane.

"Over there," said Mary, who swiped a hand across her tears and then pointed.

"No. Oh, no. It seems to have disappeared. Everybody spread out and look," said Sadie. *No, no, no. We can't get lost out here. That would make everything worse. And nobody, except Bram and Ava, even knows we are here. They wouldn't miss us for days.*

"Here is a little crushed grass. I think this must be it," said Jane.

"Wheeww." "I guess it's a deer trail and the speedy jumpers bounded as much as they walked. Keep checking, as you go. She may have dropped more bows," said Sadie.

Chapter Fifty-Three

May 12, 1865

Sunrise at an Old Smokehouse

Where in the world am I? Martha opened her eyes in the dim interior. She smelled the building's history of smoky fires and meat and the horror of the previous day came flooding back.

"Scritch, scritch, scratch."

I'm not alone. Better watch out, little critter. I'm hungry enough to roast you for breakfast.

Oh, these old bones feel so creaky. That's what happens when you sleep on lumpy hard ground. She slowly rose to her feet. *I am thankful that my captor did not come during the night.*

Something to eat and drink are the first order of business for today. So, no fire. I have to find some of those ribbons I dropped.

No time like the present. She carried a fist-sized rock in either hand and continued her search.

The sun was high in the sky when she finally scuffed through some leaves and found a blue ribbon. *Thank you, God. I was beginning to think I dreamed dropping the bows from my gown.*

She stood very still and looked all around her at the ground. *Where's the track? That looks like a faint trail over there and it goes south. I'll just have to chance it.*

Martha began kick-walking, but she tired quickly.

I need a rest.

My head is a little woozy. She sat on a stump, but presently got up and started again.

After a few minutes she turned up another blue bow, dirty. *Hallelujah. I'm going the right way.*

She struggled through the brush a while longer. *Ah, a clearing. I can sit on a log.* She sat, bent forward, with her head on her knees, eyes closed.

Blue jays. I hear blue jays.

And a cardinal calling his dog.

Voices. Now, I hear voices.

Probably dreaming.

I'm hungry and oh-so-thirsty.

It sounds like Mary.

Have I died?

Sadie, who was in front, crunching the grass down for the others, looked ahead to the clearing and saw the swath of blue cloth. *What in tarnation is that? Martha?*

"Huzzah. We've done it. She's here in the woods." She crashed through the underbrush to the clearing, where she scooped up the older woman in a close embrace.

Martha blinked. Jane and Mary made it a four-way hug.

Mary said, through joyful tears, "Oh, sister. What a wonderful day when we indulged in extravagant spending on those matching nightgowns with ribbons."

Sadie said, "Where have you been? Your face and hands are black. What is that? Soot?"

Martha said, "Um, yes, soot. I made a signal fire, but nobody came. Sadie, I recognized the kidnapper's perfume. It was the same as the man who passed me on the veranda the night Luther was killed." She coughed. "I am so hungry and thirsty."

"What have you been eating and drinking?" said Jane.

Martha said, weakly, "Drinking? Does anybody have something to drink?"

Jane opened a jar of fresh water for her and she gulped it down. "Try some of these biscuits. I made them this morning."

Martha took them with trembling fingers and finished the lot. They broke out the rest of the food and water and fed the famished escapee.

When she finished, Martha said, "I really need a bath. I can't go into the hotel looking like this."

Mary said, "Why don't we go down to the lake. At least you could get rid of the soot."

"Yes. I want to float in Lake Monroe."

"Not without guards to keep away the alligators," said Sadie.

Jane said, "I will watch out for you, Martha. Can you swim, Sadie?"

"Yes. All right. I will, too. But we must take sticks with us." *And a LeMat revolver.*

"We could go to the sulphur springs," said Mary.

Martha revived. She said, "Oh, let's do. There's that pool over by the shell mound where the old hotel used to be."

Mary said, "Our bathing costumes are at the hotel. But I don't see why we would need them. There's never anybody about there."

"Then, lead the way," said Martha.

CHAPTER FIFTY-FOUR

May 12, 1865

EVENING AT BROCK HOUSE

"..and he needs a complimentary room for a night," said Mac. "It's important business, Guillaume," said Mac.

"Great Caesar's ghost. How am I supposed to turn a profit, with you housing dead bodies, plague-ridden sailors, and murder investigation witnesses here all the time?" Mr. Lavigne said, in a huffy voice. He looked down his nose at the prospective guest waiting just outside his office door.

"Not all the time. Only for tonight," Mac said, in a soothing tone.

"All right. Just this once."

"Thank you. Where will I find Sadie?" Mac said.

With a sniff, he said, "Miss Snow is off today."

"But this isn't her day off."

"She had a pressing need. I'll let her tell you about it. If that's all, I have work to do."

Mac left him. "Come on, Curly. Let me introduce you to Fluffy on the veranda."

"Ohhh. Sounds like one of them burly-que dancers. Is she purdy?"

"She's pretty. Fluffy's our house cat, not a dancer, though she may dance around you, if she fancies you," Mac said, with a twinkle. "Give me a few minutes to talk to Sadie's friend."

"Shoot. I might just go soak at the old sulphur springs, while you arrange our lineup. I'll be back fer supper and the viewin'."

"Fine." Mac went to the kitchen to find Jane.

He smiled at Mrs. Flowers, the aproned dumpling of a woman, who was bending over her steaming pots. At his inquiry, she shook her white-capped head and said, "Lovely to see you, Mac, but no. No. Jane didn't come in today. I've had to do with the new girl, who is no Jane."

"What's going on, Mrs. Flowers?"

"I'm sure I don't know, sir," she said with a mournful look.

At the sulphur springs the faint smell of rotten eggs reached them before they heard the splash of water. "Whew. No wonder people don't come here. Are you sure you want to go near that smelly place?" said Jane.

Stacked melon-sized chunks of coquina limestone surrounded the pool and a trickle of water dribbled into the 'V' of a shallow stream leading down toward the lake. "You'll get used to it. It's supposed to be good for you," said Martha. "I've been told that folks came here for their health."

"Then why are the hotel and all the healthy bathers gone?" said Jane.

No one answered. "That sparkling spring water looks wonderfully refreshing, but it's too shallow to swim. I'm just going to wade," said Mary.

"Look at that. It's so clear I can see the bottom, and the white sand dancing around in the natural fountain below the surface " Sadie said. "Too bad it's only knee deep. I'm hot. Let's go wading."

They sat on steps shaped from slabs of moss-covered limestone to remove their boots and socks. "Ouch. I'm sitting on sharp little pieces sticking out of the stone. It's like fragments of shells all glued together. Don't scoot on them," Sadie said.

"The last one in's a hot, wet noodle," Jane said.

"Aack. Glub."

Jane said, "I'm swimming. Glad you suggested trousers, Sadie. At least I don't have a skirt billowing out to entangle me. I can't touch bottom. 'Gasp.' Cold, too."

"Really?" Sadie said. "Then I'm shedding the rest of these clothes. Let freedom reign."

"Me, too," said Martha. "But I'm throwing in this filthy nightgown. It can only improve with rinsing. I guess I won't toss my house slippers, though. I don't want to squish back to Brock House in soggy footwear."

"Sister, you'll be sopping. You can't go into the hotel wet."

"I'll dry by the time I walk all the way back there, Mary. Besides, it isn't proper to be walking around in the public areas of the hotel in my nightie, either, but I pretty much have to," said Martha. "Unless we wait until dark to sneak back in," she added.

Soon all were splashing and floating under the over-hanging palms. "Ahh. I'm beginning to relax for the first time in two days," said Martha, as she switched from floating on her back to kicking and crawling across the surface.

Sadie said, "This is tremendous. Why don't people come here all the time?"

"I guess we are the only ones who know about it," said Jane.

"Oh, no you are not. Who do you think keeps the stones stacked and trims up them weeds?" said a male voice from the bushes. "Ladies, are you aware that a snake is swimming with you?"

"Snake?" shouted Sadie, and she commenced thrashing. "Where?"

"Over there, where the wall curves. But I wouldn't worry about him none. He's probably more afeared of you than you are sceert of him."

As the fright from the snake subsided, the worry about their position as naked ladies arose. "Who are you and what are you doing here? This place is private," Sadie said.

"I just come here to get a little relief from my old rheumatism. I'm a gentleman and will turn away whilst you ladies come out and dress. But I need to soak these bones."

"How do we know we can trust you?" said Martha.

"You don't. But I don't see as how you have much choice about it, now do you?"

Martha captured her floating nightgown and shrugged it over her head. She said, "All right. I'm coming out."

The other three scrambled out, dripping. Sadie quickly put on her clothes. Now dressed, the women bristled. "Come out, you miserable cur. How long have you been spying on us?" said Sadie.

The man came out from behind the tree, where he had been waiting.

Martha said, "Wipe that smirk from your face."

"I've seen you before," said Sadie. "Curly. From the Palatka general store."

"Guilty as charged, ma'am." He looked down at his feet. "I ain't done nothing wrong. When the *Darlington* docked an hour ago at Enterprise, I decided to come visit the old sulfur springs."

Mmmm. That means that the Katie Asbell and all six-foot-two powerful inches of Noah will be back in two days.

"The *Darlington* is back? I didn't hear any whistle," said Mary.

"I 'spect you was having too much fun carrying on here." He scratched his head. "You'll be a-wantin' to get on back," said Curly. "It'll be gettin' dark soon."

"Whip-poor-will. Whip-poor-will."

Bird song echoed through the woods.

"Yes. We will. Let's go," said Sadie and they trooped off toward Brock House. At the sight of the shell road, Jane said, "We could all spend the night at Snow Bird Cottage. We don't have extra beds, but we could make you comfortable. It's not so far to walk."

"That's a kind offer, but I want my own things just now. I'm sure you understand," said Martha.

"Yes. We'll tiptoe in the back door and nobody will see us in this state," said Mary. "Tomorrow, we'll act like nothing happened."

"Yes, we can see the wisdom in that," Sadie said. "I'll just accompany them to the hotel, Jane. I need to see Mac."

"All right. Meanwhile, I'll prepare a bite of supper for us," said Jane.

Accordingly, when they reached the cottage, Jane said her good-byes and made for their kitchen,

"Thank you, Jane. I won't be long," Sadie said, as she and the Merritt sisters returned to the road.

Dusk was giving way to dark, as they approached the rear door of Brock House. With a sigh of relief, Martha turned the knob. "It's stuck."

Sadie said, "Here let me try." She jiggled the knob. *Oh, perfect. Not stuck.* "It's locked. I'm afraid we'll have to creep in the front door. *Oh folly, fudge, and flummediddle. Dripping into Brock House.*

Mac made his way to the veranda. *Do I approach the three main suspects and ask them to sit together? I was going to get Sadie to invite them to join her on some pretext, since she knows them all. Where is she?*

"Hello, Fluffy." The cat wove her way around and through his legs, rubbing as she went. "Your way of claiming me, is that it?" *Mine, mine, mine.* He peered out into the darkness to find the cause of an approaching sound.

Sadie, trailed by the two slightly bedraggled older ladies made their way around the building unseen and started up the front steps. "Good evening, Miss Snow. You're the very person I need to see," said Mac.

"Oh, Mac. Don't pop out at me from the dark, like that. You startled me," she said.

"Just standing. No popping here, young lady. Ahh. Martha and Mary." He looked them up and down. "I see Sadie has been leading you astray," he said, with a wry grin.

"Quite the contrary, Mac. She has saved the day. But that story will have to wait. Come along, sister," Martha said. With that, she marched past like an empress dressed in silks and ermine, rather than an exhausted little lady in her soiled and torn night dress.

"Sadie, will you help me? I need to ensure that the Maases, Neville Beaumont, Buck and Kat Stotts all come to dinner. And it would be convenient if they were to sit together."

"Why? Kat says she's ready to leave for New York. But she isn't on your suspect list, is she?"

"No, but I need the three men together, and their ladies usually accompany them. It's about that silver belt buckle Christian was wearing. I think one of them sold it at the Palatka General Store. Curly is here to see if he can identify the seller. That is, he's supposed to be here. Where in tarnation is that man?"

"He'll be along soon, I think. We, uh, met him at the springs and he was going to 'soak,' last he said. I'll go gather the others at one table and save seats for you and Curly. And, Mac, once you are all situated, I'll be going back to Snow Bird Cottage for my supper. I have so much to tell you, but it will have to wait. Meet me here bright and early in the morning?"

"Yes, of course. Bring your books and questions. That's our agreement."

"I may need an extra candle tonight. I have to catch up on my reading. It's been hard to concentrate with all that has happened since you left." She groaned. "The more I investigate, the more questions I find, Mac."

"Yes, it often works that way. But I think we are about due for a breakthrough."

"The one with the red silk waistcoat. Calls hisself Neville."

"Are you sure?" Mac said.

"Positive," said Curly. "He's hoity-toity. Thinks he's better 'n ever'body else. Was right put out, when I didn't give him a big price for that 'ar buckle."

"Thank you, Curly. That's all I need from you. We'll get you back to Palatka with the next steamer."

Back in the dining room Mac cornered Neville and said, "Mr. Beaumont, please accompany me to the veranda. I have some questions for you."

"As charming as that sounds, I must regretfully decline. I've had a long day and plan to retire early."

"Make no mistake. You should consider this more of an order, than a request. This dining room is much too public for what we have to discuss."

With a sigh, he said, "Oh, all right. Since you put it that way."

Once seated in straight-back chairs looking out over the lawn and lake, Mac pulled the silver buckle from his pocket and said, "What can you tell me about this buckle?"

"Why, nothing. I would never wear anything so garish."

"Are you sure? We have a witness who says you sold him this item, which belonged to the murdered man, Luther Greim."

Neville said, in a loud belligerent voice, "That's ridiculous. I never did any such thing."

"Mr. Beaumont, did you kill Luther Greim, and, noting its value, remove this silver ornament from his body, before dumping him into Lake Monroe?

Neville exploded up out of his chair. "How dare you accuse me of murder. I have powerful friends. I'm a prominent citizen and will not be bullied."

"Blustering will do you no good. Sit back down, Neville. We know you sold it. Now tell me how you got this buckle."

With a sullen look on his face, he sat. "Now that I get a closer look, I do remember it. That's the thing I found on the ground next to a tree in the woods, when we were hunting."

"What did you do with it?"

"I just picked it up and dropped it into my pocket."

"Who else saw you find it?"

"No one. We were hunting."

"Then what?"

"I was rummaging around in my pockets looking for money and found it there, when I was in the store in Palatka. I thought I might as well sell it, but the old coot didn't give me a third of what it's worth."

This brought a wry smile to Mac's face. *Curly wouldn't appreciate the soubriquet.* "Ahh. How do you think a murdered man's belt came to be under a tree in the woods?"

"I don't know and I don't care. That's your business."

"I see… No need to detain you further, just now. I will let you get to bed, Mr. Beaumont. Thank you for your time. Please don't leave Enterprise until our investigation is complete."

"Hmph." Neville stomped back into the hotel.

Is he telling the truth? If so, how did it get under a tree in the woods?

Did Luther Greim, in his drunken stupor and after being attacked in his cabin by somebody with a hammer, stumble off the steamer and into the woods? And take off his belt?

Maybe he attacked somebody else with the hammer, leaving blood evidence in his cabin. Then he ran off into the woods. Why? Was it a chase? Did he toss that person into the river? I suppose the alligators could have eaten all evidence of another person. But who was it? Nobody is reported missing.

The question still remains. How did Luther Greim end up in the river?

Chapter Fifty-Five

May 13, 1865 Early Morning

At Brock House Hotel

S adie found Mac's mug still on the shelf in the staff dining room. She brewed his favorite tea and carried two steaming cups and her heavy book bag to the front veranda.

Mmm. She inhaled deeply. *Nothing quite like a cup of spicy tea early in the morning to get my mind working.*

"Oh. I see that Fluffy is asleep on your lap. That explains your lack of a beverage. Here you are." She offered him the cup.

"Thanks. Mmm. My favorite."

After a full debriefing on happenings of the previous day, Mac answered her questions and they discussed philosophy, math, biology, and history. He gave her new assignments and then said, "I think the kidnapping was done by the same person who killed Luther Greim."

The tabby cat yawned and stretched languidly on his lap, reaching out first one paw and then the other.

"What makes you say that?"

"Martha told us about seeing someone creeping from the hotel out to the steamer the night Greim was killed." He stroked the softly-purring Fluffy. "I believe our killer thinks she knows more and would like to have her out of the way. She could have died in that shed."

"But why now? Martha told us about that days ago."

"Maybe he's had a chance to worry about what she knows. It's a 'better-safe-than-sorry' move on his part. And if our killer could get some extra money, while eliminating a threat, so much the better for him, from his point of view." Fluffy launched herself from his lap and stalked off into the high grass in front of the hotel.

"Mac, I'm pretty good friends with all of our suspects. I'm finding it hard to imagine any of them doing such a thing."

"You think they are too 'nice' for kidnapping? Or to commit murder? What you need to understand, Sadie, is that anyone can commit murder, given the right circumstances."

"Oh, Mac, you are awful. And you are wrong. Yes, maybe the accidental kind of death, like I push you and you fall and hit your head on a rock. That could happen to most of us."

"Yes, and preplanned murder can 'happen' with most people, too. I think it goes back to our basic primal instinct for survival."

"So, you think that anyone could look at me and decide, 'You are in my way, so I'll get rid of you. 'Bonk?' No. Only a person who is very sick would reason that way. Our society has instilled in everyone rules against that sort of thing."

"And we've always had those who don't follow the rules."

"Yes, but 'Thou shalt not kill' is a very important rule."

"Do this job long enough and you will understand that people differ in their ability or willingness to follow rules." Mac said, "But I'm glad you can still see the good in everyone, Sadie." Fluffy trotted up the front steps and proudly deposited at Mac's feet from her jaws her gift of a lifeless red male cardinal.

Sadie gasped, as she looked at the once- beautiful limp body and slightly soggy red feathers. She said, "Oh, Fluffy. Bad cat."

"She's a hunter, dear girl. That is her way to say she appreciates us. I'll bury it in a few minutes. Now, how are we going to flush out this killer before he strikes again?"

Sadie shivered and looked away. After a moment, she said, "Noah and the *Katie Asbell* are due back tomorrow evening. What if we..."

Sadie was a model employee all day long. She cleaned and smiled at everyone, leaving no hint of anything having been amiss at the hotel. *I'm acting again-playing the part of a happy carefree young woman.*

When she finished, she dropped off her cleaning supplies and made her way to Hattie Brock's rooms.

"Oh, Sadie. Come in," said Jacob's daughter, practically gushing. "I heard about your rescue of Martha. Thank you for saving the reputation of our hotel. We want to do something for you to reward you for your wonderful help and leadership. What can we do?"

"How did you find out about it? It's supposed to be a secret."

"Oh, you know how hard it is to keep a secret around here. All it takes is a whisper of an early morning excursion by ladies and 'whoosh.' It's all over. But you have arranged a spectacularly good outcome. What can we do for you?"

"Well, I do really need something right now. Do you have any writing paper?"

"Good heavens, girl. Writing paper? Is that all you want? We have plenty of that. Will my ivory rag paper do? It's very plain with no monogram."

"Perfect. And can you spare a quill pen and ink? I have to write some notes. I could just write them here, if I wouldn't be imposing."

"Does this have to do with the kidnapping?"

"Yes, I think so. But I can't tell you about it yet."

"Good. We will provide anything you need to get that blighter. Come sit here at my desk by the window and help yourself to our writing materials."

After Sadie left Hattie's private rooms that evening Hattie said to her sister, "I couldn't help but notice the names on Sadie's envelopes."

"Yes. She wrote separate letters to Bram and Ava Maas, Buck and Kat Stotts, Neville Beaumont, and the Merritt sisters, Martha and Mary. Interesting, that."

Later from his lounger on the veranda, Mac said, "I hope the *Katie Asbell* arrives on schedule."

Sadie said, "Don't worry so much, Mac. Noah says that 'neither Hell nor high water' will keep him from his scheduled route. He's hoping to make enough this season to pay off his boat."

"Woot, woot, woooot." The signature whistle sounded.

Mac said, "There she is." He pulled out his pocket watch and peered down. "Right on time."

"You go on to the dining room. I'll go tell Noah what we're up to, Mac."

"Permission to come aboard," said Sadie, after the steamer was made fast at the dock. "Hi, Adam. How was your trip?"

"Uneventful, Miss Snow. The best kind."

"I need a word with Noah. Do you know where he is right now?"

"I believe he went up to the bridge, Miss."

"Thank you. I'll just make my way up." *And it will be a private place for our conversation.*

"Sadie. What a surprise," said Noah, with a smile, when she stepped into the wheelhouse. "Shorty, look who's here."

"Good evening, gentlemen. I need a private word, Noah. May we step onto the hurricane deck?" *Is my heart racing because of Noah? Or is it because tonight I'll very probably be in a room with a killer?*

"Uhh, all right. Will you finish these calculations for me, Shorty?"

"Sure, Noah. Go ahead."

Over the noisy wind on the uppermost deck Sadie said, "Mac and I are hoping to draw out the murderer tonight by telling our suspects that in Luther Greim's cabin aboard your boat you found new evidence, which points to the identity of the killer. We'd like to wait there tonight and see who turns up."

"That sounds dangerous, Sadie. Can't you devise a plan that doesn't put you in jeopardy?"

Oh, for heaven sake. What am I? A marshmallow? "No, we cannot. This is our plan and we are sticking to it."

"This person killed once. What's to stop them from killing you and Mac?"

"Uhh. You? That is, I was hoping you might help with that." *Considering that you look to be more than 200 pounds of hard muscle.*

"Absolutely. If you insist on doing this, I'll keep my men on deck tonight. Most of them stay here anyway. And we'll patrol with firearms."

"No patrols. No firearms, unless you are hidden. This is our one shot to draw this villain out into the open. I don't want to spook him."

"Okay. But be careful."

"Noah, I can take care of myself."

"I'm beginning to see that, Sadie."

After dinner, Sadie wordlessly slipped a note to each of seven suspects. Every time, she put a finger to her lips as a caution for secrecy. *All done. Now to sneak onto the boat and meet Mac.*

In a very quiet voice, Mac said, "I brought the LeMat gun." He sat in the dark on Luther Grime's bunk.

Sadie, slightly hidden in a straight back chair, in the even-darker shadows beside a tiny shelf in the cramped room, said, "I've unstrapped the five-shooter that Kate gave me and have it here on my lap. I hope I don't need it." She kept her eyes on the door, which they'd left slightly ajar.

"All right. Keep your finger out of the trigger guard. And let's remind ourselves not to get a false sense of security from our weapons," he said, in an almost inaudible voice. A few minutes elapsed and then he said, "We may have a long wait. But a fair wind has kicked up outside, and I think we can converse, if we do it very quietly."

Now they spoke in the barest whispers as the wind whipped flags and caused the rigging to slap and sing. "I won't pretend that I think we are safe, Mac. But it's worth it if we can catch this villain. Was 'springing out with guns ready' a regular part of your life when you were working out of Chicago?"

"No, not really. You have seen for yourself that most investigations involve many interviews, plus a great amount of clerical and otherwise uninteresting work."

"How did you come to be working for Alan Pinkerton?"

"I married someone with relatives in Chicago and she wanted to move back there. I needed a job and Alan was hiring."

"You mean you are not a native of the glamorous 'city in a garden?'"

"I consider myself a native of Chicago by way of Hogtown, Florida."

"What?" she said, in surprise and confusion.

"Shhhh. Quietly. Yes, I am a Florida boy. Hogtown is about 45 miles due west of Palatka and 50 miles south of Alligator, the northern terminus of the railroad from Jacksonville. She was visiting her uncle's estate and I was home from college. We met at a country dance and it was love at first sight. I'd have followed her anywhere."

"You followed her to Chicago?"

"Yes, we married and our beautiful daughter was born the following year."

"Lovely. A wife and daughter... sounds like an idyllic life."

"It was, until I got too close to unmasking a major railroad robbery ring in Boston. The leader targeted and killed the love of my life and our sweet baby, Jacqueline."

"Oh, Mac. That's dreadful. I am so sorry. I didn't know. I.." *Just stop talking. Be quiet.*

They sat in silence. Wind whistled in the rigging. A thin spattering of raindrops fell onto the deck outside. The boat rocked. Somewhere outside a spar squeaked to and fro. Monotony set in.

Then the door swung open slowly. A large manly form was silhouetted against the night sky and then crept forward into the cabin and pushed the door closed behind him.

Sadie picked up her five-shooter and covered it with a fold of her knee length skirt. A match struck, bringing a momentary phosphorus smell to the small space and then a flare of light from the lamp on the table.

"Bram."

"Mac, Sadie. What are you doing here?"

"I think a better question is, what are you doing here, Bram?"

"Well, Sadie said in her note that there is new evidence pointing to the killer. I wanted to see it for myself. Where is it?" He looked around.

"Because you killed Luther and wondered what you had left behind?"

"Good grief, no. I thought I might be able to, uhh, help you identify the killer."

"Right. Now you listen here..."

Sadie said, "No, wait Mac. Let me. You know who it is, don't you Bram? Or you think you know. You are afraid it was Ava, because Luther was responsible for encouraging her brother's gang activity."

Bram stared at her. "How do you know what I'm thinking? No, I didn't kill Luther. But I might have, if I'd had the opportunity. He was a real blight on society. But, dear Ava..."

"You don't really think she did it, do you Bram? But there is that slight little niggling doubt."

His eyes widened. "You are unnatural, woman. Stop doing that."

Mac said, "This is all very touching, Mr. Maas. But the fact remains that you came looking for evidence... evidence that you hoped to suppress. You could have killed Luther Greim. Come with me to the Captain's quarters to give a written statement." He twisted the man's arm up behind his back and started out the door.

He turned back to Sadie. "It will be very crowded in the captain's quarters. Do you mind remaining here?"

Are you kidding? A quiet break will be welcome. "As it should take only a short time, I'll just sit here and rest my eyes until you return, Mac." She stood and extinguished the lamp.

She had been there only five minutes when she heard someone quietly rattling the door knob. The door creaked open and a short figure tiptoed forward, pushing ahead first one side of a bubble skirt, then the other.

"Ava, I wondered if you'd come."

"Oh, my goodness. I must be sleepwalking." She tried to retreat, but was hindered by her voluminous dress.

"Stay where you are. I'll light the lamp." Moments later, in the cozy yellow glow, Sadie said, "Ava, have a seat on the bunk. Tell me why you came... Did you kill Luther Greim? Maybe it was an accident?"

"Sadie. How could you think such a thing? It's no secret that I hated Luther. He ruined my brother's life. But, to kill him? That would make me no better than he was."

"And I should believe you because...?"

"Because it's true. I don't care what new evidence you have. It won't point to me. Are you listening? I'll tell you again. I didn't do it."

"Then why did you come here?"

"Bram went out to smoke a cigar and I, um, I'm curious about what you found that points to the killer. Where is it?"

"Just curious? Isn't it true that you think Bram might have done this, out of love for you and your brother? Didn't you decide to destroy any evidence that would point to him?"

"No. He's no murderer. He's kind, and thoughtful...

The door opened. Mac said, "Sadie, I... what in the Sam Hill is this?"

"Ava wants to go up to Noah's office and give you a written statement, Mac. You tell him the truth, Ava. Tell him everything you know about Luther Greim. This is a murder investigation and details matter."

"I, I don't know."

"Come with me, Mrs. Maas." Mac led her away into the night.

This is miserable. What good is it doing? None. We may have put ourselves in harm's way for nothing. How can we tell if any of them are telling the truth? Sadie sat in silence watching the flame dance.

Her little puddle of light was endangered when the door opened once again and a gust the wind blew in. *Oh folly, fudge, and flummediddle. What now?*

"Sadie? What are you doing here? Your letter said you would be waiting for me at the last bench in the side garden."

"You sound disappointed to see me, Kat. Do you want to tell me what you are doing here?"

The mother-to-be burst into tears. "I didn't really w-want to c-come. But I had to f-find out... find out for myself. You said there is proof positive of the killer's identity. Who is it?"

"Are you worried that Buck might've done it? said Sadie gently.

"Maybe. No. I, I don't know."

"Were you going to destroy evidence?"

"No. Of course not. Well... that depends."

"On what?"

"On who did it."

Mac entered the room and showed no surprise at having caught a third suspect in their trap. "Good evening, Mrs. Stotts. May I have a word with you outside, Miss Snow?"

She followed him outside into the windy passageway and closed the door behind her.

"What in the world did you say in those letters to get all of them here? We were supposed to get only the killer here."

"I told them all separately that in Luther's cabin on the steamer there is new evidence pointing to the killer's identity. I asked them to meet me at the last bench in the hotel side garden to discuss how to proceed."

"Good heavens. Why, that sounds like it could be an extortion letter."

"Oh, no. I didn't think of it like that."

"I better go check the side garden for killers," said Mac. "Will you take Kat's statement, please?"

"Me? What do I do?"

"Just give her a paper and pen and ask her to write down everything that happened between Luther's exit from the salon the night of April 25 and now. We want only what's related to Luther. Make sure she includes any history she might have had with him and that she signs it. Then you can release her."

"All right. I can do that." She went back into Luther's cabin.

Mac turned and, with the aid of his silver-tipped ebony cane, slowly made his way down the gang plank. All was silent, except for the lapping of the lake water and a pair of nesting owls.

"Who, who, wh, whoooo."

All my nerves are being forced, as if at bayonet point, to stand at attention.

On high alert, he tapped quietly on the path as he proceeded around the side of Brock House. The revolver was a reassuring weight in his hand.

This Lemat gun at my side makes me feel calmer than I have any right to be.

I'm ready for you. Show yourself.

The former Pinkerton man checked every bench. *If someone came to meet Sadie, they have now left.*

What in tarnation am I doing, holding my breath?

He sighed, a mixture of frustration and relief.

OK. Back to the stern-wheeler.

He still kept a lookout for a villain.

Earlier Neville let his lantern swing from side to side as he strode down the sandy pathway of the Brock House side garden. *Well, there's the back bench, but where is Sadie? What is she playing at? This letter looks like a veiled attempt to extort money from me. Would she really think she could do that? She'd be crazy to try it.*

In the background he heard an owl. "Who, who, wh, whooo." He sat down to ponder.

She's a beautiful woman. That fiery redhead would look good beside me in the Georgia governor's mansion. But, how dare she keep me waiting like this.

From the shrouded pathway, the sound of approaching footfalls broke his reverie.

"Swish, swish. Crunch."

"Ahh, there you are. It's about time. Where have you been? I was just getting ready to leave. I'm not in the habit of waiting on others, even ones as pretty as you."

Buck Stotts' bald pate and astonishing handlebar mustache came into the circle of light. He said, "Beaumont? Is that you? What are you doing here?"

"I'm meeting someone here, Buck. Just get along with you."

"Oh, ho. Sadie has you on the hook, too. Well, tell her I don't have any extra money to contribute to her and I don't care who the new evidence points to. As sure as I'm taller than a bulrush, it doesn't point to me. Good night."

"You have it all wrong. I'm just curious about what she wants. But I've lingered here long enough. I am going back inside now."

CHAPTER FIFTY-SIX

May 14, 1865 Morning

AT BROCK HOUSE

This morning, when getting ready for work, Sadie had added her long red, orange, and peach silk scarf to the floor-length plain white dress that suited Lavigne's specifications. *When I look down at the swirls, I forget, for just a moment, about the marshal.*

On the front veranda of Brock House, with her notebooks and questions, she sat down, next to Mac. "What happened after I went home?"

"Noah posted a discreet guard last night, but no one else showed up after we left," said Mac. "Let's concentrate on your lessons first. Then we'll talk about what happened last night."

"All right. But I'm really disappointed. And it's all my fault for writing that letter wrong."

"No. I've been thinking about it. You did fine. I'll tell you my thoughts later, but we might yet have some results out of that debacle last night. Now, about your philosophy reading... does anyone else's happiness affect your own?"

"Yes. We are all in this world together and..."

Noah bounded up the front steps of Brock House and strode to where they sat. "I'm sorry if I'm interrupting, but I must get going for Palatka and I thought you needed to hear this. The provost marshal in Jacksonville said he has finally cleared his books and is coming on the Darlington the day after tomorrow! I didn't mention it last night, because you were both focused on catching the killer. But I figured you'd want to know. Sadie, he is preparing a warrant for your arrest."

"No, no, no, no." She looked away from the two men. Nothing disturbed the quiet, except for a gust of soft breeze and the sound of a line slapping on the deck of the *Katie Asbell.* "Our trap got us nothing last night. We're no closer to catching this murderer. Oh Mac," she said, in a small voice. "What am I going to do? I've failed miserably and I'm going to be arrested for something I didn't do."

Noah reached down and kissed her on the top of her head. "I have to go, but I'll be back. The other evidence, blood evidence, which Mac found in that cabin, and the lack of it in yours, will convince the marshal that you didn't do it.

"I pray you are right," she said.

He rested his hand briefly on her shoulder. Then he was gone.

"I think it's best if you don't mention this to anyone," said Mac.

"My thoughts, exactly," she said.

"We will continue with your lessons, as if nothing is amiss. Can you tell me what Mendel's pea experiment was about?"

She plastered on a smile, then held up her textbook and said, "He cross-pollinated them to discover how traits are inherited between generations."

"And what traits did he observe in the plants?"

"He looked at the pea shape, round or wrinkled, and color of the peas, yellow or green. He noted the pod shapes, constricted or inflated, and the pod color, green or yellow. Then he categorized them into the flower colors, purple or white, and plant size, tall or dwarf. Last he looked at the position of the flowers, axial ones close to the center of the plant, or terminal ones at the ends of stems."

The hour passed quickly. Lessons were complete for the morning, when Martha stepped out onto the veranda. "Good morning, Sadie. Oh, I see Fluffy has found a warm spot in your lap. She's resting up from a night of mousing, no doubt. I was too tired to meet you last evening. But, tell me, who is the killer? Do you have him in custody?"

"You know we can't talk about that, Martha," said Mac.

"Oh, all right. Be that way. I'll pump Sadie, while she cleans our room."

"That won't do you any good. She's sworn to secrecy."

"Hmmph." The lady turned and traipsed off.

Sadie said, "She will, too. If it weren't such a serious topic, I'd laugh. And I do have to go to work." She gathered her things and took them to the staff room, where she stowed them in the assigned cabinet.

Aproned and armed with her cart bearing tools of the trade, she paused outside the Maas's room. *I wonder if either of them will mention last night?*

"Knock, knock."

"Housekeeping."

Ava opened the door. "Sadie, come in. Bram is off hunting again with Buck and Gator Simmons. I do declare, that man would live in the woods, if he could." She giggled self-consciously. "Oh, you can help me look for my book."

"What book?"

"*Leaves of Grass* by Walt Whitman. Have you read it?"

"No. *But I know the author.*

"I've had a devil of a time getting my hands on a copy. I tried to get some for our emporium in New York, but the printers always seemed to be out of copies. And I can see why. Parts of it are just scandalous."

Not talking about last night, then. Sadie started her cleaning regimen. "Ava, did you really come last night thinking you would find evidence that Bram killed that obnoxious man?"

"No," Ava said, looking sideways at Sadie. "I, I am sure he would never kill anyone. But some kind of accident could have happened. That might make him look like he had killed Luther. I know he loathed the man. And I'm sure that Luther wouldn't have hesitated to kill Bram. If they struggled and Luther fell and died, then Bram would feel justified in quietly getting rid of him."

"And you would feel justified in erasing any evidence that points to Bram?"

"He's my husband and I love him. I'm weary of all these questions. I must go to the back parlor and see if I left my book there. Carry on with your work. Goodbye."

"'Bye." *Whew. She gives a good imitation of a whirlwind, when she wants to. Is she hiding something? It's hard to imagine her, or the two of them together, as murderers.*

Sadie thought about her imminent arrest and the botched trap of last night, as she cleaned four empty rooms that morning. *I could probably find a way to run away. But what good would that do? And I don't want to. I like it here. Oh, Aunt Cora, what would you do? Stand and fight, I think.*

One that wasn't empty was that of Neville Beaumont. When she knocked, he opened his door. "Come right in, Sadie. I was wondering if you would be here this morning." He motioned her in.

"Why wouldn't I be here, Neville? I work here."

"Yes, I know. But, you wrote, asking me to meet you in the side garden. When you didn't come, I was worried. I thought maybe a gator had gotten you." He slammed the door behind her.

"About that, Neville. I..."

He spoke over her, in a low fierce voice that was almost a hiss. "How dare you summon me and then not show up? I've never been more angry. Angry and embarrassed. Buck showed up and obviously you wrote to him, too. I don't know what you're playing at, Sadie. But know this. You are not playing me. Whatever fond feelings I've had for you in the past are gone."

Well, I guess the New York trip as his personal assistant is no longer on offer. "Neville, let me explain."

"I don't want to hear anything you have to say. Clean the room and then get out. I'm leaving." He stormed out and pushed the door so hard that it closed, rebounded open, and then swung closed again behind him.

Folly, fudge, and flummediddle. So much for Kate's idea of getting close to the suspects. And look at this mess. I remember the same jumble the very first time I cleaned his room. Things strewn everywhere. And the mud. He must've been walking through a pig lot... or a swamp. I might as well get busy and, as he said, clean the room.

Articles of clothing, discarded atop crumpled books and brochures, littered the floor. Half-eaten fruit and pastries topped the piles. *I need a shovel for this lot.*

She picked up everything, reading correspondence that came her way. Nothing useful here. *Hmmm. The first time I did this a note fell out of one of the pockets. I'll have to see if it's at the cottage.*

Then she attacked the mucky floor. *He will have to deal with his sand-and-muck-encrusted boots on his own. I wonder where he has been to get this dirty. Not hunting with Buck and Bram?*

Sadie finished for the day, got a bite of supper in the employees' dining room, and then headed for the veranda to see Mac. *Maybe he has some ideas for dealing with the marshal tomorrow.*

She was just poised to sink into a lounge chair when Bram, Buck, and Gator Simmons came around the side of the building making a great ruckus.

"I don't need no doctorin'. It'll get well on its own," said the weather-beaten old guide.

Dragging him along, like a mother cat with a kitten, Buck said, "Look at that arm, man. You can't go around with it bent like that."

Bram, tugging on the other side of him, brought the withered fellow up the steps. They stopped in front of Sadie. "He was walking in front of me and stepped on a branch that broke under his weight. It catapulted him forward. To break his fall, he threw his arms out in front of him. I heard a snap and that must've been his arm breaking."

"Ow," said the injured old codger, whose face had blanched of all color.

"It looks swollen... and deformed. Can you turn your arm from palm up to palm down?"

"No, Miss. I can't turn it no ways," he said in a faint voice.

"Can you help him?" said Buck.

"Yes," said Sadie. She stood and gave orders. "Take him to the kitchen, please. Give him a large glass of whiskey. And then that arm needs to be washed with plenty of soap and hot water. While you're at it, wash all of him and his clothes. I'll get my bag with some pain medicine and go get some medicinal leaves from a plant I noticed in the woods behind the hotel."

When she arrived in the kitchen, he was seated on a stool in the corner and dressed in clean clothes belonging to Percy. His tattered, but freshly laundered, overalls and shirt were pegged on a line hastily strung up behind the stove. *He still looks like he might faint any minute.*

She poured a maximum dose of pain medication into a small glass and handed it to him. "Here, Gator. Drink this. It tastes sweet and it will make you feel better."

He drank obediently.

"Bear with me. This should only take a little while." Sadie tipped a gnarled root and a handful of fresh large fuzzy comfrey leaves from a collecting pouch into a pan of water and swished them around to remove sand and debris.

Then she lifted them from the water and laid the damp plant matter onto a chopping board. With a large sharp cleaver, she minced it all as fine as possible. The result was a green, gooey, sticky, and slightly lumpy paste.

Now comes the hard part. "We have to straighten his arm, gentlemen. Let me tell you what we'll do, before we do it. Buck, you'll stand behind him and hold him firmly, not too tight, under his arms. Bram, hold his left shoulder very steady. I'm going to pull on his wrist until the bones align."

Bram said, "Begging your pardon, Miss Sadie, but have you ever done this before?"

"Yes. I've done it a number of times in the hospital in Wash...uhh, where I washed patients and set broken arms during the war. Don't worry. It won't hurt him, but he might faint."

Watch your tongue, Sadie. Though, I guess my past in Washington will all come out, if I'm arrested.

It worked, just as Sadie said. Gator moaned once. "Angh." Then it was all over and he was at peace.

Sadie applied comfrey paste to the forearm and bound it with clean cloth. "Let me just get you a mug of broth now," she told him.

When she handed him a cup of warm bone broth from the stove, his watery blue eyes looked up into her bright green ones with thanks. "Could you eat something more?"

He shook his head in a negative.

To the onlookers, she said, "Please help me make him comfortable in the store room, where Christian recovered from his fever. I will stay there tonight to give him pain medication as he needs it. We can change his bandage and strengthen him with some good breakfast in the morning."

When they were finished and the others had gone, she said, "I'm going out for a few minutes. I'll be back. Please just rest."

She went once again to the woods and chose a straight small branch, larger than a man's forearm. On the veranda she found Mac.

"Would you do me a favor, please, Mac? I know you have chisels and a knife suitable for whittling. I need a flat strong piece of wood that would span from Gator's elbow to his wrist. Could you fashion such a thing for me?"

"I suppose I could manage that. When do you want it?"

"Would in the morning be too soon?"

CHAPTER FIFTY-SEVEN

May 15, 1865 Morning

AT BROCK HOUSE

After an uneventful night, the morning dawned misty and cool, with the sky overcast. *The marshal will be here tonight. I guess this is my last day of freedom,* thought Sadie from her straight-back chair in the corner of the store room. *I wonder if he'll think it necessary to make a public spectacle of me.*

She sat staring at the craggy brows, drooping salt and pepper mustache, and leathery wrinkled face of the sleeping man on the cot. A groan came from deep within him.

He opened his eyes and looked around the room. "Mornin', Miss. Thankee fer yer med'cine. It hurts like the divvil."

"Okay. I will get you some laudanum." She retrieved a bottle from her bag and poured a large spoonful of the bitter medication. "Open your mouth and take this. It should make you feel better. Can you eat something more than broth this morning?"

"Yessum, I'm that hungry."

"Right. I'll get some breakfast for you. Meanwhile change into your own clothes, so we can give back Percy's. I can help with that shirt, if you like. Don't worry about the bandage. I'm going to change it and add some fresh comfrey after you eat."

"Yessum. I can manage. I'm beholden to ye."

"I'll be back shortly." Sadie walked briskly to the woods behind the hotel. She stopped and picked four large fat fuzzy leaves. *I can take only three or four from this plant. Any more would kill it. This will do for now, but I'll have to go to the cottage and get some comfrey from the herb garden for the next batch.*

She took them to the pump behind Brock House and washed them.

As she approached the hotel kitchen with her drippy greenery, Sadie smelled smoked ham and something sweet and spicy. "Mrs. Flowers, what smells so good in here?"

"That would be my sticky buns. They're just coming out of the oven. What have you got there?"

"This is to help heal Gator's arm. May I use a corner of your chopping block and a sharp knife? Oh, and I need a cup to hold the resulting paste."

"Indeed, you may, my dear. You know where everything is. Thanks for taking care of that fellow. There's not many as would bother."

Sadie stroked the velvety leaves between her fingers for a moment, then made her paste. She washed the knife, and returned it to its place. "May I please have a plate for Gator and one for myself? He needs meat to strengthen his bones. And I think we would both love your cinnamon rolls."

"All righty. Here. Careful. They're hot." She offered a plate with two enormous cinnamon buns gleaming with sugar icing. "Go ahead and fix a couple of plates. Add some of that gravy, too."

Sadie brewed tea and prepared heaping plates.

When she arrived back at the store room with her heavy tray, Gator, dressed in his frayed overalls and shirt, sat on the side of his cot. Sadie unveiled the breakfast tray. A cloud of steam escaped. *Mmm. That smells heavenly.*

His already watery blue eyes filled with tears. Sadie pretended not to notice. She set the box that served as a table, with his plate, in front of him.

"Let's eat and then get your bandage changed."

After their meal, she unwrapped his arm. "The swelling has gone down and there is no sign of infection, but you will have to be careful and not bump it. I think I have something that will help. I'll be right back."

She hurried to the front of the hotel and stepped out and onto the veranda in time to see Mac putting the finishing touches on a narrow flat board to stabilize Gator's arm.

"That's perfect, Mac. Thank you. It will let him move around, and keep that arm still."

He handed her the splint and said, "How are you this morning, Sadie?"

"I read some by candlelight last night, while I sat with Gator. But, may we skip lessons today, please? I need to go back to the cottage to get some comfrey and some more pain medicine."

"Yes, if that's what you have to do."

"To be honest, I'm afraid, Mac. I'm afraid of my future at the hands of this marshal. And if I'm convicted of killing Luther, then the real murderer will be running around loose."

"We are going to catch the true culprit, Sadie. Just carry on as if nothing is wrong. It will take your mind off of those things."

"I can do that. I have my hands full, what with Gator and the cleaning. I need to get back and dress his wound."

"All right. Perhaps we can continue your lessons this evening while we wait here for the *Darlington.*"

"Yes. Thank you." She went back inside and made a quick detour to the office of the manager, Mr. Lavigne. She knocked lightly at the door.

"Come in. Oh, it's you, Sadie," he said, between puffs on his pipe. He blew two smoke rings.

"Sir, I thought you would like to know that Gator Simmons was brought to us last night in shock with a broken arm. He is in the store room where Christian recovered. We both had breakfast from the kitchen this morning. You can take that cost out of my wages. I have to hurry back to my cottage for some more medicine for him, but I'll be right back and begin my regular duties."

"Well, I should hope so. If you don't start on time, I'll be forced to dock your pay. And what made you take it upon yourself to treat that, that, *that 'wrangler'* in my hotel?"

"There was really no other place, sir. And it didn't cost you anything. He provides a great service by taking guests hunting and fishing. Guests might even consider it a kindness to their guide."

"Well, uh, I, oh I guess when you put it like that, it's all right, this time. But don't do it again. This is a hotel, not a hospital."

"Yes, sir. I understand. Thank you, sir." She exited, stopped to get a fresh hand towel and basin of water, then hurried on to the store room.

"Gator, let's get that dressing changed. This splint will immobilize your forearm until the bone knits together again." She wiped off last night's comfrey, cleaned the wound, and applied the fresh paste. With the last of her bandage roll, she rewrapped the arm, incorporating the wooden brace. With muslin from her bag, she fashioned and applied a sling, to immobilize his arm.

"There. You'll be good as new in no time. I'm going to my cottage to get some more medicine and bandage material. Then I'll be back... to clean. It's my job here. But I'll check in on you from time to time. Now, you just rest."

She picked up her medicine bag and the remains of their breakfast. When she opened the storage room door, she was surprised to see Neville. "Hi. What are you doing here so early in the morning?"

Neville pulled back, out of her way to let her pass. "I'm just exploring the back halls of this hotel," he said, with an enormous laugh. "Care to join me?"

"No, thanks. I can't right now, Neville."

"Always busy, aren't you?" he said.

"I am, yes. I'm really busy, right now. We'll talk later. Bye."

She carried the food tray to the kitchen, where she handed it to the dish washer. "Thanks, Percy."

He tossed his tight blond curls, and said quietly, "'Tain't no trouble, Miss Sadie." A shy smile lit his shiny chocolate-brown face.

She beamed at him. Then she went out the kitchen door and into the warm Florida sunshine. The marshal's number-one murder suspect headed to her cottage as fast as she could go.

Whew. Can't remember when I walked at this pace. If I were a horse, it would be called 'trotting.'

I have the strangest feeling that someone is watching me. Silly.

At noon the front door of Brock House opened. Sweet-smelling pipe smoke preceded Guillaume Lavigne.

He stepped out onto the veranda. "Mac, Sadie was supposed to be back to start her shift, but Daisy hasn't seen hide nor hair of her. And that red hair is hard to miss. Do you know where she is?"

"No. The last I heard she was getting medical supplies from her cottage. She said she was coming right back."

"Yes, that's what the girl told me, too. Heaven knows I've been patient with her wild behaviors, because she's a good worker and gets along with the guests. But if she can't get to work on time, I'll have to find somebody else, Mac."

"Sadie has integrity, Guillaume. She does what she says she will do. I'm sure she has just been held up and will be here soon."

"I'm not so sure." The manager shoved his meerschaum back into his mouth and marched away.

Mac stroked the cat, who was curled in his lap. "She does have integrity, doesn't she, Fluffy? Sadie wouldn't run away. It's not in her character."

'Meow.' Fluffy yawned.

"I know. You agree with me, my very soft companion. Don't tell anybody, but I have failed her. I succeeded in getting her to work with me to find the killer, and all that did was put her in harm's way. Now my failure to find the real killer means she's facing a murder charge."

Our pretty redhead also said she would not leave.

"Where is she, Fluffy? Our neighbors are really far away, but maybe she met a neighbor who needed her help?

"Is she in trouble? Maybe she had an accident between here and the cottage and is hurt, lying in the road?

"We do have panthers here. Has a panther or some other wild animal attacked her?

"Or worse, did that intruder, who keeps getting into her cottage, go after her again?"

Her integrity will insist that she stand and face the charges. I believe she's as good as her word.

All that leaves is — trouble.

CHAPTER FIFTY-EIGHT

May 15, 1865 Morning

AT SNOW BIRD COTTAGE AND WOODS

O n her way to the cottage, Sadie peered into the woods beside the road as she neared the cottage. *I can't shake this feeling. Could somebody be out here? I see a lot of hiding places, but they are very snaky.*

She unlocked the front door. *Where did I put those newly rolled bandages?* She hesitated a minute before entering. *Oh, yes. In my bureau, with other linens.*

In her bedroom she rummaged around in her drawer. *What is this?* She pulled out a folded sheet of paper. *Oh. This was on the floor in Neville Beaumont's room.* She unfolded the note and read:

"The boss says soon as you announce your candidacy, will gather funds for your push for governor. That's the least we can do for his baby brother. Will send a couple of our Bowery boys to hand over cash in favorite brothel in New Orleans. Remember Amsterdam House? Been too long since we've seen you there. But, looks like playing at being a rich planter in Georgia may elevate you yet."

O, folly, fudge, and flummediddle. The boss of the Bowery Boys *gang is 'Bill the Butcher.'* She smacked her forehead. Bowery Boys — that's one of the most vicious gangs in New York.

If I read this correctly, Neville is the little brother of a really awful man. Maybe that's why I've never liked him very much. Did he leave New York to get away from that gang? It sounds like they are still on very good terms. This is an offer to give him money to get elected as a powerful leader.

"Ugh." *I can't stop to think about it now. Get a move on. Must get back to Brock House.*

She grabbed two rolls of bandages and shoved them into her bag. *I saw some laudanum on one of those shelves in the closet. Ah. There it is.* She stuffed that in, as well. Now *to dig some comfrey.*

I guess I better take off this ankle holster with Kate's five-shooter. I don't want to stomp down on the spade and have this thing go off. She bent over, lifted her floor-length skirt, removed the small gun strapped to her lower leg, and laid it on her bedside table.

Okay. Now I need garden tools from the shed. She went out the back door and around to the shed, where she grabbed a pair of clippers and her trusty shovel. *Hmm. Better take this basket, too.*

A few minutes later she was at the back of the garden, just adding a small comfrey root to her basket filled with broad oblong hairy leaves of the plant known as comfrey or boneset. *Aunt Cora's plant is so much bigger than that one behind the hotel. I suppose it will grow to five feet like this one, given time and enough water.*

She heard a noise and looked up.

"Well, there you are again. Busy, busy." The sonorous baritone voice, with a hint of sarcasm, was that of Neville Beaumont. He stood near her back door and started down the garden path toward her.

"What are you doing here, Neville?" She grabbed up her basket and carried it to the enormous square potting bench.

He strode up to the other side of it and said, "Look what I found." He raised his hand up high. From it dangled her ankle holster and gun.

"Put that down. How dare you go in my house." *The table's too wide to reach him.* She moved around it.

"Why don't you just come and get it, if you want it so bad." He edged around away from her.

"Give it here, Neville. It's not yours."

"No, that nosy friend of Mac's gave it to you."

She moved toward him and ,tried to grab it. "What in the Sam Hill are you playing at?" He dodged away. "Ha, ha. Catch me if you can."

"Neville. Give it here. I'm not joking." She rushed him.

"I'm not either, darlin' Ha, ha. You can't catch me." He pulled away toward the other side.

Her voice rose an octave. "Now. I want it now, before you hurt one of us." She moved around. *Grab it. Fast.*

He jumped away. "Ha. You don't get it that easy."

"Quit this silliness." She vaulted onto the tabletop.

"Oh, ho. You'll never get it like that." He held her gun aloft and charged into the woods behind the cottage.

"You idiot. Watch out for snakes in there, city boy. At least you'll scare them all away before I get to you. And get to you, I will." She took off after him.

How can he punch through this so fast? Chest-high palmettos, oaks large and small, palms, and dense undergrowth of thorny vines created what appeared to be an impenetrable wall.

Ahh. He seems to be following a vague path. Must be an animal track. "Neville. Stop. This is madness."

"Ha, ha. Come and get it, smarty pants." He crashed through the brush.

"Don't be childish. Just stop and give it back." Her long skirt tangled in a bull thorn that scratched her legs. *Aargh. I could do with a pair of pants, right now. Leather pants sound perfect.*

She stopped and tied her skirt between her legs, exposing her bare ankles and lower calves. "Neville, just stop. You've had your laugh. This is not funny anymore."

"What? You can't keep up? You won't get your pretty little five-shooter, then. Ha, ha. I may throw it into the bushes where you'll never find it."

There he is, still holding my pistol. "You better not. I'll catch you, you stinker. And when I do, I'm going to smack you so hard." She redoubled her effort. *I seem to be going up. Is this a ridge? Whew. Didn't know there were any hills in Florida.*

"You going to throw me down like you did Luther on the steamer?"

"What? That's crazy. Come back here. "*All I can see is the back of his head, but that's enough. I'm gaining.* She charged under a low hanging bush and churned in his direction.

"Ouch, ouch, ouch."

"Oh, look over there. A big patch of briars. Perfect. Ha,ha, haaa."

He disappeared from view. She rushed after him. Sweat trickled down her face. "Why are you doing this?"

The terrain cleared. *I can see you now, you rotter.* She ran over sand strewn with dried palmetto fronds.

Then,

"Eeek. Aaa!"

The ground gave way beneath her.

"Fwumph. Kasploosh!"

She fell in a heap.

What?

What happened?

Sadie lay stunned. Then she opened her eyes and blinked away mud. She snorted water out of her nose, spat out something slightly brackish, and looked up.

Blue sky. High sand walls. Eww... I'm wet and mucky. I'm in a pit? Am I really in a hole in the ground?

Neville's face came into view at the top of the sand. He grinned. "How are you doing down there?"

How am I doing down here? She wiggled her fingers and toes.

"Ow."

Try the arms and legs.

She splashed about. "Ouch. Ouch. Not good. Neville. Help. Mosquitos are swarming me. Get me out of here."

"Yes. I hear that our troops complained of those blood sucking gallinippers, too. You want out already? You just got there."

"Oh, Neville. Really. I'm not joking. I hurt my left arm and ankle when I fell."

"You will get no sympathy from me."

"How can you say that? I'm injured."

"And you will be worse real soon. Ha, ha, ha."

"What do you mean?"

"I mean I'm not letting some stupid actress from Washington ruin my career in politics."

"I don't know what you are talking about."

"Don't play dumb with me, Evangeline Bright."

She lay, listening to blue jays scolding them from the surrounding woods.

Gallinippers buzzed round her ear.

"How did you know?"

"I thought there was something familiar about you, the first day I saw you. You were changing clothes in a most unladylike way. Then I remembered. I travel to Washington, too."

"Even so, I don't have plans to stop your campaign for governor. I've never done anything to you, except reject your offer of a job."

"Ha. Not buying it. You called me 'city boy.' Why was that?"

"Um, I..."

"I thought so. You are a right nosy bitch, Evangeline, or whoever you are. You found out about my brother, Bill, didn't you?"

"Um, Bill?"

You will be as much of a threat to me as Luther. Sooner or later you will open your big fat mouth and tell the world who I am."

"Oh folly, fudge, and flummediddle."

"Don't say such ridiculous things."

"Did you kill Luther?"

"Of course, I killed him. And you're never going to tell anyone."

"I should have guessed. Luther was blackmailing you, wasn't he?"

"He wasn't, but it was only a matter of time until he thought of it. And I handled him neatly, until you started poking your nose in."

"Are you my intruder at Snow Bird Cottage?"

"Oh, yes. I was having so much fun playing with you, before dispatching you, like a cat with a mouse. 'Bap' and watch the mouse run. Ha, ha, ha."

"You did all those awful things to me just for fun?"

"Yes. I tried scaring you, by moving that weird little knife around. When that didn't work, I tried killing the squirrel and hanging it, dripping with blood, where you'd find it. I figured the blood would scare you off. That should've done it. But, no. Then I had the gator wrangler put a big alligator in your cottage."

Her voice rose. "That was you? What a horrible thing to do. Poor unsuspecting Jane. She could have been killed!"

"Yes, and maybe that might have stopped you, finally. But you had to go and get a gun. Now, because you killed the stupid gator and bragged about tanning its hide for shoes, you're on your way to becoming a folk hero, you meddling bitch."

"You aren't going to help me out of this pit, are you?"

"No. It's a great pit, though, isn't it? It's for catching wild hogs, you know. I caught a wild woman. Ha, ha, ha." He paused. "You are going to die in that hog hole."

"Neville, I ..."

"And it was so convenient. It was beautiful. Right there waiting for me. All I had to do was deepen it some and cover it."

"That's why your boots were so muddy."

"Yes. I did carry some of this hole back to my room. But nobody seemed to care."

"You can't just leave me here."

"Oh, I can. Did you know that these handy holes saved the homesteaders ammunition during the war? According to Gator, they smoked and ate plenty of hogs, without shooting a single one. They just killed them in these pits."

"You knew Luther before your trip on the steamboat, didn't you?"

"Now that you can't give away my secret, I'll tell you. Luther was a customer at the bordello where my cronies and I went regularly. He saw me there once. We were enemies from rival gangs."

"The Dead Rabbits?"

"Yes. He would have ruined me in a heartbeat. It's not good for a politician to be seen in a brothel. I wasn't going to let that bit of trash ruin my political career. And you won't be telling anyone, either."

"I- I can keep quiet."

"I'm surprised you haven't noticed that you have company. Look floating in the corner over there." He pointed.

Company?

A sinewy knot of shed snakeskins.

No.

Not skins.

SNAKES.

RATTLERS.

"You'll never tell anyone that I killed Luther. You will be all swollen and covered in vomit by the time they find you. Not a good look for a classy girl like you."

Sadie looked across at the unmoving snakes. Her breath came in shallow rapid gasps.

She was a small child again, crying in anguish over her lost puppy, lying dead. From beside the pup, a huge six-foot-long rattlesnake retreated.

"Wake up and get busy, you lazy snakes," Neville shouted. "They were wiggling like crazy yesterday, when I dumped them in there. I'll be back in two or three days. I'm sure they'll get you before then. Buh, bye."

Sadie told herself, *Stop it, This is no time to freeze.* She looked again at the snakes. They were lethargic. *Are they mating?*

You have to get out of here, before these snakes discover you.

A big deep breath helped clear her thinking. *This hog hole must be eight feet deep and as wide.*

She scrabbled, as high as she could reach with her fingernails, into the walls of sand and crumbled shell. A handful splashed into the 18 inches of water covering her feet. Where she dug in, the sand came out easily. Too easily. *Fingerholds collapse in this soft sand. Maybe I can bring down enough to make a little hill to stand on.*

She continued to scrape at the wall above her. *It's working. If only I could dig faster.*

Half of a relatively intact clam shell loosened and fell amidst the shell hash. *Yay. Thank you, God. A tool.*

She grabbed it up, then stepped back and surveyed her work.

The little pile at her feet was too short to elevate her enough to get out and also not high enough to get her up above the water and snakes. *But it's a start. Hurry.*

She redoubled her efforts and soon she had removed a couple of bushels of dirt above her head. *Oh, no.* The pygmy rattlesnake swam slowly in her direction.

No.

I'm not done yet.

Go away.

She swirled the water at her feet. It swam slowly in the other direction.

Dig. Dig. Dig.

Ha. A little higher up.

"Scrabble. Scoop...FWUMPH."

Two more bushels came down.

"Ptooey." She spat out sharp shell bits and muck.

Sadie scraped it into a mound and climbed on top. *Still in this nasty water.*

Don't think about the snakes.

She immediately thought about the snakes.

Maybe the falling sand will keep the rattlesnakes away.

Sadie dug furiously about a foot below the top.

Oh, no. That whole shelf above me looks like it's cracking. and about to...

"EEeek. *Fall. down...*"

"KaFWUMP."

"Thump."

"Splash."

...collapse right on top of me.

What more could go wrong?

She had scrunched her eyes closed tight. Now she opened them, brushed at the sand on her face.

Oh. Sand in my eyes. She rubbed at it.

Ow.

"No," she cried. *Scratchy.*

Tears welled up.

Fat drops splashed a trail down her cheeks.

She sat on her hill, in the brackish water. Pulling knees to her chin, she curled into a ball.

This is so awful.

I'm never going to get out of here.

She bawled like a baby.

Minutes later, tears cleared her eyes.

She looked over at the snakes.

They look like three ropes floating, coiled around one another. They remained in a corner, well beyond her feet, and seemed undisturbed by the falling sand.

Wait. This is a blessing. It's making a kind of ramp.

Okay. Let's climb higher. She shook the dirt out of her hair and clothes.

She scrambled higher up the pile.

Ahh, finally. Out of the water.

This is going to work. She resumed digging.

When the next load fell, she was ready.

Yay. My ramp to freedom is ready.

But as she climbed, the sand shifted under her. She slid backwards and lower.

"Oh, folly, fudge, and flummediddle."

Still. Stay still.

She sighed. *I'm so, so tired. It feels like I've been digging for hours.*

Maybe fear is helping that along. Relax. It is what it is.

Think.

Okay. What can I see?

Sand.

More sand.

A small tree.

Trees have roots underground. I need one big enough to stand on and climb out of here.

She dug more carefully now. *My friendly neighborhood reptiles seem to be asleep.*

Joking to keep from turning into a blubbering idiot.

Dig.

Eureka. A root.

Soon she was standing with her eyes above the ground. A sapling grew not more than a foot away from the edge of her hog pit.

Thank you, God, for this tree and its strong foundation.

All right. Time to climb out of here.

She scrambled with all her might, but couldn't get out. *Do I have to go back and dig more to add stairs to my ramp? The snakes will get me. They're already moving more.*

The snakes now circled the base of her ramp. Her only defense was to throw sand and shells at them.

This is exhausting and won't slow them for long. What I really need is a rope to tie around that tree.

She clutched her throat, where her long, bedraggled scarf dangled.

My scarf!

Sadie unwound the long, red, muddy silk scarf. *Lord, I'm thankful for the swirly scarf. Now, where is my big digging shell?*

She tied the heavy clam shell into the end of her scarf. With her hand as high as she could hold it, she twirled her scarf around her head.

Now let the scarf out to its full length. Here goes. She leaned toward the tree and hurled the loose end of the piece of silk with its shell. It looped around the sapling and swung on around toward her.

Yay. Got it. She caught the returning shell.

Now, tugging on both ends of the very strong silk, Sadie pulled herself up the sandy ramp she had created.

Finally.

My swirly scarf saved the day. Can't bear to put the mucky thing around my neck again. She wound it around her waist like a belt.

"That was a good trick," said a voice behind her.

Chapter Fifty-Nine

May 15, 1865

In the Woods Behind Snow Bird Cottage and the Shell Mound

"Neville. There is no way..." She spun around to face him.

It wasn't Neville standing there. She backed away.

"Gator. What are you doing here?"

"I uh...."

"You're supposed to be resting."

"Well, truth be told, when you didn't come back, I got right worried."

"You were worried about me? Why?"

"I was a'feelin' bad for puttin' that gator in your cottage. Mr. Beaumont, he said it would be real funny. I figured it'd make plenty a mess, thrashin' about and breakin' things, afore you shooed it out. But, I heared thet it like ta et you, an' you shot the poor dumb critter."

"I did, and a good thing too."

"Then he offered me a big price if I could ketch him some rattlers. He didn't want the pretty skins. He wanted 'em 'live. So, I got 'em, but I was mighty curious what he wanted 'em fer."

"I wondered how he got three rattlesnakes in there with me. You probably showed him this hog pit, didn't you?"

"Yes, Miss. He axed a powerful lotta questions about them holes."

I can imagine. He thinks he's pretty smart — smart enough to get away with murder. "Gator, I need to find him. He just confessed to killing Luther Greim, a man on our steamer."

"Well he's right easy to track, Miss... like a bear crashin' through the woods."

"Is that how you found me?"

"Yes. Mr. Mac was verra worried, too, when you was gone. He sent me to your cottage, and I tracked you from there."

"But, your arm..."

He grinned. "Like you said, it'll be good as new, afore long. Whyn't we go ketch thet sidewinder? Looks like he got hisself lost agin. His tracks ain't leadin' to the hotel."

"I can't get any dirtier than I am right now. And maybe the mud will keep the gallinippers away. Let's go."

Gator led off toward the south and east.

"Whew." *He moves fast. And quietly. He wouldn't lead me deep into the woods and then leave me lost. Would he? I was lost to begin with. Can't get any more lost.*

And he wouldn't do that.

A little voice inside her said, "Never underestimate the power of money to motivate."

After half an hour of slipping through the woods, Gator said, "Looks as how he's headed fer the shell mound."

"Oh, no. It's as tall as a building. Couldn't he climb it and see us coming?"

"No way he cud ken we're comin' fer 'im, Miss. And they's a good many tall trees ta keep 'im from seein' it 'til he's right up on it. I reckon we'll ketch 'im unawares."

"Good. Because he has my five-shooter gun. Do you have a weapon?"

"Only my head, Miss. But thet works passable good."

Ha. To survive and thrive out here, his thinking must be sharp. "If I throw that villain to the ground, can you go back to the hotel and get help to arrest him?"

"Yes, Miss."

How long that will take? I'm so tired. I don't want a wrestling match with Neville. He might be pretty tired, too. But he'll be fighting for his life. Maybe I can sit on him. Muddy up his fancy clothes. Ha. I would like that. "How far is the mound, Gator?"

"Not more 'n another 20 minutes, Miss."

They soldiered on. She stumbled between trees and around bushes. Eventually the underbrush became less dense. They could see a good distance away. "Shh. Gator, I think

I can hear him, stomping through the brush. Let's try to get to him before he finds the mound." *Hurry. Watch out for that long bullthorn vine, dangling from the oak tree.*

She ducked to the right... directly into a bush, disturbing an enormous wasps' nest. The papery ball fell. Out came a cloud of angry wasps. "Aaa." She ran.

Furious, the insects swarmed after her. "Zap."

"Zap."

"Zap."

"Aaaaaa."

She slapped and dodged.

Still they chased her.

"Gator, help."

"Pull up your dress, Miss."

One doesn't pull up one's skirt in polite society, said the small ever-present voice in her head.

Oh, sit down in the back seat and be quiet. Nobody cares what my petticoat looks like.

She pulled her hem up over her head, leaving only her eyes and her fingertips unshield-ed.

She followed Gator in this manner for several minutes. "Surely, Neville heard that. So much for sneaking up on him."

"There he is, Miss. He kens something's awry. Go get 'im."

Sadie let her skirt drop.

She rushed toward the murderer.

"Evangeline. The wrangler rescued you. It won't do you any good." He pulled back his fist and punched her in the face.

"Unngh." She staggered back. Blood gushed from her nose.

Neville scrambled up the mound.

Why is he going up?

"Come on, Gator."

Ow. Ow. Ewww. Blood is splattering down my formerly-white dress front.

She slipped and skated on the shell hash, then pitched forward.

All right. I can move faster on hands and knees.

On all fours, they slithered up, then slid back halfway.

I can almost reach him.

"Boom."

A bullet whistled above her head. It thudded into the shells behind her.

That's why he went up. He's trying to shoot me... with my own gun.

We're sitting ducks.

He has four more bullets. Keep him guessing.

She crab-walked to her left. "Neville. Give up._"

"No. I will kill you and go on my way."

"Kaboom." A crater appeared ten feet away from her.

Not at this rate, you won't. Thank God you never learned to shoot.

She again moved sideways, away from the crater. "It won't help, Neville. Mac knows."

"He can't know."

"Yes, he does. And the provost marshal is coming in on the *Darlington*. He should be getting in any minute now."

"You're lying."

"No, I'm not. I think I hear the whistle now. As soon as Mac tells the marshal, they'll send an army of men to hunt you."

"Not me. I'm a very important person. When you are missing no one will care. And they won't suspect a candidate for governor. I'm finally going to kill you. I should've done it as soon as you found out I killed Luther."

"Boom."

CHAPTER SIXTY

May 15, 1865, a Few Minutes Earlier

ABOARD THE "DARLINGTON"

"**C**rack." Aboard the *Darlington* it was muffled. The shot could barely be heard over the noise of the engines and paddle wheel. But Noah had reason to be alert. He said, "Jacob, did you hear that?"

"It's probably just a hunter, Noah."

"At this time of the evening?"

"Crack."

"I heard it that time. But, why the fuss?"

"Quick, man. It's dusk. Hunters would be headed home, not trying to bag a deer that they would have to dress in the dark. A murderer is on the loose. It's coming from the shell mound. Go."

"All right. It'll only take another minute. I still think..."

"Over there. That's good. Let down the gang plank. Yes. Right on the lakeshore." The movable bridge settled onto the sand. Noah shouldered his rifle and charged toward shore. He hit the sand, slammed into the brush, and headed toward the sound of the shots.

God, help me. If I'm right and she found the killer, he might have silenced her already. Or she might be fighting for her life. God, keep her alive.

Now he could see the shell mound.

And halfway up, Sadie. She's moving. Thank you, God.

Is that? Looks like Gator. Crouching. Out in the open. No cover.

A loud voice rang out from atop the shell mound, "... I'm a very important person. When you are missing, no one will care. And they won't suspect a candidate for governor. I'm finally going to kill you. I should've done it as soon as you found out I killed Luther."

Neville Beaumont!

"Boom."

No.

Sadie's voice came. "Neville, stop."

He missed!

Well, I won't.

He took careful aim, took a big breath, then exhaled slowly. *Do I kill him or let him live? He deserves to die. But "Vengeance is mine," said the Lord.* "Crack."

Neville dropped the pistol and fell to his knees, swearing and clutching his thigh, through his flapping pants leg.

Noah lowered his Whitworth and let out the remainder of his breath. Behind him all the passengers from the *Darlington* surged forward to congratulate him on his accurate long-range shot.

The marshal said in a loud voice to his deputies, "All right, boys." He pointed. "You and you, go back to the *Darlington* and find a plank or something we can use to strap down and transport this villain. Not that he deserves to be carried. The rest of you follow me. I'll head on up the hill to arrest that blighter." He turned and hastened toward the mound.

"What are you all doing here?" said Noah.

Jacob Brock said, "With the *Darlington* essentially 'docked' right out there, all the passengers wanted to see what made you run off into the woods like that."

"Did all of you hear Neville's threats and confession to murder?"

"Oh, yes. Every word. Shocking. Just shocking," said Mary Merritt, who, with her sister, now often rode the *Darlington* for pleasure.

Not quite believing that all these people had seen the confrontation on the mound, Noah said, "Thank you for being so quiet. I concentrated so hard that I didn't know you were there."

"Don't be thanking us. We had no choice. After we heard his confession, all we could do was hold our breath to see what would happen next," said Martha Merritt.

Noah said, "That's amazing. Thirty people all listened in silence. I didn't hear a peep. And that means we have thirty witnesses to Neville's confession."

A voice ringing with amazement and disbelief said, "Noah! You're here? I thought the *Katie Asbell* was in Jacksonville this evening."

"She is, but I'm not." Without thinking, he just enclosed his lady sleuth in a giant bear hug. "Thank. God. You're safe."

She wiggled within his arms. "Noah. Not so tight. I can't breathe."

He laughed and loosened his grip.

Sadie said, "But, how are you here? You left Enterprise two days ago. It takes four days to get to Jacksonville and back."

He looked down at her black eyes, red nose, begrimed face, and bloodied dress. *I love this girl, with her red hair all askew. Her spirit, uncommon good sense, and commitment to her task, not to mention those bright green eyes, set her apart.* "It's simple, really. Shorty is piloting her."

She gasped. "You let Shorty take your pride and joy?"

"We docked in Palatka last night alongside the *Darlington* and I saw the marshal. We discussed the murder. I showed him the blood spatter evidence in Luther's cabin aboard the *Katie Asbell*. I also explained the lack of blood in your cabin, where that claw hammer with dried blood was found. He was not swayed." He sighed.

Noah said, "It seemed that his mind was already made up about the whole thing. He had you tried and hanged. I couldn't persuade him to consider other possibilities. I sent Shorty on to Jacksonville and came back here with Jacob on the *Darlington,* because I was worried about you."

She looked up at him and he could see, in her eyes, the moment that the truth dawned on her. "That shot. The mysterious bullet that came out of nowhere to take Neville down... it was yours, wasn't it?"

"Yup. My trusty 'Whitworth one-shot' never fails me."

"Noah, it looks like you really did save me, this time. Thank you." She hugged him back. They clung together longer than normal, then finally moved apart.

He squeezed her hand. "I'll be thinking about appropriate ways for you to show me your appreciation." He laughed. *Is that a blush on her face, under all that smeared mud?*

"We did it, Noah. We captured the killer. He left me to be bitten by rattlesnakes." She shuddered, then looked up into his eyes. "The blackguard expected me to die in agony. And when he thought I couldn't tell anyone, he confessed to killing Luther."

Noah said, "That rotter. He won't wiggle out of this. We have a boatload of witnesses to his confession."

"He had the gall to boast about the awful things he did to me. He was my nasty intruder at Snow Bird Cottage. It feels wonderful to be free of him. Now that he's in custody, I may not even need new locks."

"Oh, you are getting new locks. Jacob has them aboard the *Darlington*. Kate sent them for you."

"Really? She is a kind friend. Speaking of kind friends, where is Gator?"

"Over here, Miss." His formerly clean sling looked worse for the wear. He held his battered palm frond hat by his side and looked down at his calloused bare feet.

"I couldn't have found him without you, Gator. Thank you."

"Glad ta help. I'm goin' now. I reckon we done good."

"We did, thanks to your excellent tracking."

"And we're right lucky that he's a terr'ble shot," he said, with a gleam in his eye.

"We sure are. I've been thanking God for that for the last hour. How's your arm? Still hurting?"

"Yes, some."

"If it gets too bad, come to the hotel and see me. I'll give you something for it."

"Right. I reckon it'll heal up real good. Thank ye." Then he disappeared behind a nearby palm and was gone.

"Hoot. Hoot."

Noah said, "It sounds like the *Darlington* is leaving. Do you want to ride back to the hotel?" The crowd had dispersed and they found themselves alone.

"Oh, could I? I'm so tired I can barely wiggle."

"Yes, I'm sure Jacob will welcome you aboard the *Darlington* for the five-minute ride to the hotel," said Noah.

"On second thought, I'm a mess. And I'm not far from home. The shell mound is the place where Mac taught me to shoot the LeMat gun. My cottage is only minutes from here. Could you possibly walk me home? I'm ashamed to be seen like this, in front of everyone at the hotel."

"I'd be honored. Let me just run and tell Jacob not to wait for us. I'll be back in two shakes of a lamb's tail." He took off at a jog on what was now a well trampled pathway to the road and the beach beyond, where the *Darlington* lay anchored.

Sadie kicked a downed tree trunk to rid it of residents. *All lizards, frogs, crickets, scorpions, and snakes — OUT.* Then, she sank down and closed her eyes.

That's where he found her minutes later, when he returned. "You look tired. Are you sure you want to walk to the cottage?"

"Yes. I'm just thanking God for protection during this wild adventure. And thank you for caring enough to come back to Enterprise early. You stopped a man who has murdered at least once and was planning to do it again."

"Sadie, I..." He shook his head. *You are coming over all shy? Get a grip, man.* "Are you ready to go?" He offered his hand to help her up.

At his touch, sparks seemed to fizz between their hands. She rose slowly. *Still effervescing. Act normal.*

They held hands as they walked back to her cottage under a rosy sky. "I hope Jane is home. My cinnamon bun with that lovely sugar icing from breakfast is a distant memory. I'm famished and she always has something good on hand."

He laughed. "When are you going to talk about what happened today?"

"Not now. I'm just too tired. Perhaps in the morning I can tell you and Mac... and the marshal, if he's interested."

"Oh, I suspect he'll insist on it. And I guess I'll stay in Enterprise until Shorty gets here with the *Katie Asbell.*"

"I have to work tomorrow, but Wednesday, that's the day after tomorrow, right? is my day off." She shook her head at her own fuzzy thinking.

"Yup. I thought we could do something fun. Think about it. What would you like to do, now that you're a free woman?" His eyes gleamed in the blue twilight.

The moon was a giant silver ball peeking from behind her cottage, when they finally arrived. Lightning bugs blinked in the yard, stars shone above, and their resident owl family "who who-ed," back-and-forth.

In the moonlight, a yellow lamp gleamed from the living room window. They took the front steps at a slow pace. "Jane?" She tried the front door knob and the door opened. "Jane?"

"Sadie. Where have you been? You look terrible. What happened?"

"I'll tell you later. Right now, I need a bath and food. I could eat a horse."

"We don't have any horse, but we do have some very good smoked ham with gravy and biscuits," said Jane.

She eyed Noah. "Come in, you two. Sadie, get out of those awful clothes and I'll bring you hot water to wash. Noah, have a seat and tell me what you can, while I work."

"Aye, aye, cap'ain," he said, in a bemused voice.

Sadie said, "Oh, folly, fudge, and flumediddle. Is the reservoir on my outside shower full?"

"Why, yes. It is."

Sadie marched to the back door, opened it, and walked out.

"What in the world?" said Noah.

Jane went to look. Sadie, fully clothed, and with hands raised to her hair, stood under the full flow of warm water from the overhead sprinkler.

Jane scooted inside and returned moments later with a robe and towel for Sadie.

"Is everything all right?" said Noah.

"It's getting that way," said Jane. "We'll eat in about ten minutes."

My mother taught me to set the table. We are all in this together. I'll just get down some plates and silverware, thought Noah.

Meanwhile, Jane delivered the linens to Sadie and helped her remove her sopping clothes. "You look exhausted. Here. Sit. Let me rub your hair dry for you."

After Sadie combed through her red locks, Jane said, "Feeling any better?"

"Yes. I believe I do. Let's eat." They moved toward the dining room.

"I'll bring it, and I have a surprise for you."

In the dining room, Jane seemed pleased that Noah had set the table with their everyday dishes. "Thank you, Noah."

She returned with a heaping platter. Three fried eggs held pride of place on top.

"Eggs. Where did you get eggs?" said Sadie.

"That's my surprise. Last week Jacob brought chickens and I got leghorns for us — three hens and a rooster. They are pretty good layers. I've been feeding them leftovers from the hotel."

Through a mouth full of ham and egg, Sadie said, "Where are they?"

"I'm keeping them in the boat shed right now. We need a chicken coop and a run for them." She turned to Noah. "By the way, did you book a room at Brock House? I heard Mrs. Flowers say that they are at full capacity, with the marshal and his junior officers."

"Oh, no. I didn't think of that."

"I heard talk about it. They said there's not an empty bed anywhere in town. Zeb Greene is still working on his little boarding house, but he's not ready to open yet. I'm thirsty. Would you go get us another pitcher of water from the kitchen pump out back, please, Noah?"

"Certainly. I'll be right back."

After he left, Jane said, "May we offer him some quilts and a place to sleep on the floor, Sadie?"

"I don't see why not. It's the least I can do, after he saved my life. I'll issue the invitation."

Jane's eyebrows shot up inquiringly, but she said nothing.

When he returned, Sadie said, "We can offer our parlor floor and some blankets for the night."

"I wouldn't want to put you out any."

"Where else are you going to sleep?"

"The woods? In your boat?"

"Nonsense. Unless you want to be eaten by a bear or wake up as a hunchback, you won't argue," said Sadie.

"Well, then, thank you. I really don't want to walk back to the hotel and beg for a room."

Jane showed him to the parlor, where she handed him sheets, a thick comforter with blankets, and a pillow.

"This is most gracious of you. Thank you."

"Don't mention it. Good night, Noah. Sleep well," said Sadie.

"Sweet dreams, Sadie, Jane. I'll see you in the morning."

They retired for the night. He arranged his bed clothes, snuffed out his candle, and lay in the moonlight, which streamed in through the window. "Whip-por-will. Whip-por-will."

What a day. What a woman. I can't let her get away.

But I have to be here more than one evening out of four.

How can I do that and still run my business?

CHAPTER SIXTY-ONE

May 16, 1865 Morning

AT SNOW BIRD COTTAGE AND BROCK HOUSE HOTEL

N oah opened his eyes in the pale dawn light. *Mmm. Might as well get up.* He rose and folded his blankets and comforter. After stacking the bed clothes on a dresser, he yawned, stretched toward the ceiling, then headed for the front porch.

What a view. That big sky overhead is purple, orange, and blue, with all of it mirrored on Lake Monroe as far as I can see.

A light breeze came in off the lake and blew his hair across his face. *Wonder if they have any coffee?*

He went to the kitchen and ducked his head under the flow of water from the pump. After a vigorous wash, he went outside and brought in some kindling and a couple of oak logs. Soon the cooking fire was crackling.

Now, if I were a coffee pot, where would I be? He searched high and low. *No pot. They must keep it someplace special. I'll just start some water boiling in a regular pot.* That done, he looked for the coffee beans among the many labeled jars on the shelves.

He was still looking, when Jane came in. "Good morning. Can I help you find something?"

"I was just going to surprise you with a pot of coffee. But I can't find the pot or the beans."

"We have some delicious teas. Why would you want to drink that bitter coffee, when you can have tea?"

"Oh, I suppose I just got used to it. During the war, the government issued coffee as part of the standard rations. The British don't have a monopoly on coffee, like they do on tea."

"I saw some consumption of coffee in Cuba. But we don't hold with such, here. We have pekoe and souchong. Which would you prefer?"

"I've never had souchong tea. I'll have some of that. May I help you make it?"

"No. Shoo. Out of my kitchen. Thank you for starting the cooking fire. Now, go keep Sadie company on the front porch."

Why didn't I think of that? "Yes, Miss."

He looked at her. *The sun sparkles on that hair... like red gold.* Sadie looked out over the lake, as she sat rhythmically combing. Noah watched for several moments, before he said, "Good morning. Your hair seems much shorter than what I imagined it to be. I like it shoulder length, but how do you twist it around into a bun?" *I would like it any length, actually. Shoot. You could be bald, for all I care.*

"Ninety-six, ninety-seven, ninety-eight... Um, I have a story about that. I'll tell you someday."

"Bong."

Jane appeared in the doorway.

"Did you just hit the bottom of a pot with a metal spoon?" Sadie said.

"Yes. I couldn't find our bell. Breakfast is on the table. Come and eat."

The three feasted once again on smoked ham, gravy, and biscuits. A treat for their breakfast was fresh raspberries from the garden.

After clearing up, they walked together along the road strewn with wild purple-blue morning glories. The bright flowers and good company made this stroll to Brock House seem short.

Sadie said, "I wonder where they're holding Neville?"

"Probably in the storeroom, with half a platoon of guards," said Noah.

"Will the marshal be working with Mac?" said Jane.

Noah said, "Probably. That would be respectful of his status as a former Pinkerton agent. He did take on this investigation as a contribution to the community."

"We are about to find out," said Sadie.

Mac sat chatting on the front veranda with a very upright middle-aged man in a blue Union army uniform. His left coat sleeve and shirt sleeve were pinned under and he had dark circles under his tired-looking blue eyes. "and John Lloyd, who leased her tavern near Washington, testified that Mary Surrott hid carbines there and told him to 'get the shooting irons ready.' That'll hang her, Mac."

Sadie's heart raced at mention of the Lincoln conspiracy trial. Mac looked up and said, "Mornin', folks. Ladies, let me introduce Colonel Brown. Colonel, this is Jane Marsh and Sadie Snow. You've met Captain Asbell."

They exchanged pleasantries. Then Mac said, "Sadie, the Maases and the Merritts just loaded mountains of luggage aboard the steamer. They are all going home. And you'll be happy to know that Buck is aboard this morning on his way to New York. He says he's going to fetch Kat and take her to meet his wife Naomi, at his homestead south of Brooksville."

She managed a smile. "Good. He talked about his other children, a son and a daughter. I hope they turn out to be good playmates for this baby."

"Mmm. Only time will tell. On other matters, the colonel needs your statement, Sadie, about what happened prior to capturing Neville Beaumont. Noah, it will be useful for you to stay, too. We must be speedy."

Jane said, "Good day, gentlemen. I'm going on to work."

The Colonel stood and tipped his hat.

Sadie told of Neville taking her five-shooter, the deadly hog hole and rattlers, and tracking him through the dense overgrowth to the shell mound. *Tiresome story... and I'm getting weary telling it.* "If that's all, I have work to do."

"Before you go, you might like to watch Mr. Beaumont being marched onto the *Darlington.* He is going back in shackles to Jacksonville to face trial. You will have to tell your story once more. But I feel certain you will receive justice," said Colonel Brown."

A commotion arose from the side of the hotel. *Neville!* The prisoner bucked and hurled loud abusive shouts at his captors.

What in the Sam Hill? He is actually wearing his black top hat! How does he get it to stay on, with all his gyrations?

Neville's wrists were chained together in front of him.

Sadie said, " He sure is putting up a fight."

Neville Beaumont had abandoned all pretense. His polite manners forgotten, he drew back his lips in a snarl and yanked on the two ropes by which his captors were attempting to lead him to the ship. He hurled himself around like a wild hog trying to escape. "You mangy curs. You'll be sorry you ever messed with me. This is rubbish. My rivals for the governorship are behind this." He jerked from side to side, pulling a tall lanky captor to his knees on the rickety weathered dock.

"Don't worry. I got him, Slim," hollered the soldier holding the second rope. He looked like a young blond child.

Slim regained his footing, shortened his hold on the rope, and gave it a furious tug. A short and stolid soldier they called Zach prodded Neville, none too gently, from behind with his bayonet. He yelled at Neville, "Stop that afore I jab yuh real hard."

Neville erupted in a frenzy of poking elbows. He head-butted Slim.

Zach shouted, "If'n yuh don' quit it, we'll hogtie yuh. An' then we have ta wrestle yuh aboard. We're not too good at carryin', mind. Cain't say as we mightn't let yuh drop some."

"You dare do this to me? You rats. I'll get you. Watch out. My buddies will get your wives... and children. I have powerful friends. I'll soon be out of your stinkin' jail. Then look out. I am coming after you, you mongrels." He shook raised fists at his captors.

Amidst furious protests, the loud prisoner half walked and was half dragged to the ship.

"With that fancy embroidered-red-silk-lined coat flapping around him, he's the dandiest prisoner ever to stump along in leg irons," said Mac, with a laugh.

Sadie said, "Thank you, Colonel. It's satisfying to see him going to jail, where he can't hurt anyone else. For that, I will tell my story again -- as many times as you need." She stood and started for the door. "I'll be right back with my books, Mac."

Colonel Brown stood and shook hands all around. "Goodbye, folks. Better be on my way."

Mac said, "Thank you for coming Colonel. I'm happy to leave the matter in your capable hands."

"Gentlemen," said Noah. He followed Sadie.

They found themselves in a deserted corridor. As she stood looking up at him, he swept a kiss across her forehead.

"Zing." *How does he do that? Whew.*

She reached up and brushed her mouth lightly against his minty lips.

"Flash." He felt a jolt all the way down to his toes. After a gasp for breath, he returned the gesture and let his lips linger.

The kiss seemed to hold them both bound together in a sweet never — ending moment in time.

They heard the laugh of a hotel guest approaching and they moved apart. She said, "Oh. My. I..."

Kate Warne rushed up to them. "Oh, hello you two. Sadie. Just the person we're looking for. This is my boss and good friend, Alan Pinkerton. Alan, this is Noah Asbell, owner and captain of the *Katie Asbell* and Sadie Snow, who just caught her first murderer."

"Pleased to meet you, sir," said Noah.

"This is a pleasant surprise." The two ladies embraced.

"We ran into our old friend, Captain Coxetter, in Charleston and convinced him to bring us here at speed aboard the British-built runner, *Herald*."

Sadie said, "Kate, I am delighted to see you again and to meet Alan. But I can't help being curious. What brought you all the way down here again?"

"Back in Chicago, I talked about you so much, that Alan wanted to meet you," Kate said.

"And now that I've met you, I agree with her," he said. "You would be a valuable Pinkerton agent. We are negotiating to provide security to a new southern railroad and will need more southern agents. Nothing is finalized yet, but we feel certain that we'll soon be in a position to offer you employment as a field agent. We'd like you to work with us."

THE END, and perhaps a new beginning?

Want to read more of Sadie Snow's crime-solving adventures? Fear not! Coming Soon— the un-put-down-able *Death by Séance* --Full of mystery and intrigue, with ghostly twists and turns!

Fictitious Characters vs. Real-Life People as Depicted in this Novel

Fictitious Characters

Evangeline Bright>Charles Snow>Sadie Snow, actress and budding sleuth. I gave Sadie characteristics of various real-life residents of a West Florida plantation, called Chinsegut Hill.

The last name "Snow" came from a plantation family who lived there just after the Civil War. Elizabeth Robins, actress and author, who, with her brother, owned the plantation in the early 1900's, was my inspiration for Sadie. You can visit the sumptuous antebellum plantation house, which is located five and a half miles north of Brooksville, Florida.

Interesting real-life history of Chinsegut Hill: In 1842 Colonel Bird Pearson acquired the original land grant for 160 acres. He had a ship's carpenter build a log cabin, which was framed with hand-hewn 12-inch cypress, and encircled by a defensive fence.

In the 1850s, new owner Francis Ederington, a planter from South Carolina, built a two-story home southwest of the original building. He and his wife, Precious Ann, raised ten children there.

Their eldest daughter, Charlotte Ederington, married dentist Joseph Russell Snow, after the Civil War. They renamed the plantation "Snow Hill." Joseph served in the Florida House of Representatives, and the 1885 census states the family grew corn and sweet potatoes.

In 1904, world traveler and adventurer Colonel Raymond Robins and his sister, Elizabeth Robins, who was an acclaimed actress and author, purchased the property and renamed it "Chinsegut Hill." Robins had been an advisor to five different presidents and he, as well as his sister and his wife, had a wide range of national and international political and social connections. They entertained many famous people at their home. Robins, in his will, deeded 2000 acres to the US government for education. Upon his death, Chinsegut Hill became the property of the University of Florida.

More Fictitious Characters

Charles Snow, the alias chosen by Sadie Snow, when she traveled as a man.

Noah Asbell, owner and captain of the fictitious stern-wheeler steamboat, *Katie Asbell*. Katie Asbell was the real-life name of my wonderful maternal grandmother.

Jane Marsh, sidekick and former slave. She is the daughter of a fictitious rageaholic Spanish plantation owner in Cuba.

Michael MacNally (Mac), former Pinkerton detective and Sadie's mentor. He stands for justice, integrity, compassion, and wisdom. Respect for others and for their different practices and beliefs are important to him.

Luther Greim, compulsive gambler aboard the steamer, *Katie Asbell*.

Buck Stotts, salesman and ladies' man.

Neville Beaumont, plantation owner and aspiring politician.

Christian, cabin boy aboard the *Katie Asbell*.

Martha Merritt, along with sister Mary, is heiress to Cypress Pointe Plantation in Eau Gallie, near Saint Augustine, Florida. Previously she was a New York journalist with the *New York World*.

Mary Merritt Menendez, widow of prominent physician Dr. Menendez, is heiress to the Eau Gallie plantation.

Ava Maas, owner and operator of a large family mercantile store in New York City and wife of Bram Maas.

Bram Maas, wealthy Dutch merchant, from northern New York.

Kat Ashley, governess for the fictitious family of Doctor Alvarez, south of Saint Augustine.

Guillaume Lavigne, Brock House manager.

Daisy Miller, Brock House head housekeeper.

Aunt Cora Bird, Sadie's aunt and owner of Snow Bird Cottage. Author of popular women's fiction and tracts on women's suffrage and abolition of slavery (written under pseudonym), activist.

***E.W. Hall,* ocean-going sidewheeler.** I named this steamer in honor of my dad.

Percy, negro dishwasher and serving boy with tight blond curls.

Colonel Brown, provost marshal, stationed in Jacksonville.

Real-Life Characters and Places in Order of their Appearance

These characters and places were a real part of history in 1865. In keeping with their real personalities, I ascribed to them fictitious interactions with my fictitious characters.

Ford's Theatre, 511 10th St., Northwest in Washington DC was the site of President Lincoln's assassination.

Will Ferguson, call boy at Ford's Theatre April 15, 1865.

John Wilkes Booth, (May 10, 1838-April 26,1865) famous actor, who assassinated President Lincoln. In 1865, he was the highest paid actor in the world. He was considered the foremost *Hamlet* of his day.

Edwin Booth, (November 13, 1833-June 7, 1893) John's brother. He owned the acting company putting on the play at Ford's Theatre and was a well-known actor.

Harry Hawk, (April 28, 1837-May 28, 1916) sole actor on the stage at Ford's Theatre, when Abraham Lincoln was shot. He was arrested on $1000 bond.

Petersen's Boarding House on 10th St. in Washington D.C. Is across the street from Ford's Theatre and is available for tours. Many visiting actors and actresses stayed there because it was convenient to the theater.

Edwin Stanton, (December 19, 1814-December 24, 1869) Pittsburgh lawyer who served as Secretary of War, questioned witnesses in the back parlor of Petersen's Boarding House.

Laura Keene, (July 20, 1826-November 4, 1873) actress, entrepreneur, playwright, director, and theater manager. She starred in *Our American Cousin* the night President Lincoln was assassinated.

Abraham Lincoln, (February 12, 1809-April 15, 1865) President of the United States. He was carried to Petersen's Boarding House after the fatal shooting and died the next day.

Mary Todd Lincoln, (December 13, 1818-July 16, 1882) President Lincoln's wife.

Walt Whitman, (May 31, 1819-March 26, 1892) U.S. poet, journalist, and essayist. During the Civil War, his brother became ill and the poet went to Washington to nurse him. After his brother recovered, Whitman continued nursing in various Washington hospitals.

Doctor Mary Walker, (November 26, 1832-1919) American abolitionist, prohibitionist, prisoner of war, and surgeon. In 1855, she earned her medical degree at Syracuse medical college in New York, married, and set up a medical practice. In September 1863, Dr. Walker became the first female U.S. Army surgeon, served in the Civil War, received the medal of honor, and wore pants. Her unconventional dress, knee-length skirt over long pants, caused raised eyebrows and the occasional coarse comment.

Helen Getty, a 130-foot sidewheeler steamer with cabin space for 80 passengers.

Marshal House Hotel, prominent Savannah, Georgia hotel.

Enterprise, Florida is a flourishing city in Central Florida.

John Carroll Houston, (April 3, 1842-February 22, 1918) one of first permanent settlers and mayor of Eau Gallie, Florida.

Robert Gamble Plantation, originally 3,500 acres of sugarcane south of Tampa on the Little Manatee River. Robert Gamble House in Ellenton, Florida off US 301, is a Florida State Park.

Jacob Brock, (July 5,1810-September 22, 1876) prominent steamboat captain and a pioneer in the early establishment of Enterprise, Florida. He established the first regular paddlewheel transportation routes on the St. Johns River and built the famous Brock House Hotel.

Jennie Brock and Hattie Brock, daughters of Jacob Brock.

Harriet Beecher Stowe, (June 14, 1811-July 1, 1896) Author of best-selling book, "Uncle Tom's Cabin," and her husband Reverend Calvin Ellis Stowe, professor of Biblical Literature at Bowdoin College," traveled on the St. John's after the Civil War and purchased property at Mandarin, Florida, on the river.

Cornelius Taylor, (1785- 1849) in 1841 built a boardinghouse on top of the shell mound near the spot where Jacob Brock later built his Brock House Hotel in Enterprise, Florida.

LeMat gun, . 42 or . 36 caliber 9-shot cap and ball black powder revolver, which also had a secondary 20 gauge smooth- bore barrel, capable of shooting buckshot. Built by Jean Alexandre LeMat of France, US patent 1856. LeMat was a resident of New Orleans, Louisiana.

Kate Warne, (1833 -January 28, 1868) American law enforcement officer known as the first female detective in 1856 in the Pinkerton detective agency. She discovered a plot to assassinate Abraham Lincoln before his inauguration. She created and implemented a plan that averted the assassination attempt.

Sam Felton, president of the Philadelphia, Wilmington, and Baltimore Railroad.

The Bowery Boys and the Dead Rabbits were fierce rival New York gangs. Bill "The butcher" Poole was a feared Bowery Boys leader.

Captain Louis Coxetter, very successful privateersman and blockade runner in the British-built runner, *Herald*. The North put a price on his head for being a "pirate." After the war he returned to the Charleston-Palatka run until 1873,

Recipe

JANE'S CRISPY FRIED ALLIGATOR-MAKES 6 SERVINGS

Ingredients:

1 pound boneless alligator, fresh or frozen

3 garlic cloves, minced very fine

3 tablespoons grated onion

1/2 bell pepper, grated

1/2 stalk celery, grated

1 tablespoon chili powder

1 teaspoon dried thyme

1/4 teaspoon cayenne pepper

1/4 teaspoon black pepper

1/4 teaspoon paprika

1 tablespoon spicy mustard sauce(prepared mustard)

1 cup buttermilk

1 large egg

3 cups lard

2 cups flour

Procedure:

With a tea towel, pat the meat dry. Put it in a bowl and toss with the next 9 ingredients (seasonings). Coat evenly, Cover and allow to rest on the countertop at least 10 minutes.

Heat the lard in a large cast iron skillet. It will be ready to fry when many bubbles form around a wooden spoon inserted into the hot grease and the bubbles float up.

In another bowl, whisk together buttermilk, mustard, and egg.

Remove the alligator from seasonings bowl, and put the pieces on a plate.

Add 2 cups flour to the seasonings bowl. Stir well.

Dip the alligator in the flour and shake off. Then add into the buttermilk mixture and shake off. Then back into the flour and shake off. Put on clean plate. Repeat the process until all is done.

Add the alligator pieces to the skillet in batches. Start with larger pieces. Shake off excess flour before adding pieces to the oil. Don't overcrowd the skillet. Avoid overheating your lard.

Cook till crispy brown and cooked through. About 8 to 10 minutes. Use tongs to turn the pieces. Transfer pieces to a plate lined with a tea towel. Repeat until all pieces are cooked.

Recipe

Jane's Corn Soufflé-Makes 8 Servings

Ingredients:

Two cups cooked corn, cut from the cob

1 teaspoon salt

1 tablespoon sugar

2 cups heavy cream

1 tablespoon cornstarch

Three eggs, well beaten

4 tablespoons melted butter

Instructions:

Get oven hot (Marsha says 350° Fahrenheit). Mix salt, sugar, heavy cream, and corn starch. Fully dissolve corn starch. Add to the corn. Add beaten eggs and melted butter. Mix quickly. Pour into a buttered casserole dish and bake for 45 minutes.

Notes from the Author

Thank you!

Thank you for reading "Death by Alligator." I never thought I would enjoy researching for a historical novel, but I loved it. It was so much fun to find out new facts about that era, and my family says they didn't get tired of hearing, "Did you know...." I hope the book gave you joy, some interesting information about life in the United States just after the Civil War, an intriguing puzzle, and a few laughs. The world needs more kind writers and I aim to be one of them.

If you enjoyed "Death by Alligator," I'd be grateful if you would leave a review. Reviews help me, so the next book is even better. And reviews help others find the book.

If you want me to contact you when the next book is available, please go to www.marshawhitneybooks.com, where you can sign up for updates and a free story.